Drained

KERRY BERNARD

CHAMPAGNE BOOK GROUP

Drained

This is a work of fiction. The characters, incidents and dialogues in this book are of the author's imagination and are not to be construed as real. Any resemblance to actual events or persons, living or dead, is completely coincidental.

Published by Champagne Book Group
712 SE Winchell Drive, Depoe Bay OR 97341 U.S.A.

~~~

First Edition 2023

pISBN: 978-1-959036-34-0

Cover Art by Sevannah Storm

www.champagnebooks.com

Version_1

To Ed. Thanks for the wish.

Dear Reader:

I can't express how delighted I am that you're reading these words.

Drained was a long time coming. It's a complete rewrite of my very first attempt at a novel. That first novel was four times its length, full of grammatical errors, and peppered with stilted dialogue. Unpublishable. I moved on to other things.

But its characters never left me. They lingered, changing ages, sexes, and relationships. And the story grew with me over the years as I improved my writing. It represented the difference between the paths I had seen for myself and the paths I walked. It became the story I most wanted to tell.

So I did, and *Drained* resulted.

I'm beyond thrilled to share it with you.

Kerry

Chapter One

If her spell failed, the child would die—bone wilt progressed too quickly for a second chance.

So Sarlona stood neck-deep in the ocean at midnight and prayed Tydras would grant her enough power to cure the little girl at dawn.

He answered by sending Marrow from the depths, the stars, and the full moon's glittering path. Each ethereal strand of magical energy settled in her shaking bones until her insides ached and thrummed.

She could do it. She could heal the child.

Licking the salt from her lips, Sarlona headed for shore.

She froze after three floundering steps. There, in the ritual circle she'd crafted of sea-worn stone and sand-drawn runes, waited a man, his broad shoulders draped in moonlight.

He watched her.

She swiveled to the expanse of blues and blacks alive with starlight and flitting silver shards. He'd leave. It never hurt to spend a few extra minutes with Tydras anyway.

Miles to the southwest, Crescent Point Light flickered, marking the horizon. She lifted her feet and floated, gazing at His heaven, the Shimmering Sands. The moon's trail danced up to its gates—that distant line one could sail toward without ever getting closer. She fixed her gaze there and let her mind go blank.

Peaceful as Tydras's realm was, if she lingered, He might call her to Him that very night.

She spun to the pale beach, and her heart sank. A shiver clawed up her spine.

The man remained.

There were only so many reasons for a stranger to stand between a naked woman and her clothes on a cold autumn night.

With a deep breath, she tiptoed for shore. She was Sylvanus's apprentice, likely the most skilled nineteen-year-old caster in Aven. Marrow saturated her every fiber, ready to burst free. *Itching* to be unleashed, whether to work miracles or devastate. She had nothing to fear but a red face and the consequences of wasting Marrow when a sick child needed every scrap.

A wave broke on her shoulders and slapped her head. Her toes dragged across the sand as it rumbled on, leaving an empty fizzing behind it. "All right," she whispered. After another deep breath, she slogged to the beach.

She tried to keep her head high and walk with authority, to stand tall and keep her hands at her sides. The frigid air, colder than the water, made her want to wrap her arms around herself and double over.

Some relief hit her with the last rolling wave. She recognized the man as Glaucus. The sick girl's grandfather. They'd met the previous morning when he'd come seeking Sylvanus for help. With her mentor visiting Keystone, healing the child fell to Sarlona.

She marched nearer and started to cross her arms before thinking better of it. "We were supposed to meet at *dawn. In town*." But her gaze widened at the possibility the bone wilt had progressed faster than expected. Perhaps the young girl needed her *now*.

Or maybe it was too late. "Is your granddaughter okay?"

He nodded and finally turned. "She'll be just fine," he said, treading across her diligently drawn ogham to the dry sand where she'd left her things. He grabbed her cloak.

"She'll be *fine?*"

Bone wilt didn't resolve on its own. Potions and scrolls couldn't cure it. Perhaps he'd mistaken another ailment for the deadly disease.

"Yes." He held out her cloak.

She didn't step any closer to retrieve it.

He looked different. And not just because he'd donned a gleaming steel breastplate and strapped a longsword to his back. His stormy eyes blazed with life that wasn't there before. He stood straighter. His dark skin appeared richer and firmer, and his long, gray hair had grown silvery. A short-sleeved tunic revealed muscular arms, and he wore his cloak behind his shoulders despite the cold.

Maybe the dim light played tricks on her eyes, but Sylvanus had taught her to trust her instincts.

Unconcerned with conserving every magical morsel, she summoned her inner robes instead of her cloak. The white silk flew to her like an obedient ghost. She slipped her arms inside and tied the garment closed with the flying leather snake that followed. "Is that why you've come? To tell me that?"

"No." He refolded her cloak and tossed it higher up the beach. "I've come to take you to Ashmore."

"In Gulway?" She had never been to Ashmore and had no reason to go. The tiny, out-of-the-way fief lay in a neighboring barony. Sylvanus bore no direct responsibility for the land or the people there. So, neither did she. "Why?"

Wearing a soft smile, he stared at her. "Because Sarlona, Ashmore is your new home."

She started to shake her head but sensed movement behind her. Something huge. She ducked to the side, putting him and the second entity in front of her.

What appeared to be a massive demon circled to his side. Its sharp horns silhouetted in the moonlight, and its eyes glowed hellfire red.

"You don't have to be afraid." The demon's words tangled in a gravelly Northland accent. "We don't *want* to hurt you."

"Why would *I* be afraid?" she asked, strangling the warble from her voice.

She threw an orb of light into existence above Glaucus and the demon. The pair shielded their eyes, squinting. Neither went screaming to the hells.

She squinted too, less from the light than trying to figure out what stood in front of her. The orb's bright, white glow *had* made the demon vanish. What towered in its place appeared human. No sharp horns grew from its head, only from a black leather helm. And the fire in its eyes had calmed to a dull blue.

It was a Northlander and a woman.

More muscular than any man Sarlona had ever seen and swathed in animal parts with a double-bladed battle axe peeking over one hulking shoulder, the woman appeared as fearsome as the demon.

"What... What the hells is this?" Fear drove the cold away, but Sarlona's numbed toes dragged in the hard sand as she retreated. "Who are you?"

The woman doffed the helm, revealing a shoulder-length mess of blonde hair. "My name is Dagmar." She nodded at Glaucus. "Glaucus is my father and the Lord of Ashmore."

Dagmar's size argued against the possibility that a Northland king hadn't sired her, and the pair's skin tones sat on opposite ends of the spectrum.

Sarlona raised her brow at him. "Ashmore needs a druid?" If he was a Lord of Aven, it might be unwise to deny him. She didn't have to go with him, though. Most of his authority lay in another barony.

His eyes twinkled with mirth. "We need *you*, Sarlona."

The way he said it sent a pulse of warmth across her icy skin. No one spoke to her that sweetly. "Milord, I don't understand…"

"You will." He held out his hand. "Come along, now," he said, his tone firm and gentle, his body language inviting.

"I'm not…" Had his daughter not appeared so brutal, Sarlona might have gone to him. "I'm not going with you…" She turned to the path cutting through the tall dune grass from the beach and spun into Dagmar.

Sarlona shoved her with a blast of kinetic magic that would have sent a moose end over end. It only moved the Northlander a few paces, and she landed lightly on her feet. Those demonic eyes returned. Yellow this time. The eyes had been no trick of the light.

"What the hells are you?" Fear clawed at Sarlona's chest.

It just about ripped her heart out when she glanced down. The Northlander had clapped a thin silver bangle onto Sarlona's wrist. An anchor cuff—a restraint to prevent teleportation and acceleration spells. She gulped air like a fish on the deck of a boat.

He and Dagmar glanced at each other. After a moment, his eyes caught fire too—a glowing lavender. "We're lorkai."

He might as well have stuck his blade through Sarlona.

Her legs wouldn't work to retreat. She shook her head. "Spell-drinkers aren't real…"

The pair's retort was to stand there, staring, with hungry, luminescent eyes.

She understood what they wanted now, to imprison her in Ashmore and drink her Marrow. To keep her like a dairy cow.

"I'm not going with you," she whispered.

"You'll like Ashmore." Dagmar swaggered forward. "You can rest there. No more foraging for your breakfast. No more fasts and vigils. No more lonely nights in the woods in hopeless pursuit of pleasing a cold, old man."

Sarlona lifted her hands, trying to think of what spell might convince the lorkai to seek another victim.

"We'll take good care of you, little one," Glaucus said in the gentlest of voices. His irises flared a violent, blazing pink.

She edged backward as if moving slowly enough might prevent the monsters from noticing her withdrawal. Her voice wouldn't obey her. Without it, she had no chance of escaping.

He crept toward her like a panther closing in on a fawn. "It doesn't hurt, Sarlona."

She shuddered. Then a breeze, a few degrees warmer than the

ambient air, puffed off the sea and wrapped around her. The salt went through her, tinged with fish and sulfur from decomposing seaweed. The waves rumbled again.

"My blood is in these sands." She called the Marrow from her center to her hands. "My bones are destined to become them. I can't leave them."

"Oh, Sarlona..." Dagmar tossed the helm up the beach to join Sarlona's things. "We can put your blood in *lots* of places."

"Daggy..." He flashed her a withering glare with electric blue eyes, but if the Northlander wilted, she still stood a head taller than everyone else.

Sarlona's fingertips flared to match his eyes.

Dagmar shook out her shoulders and grinned. Her irises fluoresced green. "I'm curious to see what Sarlona can do with more than a bitter old druid's approval at stake." She charged, drawing her axe and winding up.

"Carapace," Sarlona whispered when Dagmar swung.

The axe crashed to a stop half an inch from Sarlona's cheek. Flecks of silver light danced into her vision to join the many stars above before falling like snow and fluttering off.

Dagmar let the axe head sink to the sand and leaned on the handle. "How long can you hold that shield?"

About two hours against blows like that if Sarlona didn't cast anything else or suffer a concussion first.

"How long do you think I can swing an axe?"

Indefinitely, if she had to guess.

"Sarlona," he called past the Northlander. "We need only touch you, and it's over," His voice was tender and pleading. "So come now, get dressed. We'll get you warmed up, and in the morning, in daylight, we'll chat. You'll see that Ashmore is where you belong."

The way he spoke made her feel like she'd been cold for years. Every part of her trembled.

She shook her head.

Dagmar wound up again. When she started to swing, Sarlona telekinetically snatched the axe head and yanked. The weapon should have sailed up the beach. Instead, it caught as though snagged on a branch. Dagmar shifted her weight forward and ripped the axe through with a vicious uppercut.

The axe connected just under Sarlona's chin, tipping her head back and bringing her up on her toes. She had been wrong. Her carapace wouldn't last two hours.

"Little one..." He drew his sword. "What do you think will

happen with the blow that breaks your barrier?"

"Give it up, Glaucus. We might as well show her we can bring her down when she's at full strength." Dagmar locked her luminescent yellow irises with Sarlona's. "And keep her alive when she's in pieces. Then she'll understand."

Sarlona thrust her palm, and a stream of fire, at Dagmar's face.

The axe descended from behind, striking between Sarlona's shoulders and along her neck, bobbing her head. Before she could straighten, he thrust his longsword at her gut.

She blasted both lorkai back and swept her arms outward. With a wet rumble, the sand around her opened into a wide, watery chasm, swallowing the lorkai but leaving her atop a narrow pillar. She clasped her hands, slamming the crumbling walls closed.

Just like that, peace swept over the beach. Tydras's sandy mortar lay smooth above the buried monsters, any sign they'd ever trod there erased.

She couldn't count on it staying that way.

Chapter Two

Sarlona sprinted up the beach, only slowing to a jog once her legs burned from powering across the shifting sand to the dune grass. She dropped her carapace, glanced at the night sky, and imagined herself there, catching the still air between her fingers. Those fingers elongated as she shrunk.

Shortening legs brought her to a stop, and the stars dimmed and blurred. Numbed flesh found relief beneath short fur. Her ears slid up higher on her head and expanded. She cried out, and a new, auditory landscape joined the visual one.

This landscape had Glaucus standing huge in front of her, with his sword raised.

She slammed her carapace spell into place with a hideous half-voice, half-squeak, abandoning the bat transformation. The blade bounced off her barrier.

Other than being plastered head to toe in sand, one would never have known he had been crushed under tons of beach. "You'll have to kill us, Sarlona." He extended his hand. "If that seems too awful, join us in Ashmore."

She whipped her hand around in a spiral, and the wind rose in a violent whirl, taking the loose sand to throw as a weapon. The initial blast knocked him aside and sucked his cloak into the sky.

He threw one forearm in front of his face and strained to regain the step he'd lost.

She brought her arms out wide and put her core into it. The funnel widened, and he tossed his sword. He leaned into the wind until his knees and hands hit the dark sand left behind.

To her horror, he sprouted new swords from his wrists. An ivory blade flipped out from the underside of each forearm like a folding knife. He plunged them into the ground and tucked his face into his shoulder.

She ran for the water with the wind-driven sand grinding at her carapace and a gale roaring in her ears.

And collided with Dagmar's axe.

It connected with her barrier an inch from her temple. She tumbled, landing on one hip.

When Dagmar wound up, Sarlona jabbed at the monster, unleashing a blast of lightning. It hit Dagmar square in the chest and threw her into the windstorm.

Sarlona climbed to her feet while the earsplitting crack shook the sand. The Northlander seized with electricity and rolled in the wind. A seed of hope sprouted in Sarlona's gut. But she couldn't hold a carapace and a storm *and* fire offensive spells for long.

She reverse jogged at the sea and fired a second, much larger bolt. It split into hundreds of blue tendrils as it smashed into the sandstorm. She didn't check how many caught a lorkai. Dashing for the water, she let the storm go and hoped the massive cage-like maze of petrified lightning would entangle the monsters for a minute.

Another pseudo-peace descended on the beach. Only the crashing surf and the slap of her feet against the saturated sand broke the silence.

The second her toes hit the water, she lowered her carapace. A glassy shattering rang in her shrinking ears as she fell onto her stomach with withered legs and arms. The cold melted. Flesh and blubber swallowed her limbs and left her undulating to throw herself forward. One more flop and she could float and swim.

When her spine elongated, and she lifted her front for that final thrust, pain exploded in her right flipper-foot. The seal vanished, leaving human Sarlona to rip her foot off the longsword that pinned it through the sole to the sand.

"Carapace," she shrieked, scrambling forward, and flipped over.

He hit the shielding instead of her ankle.

Her heart raced, insides thinning while the water around her grew darker.

"I can heal it with a touch." He crouched as the remnants of a wave washed her onto her side. "Let down your barrier."

Dagmar appeared at his side, looming over them. A whiff of singed hair preceded her.

Sarlona needed help.

She asked for it in the school of minnows that filtered in to investigate her blood. They darted for the depths at her behest.

Clutching her foot together beneath the water, she imagined it whole, painless, unbloodied. Green light seeped from her hands, and the halves became one.

He remained on his haunches, stroking the side of her calf or the water half an inch above it. Dagmar rested one huge hand on the barrier over her head, then caressed the carapace above Sarlona's cheek.

As long as she couldn't feel them, and they couldn't drain her Marrow, she could tolerate their touch while she waited to see if Tydras would offer aid.

"You know... The stronger the caster, the better you taste," Dagmar said. "We're going to *so* enjoy you, Sarlona." The ache in her voice made Sarlona shiver. The monster bent low to whisper near Sarlona's head. Dagmar's fingertips lit up manna blue as she ran them from Sarlona's cheek over a breast to her hip. "I'll let you choose where I put my hands to feed the first time."

Dizziness accompanied the chill that engulfed Sarlona. She almost sighed with relief when Dagmar straightened and wound up with her axe.

Sarlona grabbed both lorkai by the ankles with the most vicious undertow she could conjure. Dagmar collapsed onto one knee, and the axe embedded harmlessly in the sand. Glaucus toppled flat on the water and caught himself with his hands.

Good enough.

When she got to her feet, Sarlona hit them with a rip current stronger and wider than that beach had ever seen. In seconds, the frothing water sucked him out through the surf. A blast of fire at Dagmar's left hand made her release her grip on the axe, and she followed him.

To Sarlona's dismay, the lorkai didn't go so far out to sea as the current she'd created. Glaucus dove under the surface and popped up a minute later to the side of it. Dagmar swam across it, despite how Sarlona augmented its angle.

The lorkai arrived at the surf simultaneously, and Sarlona grew the next wave to creep up behind them. She raised it to about three times Dagmar's height and slammed it on top of them. Other than making their glowing eyes disappear for a few seconds, it didn't do much. Exaggerating the undertow as the water receded did more, taking the steps they had gained.

That would do. Sarlona sensed them near—the denizens of Tydras's realm. She told the nearest, the largest, what she needed.

Taller and heavier, Dagmar gained her feet first. She waded for Sarlona, each step steadier than the last. With a flick of her wrists, the same strange ivory blades Glaucus had borne flipped out of her forearms.

He disappeared beneath the surface behind the Northlander. Sarlona held her hands out to the moon, then drew them in. All the light sparkling on the water came with them. The night deepened. For a second, the sea mirrored the black abyss. Complete with tentacles, one broke the surface where Glaucus had been, then dove under.

She drove her fists, full of white light, at Dagmar. The monster flinched and turned aside, avoiding half the moonbeam. The blast only knocked her shoulder and singed her cheek. That was fine.

Influencing a kraken and a shark to attack at once wasn't easy. Especially since the lorkai seemed to have no scent. But the kraken saw them well enough, and the shark sensed their movements.

Sarlona urged the kraken to slither its tentacles around Glaucus's throat and limbs and pull him to its razor-sharp beak, to drag him deeper and envelop more of him. Then pull him apart. The shark Sarlona told to sunder Dagmar into small enough pieces for an eighteen-foot fish to swallow.

The fin rose off to Dagmar's right and grew to the size of a sail, cutting its way toward her.

She got to Sarlona before the shark met Dagmar. The Northlander sliced hard with her claws, those bony, short swords with a slight curve and serrated bottom that protruded from the undersides of her wrists. She struck three times inside a second.

The blows came as mightily as they had with the axe and wore far more on the carapace than steel. Sarlona wasn't sure she'd withstand a dozen more hits. Thankfully, she wouldn't have to.

Dagmar swiveled when the shark breached, and a set of jaws, decorated with two dead eyes and borne on two-thousand pounds of fish, lunged at her.

Even with her carapace up, Tydras's favor, and Dagmar between them, Sarlona's adrenaline surged as those rows of serrated teeth hurtled at Dagmar.

She caught the creature by the nose, deflecting its jaws upward and skewering its snout. Her left claw jammed into the shark's mouth in an uppercut. The white blade's tip popped out the top of the shark's head in a spray of blood.

The lorkai ripped her claws free, and the shark stilled after one weak thrash.

A beautiful example of Tydras's most sacred animal slaughtered in a second.

Sarlona gaped at the fish while it floated dead and rolled shoreward on bloody foam.

Spitting ancient obscenities, Glaucus burst from the water. A tentacle pursued him, but he caught it, and it coiled around his arm instead of his throat. He backpedaled toward land.

It took Sarlona a moment to realize the kraken wasn't going to drag him into the depths. He would tow the kraken onto the beach.

With the tentacle over his shoulder like a rope, he pivoted. A moment later, more tentacles appeared, two with the ends severed, followed by the kraken's mantle.

When he slogged to hip-deep water, Sarlona spurred the largest jellyfish she'd summoned to snare him in its stinging tendrils. Cursing, he ripped the delicate appendages from his hip and thigh.

"I'm losing my patience for this, Sarlona," he said a second before a giant tentacle wrapped around his face.

He sounded like Sylvanus, but Glaucus's warning closed a much colder fist in her gut.

Swinging his sword behind his head, he sliced off the tentacle around his face. He hauled on the creature until he had it in knee-deep water. There, he severed every tentacle that came close, then he plunged one claw deep into the kraken above the beak.

The creature's flailing tentacle stubs slumped. Its bone-shaped pupils shrank to slits in its saucer-like eyes. The life left them. That didn't stop them from staring at her with accusation. The kraken twitched when Glaucus tore his claw free to the sickening crunch of ripping flesh.

He peeled the remaining tentacle off his arm. "This is enough, isn't it?"

Maybe it was. How many of Tydras's creatures would she command to die for her? What destruction would she do to the shore?

As Dagmar waded closer, four fins appeared, smaller fins than the last but each sharing the same ominous shape. The sharks circled Sarlona, bellies grazing the sand, ready to rip into anything that came too close.

Dagmar skewered the first in her path like she was spearfishing.

Sarlona couldn't summon the courage to send the rest out to sea. Instead, she called every fish and invertebrate with sharp teeth or toxic spines within range to set upon the lorkai.

When Dagmar struck, the surf roiled with fins of all sizes, flying teeth, and poisons. None offered Sarlona's carapace more than a second's reprieve. Each were cut down, shrugged off, or outright ignored. And the fiery moths Sarlona conjured to target the lorkai's eyes seemed only to irritate them.

She needed to risk a big spell or transformation again. But just when she resolved to try to pinch the lorkai between a wall of sand and of water, a spear tip burst through the front of Dagmar's shoulder.

The Northlander growled with pure rage, an inhuman sound that sent a shiver up Sarlona's shaking spine. As Dagmar wrested the long spear the rest of the way through her shoulder, Sarlona spotted its thrower. The moon hung behind him, casting a shadow over his face, but she recognized the silhouette of Vosvoshish's shoulders and his short, three-pronged crown.

The seventh prince of King Zoshinzin's Shoal had come to her rescue with his pod of warriors. One of those minnows had found Tydras's children.

All at once, the merpeople burst from the water, lunging with spears and tridents at the lorkai. Glaucus and Dagmar parried every jab with their weapon-like appendages. Sarlona redoubled her efforts to land insect-shaped fire on lorkai heads, hoping to drive them underwater where the merpeople had an advantage.

The piscine warriors were no match for the pair of spell-sucking monsters.

Dagmar batted Vosvoshish's trident aside and ran her claw through his sternum. Vosvoshish let out a garbled scream, and she lifted his skewered torso. The ghastly sound grew more inhuman as she yanked him down by the arm. She eyed Sarlona while she carved through his ribcage. He stopped screaming and moving before the claw came out through his shoulder.

Vosvoshish was too dead for Sarlona to heal with the magic she had left. His corpse bobbed in the water, split through the heart with half his left side peeling off.

Dagmar, soaked with as much blood as seawater and eyes glowing as red as any demon's, grinned at Sarlona. Beside Glaucus, a woman's torso drifted from a fish-like tail on a dark plume. A man floated facedown nearby with a spear through his ribs.

All dead because of her.

The stars went dark, and Sarlona sank to her throat. The splashes from the two surviving mermen finning over to dive and flee sounded miles away. The rumble of the waves told her to sleep. Instead, she vomited.

The lorkai would win. And there'd be no mercy in Ashmore. Just violence and suffering.

Stumbling to shore, she dismissed the remaining denizens. She couldn't soak in Vosvoshish's blood and the thick stew of the butchered life she was supposed to help protect.

Her legs gave out a few yards beyond the water. The lorkai meandered after her, wringing out their hair and squeezing what water they could from their torn clothing.

"Ready for your rubdown?" Dagmar asked with a wicked grin.

Sarlona dug her fingers into the sand. Shakily, she stood, raising her arms. She imagined the Veil lifting and asked Tydras to send one more thing to help her—the drowned dead.

She wasn't supposed to do that.

A few men staggered from the dunes. Ancient skeletons that might have lain buried for decades, or maybe whose bone dust had washed in.

Most emerged from the waves. Pale, white-eyed sailors and pirates in tattered clothing marched ashore. Men and women in less distinctive attire stumbled through the surf. A schoolhouse's worth of children crawled from the foam. They were all Sarlona's mindless servants. Bodies to throw at the lorkai.

Dagmar glanced from the waves to Sarlona. "Sarlona... I didn't think you had it in you."

"That's her last big one," Glaucus said as the first sea-bloated corpse groped for him. A swipe of one blade cut it in two. The top half crawled at him and grabbed his boot. He lopped its head off. "I'll hold them."

Dagmar was on her before Sarlona could drop her carapace never mind transform into a bat. The two skeletons that shambled from the dunes tried to rescue her. The first to grasp at the monster lost its arms. Dagmar ripped the skull off the second. Then got three strikes in on the carapace prior to recoiling under Sarlona's puff of fire.

That was it. He cut the dead down as fast as they shambled from the water. Sarlona crumpled to her knees. The cold stabbed deep into her rattling bones.

Waiting for the carapace to break, she shut her eyes. She held it not to delay the inevitable but to give herself a minute to pray. To beg Tydras and all her Gods to see her through whatever lay ahead. Or take her to the Shimmering Sands or another Otherrealm to rest. She tried to feel herself there—the warm sand, shimmering blue, and the comforting perpetual rumble.

The seventh wave in a set crashed louder than the ones before it. Tydras spoke in it. His voice conveyed no hope or reassurance.

It did give her one more spell.

Sarlona opened her eyes to find the tip of Dagmar's claw trailing across her carapace, right over her throat. She stared past the monster to the sea, at the most distant ripple, and drew in every vapor of loose Marrow in the ether, channeling it into raising that wave.

As it glided closer, the wall of water grew to five times higher than any crest Sarlona had ever dove under, and the tide receded lower than she'd ever seen it. The wave sucked up Vosvoshish's half-split corpse amid parts of Tydras's sacred animals.

A piece of Sarlona's heart floated off with them.

"Her last big one, huh?" Dagmar glanced at a wave that had to appear monstrous even to monsters.

"Please, Tydras," Sarlona whispered as the night of the sea loomed over them. She prayed He'd either wash her far from the lorkai or take her now into the Shimmering Sands.

Glaucus crouched and drove his claws into the sand. Dagmar followed his example.

While the wave hung over them, he glanced at Sarlona. "It'll be okay."

The water hit her like nothing ever had, smashing her carapace to mist and slamming her into the sand. She tumbled and bounced under its crushing force until the world left her.

~ * ~

Consciousness returned with warmth radiating from Tydras's powerful arms. He'd taken Sarlona home to rest forever in his embrace of fine, silky sand and rolling summer waves under a sparkling sun.

The illusion shattered as her vision solidified. The light above radiated from glowing yellow eyes, not the sun. Dagmar's steady gait rocked Sarlona, not lapping waters. It wasn't peace that held her still and silent in muscular arms but paralysis. Maybe the wave had broken her neck.

"It's over now." Dagmar slogged the last few steps out of water.

Sarlona's eyes, at least, obeyed her. She stared up the beach rather than view the monster's stern face. Packed rock and pebbles bobbed in her vision with the lorkai's steps, stretching its length. The wave had eaten the sand.

She regretted that.

Dagmar crossed the field of wet, sandy stone without a stumble to the dunes where the water had flowed but not beaten. Glaucus waited among the tufts of sharp grass.

Dagmar dumped her at his feet.

Smiling, he lowered to his knees. "It will be all right." His hands flared with blue light as he took her arm, and his eyes changed to match them.

He'd lied.

It hurt, like Sarlona had not only overdone it—she had—but tried a big new spell that came out wrong. It hurt like when she swallowed a mouthful of dry bread, and it got stuck on the way down. Except the feeling permeated her being. A cold, ghostly claw seemed to plunge into her soul. The sensation deepened as Dagmar's fingers alighted on Sarlona's cheeks.

His grip loosened, and he trailed his fingertips up and down her arm. Her muscles lost all tension, and a warm tingling washed from her toes to her crown, drowning most of the pain. Her eyelids grew heavy, despite her thrashing heart, helpless as the strange monsters held her down and caressed her skin.

She closed her eyes.

Chapter Three

A fresh bolt of fear hit Sarlona the instant her eyes opened. She lay in a strange bed with an unfamiliar knotted pine ceiling overhead. None of it had been a dream.

Throwing aside the covers, she sat up too fast. Her head swam and didn't find dry land until she drove her bare feet onto the cold plank floor.

"Okay...," she whispered and wished she hadn't made a sound.

It took far more effort to get to her feet than it should have. Maybe she'd bashed her head when the wave hit. Or perhaps the lorkai had done more to her than take her Marrow. But she feared the sick, weak sensation weighing her down had to do with the room.

She called what Marrow she'd regenerated to her hands, but it didn't come. It felt as sluggish as she did and flowed to her fingertips like molasses. "Shit."

She tried to conjure a flame, but it fizzled into a wisp of smoke. The moisture in the air wouldn't obey her to form ice. Finally, she cast a scan spell. It took five times the Marrow it should have, twice the concentration, and it came out weak and tenuous, but it confirmed her suspicions—the chamber was heavily warded. If she'd had every scrap of Marrow she could hold, she doubted she could blast her way out. That buried to the hilt the dagger of dread in her chest.

She couldn't imagine who could put up wards that strong. Or what the lorkai had done to them to compel them to install such magic.

She teetered to the chamber's window. There, the midday light spilled across her chilled skin. The life-giving sun. That mild warmth of the autumn sunshine, the scarlet maple leaves along a distant tree line, and the perfect blue of the cloudless sky... Something about them cured her vertigo.

They didn't make the window any lower to the ground. Her

prison was on the third story with nothing below the window to drop onto or grab. If she jumped down into the yard, she'd break her legs. The chamber was on the front side of the building, anyway. Someone would witness her escape attempt. Never mind the long nails pinning the window shut.

At least it gave her a partial lay of the land. The estate was surrounded by a log palisade twice her height, its gate about two hundred yards straight out from the building. The doors were shut and barred with no cover nearby. She spotted ways to scale the wall off to the sides, though.

If she could climb onto the roof of either the small stable on the left or the chicken coop on the right using the barrels and crates lining the yard, she could get over the wall. Then just a quarter mile or so of meadow stretched before the forest...

Her panic and the hundred reasons she'd never make it to the woods rose, hastening her breaths. She had to get out of the room first, then she could worry about escaping the grounds.

Without much hope it would open, she crept to the door. Her fingers trembled against the cold brass handle. Gingerly, she turned it, fearing the slightest rattle would draw the lorkai's attention and earn her an extra touch.

The door opened without a squeak. All her hope tumbled to the ground like an arrow-pierced pheasant when she peeked beyond it.

A tall man with a befittingly massive sword on his back leaned beside the doorway, staring down at her. She recoiled, retreating into the room.

He filled the door's frame with his own. "Good afternoon, Sarlona." His smile showed off his tusks. "My name's Gorgil. I'm Ashmore's guard captain." He had a slender build for a man with orc blood, but she didn't doubt he could work his sword without any trouble. It's nice to finally meet you."

She contemplated his use of "finally" and hoped he wouldn't come further into the room.

He didn't, except to hang inward on the door frame. "Is there anything I can get for you?" His face softened, and he used the gentlest voice that a human-orc man with a blade that big could. "You must be hungry by now."

If she was, other sensations screamed over it. "Can I use the privy?"

He scratched his head, then pointed to the far side of the bureau that sat against the same wall the door was on. "You have a chamber pot over there."

She took that as a no.

His deep brown stare drifted down from her face. "There are clothes for you in the bureau."

She glanced down. Someone had dressed her in a thin, white slip befitting a sacrificial virgin. At least she wasn't nude. "Okay," she whispered, face burning. "I'll put the clothes on."

He got the hint, offered her one more smile, then closed the door with his retreat.

She exhaled.

On the verge of pissing herself, she located the chamber pot tucked against the bureau and prayed no one would enter the room while she used it. After her first opportunity for humiliation without interruption, she set about her second.

The heavy bureau contained clothes, but she couldn't believe they were for her. Instead of robes, she found linen pants, short-sleeved tunics, and a sculpted leather chest piece. All in black and of higher quality than anything she'd ever owned.

After some hand wringing, she tore off the slip and raced to dress. The clothing fit too well. As if they'd been tailored. She ignored stockings and boots in the bottom drawer. If she did make it outside, she'd need her feet bare...

The door flashed open and shut without a sound.

"You look lovely," Glaucus said.

She lurched with a shot of adrenaline. Trying to sound amicable, she raised her hands half in surrender and half in a bid to stop him where he was. "Please, milord."

"It's all right, Sarlona." His tone made her want to believe him. "I thought you might like to talk now."

If she could slow her thrashing heart and catch enough breath to speak. He wasn't a large man—*monster*—just muscular for his apparent age. Still, indoors and without Dagmar beside him, he cut an imposing figure.

While terrified at what she might see when she reopened them, she closed her eyes. She counted to four as she breathed in, then searched for that space at the top of her breath. Nodding, she exhaled.

When she opened her eyes, he stood where she'd left him. "How long do you intend to imprison me here?"

"Until you stop thinking of Ashmore as your prison and accept it as your home." He crept closer.

Her dread tightened like a noose. "I could meet you once a fortnight." It was too much to keep her from begging. Tapped out and trapped in that room, she wasn't the second most powerful druid in Aven, but a scared, kidnapped girl. "You could have what you need then... And still let me go home..."

She winced at how pathetic she sounded and at the idea of strolling into an inn twice a month to be molested by monsters. But it beat being kept in Ashmore, subjected to it at their whim.

Smiling, he shook his head. "It's your company we desire."

He lied. She was food. Her voice cracked, and her eyes watered. "Will you let me see my family?"

Frowning, he clasped his hands in front of his belt. "No. Never... For that, I truly am sorry."

His tone sounded sincere. That didn't keep the tears at bay. She wiped them before they traversed her cheeks and gritted against a sob.

He tilted his head as if that would help him see her eyes beneath her tears. "I will check on them for you, every so often. If you like..."

Her gaze hurtled from the floor to his face. "*No.* No. Stay away from them." She hadn't meant to shout. "Please."

"All right."

If he intended to keep her from her family... He might never let her return to her true home either. "I need the sea..." The Gods were supposed to be her supreme concern. She should have asked about the ocean first. Like a stranded starfish, she'd desiccate without it.

"You will touch it again... someday," he answered. "You'll also form a relationship with the land here."

That restored some hope. She'd be allowed outside, enough to commune with the land. Maybe the lorkai did just need a druid. It made sense they'd abduct one. No caster would go with them willingly.

Which made her wonder something else... "Who put up these wards?"

"A dark mage in my employ."

"How—?"

"You can ask him when you meet," he answered before her question had fully formed. "I'm sure you've discovered few spells will work in here, and none will help you escape." For a minute, he was silent. "Is there nothing else?"

Nothing but desperate pleas came to mind.

"Then let me tell you." His tone changed from a grandfatherly one to a lord's.

Cringing, she braced herself.

"You understand that with my touch, I command every particle that makes up your body?"

She did now. Her entire being pulsed with her pounding heart. Cotton stuffed her mouth. "Yes," she croaked.

"Good. Then know you will obey me. By choice or compulsion."

Swallowing hard, a stream of terrible things he might force her to do flowed through her head—degrading and violent acts. She might survive being his toy. If he meant to control her magic and put it to evil purposes, however... If he made her hurt people... She prayed he wasn't as awful as he could be.

"You'll eat at least twice a day, or I'll hold your hand and do it for you."

Despondent or not, she could do that.

"You'll sleep at night, or I'll put you to sleep."

He might have to, but she'd try to avoid it.

"You'll bathe, or I'll order my men to bathe you."

Paling, she nodded enthusiastically.

"You'll be allowed fresh air and exercise under guard."

"Thank you," she whispered.

"But until I trust you, you'll spend most of your time in this chamber."

Better a bedroom than the chains she might have expected. Preferable to a dungeon cell.

He stepped nearer, and she fought not to retreat. "I'm not a cruel man, Sarlona." His voice had gentled for that sentence.

How could he not be? To take her from her home and prevent her from ever returning? "And Dagmar?"

One corner of his mouth rose. "Well... She's not a man anyway."

She supposed that was something.

"She likes you." He waited until she met his stare. "I won't punish you for your inevitable escape attempts." His voice harshened again. "Unless you injure my men," he warned. "They have orders to stop your departure, by any means, short of death."

If the rest of his men were anything like Gorgil, she didn't have a chance of prevailing in a physical confrontation. Not unless she could accumulate some Marrow outside that room...

"Understand?"

"Yes, milord."

"Wonderful." The grandfatherly tone returned with a pleasant smile. "Now, come here." He held out one hand, beckoning.

The blood drained from her. "Already? Please..."

"Sarlona..." His voice was a summer breeze. "Obey."

"Okay." It wasn't like she could avoid him. The path out lay through him, and he could snatch her in a blink.

She tottered to him, offering a trembling hand.

He took it, cradling it between his palms. The sensation of being held spread from her hand to afflict her whole body. "With our abilities, we can make you feel anything, Sarlona..."

Everything tingled, ignited. "Please..."

"Great pleasure..."

Ecstasy washed over her. Her eyes rolled, and her knees weakened. A soft groan slipped from her parted lips. "Milord..."

"Just Glaucus, little one," he whispered.

The warm butterflies he'd put inside her left no room for embarrassment. He made them flutter for a full minute before they flew off.

"Or...great pain."

Her eyes widened. "No, please." She yanked to retract her hand, but it didn't budge. If he could make her feel that sublime...

He hugged her, patting her back. "It's all right... I wouldn't do that to you."

Tears sprang into her eyes. "Thank you," she said, defeated.

He released her hand to cup her cheek and made her gaze into his storm-gray eyes. "We're going to take good care of you, Sarlona."

They would. Of course, they would. Prize livestock was hard to come by.

His eyes and fingertips flared electric blue.

Chapter Four

Benton watched from the threshold, leaning against the doorframe as Glaucus's fingertips lit up like blue flame on the girl's cheek.

Her frantic eyes, the one part of her the lorkai allowed to move, caught Benton and pleaded for help.

He ignored their tug, flashed a smile, and glanced down to escape them.

Glaucus knew he was there. The lorkai would have heard Benton long before he opened the door. He tapped his half-empty cup against his hip, opposite his spell-sucking sword, waiting for the Lord of Ashmore to acknowledge him.

"What is it, Benton?" Glaucus finally asked without turning around or taking his hands off her.

He sipped his ale, then answered, "Gregor's at the gate with a couple villagers."

"For what purpose?"

"They're complainin' about orcs and sheep and other shit I don't care about."

Glaucus sighed, withdrawing his hand from her face. She stumbled with a gasp and tried to suck in her tears.

"I had better address that." The old lorkai's eyes and fingertips cooled. "Why don't you keep Sarlona company?"

Benton coughed his next swill back into his cup. "'Cuz I'm off duty." That, and he didn't want to get to know her.

Glaucus smirked. "You can drink and be company. Show her around her new home, won't you?"

"You mean, outsida this room?"

He nodded. "Just keep her within the palisade." His answer seemed to breathe a puff of life into her.

Benton stared her in the face. Taking her out sounded like a pain in the ass. "How hard am I allowed to hit her? If she throws somethin'..."

Her eyes didn't grow wide enough. He needed her to know he meant business.

"Half as hard as you'd fancy Dagmar hitting you." Glaucus pivoted to Sarlona. "Please excuse me." She winced when he grasped her chin. "Behave yourself now."

The old lorkai vanished, and Benton sauntered into the room. "Had some excitement there last night, huh, darlin'? And not the good kind."

She only glanced in his direction.

He sidled closer and eyed her up and down now that she wasn't unconscious and hidden beneath the covers. She was lean and muscular, though nothing like Dagmar. Sandy-gold hair came to rest on shoulders that were the same width as her hips.

He liked the looks of her well enough. Everything but the red, watery eyes.

"Are you one of them?" Her voice wavered with her tremble.

There had been occasions when he enjoyed seeing fear on a woman's face. It didn't do it for him this time. He took another drink and stared for a few more seconds. "The lorkai? No, sweetheart. I'm all man."

She seemed to remember she had hands then and peered at them like they had something to say.

He'd been warned what she could do with them when she had the juice to do it.

But her gaze jumped to him, and his hand hopped from his hilt. "You work for them?"

"Yup." She didn't need to know the details of that arrangement. The question reminded him how afraid he'd been when he'd first agreed to it. When he'd first arrived in Ashmore. "Pretty scared about now, huh darlin'?"

She wiped her eyes with her palms and sniffed. "Yeah."

"I was too. It turned out all right." Of course, he wasn't a caster, and Glaucus had saved his life, not stolen it. Never mind that he'd been accustomed to monsters. Albeit of a different sort.

She stared at the plain wooden walls as if the grain might hold a secret. "You aren't magical..."

"No, but I got enough Marrow to be." Glaucus had told him that. Benton tried not to think about how different his life might have been if he'd known it as a boy.

She finally peeked in his direction again. "Is that why you're here?"

"I'm here because I'm good with a blade."

Her gaze darted to his hilt, then crawled up to his eyes. Women liked his eyes. "Glaucus doesn't keep *you* drained?"

"No." He thanked the gods for that. The two lorkai almost never ate in…until now. He grinned. "Course, he don't get me off, either."

"He didn't—" She grew redder than he'd seen a person change. "That wasn't…" She just about whispered the last word, "sexual."

He laughed. Of course, Glaucus playing with her insides wasn't funny. Watching her squirm was. "Oh darlin', maybe you will be fun."

"I have a name," she said with as much force as he'd heard out of her yet.

Benton didn't want to believe her, despite how pretty it sounded. "Yeah, sweetheart?" He finished his drink as she glared at him. She was going to be fun. "All right… Lucky for you I got just the cure for handsy, lorkai horseshit."

She crossed her arms. "Is it ale?"

"Yup." He shook his empty cup. "Cures everything. Come on, darlin'," he said, waving her at the door.

She glowered at him as he stepped aside, and he leered when she passed. He grasped for her shoulder when she crossed the threshold, but she ducked under his hand.

"Oh gods, that's better." Stopping just beyond the threshold, she inhaled like she hadn't been able to breathe until she breached the doorway. She peered into the room. "Those wards are horrible."

He didn't doubt her, he wouldn't expect any less from Amenduil, but he didn't truly feel them. "Gonna light me on fire now?"

Though her eyes still watered, the life had come into them. "I don't have any Marrow left."

It wasn't the answer he'd hoped for. Or the truth, he suspected.

"All right, that's Dagmar's chamber," he said, pointing to the door across from and to the right of her cage. "I'd keep the hells out of there if you can help it. The one at the end of the hall is Glaucus's."

He grabbed her around her upper arm and tugged her in the other direction. She scowled at his scarred hand like he might suck the life out of her like a lorkai but came along.

"Glaucus's study," he said, stopping at the wide, hickory door at the outside center of the hall. His cup clinked against the wrought iron knob as he opened the door just far enough to see bookshelves. "If he calls you in there, it's usually to tell you somethin' you ain't gonna like hearin'." He shut the door and dragged her to the stairway.

She jerked against his grip. "Will you please let go of me?"

"Nope."

She leaned away. "You smell like ale and emberleaf and—"

"Man?"

"Yeah."

He had at least seventy-five pounds on her. A stiff yank put her in his arms.

Her hot breath and the vibration of her voice pricked his sternum, but he couldn't make out the curse she grumbled. A soft, unexpected sensation bloomed in his chest.

"Let's see what you smell like, darlin'." He inhaled against the top of her head. The sandy waves held the scent of soil, salt, and sun-warmed skin. "Like... I don't know. Druid-y shit, I guess."

That seemed like enough. He opened his arms.

She spun and hopped back. The only water left in her eyes was the storming sea. "Don't touch me." She looked like she might sprout fangs.

"Or what, darlin'?" he said, stepping toward her.

He drew his sword the instant she raised her right hand. With a short outward chop, she flung a yellow-green sheet of viscous fluid at him. He brought his weapon up and across in a flash, and the sword devoured the goo without letting a drop pass by. Pure instinct made him flick the blade at her, returning her spell. He prayed the snot-colored liquid his sword spit at her wasn't acid as it splattered across her front.

It never hit her skin, whatever it was. It bounced off the shield she'd put about half an inch in front of her. The fluid vaporized as rings of large, razor-sharp sharks' teeth sprouted in thin air, encircling her at the ankles, knees, hips, navel, chest, throat, and crown. They spun around her like man-eating bilge hoops.

"There it is." He let the cup he'd forgotten to drop clang to the floor. "I cockin' knew it. Don't have any Marrow, huh? Can't ever trust a robe."

She stared at him or maybe at his lorkai-like sword. "I don't want to fight," she said, lowering her hands.

He straightened and let his blade sink.

"Please, Benton. I'll behave if you do." Her tone wasn't pleading, but her eyes were. Though they still resembled the sea, the storm in them had calmed.

Benton had never seen blue quite that deep. "You're askin' a lot outta me, sweetheart." Her rotating rings of flesh-rending dentin vanished as he shoved his sword into its scabbard. "Walk in front then." Snatching up his cup from the worn floorboards, he ordered her ahead. "First floor, then right." He motioned to the stairwell behind them.

They descended the stairs, and he guided her through the great hall, which wasn't so great, into the unoccupied kitchen.

She gaped at the room, a quarter of which was taken up by the massive iron stove.

He went straight for the keg. "What?"

She ran a finger through the flour dust atop the counter. "It's just so normal. The bread and garlic and apples…"

"Well, the lorkai gotta feed us, don't they?" he said, halfway into filling his cup.

Scanning the sacks, crates, and barrels tucked and stacked under and between the counters, she drifted to one of four rectangles of sunlight cast by the windows, like an old dog. "Feed many of 'us' judging by the stores."

He snorted and pulled a battered chair out from the small table in the center of the room. "There's nine guards, two lorkai, and one old maidservant. Knowin' that ain't gonna help you."

She just stared out the window.

He set his cup down and tore an end off one of the morning's loaves. "Glaucus said eat."

She swiveled just in time to catch it when he tossed the bread end at her head. He returned to the keg and filled a fresh cup while she scrutinized the bread like it had whispered to her.

"And I said drink." He set the new cup down and yanked out a second chair with one hand, half-spinning it in her direction. "Sit." He collapsed into the first chair as if he were the one having a rough day.

After inching her way to the table, she sat in a third chair disappointingly out of reach.

She tore off tidbits of bread like a bird for a minute before he slid the second cup of ale at her.

"I only drink for ritual and the high festivals."

He rolled his eyes. "C'mon darlin', it'll make you feel better."

She ogled the windows behind him. "Some fresh air would make me feel better…"

It probably would. It would also embolden if not empower her.

"Will you take me outside?" she asked, tone light and sweet.

He leaned back. "I'll do anything you want if you let me get drunk enough first."

A smile crossed her face like a songbird's shadow as she poked at her bread. He had a feeling it rarely materialized any other way.

"But not take me out of Ashmore…" She glanced at him, and he could have sworn she batted her lashes. He might have imagined that.

"Oh, I probably would… Then I'd drag you back when I sobered up."

Her one-sided and thin-lipped smile, she managed to hold longer. "You think you could? After I've regenerated?" She ripped off a tiny piece of bread and rolled it between her thumb and index finger. "Do you think your magic-absorbing sword would be enough?" Peeking up at him, she popped the ball of bread between her lips too deliberately.

He took a big drink. "I think I'd enjoy tryin'."

"I don't think you would."

Her words were quiet and devoid of arrogance, but he couldn't have her go on believing them.

"You may be able to bring the fire, sweetheart, but you ain't gonna torch anyone... I can see that plain in your eyes." He thought he did anyway. When they weren't storming or red, they appeared gentle, like something to dip a cup into and drink. "You druids are all about pretty flowers, little birds, and big trees. Nature-y shit. You don't know how to kill."

She stiffened and flushed. "*Nature* is a mother watching a father's rival devour her newborn." Low, hard, and cold, her voice didn't sound quite right forming in that long, slender throat, or passing from those delicate lips. "It's being eaten alive from the inside out. It's freezing, burning, drowning, starving. It's death and decay."

If she thought he hadn't seen nature in damn near all its ruthless glory, she was mistaken.

Her teeth showed with her words. "It's merciless. Its goal to continue itself, by any means."

But that wasn't her, probably. And while he hadn't expected anything so morbid to come out of her, it hadn't disturbed him. He sure as hells couldn't have her thinking it had, either.

"Nature and me got that in common, I guess." His gaze sought hers, so she could see he meant it, but she wouldn't give it up. "How many men you killed, darlin'?"

She wrapped her hands around her cup and stared into it.

"That's what I figured." He downed the last of his ale.

"Have you killed men?"

Pushing his chair out with a loud, grinding squeak against the floor, he rose to replenish his drink. "Plenty. They were all assholes."

"And... women?"

He glanced over his shoulder. Whatever confidence she had a minute ago had bled out of her. *Good.*

"None who weren't too stubborn to stop tryin' to put a blade in me." That wasn't entirely true. "I got uses for women."

He sucked the head off his ale and sat, waiting with dread for the next question.

She scrunched her face as though bracing for a blow. "Children?"

It was his turn to search for answers in the amber liquid. "Just one."

Chapter Five

One being a woman and the other being a caster, the two guards loitering in the barracks each seemed to share half of Sarlona's troubles. She had expected to squeeze an ounce of sympathy out of them.

They wouldn't look at her.

"Here's the druid," was Benton's introduction.

The swarthy, wiry guardswoman reclined in her chair, boots on the common room table.

"Great, longer hours." She plucked a throwing knife from her bandolier and flicked it at a target on the wall. It planted dead center.

The blond man peeked up from his book. His eyes were the same honey brown as his robes.

Benton shoved the woman's feet off the nicked-up table. "You got competition around here now, Lita."

"Or a decoy." Tipping her head to glance at Sarlona, she pulled another knife. "Sorry, hun." She threw her heels back onto the table and the knife over Benton's right shoulder.

While they traded quips that seemed more mean-spirited than chummy, Sarlona sidled closer to the man in the robes.

"Hello." She wanted to ask him how long he'd been there, how he'd survived, how he could work for lorkai, if he'd been a prisoner at first too... "I'm Sarlona."

"I know." He glanced up again but continued to hide the rest of his face in the book. "I'm Cyr."

She caught herself before asking if he'd installed the wards upstairs. He couldn't have. To create wards that powerful, one had to drip magic.

Casters like that she could feel across the room. The man in front of her was damp with it at best. "Did they abduct you too?"

"No."

"All right, c'mon, darlin'," Benton said, snatching her arm. "You want out? Let's go out." He released his grip before she could complain and gestured for the steps that led up from the dingy, windowless chamber.

She headed right at the top of the stairs and down the unadorned main hall. It was the only way to go. Another orc-human man—blockier, shorter, and greener—guarded the double doors to the outside. He wore an axe on each hip.

She expected the cold disinterest she'd received downstairs, but the man gave her a tusk-y smile when she drew close. "Well, you're too pretty to be anyone Benton dragged home, so you must be Sarlona."

A simper tugged at her lips, and she let him shake her hand.

"I'm Grub."

"Hello." Saying it was nice to meet him didn't seem appropriate.

Benton took a swig, starting on the cup he'd brought for her. "All right, outta the way, we're goin' outside." The larger man didn't budge, and Benton tried to shoulder by him without success.

Grub snorted. "I'm sure that will go well."

"Yeah, well... We're tryin' it."

Grub stepped aside, and Benton shoved through the doors. Blessed sunlight streamed in around him.

She rushed into it like any hesitation might let the shadows swallow her.

"You let me know if he bothers you," the larger man said, shutting the doors behind them.

The afternoon sun drove half the heaviness from her chest, its warm rays a balm for her spirit. Feeling more herself, she closed her eyes and turned her face to its restorative kiss. The sun told her she'd survive. If she could see it, *feel* it, she could endure. Everything could.

She drew in a slow, purifying breath. The air bore wood smoke, hay, mud, and chicken manure. Better than the must collecting in the dead trees that craftsman had warped into the Lord of Ashmore's estate. But not what she yearned for. She craved salt in the air. Or, failing that, humus, lake water, or pine. Taking another deeper breath, she delved farther—dead leaves, browned grass, and...*Benton*.

With a start, she opened her eyes.

He whispered in her ear from behind, "I'm warnin' you, darlin'." The ale on his breath was thick enough to taste. His body heat seeped into her spine and shoulders. "Those hands better not start glowin' with Marrow."

He ran a finger down the palm at her side. Gods knew why that made her flush. A strand of his black, unwashed hair spilled onto her shoulder.

"They won't," she said, recoiling.

He sipped his ale, spinning away on the balls of his feet—a maneuver that could have been lithe or drunken. Hopefully the latter.

She wandered the yard, then walked along the palisade, with him trailing behind her. Every so often, when his stare drifted from her, she snuck a sip of Marrow through her bare soles.

There weren't many ways out.

The palisade logs were straight, sharp, peeled of their bark, and difficult to climb. Her best bet was the one she'd spotted from the window, scrambling onto either the stable or the chicken coop and leaping for it.

She wasn't getting through the gate. Gorgil guarded that. "Hello, Sarlona," he said when she neared.

She forced a smile. "Hi."

The guard captain addressed her but glared at Benton. "Benton let you out, did he?"

"Glaucus said to take her around," Benton answered.

Gorgil frowned and broadened his stance. "Did he say to show her the way out?"

"Nah, but it's cute, the way she's searchin' for it. Thinkin' I don't notice."

Her heart sagged. She'd hoped he was focusing more on his cup than her eyes.

"Sarlona..." Gorgil called her attention from the jagged line where the blue sky met grayed wood. His striking brown eyes widened, and he spoke slowly as if in emphasis. "You may get out, but you won't get away."

What an awful thing to say to a caster captured by lorkai.

"She knows that," Benton said.

Maybe she did.

She meandered about the courtyard until he'd finished his fourth drink in an hour and yawned at his empty cup. Making her way to the stable, she noted what she would've described as a widow's walk on the manor's roof. She gawked at the horses as if they held some meaning to her, peering in each stall to say hello. When she got to the end, she leaned against a large crate along the stable's far end and gazed at the sky.

A gray-haired guard with a bow paced along the widow's walk.

"Who's that?" She pointed.

Benton pivoted at the roof. "That's Gupson. And a pretty useless asshole."

Sarlona had cast an invisibility spell and was halfway onto the stable's roof when he swiveled back.

"Cock." Benton snarled as she swung her legs up onto the cedar shingles. Hopping onto the crate behind her and sweeping his hand across the roof's edge, he just missed her ankle.

With no time to contemplate how hitting the top of the palisade wrong might impale her, she prayed mid-leap she wouldn't slip.

Her feet jammed painfully on either side of one sharpened log, but before all her weight came down, she jumped again, out from the wall.

"Feather." She softened her landing an instant before colliding with packed earth, rolling to absorb the rest of the impact. The expletives from the stable roof propelled her into a sprint.

She didn't dare glance over her shoulder. The louder curse, grunt, and metallic jangle told her he was following and not half as impaired as she'd hoped. Even if she was faster, she had to get out of there quick before the lorkai arrived. That required more Marrow than she had to spare. So, she took it in from the earth, a tiny sip with every fleeting step while she made a beeline for the forest.

An arrow appeared in the ground ahead of her with a thunk, forcing her to jump over it. "Carapace." She threw up her magical shell just before a second bounced off her calf.

The guards couldn't see her but judging by the accuracy of the arrows and the pounding boots behind her, they knew where she was. The disruption of dead meadow grass and the slight glow of Marrow where her skin met the earth betrayed her.

She discarded the invisibility to conserve her magical energy, and once she thought she was out of Gupson's range, she dropped the carapace too.

Another string of profanities came as a gasping growl right behind her.

"Shit." She made one last push for speed. Her thighs and lungs burned like fire, and her heart thrashed. She wouldn't make it to the forest.

Far from prepared, she slapped her hands in front of her and interlocked her thumbs to form a bird. "Flight."

Throwing her arms out to the sides as much as she could without sacrificing speed, she groped for the breeze. She imagined soaring, her fingers growing long and light, and catching the wind beneath them. Picturing a kestrel, her bones shifted and lightened. Her insides turned airy. Chipmunks manifested, scurrying across distant branches. With a scream and a flap of powerful half-arm, half-wing appendages, she leaped.

The spell flew off without her.

Instead of lifting into the air, she slammed into the ground. Her cheek hit cold earth, her bones groaned, and her breath fled her lungs.

Her head swam. She thought she'd been hit by the ram...

But something warm and unforgiving crushed her into the stiff meadow grass—Benton.

His weight lifted before a biting grip smashed her right wrist against the small of her back, and a knee pinned her between the shoulder blades. She thrashed as he tried to nab her other arm.

"Be still, gods dammit." His ragged breaths reeked of ale.

She couldn't take enough of her own, his weight making them extra elusive.

He snatched her other arm and twisted it behind her, provoking her holler. She struggled all the harder as he finagled her wrists into one hand and went for the cord on his belt.

"Repel." She used a scrap of Marrow to blast him off her and scrambled to her feet. Before she could take a step, he hooked her ankle. One yank knocked her to the ground.

He dragged her toward him, and she sent a puff of flame over his arm, just short of his face.

"Cock."

She clambered up again when he let go, but he popped to his feet just as fast and grabbed her shirt at the shoulder. He whipped her around faster than she could rip it free.

Her face exploded with pain, and everything went blank. She lay in the dead grass when the world returned with his hand on her throat. He elevated a fist, and she winced, bracing for the blow that would knock her out.

Sighing, he relaxed his grip and opened his fist. "Gods dammit, darlin'." He rolled her over, then tried to recapture her hands.

She wouldn't let him. Thrashing, she tried to kick her way out from under him. "Help me." Screaming to the Gods and the forest, she stretched her free hand at the tree line.

The Gods didn't answer. The forest did what it could.

A shot of Marrow came through her fingers. It might power a spell or two.

"Stay." She wished for fat, woody roots to wind around him and bury him in the earth. The trees were too far for her to manage it so depleted. She sent the weeds after him instead. Stringy tendrils sprouted from the soil and looped over his boots and calves.

"Dammit." He let her go, and she crawled forward.

Drawing his sword in a blink, he severed the roots around his left leg and tore his right free with a bellow.

She didn't have the strength or the focus to make the living mat ensnare him as fast as he could rip and slice the roots.

"Carapace," she whispered while climbing to her feet. Her voice was thick, and she tasted blood. Everything hurt. She had nothing left.

He stood between her and the woods. Raising his blade, he grinned. "This ain't what I wanna stick in you, darlin'," he said. "Come on now, and I won't have to."

She wanted to cry. Instead, she juked left and jumped right, trying to sprint around him. His blade dissolved her flimsy carapace and sunk into her thigh, mid-hop.

Agony hurtled through her leg, and the blade sucked out what vapors of Marrow she had remaining. It would have started on her life force had he not slipped it free. She collapsed with a shriek.

As he tied her hands, and her leg grew warmer and wetter, she screamed at herself to get up and hobble. All she could do was tremble.

"Up." He seized her under the arms and pulled her to her feet.

She howled through gritted teeth.

"Come on, sweetheart. If you can run, you can walk." He towed her along for a few seconds before she lost her feet.

The pain didn't prevent her from walking. It was the shaking, the wetness, the sight of raw red flesh peeking out from her torn pants.

"I can't," she said when he hauled her up. He grumbled and shoved his sword into its scabbard.

"Fine." He stooped and grabbed her around the haunches and the back of her knees, lifting her onto his shoulder.

The sickly-sweet smell of ale and sweat swallowed the scent of dried grass as the world flipped upside down. He started for the manor house, his shoulder driving deeper into her gut with every step. She groaned at the trail of blood dotting the brown meadow behind them. And her leg was throbbing.

He patted her ass. "You'll be all right, sweetheart. The lorkai'll fix you right up."

That wasn't much comfort.

Gorgil opened the gate wide when they approached the palisade. "See?"

She ignored the upside-down guard captain as they went by.

Benton stopped just shy of the house's entrance. "I only stuck her once. She's just bleedin' a lot."

The huge, fur-lined boots revealed the other party. Dread crushed her like a cider press.

"I'll take her now." That deep, Northland thunder rumbled up

Sarlona's spine.

"I can bring her up to her room," Benton said. "Just fix the kid's leg."

That sounded preferable to Sarlona.

"Give her to me," the unyielding voice replied.

Chapter Six

After more hesitation than Dagmar usually tolerated from him, Benton dumped Sarlona at her feet. The young woman groaned and tried to rise but climbed no farther than her hands and knees.

"She's strong as hells for a robe, you know that?" He gazed at the girl too hungrily.

Dagmar leaned closer. "Go ahead and say it."

He peered at her with a grin. "And for a woman."

"Mmhmm." When mortal, Dagmar could have knocked him out with one punch. Steel to steel, he would have given her trouble.

She pressed her lips together and stared at Sarlona. The young woman was strong for a southerner. But weaker stomached than Dagmar had hoped.

She scooped up Sarlona and threw her over a shoulder. The girl's heart rate increased from a jackrabbit's to a hummingbird's.

"For once, Benton." Dagmar patted his head, and he flinched, with good reason. "You did well."

One corner of his mouth rose, but he wouldn't meet Dagmar's gaze. His leer roamed between Sarlona's backside and the blood flowing down Dagmar's arm.

The lorkai ran her fingers along the side of his face and stroked his jaw. That captured his horrified stare—his eyes the same stunning blue as the streams that ran through Northland's glaciers. She let his heart pound in fearful confusion for a moment, then destroyed all the extraneous alcohol in his body.

"*Ah.*" He winced and writhed from under her hand. "You gods-damned bitch."

She laughed and took Sarlona inside. An instant later, she threw the girl on to the bed in her chamber.

Sarlona trembled while she righted herself and wiped the blood from her nose. She fought for air. Her tangy scent said sheer terror, rather than injury or pain.

Normally, Dagmar would've taken pride in that. Yet as she sat on the edge of the bed, it annoyed her that Sarlona didn't ask for help. Instead, while growing pale and woozier, the girl covered her wound with her bound palms and tried to call a spell that couldn't possibly answer.

Dagmar reached inward, double-checking that her eyes were set on unremarkable blue and ran a hand through her hair to tame it. "Why don't you ask me to heal you?" She spoke more hushed and at a higher pitch than came naturally, trying to seem less monstrous.

Sarlona glanced up. Her mouth opened, but no words came out. Then she pressed her hands over her leg and laid her head on her knees. Apparently, the girl preferred to curl into a ball and pass out from blood loss.

"Here." Dagmar took Sarlona's calf, coaxing her leg out straight. "Lay down."

Quaking, Sarlona sank into the fur-lined blankets.

Dagmar could have taken her hand to make her well. Instead, she unlaced the front of Sarlona's pants. The young woman jerked, trying to deflect Dagmar's powerful hands with her paling, delicate ones. Of course, she couldn't budge them. Her blackening eyes met Dagmar's, then she dropped her hands on her stomach and stared at the ceiling.

Dagmar tugged her blood-soaked pants down to her knees.

Sarlona wouldn't have bled out. The blade had passed expertly through her outermost thigh muscle, the one that attached to the kneecap, missing the femoral artery but making it difficult to walk. The mess was more from her frantic heart than the severity of her wound.

Dagmar cupped her hands around Sarlona's thigh that was the perfect balance of hard and soft. With her will alone, Dagmar knitted the muscles together, joined the blood vessels, and sealed the skin. She straightened Sarlona's nose, faded her bruises, and wiped the abrasions off her feet with the same touch.

Sarlona's color returned, the knots in her face loosened, and she sat up. Not a sliver of tension left her limbs, though. Probably because Dagmar hadn't removed her hands.

"You know I've got nothing left," she said with a kitten's mewl.

Dagmar did. That didn't stop her from running her fingertips over the girl's skin. Or kneading muscle.

Sarlona tolerated about three seconds of it before she squirmed.

"Relax…" It wasn't a suggestion. Dagmar sent the command up Sarlona's leg.

The druid wilted into the mattress. Her heart rate slowed to that of someone digging a trench rather than running for their lives, but the fear in her eyes intensified.

Dagmar's muscles itched for her to use them, and a rumble rose in her chest, but she silenced both. "That old man broke you," she said. "Keeping you alone in the wilderness for so much of your time. Without so much as a pat on the shoulder…"

She pressed her thumbs deeper into Sarlona's flesh. The red in the girl's face expanded. Adrenaline battled her endorphins.

"I was happy." Sarlona sounded out of breath and distant.

Dagmar laughed. "No, you weren't."

"I was comfortable."

"Not truly." Dagmar read Sarlona's body rather than control it as she made circles with her thumbs. "But we'll get you comfortable here."

The girl caught a groan halfway out of her mouth, and it thinned into a whine. "My leg is fine now." Her muscles had stopped quivering, but her voice hadn't. "Thank you," she added.

"There's going to be a lot of touching, Sarlona."

The young woman's eyes watered as she stared at the ceiling.

That triggered an ache in Dagmar's chest she hadn't expected. She sighed and draped a blanket over Sarlona's legs. "You'll get used to it."

"I won't." Sarlona's voice broke, and her eyes welled up, the delicate skin around them twitching as she held back the tears.

"It's your first day here…," Dagmar said. "Your first day free of Sylvanus's shackles, and your first day with people who know your value."

"You value me like my father values our best cow," Sarlona said through gritted teeth. As if such a small voice could sound menacing.

"Which is more than he values you."

The fight left Sarlona's face. Dagmar knew where to press Sarlona inside to make it hurt, just as she did outside to bring relief. She snatched one foot from under the blanket. Sarlona didn't resist.

A few well-placed fingertips turned her red. A spike of pheromones seeped into the air, sharper this time.

"No one knows you as I do," Dagmar said, and the girl's gaze drifted from the ceiling. "No one knows what you need as I do."

Sarlona gripped the blankets, white-knuckled, while Dagmar kneaded her flesh.

Then she pushed elsewhere…on Sarlona's mind.

The girl's eyes went wild. "What are you doing?" She held up her hands as if those could come between her thoughts and Dagmar's will.

She bore down until Sarlona writhed and clutched the sides of her head. "Let me in, Sarlona."

She shook her head and clenched her jaw.

Her mental protections were superb but not enough. Dagmar had been in her mind before she'd perfected them. That left her vulnerable. And if Dagmar hadn't been able to break through via telepathy, skin-to-skin with the girl, she could stroll in physiologically.

"Please don't, Dagmar," Sarlona begged through gritted teeth.

"It doesn't hurt if you let me in," Dagmar replied, pressing harder, working her way in like an awl.

Sarlona squealed when she popped through. That sound... Dagmar's hunger raged. Her desire burned. She could force that small, arousing noise from the girl again. Grope her from head to toe and make her cry out as many times as she liked. Dagmar took a deep, calming breath. Not yet.

Too aware of the threat inside to worry about the threat outside, Sarlona stilled.

Other than her gods-given right to her inner self, Dagmar didn't see what was worth begging to protect. The girl was a ball of fear, bobbing in a sea of guilt.

Fear of years of imprisonment, dread she'd never see her family or her homeland again, horror the lorkai would use their touch to torture or rape her, or worst of all, compel her to hurt people. Her body betrayed the quantity of her terror, and the specifics, one could surmise. Dagmar might have been ashamed of being so afraid, but Sarlona wasn't.

The guilt was over the death of the three merpeople and so many of Tydras's creatures. Also predictable.

Deeper, Dagmar found smaller, long-standing fears. These too were unremarkable, and Sarlona had harbored them since childhood. The lorkai already used those against her.

She kept a thin and fleeting fantasy of suicide as her darkest secret. Self-pity and a few mean-spirited words that had slipped out at her brother served as her greatest source of shame. The inevitable social blunders of someone kept so isolated supplied the rest.

Pride in her power was her greatest sin, and the knowledge she'd never live up to Sylvanus's expectations tempered it. Dagmar couldn't find a fully formed sexual fantasy anywhere. Sarlona just yearned to be loved.

So as far as minds went, hers was clean and innocent—a blooming flower in a field of rotting carnivore shit compared to the minds of Ashmore's guards and the lorkai's.

Nothing to be embarrassed about.

The only thing Sarlona had to hide were some of Sylvanus's secrets, and Dagmar couldn't care less about those.

"I missed this...," she said. "Being so close to you."

Sarlona wriggled, mind and body. But Dagmar's presence ate at her loneliness. After a time, she accepted it, and her thoughts quieted.

She lost herself for a few seconds, swallowed by the relief Dagmar's hands brought to her body, and Dagmar's mind brought to her psyche.

The lorkai had to smile at that.

Sarlona soon returned with all her discipline. Staring at one knot in the beam above her, she traveled its rings, smelled the old wood, and faded into its center until she became it.

Dagmar didn't care to be a knot or be intimate with one.

Rather than shatter Sarlona's focus or impel thoughts to the front of her mind, Dagmar receded from her consciousness. She let the girl meditate for a few minutes, listening to her heart and breaths slow. Then she sent a warm shock rippling through Sarlona's body, transforming her into a young woman.

Sarlona shook her head as if she needed to do so to set it right. "Are there other... prisoners here?"

"No." Dagmar squeezed a cry out of her, the sort that roused every type of hunger.

"I'm... You don't keep anyone else here to drain?" Sarlona sat up a bit. Her heart raced again.

"We're not keeping you to drain. You produce far more Marrow than my father and I need to sustain ourselves." Dagmar spoke with care. She had no desire to deceive the girl, but she couldn't tell her everything either. "We're draining you to keep you. What we need from you is a way to sustain our people. We're almost gone."

That scared Sarlona more of course. She shook. "How? How could I do that? What are you going to do to me?"

Dagmar slid her hands higher and locked gazes with the young woman. "Nothing you can't handle, I promise. Don't worry about that right now." She used the gentlest voice she could summon. "I want you to focus on how you feel." Massaging Sarlona's calf, she sent a hot tingle up the young woman's leg.

That diverted Sarlona's trepidation but not for long. It jumped back to what the lorkai had planned for her. "Are you going to use me in a ritual?"

"There will be a ritual."

"One that will consume me? Kill me?" She propped herself up awkwardly on one side, but Dagmar made her arms go limp, and she sank into the blankets. The sweet scent of her fear hung thick in the air.

"You might pass briefly between realms, but that won't be your end, Sarlona. You'll be okay afterward."

Sarlona fell quiet, except for the sounds Dagmar kneaded from her. Her lips remained parted like questions danced on her tongue.

"What is it?"

"Is the dark mage going to perform the ritual?" Sarlona asked. "The one who set those wards?"

No doubt the fate of her soul concerned her if shadowy magic was to send her to the next realm. "No."

"The tales say lorkai can't use magic—"

"We can't *cast*," Dagmar said. "We can use magical items, trigger-laid spells, that sort of thing." She nabbed Sarlona's other leg and scooted farther up the bed, desiring the whole girl within reach. "We won't do anything to endanger your soul."

The cloud hovering over Sarlona thinned. "When it's finished... Can I go home?"

"No." Dagmar dug her fingers in until pain mingled with release, and she wrung that sweet, arousing cry from her prey again. "The fate of the lorkai will be bound to you. And you to us."

Chapter Seven

The knock transported Sarlona from her book to her prison, where she braced herself for who might come through the door.

"Hello, little one." Glaucus appeared in the threshold, its door now open.

Some of the tension leaked from her spine.

Then Benton, the lewd killer with the hungry eyes, loose grin, and the spell-eating sword, followed him in. He stationed himself in the corner by the window and leaned into it. A second sword belt hung in one hand.

She ignored him and focused on Glaucus's smile. It was an honest one, which promised the sight of her brought him joy. She'd never had that.

He held out his hand and drew her to him with his gaze. She tucked a scrap of ribbon into the book and rose. Her heart pounded, but she needed out of that room. And he was easy to please.

If she didn't struggle or plead when he drained her, he'd take her for a walk outside the palisade afterward. She needed that forest air. So as soon as her feet would cooperate, she went to him.

He took her hand and tugged her into his arms. Hugging her from behind, he whispered in her ear. "Good girl."

His embrace brought a blissful jolt she couldn't resist.

She didn't want to like him, his attention, or crave his approval, but she understood why she did. He was a Sylvanus who was warm and affectionate and said, "Well done," instead of, "Well, you did it, however poorly…"

So Glaucus's willingness to fulfill her emotional needs drained the fight out of her before he started on her Marrow. It didn't hurt that he was handsome, for an older man, with a warrior's build.

He slid one hand under her shirt to rest on her stomach, and she wasn't sure if the delightful fluttering inside was his doing or her genuine response this time. She would have sunk into him when he kissed her throat had Benton not been staring.

The pull of Marrow from her hand and abdomen made her wince, but she nearly swooned from the rush of warmth Glaucus sent through her to drown the unpleasant sensation.

She tried not to make a sound or a face or let her legs go weak but failed at all three.

"Thank you, Sarlona." A sweet shiver crawled up her arm with his caress. "I am sorry we must keep you so weak." He kissed her behind the ear and stepped away with a squeeze of her shoulder.

A cold tremor overtook the sweet one.

"I'm afraid I couldn't make time for our walk this morning," he said, as he headed for the door.

Disappointment weighed her down like a rock.

"Benton will keep you busy."

The guardsman smiled and pushed himself off the wall.

A pang of dread joined her disappointment.

Glaucus glanced at her from the doorway. "Do as he says." He left.

Some deep part of her ached. She hated herself for that.

"Did he get you off that time?" Benton asked with a grin. Always with that stupid grin.

"Stop it," she said, staring past him.

He stepped close enough she either had to view some part of him or turn. "Kinda wanted him to, though, didn't you?"

The blood pounded in her face. She couldn't get used to the things that came out of his mouth. But she was beginning to believe their primary purpose was to change her color.

He leaned in, whispering near the side of her head. "How 'bout I finish you up, darlin'?"

Or maybe they were to jolt her heart out of rhythm. Heat flashed through her like she might pass out. Then she'd be in *real* trouble.

"No." The word came out hushed and dry, so much so, she worried he wouldn't believe she meant it.

He just handed her the extra sword and belt. "Put it on."

That didn't seem like a real thing he'd say, but warm leather and the weight of a sword attached to it tugged on her hand. Once her disbelief had worn off, she tied it around herself.

He leered at her hips. "Perfect."

She figured he just liked swords and women's hips in general.

"Go on." He motioned to the door. "We're goin' down to the

yard. I'll show you how to use that thing."

She wasn't about to argue. Any chance to leave that room was one she'd take.

Much of her heaviness faded the instant she crossed the threshold. She could breathe. Marrow sung to her in its melodic hum beyond the wooden walls. A few sips of it, and she wouldn't be weak, helpless, and hopeless. The fog around her brain and the syrup in her veins thinned. She left some of her fear in the chamber as she strode down the hall.

Another weight lifted when she stepped outside. The bracing cold and crunch of frozen, hard-packed gravel came with a vesper of Marrow. She took a deep breath, and life flowed into her with the fresh air.

"Come on." He prodded her behind the building where a small, dirt arena lay bordered by the second and third-floor overhang of the house on one side and a row of targets and training dummies on the other. A few barrels and crates stood on each end.

He walked into the middle of the dirt oval. "Okay, let's see what I've got to work with. You know a basic lunge?"

Softening her knees, she prepared for one. "Yes."

"Let's see it then, sweetheart."

She slid the dull blade from its sheath and lunged with it out straight, putting her right foot forward.

"Hold like that."

"Who am I going to be stabbing?" she asked, motionless.

He kicked her left foot into a position perpendicular to her sword arm and raised the tip of her blade when it started to droop. "You got somethin' better to do?"

Stepping clear, he looked her over, then took her hand in both of his. They were bronze, rough, and crisscrossed with about a dozen scars but gentle for the moment.

"You want it more in your fingers right behind the guard," he said, manipulating her digits into place. "The end of the grip just sorta rests on the heel of your hand."

He seemed strangely person-like in that instant.

Then he went behind her. She started when he grabbed her hips and tugged them backward. "Keep as much weight over your left leg as you can. That way, you can pull back quick."

His hands lingered, and he pushed his thumbs into a tender muscle behind each hip bone she hadn't known she had. A twinge of pain mingled with pleasure shot through her hips and gave her another start. The sensation paralyzed her.

"Your hips are real tight, darlin'." He pressed harder. His body heat coated her spine. "How 'bout I loosen 'em up for you later?"

Her skin flared with heat, and her face burned.

"All right, now try it," he said, dropping his hands from her hips.

She would have let him keep them there. That couldn't lead anywhere beneficial. After a deep breath, she lunged again, with his instructions in mind.

"Good." He came around from behind, and while his back was to her, she called a thread of Marrow from the sky. "All right, now see if you can't hit me."

She stared at him, waiting for him to draw his blade. "Don't you need your sword?"

He pulled on gloves from his pocket. "I doubt it."

"Just...stab you?" Her sword was dull and blunted, but he wasn't wearing any armor.

He never did, just leather pants and a sleeveless leather jerkin left open over his grungy shirt. If she connected solidly, it would hurt.

"If you can, sweetheart. No magic, that's all."

"Okay."

"Don't get no ideas, either." He widened his stance and crossed his arms. "I can pull this blade plenty quick. Plus Amen's keeping his eye on us. Sweet girl like you won't take that dark well."

She hadn't spotted 'Amen.' Neither did she sense any black auras or extraordinary magic nearby. He might be bluffing. Tentatively, she sent out her imperceptible magical feelers.

They were stomped out of existence like glowing, wayward ash.

That added an extra draught of dread to a full bottle. And it irritated her that Benton thought he knew her. "What makes you think I'm sweet?"

He swaggered close enough she expected to catch ale on his breath. "The taste I had after Dagmar got done with you last night."

The blood drained out of her. He'd been guarding her door the previous night.

"I'm kiddin', sweetheart."

Her chest heaved. It all seemed like too much again. "You're not funny."

"All right, stab me," he said, receding.

She lunged, aiming for his center.

He parried with his palm against the flat of the blade. "Reset."

Straightening, she lunged to the same effect.

"Reset."

She aimed to the left, but he still parried.

"Now, that ain't workin', is it?" he said. "Again."

Targeting his right thigh, she exploded out of her next lunge.

He still deflected the blade. "Advance."

She brought her hind foot forward and went into another lunge as he retreated.

"Come on... Hit me, darlin'. I've gotta've given you enough reasons by now. Advance."

She struck faster, harder, trying to get her blade in high, low, and everywhere in between. She advanced on him until his back was against the building and without a single hit. When he had nowhere to go, she lunged one more time.

He grabbed the blade and yanked. For a second, she went with it, and he snatched her around the waist, crushing her against him before she could hop clear.

Grinning, he peered at her. "Hi, darlin'."

She sighed, though the thrashing of her heart said she should scream. "Hello, Benton."

He inched one hand dangerously close to her tailbone. "Holdin' that grip like it was a club again, weren't you?"

She couldn't quash the warble that leaked into her voice. "It seems so." Every breath pressed her tighter against him.

He smelled better than usual—like leather, woodsmoke, and metal instead of ale. The warmth of his body spread into hers. Warmth she didn't have to trade Marrow for.

Magic-sucking or not, she doubted he'd be satisfied with an embrace and tried to pry herself free. "You don't strike me as the type to need a hug."

He leaned in, grinning against her cheek, and whispered in her ear, "That ain't all I need, sweetheart."

"So desperately that you'll risk being lit on fire?"

"Darlin', I can't wait to get your fires goin'," he growled into her hair.

The rare heat pulsed through her, fighting a swell of panic. Panic won. "Let go of me, Benton. I swear to gods, I will sprout quills. I—I have enough Marrow f—"

"I trust everyone's behaving themselves?" said a low, resonant voice from behind.

Benton sighed and loosened his arms. "Much as I'm capable."

Squirming away, she exhaled and spun to meet the last and most dangerous of her mortal jailors.

The dark mage wasn't what she'd envisaged. Where she had pictured black robes over a skeletal frame, stood a tall, heavyset man draped in blue silk. She'd expected dark, sunken eyes, but found bright blue-green ones accented by thick lashes. His short hair was black with streaks of silver, and he wore a grayed goatee. Despite that, he appeared young, she guessed no older than thirty. He also looked familiar.

"Greetings, Sarlona." With a cordial smile, he reached for her hand.

After hesitating, she gave it to him.

"It's lovely to see you again." He kissed her fingers.

She stared at her boot and scuffed the dirt.

Benton crossed his arms and spat at it.

"I'm sure you don't remember me, my dear. You were a child when we met." Amen clasped her hand between both of his, trapping it. "It was at the university library. You were there with your mentor."

She had accompanied Sylvanus to the University of Higher Magic in Royal City to use their library a dozen times. On the first, when she was eight, a teenage boy who'd just leveled out of his training—five years early—introduced himself to Sylvanus and took her on a tour of the campus.

"I remember you." She nodded. "Amen*duil*. You leveled out at fifteen and broke all those records..."

He smiled a touch wider and released her hand.

"Is this where you've been all this time?" She imagined him as an even greater prize to the lorkai than she, abducted as a youth and held in Ashmore for more than a decade, eventually brainwashed into staying.

"Let's not bore Benton with our catching up," he said. "Finish your lesson, and I'll visit upstairs later where we can chat in private, yes?"

"Okay."

Amenduil smiled anew and disappeared around the side of the building, heading for the stairs to the roof.

"He's trouble, sweetheart," Benton said when she spun to him. "Be careful with him."

She raised her eyebrows. "More so than you?"

He grinned. "Hard to believe, I know." The smile left his eyes. "But I ain't after your soul."

Fearing for her soul, body, and freedom all at once, she examined the dirt. "Well, I can't escape any of you, can I?"

"Nope. You might have more of a chance if you get good with a blade." He tossed her the dull sword. "Probably take out Cyr or Gupson someday."

She gripped the sword like he'd shown her and stood with her hips open and weight back.

"Advance."

They played the same game as before. Other than grazing his arm, she didn't do any better. And once he'd retreated within a stride of the wall, she lowered her weapon, afraid he'd grab her under the overhang again.

"Lunge," he demanded.

"No."

"You're that scared of me?"

As much as she hated fearing some asshole guard with a sword when she could wield a storm, she couldn't deny it. "Only while I'm drained."

He peeled himself from the wall. "Well, that's gonna be for the rest of our lives, ain't it?"

Tears sprang into her eyes. She couldn't stop them. He was right. She'd always be weak now, always at mercy of the violent men and monsters around her. She'd never truly feel like herself. Never be invigorated or reach her potential.

"No..." His voice weakened. "Now, don't start that, darlin'." He approached like she was a frightened animal. Maybe she was. "I'm sorry, sweetheart, I shouldn't have said that. I'm sure that ain't fun to think about..."

She could have laughed if she hadn't tumbled into a dark hole. That, of all things, was the one he knew he shouldn't have said.

"Come on, now... Stab me." He set his hand on her shoulder like it was coated in embers.

She nodded and wiped her eyes with her palm.

Stabbing him would help. She tried hard for at least half an hour but never landed the nasty jab in the ribs she so desired. Skimming his thigh and catching his fingers was all she could manage.

"All right, that's enough of that," he said, finally, and took her sword.

Assuming that meant they were finished, she shook out her numb arm and slicked her hair back with the sweat on her brow. He jogged to one end of the training area and cut a line in the frozen ground. After returning the sword to her, he beckoned her to follow to the other end of the makeshift arena.

"Now, I'm gonna come after you." He pointed at her. "You'd better poke me somewhere important before I get by your guard or you back over the line. Cock it up, and I'm gonna knock you around some."

He sounded serious but couldn't look it with that stupid grin. "I'm gonna enjoy it too."

She wouldn't get her blade through to his trunk. That was fine.

Maybe she deserved a beating. Maybe if she was physically injured, she could feel sorry for herself without drowning in shame and cowardice on top of it.

"Ready, darlin'?" He put his hands out in front of him and let his knees slacken.

"No."

"Tough." He leaped, grabbing for her.

She hopped back, avoiding his grasp. He lunged at her as if he had a sword, and she jumped clear.

"You're almost halfway to the line..." he said, advancing on her.

She took the bait, aiming for this throat.

He deflected the blade wide and to her right, making himself an opening.

Her eyes watered an instant after hot pain erupted across her cheek. At least he'd only slapped her.

At least. Only. She followed him to their starting point as disgusted with herself as she was with him.

Her second attempt ended like her first, and her third failure earned her a fist in the gut. He slammed her into the ground after her fourth. She was afraid to lunge after her fifth punishment—a jab to the kidney—and backed over the line.

"You must like a little pain, darlin'," he said after throwing her onto the ground again.

With everything stinging and aching, she didn't bother to shake her head. She was accustomed to pain. But all the bumps, scrapes, bruises, frostnip, and spell burn inflicted upon her were, for the most part, incidental. This felt different—violent and humiliating.

Part of her longed to return to her warded chamber and crawl into bed. For Glaucus to come in and rep lace her hurts with softness. Sick with herself, she rolled over and almost threw up. Maybe the lesson was meant to break her. Or worse, to make the lorkai approachable or even desirable.

"Benton, I don't want to do this anymore." She started to get up, but his boot drove her pelvis to the ground.

"Well, I guess you had everyone fooled," he said. "The lorkai said you were tough. I thought you were a fighter that first day."

"I'm not." To prove it, she let her arms buckle and laid her face against the icy gravel.

It brought some relief to her stinging cheek. And it smelled a lot like the tilled soil at home. A deeper longing for Mast Landing blossomed in her gut. She pressed her ear against the dirt and listened.

He lifted his boot after an extra push. "Well, you gotta be around here."

Much of the life had been stomped out of the earth beneath her, but she sensed what remained. Below the surface, worms and larvae dwelt in their lairs. Viable seeds lay ready to sprout if they were ever brought near the surface. They hummed to her.

Stealthily sipping at what strands of Marrow existed there, through her palms, cheek, ear, and the sliver of abdomen her shirt had ridden up to expose, she heard all their songs. Or imagined she did.

"Come on, darlin'. Get up. We'll getcha there." He tapped her leg with his boot.

She climbed to her feet with a groan and shadowed him to their starting point. Raising her sword point with her left arm out behind her as a counterweight, she settled into position. He advanced, and she lunged just left of center. When he brought his left hand across and twisted to push the blade wide, she juked the sword right. The tip jabbed him under the arm.

"Cock." He clutched his armpit, snarling.

She should poke him twice while she had the chance.

"Gods, that cockin' hurt."

Good. Though she worried he'd be angry when he stopped whining.

After shaking his arm out, he appeared genuinely delighted. His smile almost spread onto her face. "See? You're gettin' the hang of it, darlin'."

Starved as she was for approval, she didn't care whether she had his. "So, we can stop now?"

"Oh, no, sweetheart." His face lit up. "You gotta give me a chance to pay you back for that."

She sighed but raised her guard. As soon as she was in position, she exploded into a lunge, hoping to catch him by surprise. He pushed the flat of the blade wide with his palm, then kneed her between the legs.

Searing pain shot through where she least wanted it. "Cock." She dropped the sword and clapped her hands over her front.

"Sorry, darlin', force of habit. How come all the women around here have balls?"

"I still have to piss from somewhere." Her eyes watered from the raging sting.

He scooped up the sword and shoved it at her. "You'll be all right, sweetheart." His voice turned sickly sweet. "I'll kiss it better right when we get done."

She took the sword to throw it at him with all her strength.

He barely blocked it from hitting his face. "Ow."

"Shut up, Benton. Just shut your mouth for once." She ached to use the scraps of Marrow she'd collected to throw him like a rag doll into the side of the house. Instead, she yelled, "Imagine if Glaucus said the same things to you that you say to me."

He grimaced. "Why the hells would I do that?"

Fuming, she got in his face. "Because that's what it's like for me." She made sure to peer into his eyes, as much as she hated to. "Every time you open your cocking mouth."

"It ain't the same thing."

"It's exactly the same." She almost grabbed his arms.

He fell back a step. "He's a man. If it was D—"

"Yes, Benton. And men go inside you. That's the problem with them."

He just blinked at her for a moment. "But you're—"

"So, without my magic, I'm almost as helpless against a man like you as you are against Glaucus." She hated to admit that. "Imagine if he implied, if not told you, he wanted to cock you every time you interacted."

His gaze left her. She'd gotten through to him. "Imagine he didn't give a shit when you said you weren't interested."

He met her stare again and regained the ground he'd given up. "You know you ain't come out and said you ain't interested."

Realization dawned on her with a pang of horror. He was right. She justified it by telling herself she'd been afraid to offend him. "I haven't said I am, either. So, stop it. I've definitely told you to shut up."

He drifted too close. "You know, I wouldn't hurt you, darlin'."

She had an abundance of evidence to suggest otherwise.

Benton leaned in and brushed a strand of hair out of her face. "I can be real gentle when I wanna be," he purred.

Her heart raced. Heat bloomed in her cheeks.

He slipped off one glove and ran warm, rough fingertips from her earlobe to her collarbone. "I'll make you scream some, but it ain't gonna be from pain."

The fire in her face spread downward, but she shrugged off his hand. "It'll be for help in a second."

Sighing, he dropped his arm. "Relax, sweetheart. I ain't gonna do anything to you that you don't want." He sounded like he meant it. "Dagmar would castrate me for one thing—"

"Is that the only thing?" She tried to capture his gaze, but he wouldn't surrender it.

He shrugged. "Darlin' I'm standin' here cuz Glaucus bought my life off the gallows about one second before they were gonna pull the lever. The necks of the other men cracked as we were walkin' away."

Her heart wilted under the weight of dread and empathy. She stared at a puny seedling trying to carve a life for itself between two crates at the end of the arena. A lonely twig. An oak. The most sacred tree.

When she glanced up, his perpetual grin had left him. "I've done a lot worse than come in a little fish-cockin' druid without permission."

She'd assumed as much, given he'd claimed to have killed people, including a child. The veracity of his statement made it that much more enraging.

"Benton." Voice shaking, his name caught in her throat. She met his gaze again.

Chapter Eight

Benton backpedaled, drawing his sword. "Amen... I pissed her off good...," he shouted at the roof.

Amenduil appeared on the catwalk. "Benton... Always the instigator. Don't worry," the dark mage called. "She can't have more than two devastating spells in her."

Sarlona grinned.

"Shit," Benton said, retreating a step. He raised his sword point.

Tapping into the oak sapling, she grew a dozen of its roots to burst from the ground.

He slashed through two and avoided a third, but a fourth snatched his wrist and wrenched the sword from it. Another she urged to grab his other wrist, and two to snag his ankles. She froze them, unyielding wood rooting him to the ground, with his arms out wide above his head.

His grin returned in full force. "Got me how you want me, huh, darlin'?"

She punched him in the gut. Not as hard as she could, but enough to make him groan. The sweetness of the sound surprised her. She didn't think she wanted to hurt him. Just scare him the way he did her.

"I'm glad you like it rough, sweetheart, but—"

Another blow to the gut cut him off. She longed to shut his mouth but imagined he'd die before she accomplished that. Settling for his fear, she circled to hug him from behind.

"Trust me, darlin', this way ain't gonna work."

She ignored the spreading warmth from his body and whispered in his ear. "Benton... I could transform into a male animal. So...what do you like better, brown or white bears?"

She got her wish. His heart pounded harder, and he thrashed against the wooden fetters.

"Amen." His voice cracked. "Gods dammit."

"You're doing fine, Benton," Amenduil hollered. Amusement threaded his voice.

Perfect.

Lucky for Benton, if she had the Marrow for a transformation, she wouldn't have wasted it on him. Instead, she used another trace to commune with the tiny oakling.

The sprig burst into branches, springing into the sky and stretching above the manor house in seconds. Roots wound out halfway across the training area, then froze into gnarled ropes. Furrowed bark expanded wider than three men could join hands around.

The massive oak trapped him in its center. Sinuous, immovable primary branches held him with little more than his face exposed. He strained for a few seconds but wasn't able to budge solid oak.

Some force drew her closer to him.

She supposed she liked his face. He had a strong jaw and chin, a straight nose, and shapely eyebrows. Typical of Avenians, he had dark hair and light eyes. But his eyes were a rare blue—alive, like some of the hottest fires she'd ever conjured, and accentuated with dark lashes. His mouth was the problem. Even that looked pleasing.

She swiped a greasy strand of hair from his face, then ran her fingertips from his earlobe to his clavicle, as he'd done to her.

"Don't kill me all right, darlin'?" He sounded calm for a man locked in a tree. "I got a lotta drinks left undrunk. A lotta women left unbedded. One in particular."

She took a slow breath to avoid striking the tree with lightning. "I hate you."

"Don't lie to me darlin'. That ain't nice."

She rose on her tiptoes. Part of her wanted to kiss him. Not to see how it would feel, but to learn if he'd return the kiss or just tell her to kiss him lower. She rested her hand on the side of his head and rubbed her thumb across the perpetual stubble that adorned his cheek. There was no mistaking her intentions when she leaned in. They shared the same breath.

And he parted his lips.

She withdrew, smiling.

He chuckled and tried unsuccessfully to shake his head. "You let me know just as soon as you're ready to feel somethin' other than scared, sweetheart. I'll take good care of you."

She slapped him for all the red he'd put in her cheeks and pivoted.

"If you think that don't do it for me, darlin'—"

She raised her hand, crossing her fingers, and the oak swallowed him.

With Amenduil's view of her blocked by the oak's canopy, escaping seemed worth a try. Of course, the appearance of a mature oak poking above the roof and shading out a large section of the building had attracted attention.

She raised her arms to the light filtering through the leaves and channeled the sacred oak's potent Marrow until Gorgil and Grub jogged around the side of the house.

"Benton's in there. He's going to asphyxiate," she lied, pointing at the trunk.

Gorgil glanced from her to the tree. "So let him out."

"No."

Frowning, he nodded from Grub to the tree. He pulled his sword as the other man started hacking at the thick bark. "Back inside, Sarlona."

Ignoring him, she stared at a small mat of damp leaves that had blown in and formed against the house. Breathing warm air onto her hands, she made fists.

"Sarlona," Amenduil called, almost singing. "What are you doing, my dear?"

While she retreated from Gorgil, she opened her hands into a 'V,' then parted them upward.

From that small mat of leaves rose a giant centipede. She grew it large enough that men would seem like prey. Large enough that they'd fit between its poison-delivering, fang-like front legs. And given the cold, it hadn't eaten in weeks. Now it was warm and hungry.

The monster charged at Grub first, waving its long, whiplike antennae and rushing forward, snakelike, on dozens of clawed, chitinous legs, faster than anything that size should move. He deflected its black-tipped, venomous pincers with a desperate swipe of an axe as he dove clear. Its antennae followed him, then its head, locking onto its prey with the six black globs that made up its two eyes. It reared up, lifting its first seven segments, sharp legs poised to grab on and fangs ready to deliver their venom.

Gorgil ran for its nearest leg and brought his heavy sword down on one of its joints. The blade didn't cut far enough through the rich-brown chitin to take the leg. With a chittering hiss, the centipede spun on him. "Amen, do something," he screamed.

She whirled to the palisade, fixing her gaze on the spruce logs that made up the wall, then let her vision blur. Blocking out the pounding of boots, shouting, and crunch of thirty-or-so spear-tipped legs puncturing the frozen earth, she imagined the logs as they'd once been. She envisioned them standing tall in the forest.

Her concentration broke with a heavy thump beside her. A decaying, saturated log lay at her feet half-exploded with its impact. The oak was crumbling, rotted to its core. Branches descended as dark, wet decay.

That was Amenduil doing something.

She tried to tune it and everything out.

Benton cursed, and Lita, the guardswoman said, "Here, you idiot."

Then the quiet of the forest washed in—birdsong and a squirrel skittering over loose bark. The spruce spread out, rooted deep in forest soil. Beams of sunlight pierced the dense canopy here and there, made tangible by the heavy mist in the moist understory. Sarlona strode into it.

Glaucus's voice turned her head. Back in another world, the lorkai plunged one claw into the centipede's underside as it struck at Gorgil. One of its venomous fang-legs still drove into the guard captain's shoulder, and he collapsed with a shriek.

Glaucus snatched Gorgil by the arm and tossed him clear of the creature's mouth, then struck again. The centipede hissed, oozing a thick, sticky goo from its underside. The men nearest it, Grub and Sal, stumbled and collapsed, Sal out cold.

Over the earthy scent of the forest, she caught a hint of bitter almond. She swiveled and emerged from the forest on the other side of the palisade.

"Amenduil, Benton, fetch her," Glaucus yelled on the other side of the grove.

She transmuted the woods into a wall and ran. Every shred of Marrow she had left went into a carapace. She just had to make it to the forest. There, she could disappear from the human men without magic. And it wouldn't take her long to absorb the Marrow to power a transformation from the woods. With some luck, she might be able to fly off before one of the lorkai caught up to her.

Glancing over her shoulder, she saw the men emerge from a black portal in the palisade. Benton wouldn't catch her this time; she had too much of a head start. Well within range of a decent caster, though, Amenduil could undoubtedly hit her. She prayed her carapace would hold against him or that he didn't care enough to throw something substantial at her.

The Gods ignored her prayers once again.

With the forest just fifty yards ahead, a cloud of black sand surrounded her. The grains disintegrated her carapace, zipping through it as if it were fog. They sucked the air out of her lungs and stung her eyes. Chest heaving for breath that refused to enter with hands clapped over her face, she crashed to the ground, skidding across the brown meadow grass with a silent cry.

After a blind and breathless struggle against an unfamiliar spell, she peeled open her eyelids and inhaled.

The meadow had gone, taking every hint of color and glimmer of light with it—all replaced with the black sand in which she sank. She clawed for more solid ground and strained to hold on.

It took her a moment to realize she was back on the beach. *Her* beach but black. Inky sand and ebony waves lay under the night sky where no trace of a moon or stars hung. She was trapped halfway to the water with an incoming tide. On each wave that flowed farther up than the last, she made out hundreds of obsidian tendrils writhing over each other.

"Amenduil," she hollered into the darkness when she descended to her navel. "Please, drop it." Her plea echoed like she was in a long, empty hallway.

From the surrounding blackness, a massive entity coalesced. Its form shifted, and it faded in and out of the darkness. All but the maw. Huge ebony fangs circled a pit blacker than the other black. Its dead eyes studied her as it came closer.

"Amenduil."

A second creature stepped out of the darkness and took a shape she recognized. Benton. Or some shadowy version of him. Except for a few thin streaks of light swirling through him and his bright blue eyes, he was ebony from head to toe. He roared, but Sarlona couldn't understand him. His words came out in reverse. Or went into her ears that way.

"Help me," she shrieked, clawing at the sand.

The monster spoke too, and she recognized the calm, low, almost sweet voice…Amenduil's. She couldn't understand him either. But the man and the monster seemed to be arguing.

Meanwhile, the warm, silky sand continued to swallow her while her fingers slipped, rising to her breasts. Intrusive thoughts told her to let go. The sand wouldn't crush or smother her. She'd become it, and it would become her. Every inch that it devoured faded, allowing it to mingle softly with her shadowy remains.

As the ebony granules filled in around her throat, the darkness promised it would hold her, forever in its nocturnal embrace.

The Nocturnal Embrace—Vorakor's cult.

"No," she screamed.

She lay on the dead grass, staring up at the blue sky…and Benton, cloaked in a heavenly glow by the bright sun behind him.

Taking her under the arm, he pulled her onto her feet. "Hey, Sar. You're all right." He patted her shoulder when she hunched over, gagging. "Okay, you're all right."

She fell to her knees and retched up a thick, black mucus that fought to ooze back down her throat. Every gasp to catch her breath ached, her ribs and abdomen sore from straining so hard. She couldn't get up.

He lifted her into his arms—the second-to-last place she wanted to be.

Chapter Nine

Glaucus exited through the gate. That was the measured, dignified path from the estate. The lords of Aven were supposed to be measured and dignified. And despite being a minor lord of a backwater village and its surrounding lands, he excelled at being both.

Though, he didn't feel dignified covered in translucent, yellow-tinted goo, and his patience had worn about as thin as it could before running out. Nevertheless, his response would be calm and calculated as always. Even if irritation nipped at his nerve endings. Especially given how Marrow rich the three humans in the meadow were. All roused his hunger in ways that tested his temperance.

At least, the Marrow of neither man was to his taste. Amenduil had so much dark magic in him, he was almost non-potable. As if a trickle of the Abyssal Waters themselves had diffused into his magical energy.

Like the rest of him, Benton's Marrow seemed to bear the hint of ale.

Sarlona, however, was pure sweetness.

He heard their conversation, their breath, their heartbeats from hundreds of yards away.

"Why do you gotta throw that shit," Benton said to Amenduil. He had Sarlona in his arms. She was whole and conscious, but Glaucus sensed her distress. "When you know every cockin' spell under the sun."

Amenduil put his hand to his heart. "I lovingly crafted that one just for Sarlona. You can't expect me not to give it to her."

"You're a sick man. You know that?"

"Me?"

Glaucus sighed and picked a bright white, shining hunk of arthropod fat out of his hair. "I'm not happy with you three," he said, careful to keep his tone in check and his eyes gray.

For now, he was the Lord of Ashmore, not a monster. The words alone would dismay Sarlona for reasons she would torture herself over and Benton for reasons the swordsman didn't understand.

They wouldn't affect Amenduil.

Glaucus laid a hand on her forehead. She didn't resist him when he seeped into her body and mind. Her injuries were no more than bumps, bruises, scrapes, and strained muscles. He wiped those clean. The black filth Amenduil had put in her was more serious. Her sapphire eyes better matched a raven's plumage.

Glaucus didn't like that.

So long as the darkness was in her body and not her spirit though, he could combat that too. Without knowing what the black ooze was, he vaporized it.

She looked herself, and he helped her from Benton's grasp onto her feet. He held her hand, first to steady her, then to fetter her.

He sighed afresh and stared down Amenduil first. "Save the nightmares for darker souls. Don't pollute Sarlona's."

"It's not in my nature to discriminate, my lord," Amenduil replied with all the confidence of someone hard to hurt. "Except when it comes to Silsorians. They require extra...care."

"You'll make another exception," Glaucus insisted. "Or I may revise the terms of our agreement."

Amenduil searched him with his hyper-intelligent gaze and smiled in the way that made Dagmar punch people. "As you like, my lord."

Glaucus set his stare on Benton next. He didn't speak until the man met it. "Benton... What are you doing?" The human didn't answer, so Glaucus shrugged. "Trying to goad Dagmar into granting you an excruciating death?"

Benton's gaze returned to the dead grass. "You know I don't know why the hells I do what I do."

"Keep behaving this way, and I'll dig as deep as I must to find out."

For the most part, Glaucus allowed his men their privacy and rarely made them endure any mental invasion. None of them wished to relive the dissections they'd experienced their first nights in Ashmore. Maybe Benton, least of all.

"I'll be good," Benton said, studying the ground. "My version of it, anyhow."

Glaucus hadn't finished. "You were warned not to underestimate Sarlona."

"I was also warned not to cut pieces off her."

"Strike a balance, Benton."

Glaucus pivoted and tugged her in front of him. While he waited for her watery gaze to find his, he took her hands. "My men are not expendable... I raised Gorgil from infancy."

Her eyes grew wetter still. "Is... Is everyone okay?" she asked, voice cracking.

The horror in her face was real, however angry she had been a short time ago. However much, "everyone" was her enemy.

He nodded. "Now that I've healed them," he said. "I understand your impetus, but you will abide by the tenants of just combat. No cyanide gasses. Or animals with secretions that volatilize into them," he elaborated the end.

"I thought it was a creative and well-executed piece of spell work," Amenduil said.

Glaucus released one of her hands. "You two help clean up the yard," he told the men over his shoulder as he led her toward the gate. "I'm not angry with you, Sarlona," he said after a minute. "Have no fear of that."

"Well, I'm angry with you...," she said so quietly a human wouldn't have made out the words.

Her scent belied her words. He smelled no anger, only dread. "Are you, now?"

She glanced over her shoulder at the two men following. "You could assign other guards to me," she whispered. "Gorgil could teach me to use a sword, if I have to learn."

"Gorgil has other duties." He wasn't unsympathetic, but her distress wasn't so important as keeping her in Ashmore. She'd have to suffer greater torments before long.

"Someone else then... I..." Her whisper grew softer as she leaned close. "I can't be around Benton," she said. "Or Russ or Sal, truly."

He knew from the time he'd spent in her mind that she would have added Dagmar to the list had she believed he wouldn't take offense.

"They're too...," she hugged herself with her free arm. "Awful."

He put one arm around her and squeezed. "We don't get to choose our captors, little one."

"You choose mine."

"Yes." He nodded. "I do."

Of his men, only Benton and Amenduil could reliably keep Sarlona there. And he couldn't count on Amenduil's loyalty.

Glaucus wasn't about to tell her that. "I'm afraid Benton will continue to be the man most often standing on the other side of your door."

Shrinking, she let all her breath out. For a minute, it seemed like she wouldn't bother to take another. But while she had the discipline to stop breathing until she passed out, she wasn't the type to behave as a defiant toddler. No doubt, she had to be sick of losing consciousness in his arms as well. After a few more seconds, she inhaled, pausing for a few heartbeats at the top, then exhaled.

"You know, Sarlona," he said at normal volume as they passed through the gate. "My men aren't just charged with preventing your escape. They're charged with protecting you."

"Protecting me?" She gazed at the back of the building where

Grub and Lita were just visible, filling a cart with shovelfuls of rotted wood and centipede. "The only protection I need is from the monsters within these walls."

He removed his arm from around her shoulders and patted her head to smooth her hair.

She liked his touch. Not just because he made her body respond so positively to it. Starved of them for so many years, gestures of affection brought the blood to her cheeks without him controlling the flow. So, he gave her lots of tender touches, many fleeting reasons not to fight him or hurt herself.

"You have many enemies, Sarlona."

She stopped and stared at him, careful not to let her gaze drift from his face to Benton and Amenduil while they passed by. "I don't," she said. "I don't make trouble. I help resolve conflicts. I try to be nice to everyone..."

She had tried hard to be the diplomat Sylvanus desired her to be. Glaucus had seen that in her memories. And, until Ashmore, she'd always granted everyone the benefit of the doubt. "They're not enemies you've earned, little one. They're enemies you were born with."

"I don't know what you're talking about," she said. "My parents are farmers."

As if he didn't know more about her than she knew herself. He took her hands and bound her eyes to his. "Sarlona... People hate you."

She raised her brow as the orbs below glistened.

"Because of how powerful you are," he explained. "Because they fear you."

She shook her head and tried to free her hands. "People don't know me. Not outside of Mast Landing, Treefall, and druid circles..."

"Sylvanus sensed your power the day you were born. He took you on to try to control it before you became dangerous and the Society of Progressive Sorcerers found you. They know of you now, little one. The Council knows of you. They fear you."

"Why would the SPS Council fear me?" she asked, trying to rip her hands from his again.

He released one and tugged her into a step, toward the house. "Because you have more raw power than any of them. You'll surpass them within a decade or so. Men of great power do not like being surpassed. Especially by a woman," he said. "It's more than enough reason for half of them to want you dead."

"You're making this up," she said, shaking her head. "I've met the councilors. They were...amicable enough. One is youngish... Two are women."

"You're naïve, little one. Anyway, I said half of them."

"But—" She shrugged. "Wouldn't they also fear Amenduil?" she asked as he opened one of the heavy double doors and held it for her. "He must be stronger than a few of the councilors."

"Amenduil would be a councilor if not for his affiliations," he replied, following her inside. "He knows how to protect himself. He's been hiding for years, mostly from the Silsorian Order."

With an exaggerated hang of her head, she started up the stairs when he gestured to them.

"He can go to ground with the Embrace when he needs. You, little one, are stuck with Ashmore."

"Lucky me," she simpered then stopped halfway to the first landing. "You don't expect me to believe this is all for my own good, then?"

"No." He smiled without showing teeth. "This is all for the welfare of the lorkai. Nevertheless, you will see, eventually, that it benefits you too."

"I'll bet," she said, smirking. "How many of you spell-drinkers will I have to feed exactly?"

By the small of the back, he urged her up the stairs. "Not as many as you imagine, I'm sure."

She didn't get far before spinning. "Will you at least speak with Benton? Please."

"I will, little one." He swept her upward. "I think he's just fond of you."

At the top of the stairs, she froze. "That might make it worse."

"I understand. I'll speak to him," he promised once more.

Wrapping his hands around her shoulders, he prodded her forward. Whether conscious of it or not, she was stalling, trying to avoid returning to the warded chamber.

Snorting, she dragged her feet. "You don't understand. You're not a captive or a woman. You're not mortal."

"I have been," he told her. "Not a woman, of course... When I was still a mortal man in the Imperial Legion, I was captured and imprisoned in Gray Weald." Memories rose of the gray mist. The gray bark. And, worst of all, the gray mud. "I would never allow you to experience the things shown and done to me there, little one."

Pausing again, she met his gaze. "I'm sorry."

"It was almost eighteen hundred years ago. Besides, I wouldn't be here today if not for that time." While he nudged her along, he tried not to think about whether the Gods had decided to take the lives of his men, many whom he'd loved as sons and brothers, to give him the years

They'd stolen in the Weald. If so, he might live to be four thousand. "I never would have met Daggy." Squeezing Sarlona's shoulders, he sweetened his tone. "I never would have met you."

She sneered when he opened her door. He couldn't blame her for believing he was disingenuous. While he'd known her for years, she'd known him for only a fortnight.

"Do I have to go in there?" she asked, looking up with an expression that had never worked on Sylvanus.

"After your centipede trick? Absolutely."

"But I've burnt myself out." She leaned on the doorframe rather than enter. "Maybe…I could stay with you today?"

He smiled. "Maybe." Either his tactics were working, or she was plotting something. He tipped her chin up to capture her gaze. After a deep breath, she offered it up.

She didn't resist as he breezed into her. Just the opposite. Her heart fluttered with excitement. She didn't want to be alone, especially in that room that made her feel so weak.

Smiling wider, he eased himself out. "All right, little one." He slid his thumb over her cheek before dropping his hand. "You can read in the study while I catch up on clerical tasks."

She followed him to his study and slipped inside when he opened the door for her. Lingering near the entry, she surveyed the room from one side to the other.

"Please make yourself comfortable." He waved at a stuffed chair that sat before the snowy skin of a poor beast Dagmar had strangled, which in turn lay in front of a hearth. "Start a fire. Have a drink. Pick a book and have a seat," he said, pointing to a dusty bottle and pair of glasses on one of the few shelves that weren't packed with books.

"Thank you," she answered as he took his place at a massive oak desk in the corner opposite the hearth.

She ambled down one side of the long rectangular chamber, scanning the tall bookcases as he uncorked a bottle of ink and arranged the month's certificates.

Stopping at the far end of the room, she knelt on the padded bench set in one of the two bay windows and peered out. She leaned into the sunlight as if she couldn't get enough of it.

He shifted his attention to his papers, mentally noting the names of his subjects who had married, died, had a baby, or bartered their leased land with each other. Many had never laid eyes on him, but he knew them all except the babies intimately. He signed his name to each sheet of parchment, making real the defining moments in the brief lives of mortals whose great grandchildren's death certificates he would someday sign.

Sarlona drifted from the light and stared at the portrait hanging above and between the two windows. It featured three women—one hard and huge, one delicate and refined, and one dusky and enchanting.

"The other blonde woman was my mother, Laelia. The younger woman was my sister, Idalia. She was a druid too, in her first life."

Sarlona pivoted from the ancient painting. "They're... no more?"

"They were killed in the second Wizard War." Saying so wasn't difficult. He missed them deeply but had finished mourning many years ago.

She raised her eyebrows. "The lorkai fought?"

"The majority magical body has always taken full advantage of the lorkai and our abilities," he said with a chuckle.

"Then the SPS knows you're real? Do they know you?" She came without hesitation when he beckoned.

"We're members. Conscripted. They claim our abilities are a form of biological magic." He took a candle from the desk and held it out to her. "Do you mind?"

She glanced down, eyes narrowed with suspicion, but she pinched the wick anyway. A delicate flame danced around it when she withdrew her fingers.

"Thank you, little one," he said, returning the candle to the desk. He scooted his chair back, then patted his lap. "The speed with which you regenerate is extraordinary."

Her heart jumped into a sprint, and her cheeks flushed. She made an exasperated groan but didn't retreat. Frozen somewhere between fear of him and the desire to obey him, she stood stock-still.

He took her hand and her hip and guided her down. "I'm going to take enough to make you sleepy."

She didn't protest, just panted, even when he dipped his hand into her waistband.

He drew in, and wisps of Marrow rushed to his fingertips. Despite his insides still humming with the Marrow he'd stolen earlier, her intoxicating taste begged him to grope her with both hands and rip out everything she had.

Instead, he sipped as he explored her hipbone with his fingertips. Draining someone beyond their magical energy required care. The Marrow reserved for sustaining life was ambrosial, and if he took too much, he would kill her.

"You're hurting me," she whispered.

He wasn't causing her physical pain; he was sure of that. The sensation of having one's life force taken, however, was distressing. "I'm sorry, little one."

He summoned a tingling wave to drown out her discomfort. It swelled deep in her center, and she groaned softly as it broke and washed over her.

Once her eyelids grew heavy and her body slack, he slipped his hand away. Reveling in her warmth, her scent, the unique sound of her heartbeat, he held her.

She turned her head left, resting her cheek on his shoulder, and peered down the room through drooping lids at the family portrait. "It must have been terrible for her…losing her magic."

He adjusted Sarlona in his arms and stood. "She spoke of it being difficult… But she'd embraced her identity as lorkai by the time we met," he said while crossing the room. "The Council outlawed making the magical a century or two after mother made Dally—Idalia." He laid her on the window bench to rest in the sunlight and watch the birds. "On the grounds it was cruel."

"It *was* cruel."

"Yes," he agreed.

Chapter Ten

Dagmar took Sarlona for her walk that night. Much as she feared being alone with the Northlander, it beat being alone in that room—stifled, trapped, and exceptionally vulnerable to any monster that marched in—lorkai or man.

"He's a dog," Dagmar said when Sarlona's thoughts veered to Benton for the fourth time. "You're experienced with animals. Consider training him."

It upset Sarlona enough that the lorkai read her emotions through her physiological responses. Having them flit in and out of her head filled her with a special blend of horror, hopelessness, and rage. She had stopped fighting it, though. The destruction of her mental protections was too painful, too traumatic to keep her walls in place.

"Anyway, it's a beautiful night," Dagmar added. "Don't let him haunt your thoughts when you can use this time to restore your spirit."

It was good advice. Sarlona should be connecting with Altvina, Goddess of the Forest, and the new land she was forced to inhabit, not dwelling on the things Benton had said or how she'd reacted to them.

There, in the present, everything was okay.

Dagmar cradled Sarlona's hand in a delicate, comforting embrace. The moonlight smoothed Dagmar's hard features into a serene expression. Not a hint of anger sparkled in her eyes.

The glint off her axe, the width of her shoulders and thighs, and the steadiness of her stride all boasted that Sarlona was safe from any threat but Dagmar herself. And tonight, for once, the Northland lorkai seemed in a gentle and generous mood.

"The moon has never held the magic for me that it holds for you." Dagmar's steps didn't falter as she gazed at the sky. "But in almost seven-hundred years, its beauty hasn't diminished in the slightest."

Sarlona peeked at her. The comment seemed one of the most

honest and innocuous to come out of the monster so far.

"Is it hard to be immortal? To watch everything, every*one* come and go?" Sarlona wondered, with no envy, what it might be like, to see centuries pass by.

Dagmar glanced down with human eyes. "Not for me. I never truly loved a mortal…"

Sarlona didn't quite believe her.

"Not long enough for them to die of old age."

"You didn't have a human family?" Sarlona needed to see the humanity in Dagmar, something to justify the warmth of the woman's hand and the peace in the cold, still air.

"I had a lot of family," she replied. "Glaucus saw to it that I was disgraced before he took me. I was dead to them before he killed me."

"That's terrible."

Dagmar shrugged. "It made it easy to leave Northland."

The night deepened as they passed into the forest, and Sarlona returned Dagmar's grip to steady herself against any roots or rocks that reared up through the frozen wagon ruts.

Less and less, the leaf litter sparkled with silver streamers where the moonlight fell through the branches above. "Do you miss it?"

"I did for the first century." Sighing through her nose, Dagmar stared off into the darkness, no doubt seeing much more than Sarlona did. "Northland formed me, but this place is my home. Ashmore hasn't changed much. The guards change. The villagers change." She shrugged again. "They converted to Silsorianism."

"You do…love? Right? Lorkai, I mean." Sarlona asked. "Or are you just creatures of shadow and hunger?"

If they felt the way mortal humanoids could, maybe if they grew to know her well enough, the lorkai wouldn't do to her whatever they planned to do. Maybe they wouldn't hold her against her will for all her years.

"Of course, we do, Sarlona."

Her tone held a note of offense, and Sarlona wished she'd asked in a different way.

"Glaucus and I love each other deeply."

"Are you…?" She wasn't sure how to phrase her next question. The pair weren't married, at least not in the mortal world, but their relationship seemed different than father and child. "Mates?" she asked, face burning.

Dagmar looked down, and this time her gaze lingered. "Now and then," she answered without any hint of embarrassment. "Out of comfort and closeness. He's a bit like you… He doesn't have much of an appetite.

And I'm more often attracted to women."

Sarlona half expected a devious smile or Benton-like grin, but Dagmar's stare returned to the forest, and her attention seemed lost among the trees.

Glaucus always followed the road, but at the sharp left curve in the wagon ruts, Dagmar led Sarlona right, down an overgrown path. Hemlock boughs brushed her shoulder and hip, often kissing her face. "Where are we going?"

"To a spot I think you'll appreciate."

With the trees caressing Sarlona's arms, the forest air in her lungs, and nothing but canopy and sky overhead, the temptation to absorb enough Marrow for a few solid spells, between mental invasions, was high. But she refrained.

She didn't dare destroy the peace and maybe the forest in a vain bid for freedom that would end in a rough draining and forced unconsciousness. Instead, she made every step a grateful and cooperative one, hoping that if she were sweet enough, Dagmar would stay pleasant. Maybe the Northlander would be good-natured.

Still, when Dagmar released her hand in the thick of woods, all Sarlona longed to do was disappear into them.

"Even you can't lose a lorkai in the forest, Sarlona. Not without flying off." Dagmar's voice was big, loud, and low as always, maybe more so in the dark, silent wood, but she didn't sound angry.

"I'm sorry..."

"You never need to apologize for your thoughts," Dagmar replied. "Or much of anything." Her voice hardened. "You should apologize less."

They walked another minute before it became difficult to squeeze between branches. "Just through here." Dagmar's hand on her back commanded Sarlona to lead the way. "Straight ahead."

Sarlona pushed herself through the matrix of twigs and needles, holding onto the larger branches so they wouldn't recoil and slap Dagmar, though there was no danger of hitting the Northlander in the face.

The thicket spat them out on thin soil atop a group of boulders. Beyond lay a deep pool mirroring the moon. To the north, a brook tumbled seven feet off a rocky overhang, the clear waters hitting a tiny basalt outcrop and splitting into a series of trickles, then coalescing again in the pool. The brook continued where the pool overflowed at its southern end.

"It's beautiful," Sarlona said. The fall's grumble where it collided with rock below had announced its presence, but the pool was more enchanting than anything she'd pictured.

"I thought you'd like it." Dagmar took off her axe and laid it at the back of the sloping boulder that dipped into the basin. She sat cross-legged at the water's edge and patted the granite beside her.

Sarlona didn't hesitate to go to her side, wishing to stay in each moment rather than worry about what the next would bring. Right now, she was in the wild where she belonged. It didn't matter that she was held captive by a spell-drinker. It wouldn't until Dagmar laid hands on her. Sarlona sat just within reach and pretended the Northlander's long arm wouldn't come for her.

"Is this place not as lovely as any in the hills around Mast Landing?" Dagmar asked.

Sarlona nodded. "It is lovely, but it isn't home." Home or not, she might forge a bond with the spirits there if she could open herself enough. She pulled off her boots and plunged her feet through the skim ice that had formed along the pool's edge and into the frigid water. The cold seized her ankles like claws, sinking into her flesh and squeezing her bones. It also brought her to life, and it made her a part of that place, vaguely.

"You don't have to do that anymore," Dagmar said.

She did. In the short periods she was allowed in nature, she had to find a way to merge with it. "It's grounding," Sarlona said. "I need that." More than ever.

"You think you deserve pain." Dagmar leaned close. "You don't."

Sarlona focused on the water, trying extra hard to feel it while ignoring the bone-splitting ache that traveled up her legs. Trying to be as still as the pool.

Dagmar held out her hand, palm up. There was no threat in the gesture. No demand. "I'll warm you."

The icicles stabbing Sarlona's legs melted the instant she dropped her hand into the much larger one. She braced herself for the deep, powerful draw of Dagmar drinking, but it didn't come.

"Go for a dip, if you like," Dagmar said, slipping her hand up Sarlona's arm. Strong fingers found the most tender points around her shoulder blade. "I'll warm you up afterward."

Sarlona's heart pounded, but she bobbed her head. It would feel good to get in the water spiritually. Her soul needed that nourishment. Shedding her clothes would remove one barrier between her and the Gods. The water would act as a conduit from her body and spirit to Their wills. She grimaced. The cold would hurt like hells, though.

Standing, she took off her cloak, then chest piece, shirt,

stockings, and pants. The undergarments, it seemed, were tarred on. Who knew why? Avenian women didn't have to hide their bodies from each other, just men. Despite having to disrobe for some rituals, she opted for privacy, always.

Dagmar leaned back. "You don't have to. I'm not going to strip you bare and throw you in."

Sarlona turned from Dagmar and stared at the water dancing over the rock. Its murmur lulled Sarlona into a relative calm. The silver flashes of moonlight drew her closer.

Modesty wouldn't keep her from her Gods. All she had left was her faith.

Gazing at the water, she unhooked, then unraveled the linen wrapping from around her chest. A sense of freedom bit her with the cold. The binding fell at her feet. A few seconds later, her underdrawers joined it. Bracing herself for the icy water, she softened her knees to jump.

"Sarlona."

She glanced at Dagmar over her shoulder.

"Turn around for me."

Keeping her hands at her sides and her back straight as if Sarlona was alone with her Gods, she did as commanded. Her flush eased the air's icy bite.

"I can't wait to warm you."

Sarlona pivoted and jumped.

The water hit her like a runaway horse. It sucked all the air from her lungs in a shuddering cry she couldn't stifle. For a minute, there was only the cold. It knocked all the fear, worry, and embarrassment out of her frantic heart.

Lifting her feet off the leafy bottom to tread water rather than let them sink into the muck, she struggled to focus on the water without all its agony. She reassured herself the pool had her. The land had her. Not Dagmar.

Laying back, Sarlona let the water wash over her ears and hair and imagined it flowing through her. She pictured her water joining the pool. Envisioned being the water. She was the water. Flowing through all the world, in and over the earth, into every living plant, animal, and other creature, connecting everything—the Gods, and the Mother and Father of All.

"That's enough."

Even lorkai.

"I don't like it when you're not you," Dagmar said.

"I do." Sarlona sat up into a tread from floating. "Northlanders have gods. Didn't you ever pray?"

"Not like that." Dagmar waved her out. "Come out now. Before your spirit truly becomes part of that pool, and I have to stuff it back into you."

Sarlona's limbs had grown thick and heavy anyway. Her hands and feet were numb. And her center had surpassed shivering to near spasm.

One stroke brought her fingers within inches of the stone. Before they touched, Dagmar snatched her wrist and plucked her from the water. All the cold stayed behind in the pool.

Sarlona stood there toasty and bare in front of Dagmar, her wrist trapped in the Northlander's grip. Without their glow, she struggled to make out Dagmar's eyes in the dark. That didn't stop her chest from tightening as she imagined them drinking her in. Still, she should have been more terrified. Perhaps she'd exhausted her fear, or maybe Dagmar controlled it.

She caressed Sarlona's arm up to the shoulder, grazed her jaw, then skimmed fingers down and behind her hip. "I've been waiting so long for this."

Sarlona had no response. With each inhalation, her breasts brushed against Dagmar's hide armor. She started to shake.

Dagmar slid her hands around Sarlona's waist and neck. Leaning down, she kissed her throat. "I wish you wanted it," she whispered, and locked Sarlona in an embrace.

Wanting 'it' was out of the question, but Dagmar's warm breath and gentle kisses sent a tingle across Sarlona's skin. Heat blossomed in her core. She wished she had clothes on and that Dagmar was any humanoid but a lorkai.

The kisses climbed Sarlona's throat, to her jaw, and finally her mouth.

Softer than the rest of her, Dagmar's lips pressed against Sarlona's without roughness or aggression.

It seemed like a good kiss.

Dagmar pulled back and cradled Sarlona's face. Smiling sweetly, she peered into her eyes. When she leaned in again, she took Sarlona by the chin and coaxed her mouth further open.

This kiss was deeper and so perfectly tender, Sarlona could melt. She closed her eyes and surrendered to it.

Dagmar vomited into her mouth.

Sarlona's eyes flew open to the red glow of Dagmar's. Gagging and choking, she tried to rip herself free, but Dagmar snatched control of her body. The lorkai paralyzed Sarlona's limbs and killed her cough and gag reflexes, forcing her to swallow the thin, sweet, fiery fluid. For a full minute, Dagmar retched, her muscles knotted, back heaving, and fingers biting into Sarlona's head like an iron trap.

And she drank, mouthful after mouthful of what tasted like gin cut with maple syrup. All with her lungs thrashing to cough and tears streaming down her face.

At last, Dagmar released control and her grip. She staggered, gasping, and Sarlona collapsed to her hands and knees on the rough granite.

Dagmar hunched over and wiped a dribble of glowing blue liquid from the corner of her mouth. "The first time is the worst. Try not to fight it."

Sarlona barely made out her words. A loud thrumming drowned them out—this low, rapid vibration deep in her center. She coughed so hard her ribs ached, and her face throbbed like it would split open. Beneath the icy bite of her wet skin in the late autumn air, she ignited.

Whatever Dagmar had put in her, she needed to get it out. Sarlona shoved two fingers down her throat and gagged. Dagmar's evil fluid refused to rise.

"You can't stop it," she said, crumpling onto her haunches. "Just relax as much as you can."

The thrumming reached a fever pitch, and Sarlona screamed as the liquid tore her apart. Every muscle seized, her eyes rolled, her urine let go, and her heart lost its rhythm. The world seemed to contract on her, then expand. Blue fire flashed behind her eyelids. She burned up in it.

Chapter Eleven

Sarlona opened her eyes to a dark but familiar ceiling. Though she sensed her body and soul were still whole, relief came in a trickle rather than a flood. Something was wrong. Inside her.

She hopped out of bed and checked herself over. The lorkai had put her in the white slip again, but everything looked normal. Some strange energy whirred faintly through her bones, like Marrow, but thick and slippery. It wouldn't heed her. She didn't feel weak for once, just wrong. Her muscles itched, and her blood boiled.

Glancing out the window, she surveyed the stars. Morning would come soon. Dagmar's bile had raged through her systems hours ago. Deciding to confront the Northlander about whatever the hells she had done, Sarlona went for the door handle. It rotated, but the door wouldn't open. She yanked on it, putting her foot on the wall for leverage. Then she pounded on the door.

"It's cockin' barred. Give it up already."

She kicked the door, which did nothing but hurt her foot. "Let me out, Benton."

Metal creaked and slid against metal on the other side of the wood. She tore at the door.

Benton caught the outer handle before she could throw it wide. She tried to shoulder by him but couldn't squeeze through. "They said you gotta stay in there until Glaucus can drain you more."

"I need to talk to Dagmar." She drove her shoulder into his sternum, provoking his growl, but with one hand gripping the handle and the other on the door frame, it made the opening smaller.

"She's asleep."

"I'll wake her."

He snorted. "That's the stupidest cockin' thing I've heard outta you yet."

She tried to pry his hand off the frame. It wouldn't budge. "Glaucus then."

"He ain't ready for you."

She dug her nails into his hand.

"Shit." Benton let go but grabbed her when she tried to slip by and shoved her further into the room. "Quit askin' for trouble, darlin'. I tend to be generous with it."

"Let. Me. Out." She yearned to tear him apart. Had she been able to cast destructive spells in that room, she might have given it her all.

"If you don't knock it off, I'm comin' in." Stepping toward her, he did.

She didn't see the threat, only more space in the doorway. Seizing her arm, he stopped her dead before she stormed past and hopped his hips clear when she tried to knee him in the groin.

"Let me go." She punched his arm with her free one. He tightened his grip.

"I'm puttin' you back to bed, sweetheart." He threw her onto the bed and spun to leave. "Don't make me tie you to it."

Popping up, she punched him hard in the lower back, where his right kidney would feel it.

"Cock." He went down on one knee but snagged her and blocked the punch that came for his temple as she twisted around.

Instead of trying to wrest herself loose, she leaped at him. Her momentum knocked him onto his ass and almost over flat, but he caught her other wrist. She thrashed, trying to claw his eyes or throat. His arms barely moved.

He half-smiled as she struggled. "Come on now, don't make it hard."

Unable to use her hand to shred his face, she bit into his wrist.

"Gods dammit." Letting go with his other hand, he smacked her cheek. "What the hells has gotten into you?"

The slap knocked some of the volatile fog from her mind. She opened her mouth with copper pricking her tongue and let her arms go slack. It occurred to her she all but straddled him in nothing but a slip, and it hadn't stayed wholly in place.

"Dagmar." The name came out in a sob, tears springing into her eyes without warning.

His grip loosened. With a twitch like he tried to stop it, that stupid grin broke out. "You mean she..."

They squinted and shielded their eyes when an orb of light popped into existence in the center of the ceiling.

"Sarlona, I believe we have a date, my dear." Amenduil stood in the doorway. He appeared perfectly calm and unsurprised to find her crying on top of Benton. "Unless you wish to continue with…this?" he said, waving at them. "Do you mind, Benton?"

Benton shoved her off and onto her side. "Yeah."

Amenduil came into the room anyway. "I'm afraid you won't be able to contribute to the conversation. The subject isn't blades, booze, or badgering women into bed."

Benton sneered as he offered her a hand. "I ain't leavin' her alone with you. Not before daylight, while she's in a state."

She was perfectly capable of getting to her feet, but she took his hand anyway, and he hauled her up.

The dark mage covered his heart. "Why, Benton, if I didn't know any better, I'd say you were looking out for another."

"I got my motives."

Amenduil pulled a handkerchief from his robes and offered it to Sarlona.

She took the silky square and wiped her eyes. "It's all right. I'm okay now."

It was a lie, but the anger had subsided. And she needed to talk to Amenduil, however dangerous he was.

Benton narrowed his eyes and darted his focus between them. "All right, but if I hear anything weird, I'm comin' in. I don't care what the hells I walk in on." Winking at her, he marched toward the door. "Just holler if you need me, darlin'."

The door shut behind him, but no metallic clang or grinding of a bar sliding into place followed.

Amenduil's light dimmed to a comfortable glow. "May I?" he asked, drifting to the bed.

"Okay."

He sat, patting the mattress beside him. "Please."

She crept to his side as though he might morph into the black maw she'd seen while in the grip of his spell.

"I suppose I frightened you yesterday," he said. "I'm sorry."

His words sounded sincere. If not for the knowledge of his allegiance to a dark god and his incredible spell skill, she wouldn't have found him threatening. He projected an aura of gentleness, one, she was sure, was contrived.

She sat next to him anyway. "A lot of things have frightened me in the last day."

"Well, I didn't intend to be one of them. I often become over-enthusiastic in my reverence to our Abyssal Lord."

She cringed over the word 'our'. While Vorakor existed within the same pantheon as her Gods, no one acknowledged him in their prayers these days. Only his children did—the Nocturnal Embrace.

"Dagmar did...something to me earlier..." All the questions she had for Amenduil earlier had dissolved. All she could think of now was Dagmar's 'kiss'.

He painted on a sad smile. "You can tell me about it, Sarlona. If you'd like."

"She..." She couldn't come up with words to make Dagmar's actions any less vile. Reliving it in her mind, she started to shake. "Expelled an almost manna-like substance from her mouth... She made me swallow it."

He nodded with a dour expression. "The lorkai call it their 'quick,'" he said. "It's concentrated Marrow, a reserve in their bodies, and a great source of power."

A dark hole opened beneath her, and he hadn't summoned anything. "Why...would she...?"

"Sarlona..." His voice remained soft, but a hint of reprimand crept into his tone...and pity. "You must have figured out why you're here by now..."

She trembled harder, shaking her head.

"My dear..." He placed a steadying hand on her shoulder. "The lorkai intend to make you one of them."

Her heart stopped.

"You're here to become Dagmar's daughter."

Sarlona doubled over, unable to breathe. Or maybe she breathed too much. She slid off the bed onto her knees, still shaking her head. "No. No. No, no, no, no, no." Her knees rattled against the floor. "They can't cast. Oh, my Gods... *They can't cast.*"

Amenduil patted her back. "I'll cast a tranquilizing spell...if you like."

She tried to swipe his hand away and clutched her head. "They can't do this... Not to *me*. Why would they do this to me?"

"The greater the mortal's capacity for Marrow... The stronger the lorkai they become when turned," he said. "You'll make a miraculous monster. One poised to pull their kind from the brink of extinction."

She quaked too hard to rise but twisted on her knees. "What..." Folding over further, she curled into a ball, until the darkness stopped closing in on her vision. Then she snarled at him. "What about you?"

He helped her onto the bed beside him. "Not long after you and I first met, the lorkai found me," he said, his warm hands still around hers. "They'd drained me in my sleep and were going to turn me. So I told them about you."

"They had you. Why are you still here? Helping them?"

"Female lorkai are much more powerful than males of the same age. Males can only reproduce once," he said and squeezed her hand. "A woman like you, well made, should be able to make three or four children a century. Even in the first."

Just when she'd caught her breath, it left her again.

"I promised Lord Glaucus that if they released me, I'd return when you came of age and help hold you here. That way Dagmar could take her time with you and make you as strong as possible."

Despite the warmth in Amenduil's hands, they froze her blood. "How could you do that...To another caster...?"

He freed one hand to trail his fingers down her spine. "My dear girl, I don't wish any harm upon you. Truly, I don't. I sympathize. Nevertheless, no part of me is unwilling to sacrifice your magic to save mine."

She twisted her face in disgust, holding up her wrist with the anchor cuff that prevented her from teleporting. "You could break this and disappear," she said, certain. "You could free me... At least, crack the wards."

"I could."

"You could destroy the lorkai..." she said. "We could destroy them..."

Even as she suggested it, she wasn't sure she wanted that. But the lorkai planned to destroy her. She pictured Dagmar's claw, ripping through Vosvoshish.

They'd brought it upon themselves.

"We could," he said. "Perhaps it's likely. I still won't risk trying." Every word dripped with unobtrusive conviction and quiet self-assurance. He'd made up his mind and laid his plans years ago. "It's nothing personal, Sarlona. I cannot take any chance, however large or minuscule, of finding myself in your place. Vorakor has plans for me. I must have my magic to carry them out."

Glowering, she yanked her hand from his and slid aside. There was no escape without his help. Just destruction. Destruction that wouldn't end her but make her endure in despair for all time.

She dug her nails into her head and pulled her hair while that hopelessness swelled anew. "Why... Why me? Why not Alvianna Khalorini? Or her daughter? There are other women..."

Amenduil gave her an answer, though she hadn't been searching for one. "Few. Prominent, well-connected, politically powerful women. From families with long histories in the magical world. You, however..."

His voice pulled on her. She didn't understand how he made it do that.

"You're all alone, Sarlona."

Arguing that she had Sylvanus was pointless. She was alone. Never more than at that moment.

"Except..."

She lifted her head off her knees.

"Vorakor doesn't want you to be alone, my dear. He longs for you to be with Him."

She snapped her gaze to the window for starlight. A shiver worked its way over her, then she shook her head.

"*He* watches over you, my dear. But you must accept Him into your heart if He is to help you."

As if everything else she'd been told wasn't terrible enough.

"I'll break the cuff," he said, pulling her gaze into his. Wrapping his hands around her wrist, he glided closer. "I'll take you from this place. If...you accept Vorakor as your patron deity and join His children in the Nocturnal Embrace."

She might as well have been asked which part of her heart she wanted ripped out. As much as she wished to leave Ashmore, the thought of forsaking Tydras left her more desolate than staying. She couldn't pray to pure darkness and endanger her soul like that. And, however much they irked her at times, she couldn't use her magic to hurt Silsorians.

"I can't do that." She twisted away and stared at the floor again.

"Then it's Vorakor's will that we're both here."

Chapter Twelve

Sarlona shot to her feet at the shouting from outside. A second later, Grub's boots pounded from his post at her door. Through a crack in the boards covering the window, which she'd broken and injured herself jumping from, she watched the guards scramble about the yard. They readied horses and weapons and donned extra leather armor.

They'd never done that before.

Within minutes, they rode away at a gallop in the direction of the village.

Glaucus and Dagmar went with them.

Only Benton and Amenduil stayed, as far as Sarlona could tell. Amenduil could have teleported to wherever they were all going.

She prayed he had.

A bar on the other side of the door might be all that stood between her and freedom.

That and a drunkard's blade.

She laid her hands and forehead against the door, reaching to the other side with all her thoughts. The earthy must of rotting logs leaked into her nostrils. Decaying wood crumbled in her hands, wet and soft. She imagined it merging with the door's wood beneath the iron bar brackets.

Nothing happened.

Amenduil must have updated his wards to add decay to the list of magic severely hampered by the room. As she took a deep, wavering breath, ready to scream and cry into the wood, footsteps echoed in the hallway—Benton's.

She scurried over to the bed and tried to look like she hadn't been up to anything. The bar ground against its brackets, then creaked, swinging on its hinge.

He materialized in the threshold with a cup in his hand. He'd lost his shirt, but his black, sleeveless jerkin had made its way onto his torso, half tied. His sword belt hung lower than usual. "Where the hells is everyone?"

She shrugged. "They went out the front gate on horses."

"Must've been an orc raid somewhere then." He sipped his drink. When he brought the cup down, his grin appeared. "I guess it's just you and me, sweetheart," he said, words slow but not slurred.

She had thought a lot about what Dagmar had said. About him being an animal. She forced a smile as he came into the room. "At last."

He grinned wider, and she rose. His sword arm held his cup, so she took his off hand and tugged, trying to draw him to the door. "Take me out for some fresh air."

Losing his balance, he stumbled, but caught it as quickly and closed his hand around her wrist.

Laughing, he yanked her around so hard she stumbled and toppled onto the bed. "I ain't takin' you out with no one else here, darlin'," he said. "I'm happy to keep you company, though."

She flipped over and sat back on the mattress with a frown.

He stood between her and the door. She ran her hands through her hair, then stopped them on the sides of her head. "What am I going to do, Benton?"

They locked gazes when he peeked over his cup. "Drink and cock the handsome guardsman until it's all over?"

"What would you do?"

"Drink." Sighing, he put his cup on the bedside table. "I don't wanna think about it, Sar. I don't wanna think about what's gonna happen to you, and I sure as hells don't wanna imagine it happenin' to me," he said. "It's just the kinda shit I drink for."

"You could help me, Benton." It seemed worth a try. She rose again and took both his hands this time.

He stared at them like he'd gotten them caught in a trap. "Darlin'…"

She inched closer, and the reek of ale flooded her nostrils. "We could escape this place… together…"

His eyes widened. If he didn't like the idea, maybe it would at least scare him off…

"Sweetheart, there ain't any escape." He flipped his hands and took hers to squeeze. "Not for me. Unless it's at the end of a rope. Not for you. Till long after your eyes start glowin' like your fingertips." He skipped his hands from her fingers to her hips and slid them around the small of her back. "I can think of a few other things we could do together." Her heart beat too hard while he squished her against him. "I like the together part."

She tried to retreat from his embrace. "I'm going."

His arms tightened. "No, you ain't."

"Come with me."

"Only place I'm comin' is in you, darlin'," he said with a big grin.

A fire lit in her chest and burst onto her cheeks. Her heart leaped into a gallop. Instead of trying to rip herself free, she wondered what the lorkai would do if Benton got her pregnant. If that would buy her more time...

She'd done things more desperate in the past fortnight.

His warmth spread deep into her anyway. Her chamber had become a frozen cavern with the window broken, and her insides had iced over since Dagmar corrupted them. Any heat was welcomed.

"Get me to the woods, and I'll let you." She meant it.

His grin blossomed into a glowing smile. "Let me, and I'll get you to the woods." He crushed her against him and rammed his hips into hers.

A fuzziness danced behind her eyes. "I don't believe you."

Creeping one hand around to her front, he shrugged. He slunk his fingers up her ribs, straight up her breast, over her throat, then cradled her jaw. "There's a chance I mean it."

An infinitesimally small one. It seemed worth taking. Her dignity, privacy, and bodily autonomy were long gone anyway.

And he was warm.

He tilted her face to meet his. "Come on, darlin'. It'll be a nice distraction. You won't be thinkin' about anything except how good it feels."

All her blood seemed to go to where his hand met her face. She drifted hers to one of the delicate buckles on her chest piece and fumbled with it. Her fingers and body shook too much to work the strap.

Trailing the fingers on her jaw down the side of her throat, across her breast again, then nudging her hand clear, he took over working the buckle. He snagged the opposite buckle in his other hand and, with a jerk, unfastened both at once.

She closed her eyes and squeaked when a stiff yank undid the second set. He started on the last pair.

With his fingers occupied and his grip on thin strips of leather, she jumped backward, snatching the hilt of his sword. The blade slipped from its sheath and the straps from his fingers. Half surprised herself, she retreated against the bed as though she wasn't the one with the weapon.

He shook his head. "You're awful cruel, darlin', you know

that?" Raising his hands as she lifted the sword point, he stumbled. "Well, I guess we'll see if I taught you anything."

"Just move, Benton. Please."

"You're gonna have to step over my corpse to get out, darlin'. Think you can do that?"

She wasn't sure. But she was certain he was intoxicated. There was a chance she could get past him. She might be able to do it without running him through.

Juking right, she whirled left, struck for his right arm, then drove the blade down for his knee.

Maybe she should have stuck with the arm.

He pivoted sideways, pulling the leg she struck for behind him while sweeping the blade wide to his right with the flat of his left hand. Spinning the rest of the way, almost against her back, he grabbed her from behind.

"Drop it, darlin'." He trapped her sword arm out straight and tugged, overextending her elbow.

His sword clanged to the floor.

He let her bring her arm in, then crushed it against her side. "Just relax, sweetheart...," he whispered into her ear.

A warm shiver wiggled from where his stubble met her skin below her ear and worked its way through the rest of her. If only she couldn't taste the ale on his breath. "You're drunk..."

That didn't stop him from deftly undoing the last set of buckles on her chest protection.

"Maybe we should wait..."

"I don't wanna wait another minute, Sar." He pushed his hips against her and a hilt into her back.

His sword lay on the floor.

The wet warmth that bloomed on her side slowed her racing heart. Sighing, she glanced down, but he hadn't spilled what she'd imagined. "Benton... You're bleeding on me."

Still hugging her from behind, he held his left hand near their faces. A laceration ran from the base of his middle finger to the heel of his hand, weeping blood. "Shit, I *am* drunk."

"I'm sorry." She hadn't wanted to cut him, just escape that room.

Far less bothered by bleeding through her shirt than she was, he squeezed her. "That's all right, sweetheart."

She caught fire when he kissed her throat.

"If..."

Maybe he would take her to the woods afterward.

"I..."

His scratchy stubble and warm breath sent a tingle rippling across her skin.

It might get him more on her side. "Benton, I need…"

He snatched her hips.

It would piss off Dagmar.

"*I* need *you*," he whispered. His thumbs bore into those tender muscles again.

"Oh, Gods…" He was so warm. She longed to feel warm. "Benton… I need you to be gentle. Okay?"

Groaning, he slid his right hand into her waistband and stretched his fingers down where no one else's had been. "I'll be whatever you want, Sar."

She sucked in a sharp breath as calloused fingertips came to rest just short of inside her. A hot jolt shot through her.

He breathed beside her ear, then kissed it. "It's gonna feel good, sweetheart. I promise."

For a moment, she believed him. But as his fingers made small circles between her legs, something about his hand shoved down her pants made her itch to scream.

"You're real soft, darlin'…"

She squirmed.

The cold bit every sliver of her exposed skin. Amenduil's evil wards weighed on her spine like a pack laden with rocks, and the room's shadows appeared endless, despite its walls closing in. With each raw breath, vespers of Marrow stirred like ashes blown from a dead hearth by an icy draft—gray, lifeless, useless. The bloody bits of her clothes clung to her like leeches. She tasted Benton's ale-laden breath.

He wasn't going to hold her in a sweet embrace and kiss her deeply first. They might not even look in each other's faces. He'd just push her over the bed and… That's what men like him did.

His hand was too rough.

"You're…*not*." White-hot rage and profound irritation smothered any hint of pleasure his fingertips might have provided.

His touch felt like a mosquito in her ear but everywhere.

She exploded.

Not the way he desired, though it was warm and, unlike his fingers, wonderful.

She burst black bile. Thick, ebony fluid spilled out of her mouth and filled her eyes. It trickled from her nose and ears.

His hand retracted from its den like he'd rested it on a hot stove, and his arms opened. "Sar…" He scooped up his sword and backpedaled.

She rounded on him, and the room darkened and stilled.

The exhaustion that the chamber's warding inflicted upon her vanished. Nearly two decades of tension bled from her shoulders as something slithered out of them.

The floorboards beneath her cracked and plummeted into a lightless void, while she hovered above it.

When he scrambled for the door, she shot one of her black tendrils out and snatched him around the ankle. He hit the floor hard.

"Come back, Benton." She didn't recognize her voice. It sounded lower, more melodious, sultry. Beautiful. "I want you."

Flipping around, he severed the tentacle that had snagged him.

It didn't hurt. The amputated piece just slithered into the pit beneath her. She sent five more sable whips to collect him.

He cut through three, but the fourth wrapped around his neck, and the fifth caught his arm and stopped him from flashing his blade again. She tightened it until his wrist gave way with a faint pop. With a pained curse, he let go and the blade thunked to the planks below.

She reeled him in, out over the lightless pit that had replaced half the floor. He fought like a flapping songbird trapped in her hands—light, weak and easy to break. The tender, hot skin of his throat beneath her silky tendril made her insides flutter.

The darkening of the doorway announced a welcomed presence before she could wind more across other parts of him.

"Get rid of it, Amen." Benton looped his arm with the broken wrist over the tendril around his throat and tried to pry it off with his other hand.

"Now, why in the worlds would I do that?" Amenduil said. "Marvelous, Sarlona, my dear. Shall we go?"

Amenduil's wards didn't stop Abyssal magic. She could leave. But she just longed to go down.

Not yet.

First, she had to watch the life leave Benton's eyes. She brought him up close to her face to see them. They were stunning. More beautiful than she'd realized. Wide and wild and full of panic, they were perfect. She'd make them close forever.

Tightening the tentacle around his neck, she tugged on his leg with another. His face grew purple as he struggled to hold himself up and clawed at the black snake with the other hand. He opened his mouth, releasing spittle and a growl.

His kicks became less frantic, and his hand slipped. The light began to leave his drooping eyes. It appeared elsewhere.

Over his left ear, sunlight snuck into the dark room from between the boards on the window. It caught in her eyes, too blinding for death. Blinking hard, she loosened her conjured appendage's grip. She was supposed to remember something. Something Sylvanus had told her to do...

"I am the glimmer on the deep blue," she whispered. "I am the sun drop between the froth. I am the summer gleam on the winter sea."

Benton sucked in a raspy breath and redoubled his grip. With pure, infinite blackness below, he stared down. "Funny, all I'm gettin' is a lot of Abyssal bullshit," he croaked.

She repeated her mantra. Sylvanus had made her come up with it—words to draw her back to the light in case Tydras's cold, dark abyss ever began to hold more appeal than His Shimmering Sands.

She didn't hover over the black of the deep sea. The black beneath her now, in her, was warm. It was *the* Abyss. Vorakor's. But picturing the summer sun dancing on familiar waves still seemed to help.

Amenduil sighed. "Oh, Sarlona... How disappointing."

The tendril sloughed from Benton's foot, and the other opened its coils. "Well, don't cockin' drop me, Sar," he said, holding on for dear life.

She whispered her mantra a third time and shut her eyes. Sand warmed her toes, and the sea air kissed her lips.

When she opened her eyes, her soles pressed against cool, worn floorboards. A hint of must and wet charcoal permeated the air.

Benton hit the floor with a heavy thump and crawled until he collapsed under the window.

Shaking, she faced Amenduil. Afraid she'd give him an excuse to cast any more Vorakor on her, she slapped her palms against her thighs. There was no way past him unless he allowed it anyway. She opened her mouth to ask how any of that could have happened. How was it possible when she'd never been trained in dark magic?

He flicked his hand. "Sleep."

The spell knocked her off her feet. She rolled over twice and obeyed before coming to a stop.

Chapter Thirteen

Sarlona's family and farmhouse vaporized as she woke from her mundane dream.

Back in one of the hells, in that stifling, dark chamber, both lorkai stared at her. Emptiness hollowed out her every recess. They'd drained her while she slept.

"I wonder if two other parents in all the realms have ever wished so hard for their child to be less extraordinary..." Glaucus leaned close with parted lips, staring deep into her bleary eyes with his burning violet ones.

"Please, get away from me, I'm begging you..." Tears sprang into her voice before they showed in her eyes. He was about to do the same thing Dagmar had been doing to her. She saw it on his face.

"Who can blame them?" Dagmar said, her eyes a fiery orange. "All they wanted was to keep their daughter to themselves. Instead of sharing her with a reclusive old man."

"Don't do this to me, not to *me*."

"You're meant for this, little one." He caressed her cheek with the back of his fingers.

She recoiled and shook her head. "I was meant to be a great druid like Sylvanus."

"You will be great. But not a druid." He grasped her shoulder, then slid his hand to her throat, bringing his warm butterflies with it. "Let me kiss you, Sarlona."

The heat swelled like a wave about to break and hit her low. She rebelled against the surge. "Cock you, Glaucus. I'm not going to let you vomit your corrupted Marrow into my mouth."

He made her cry out with a sharp pang of ecstasy, and his eyes laughed. "The lorkai quick is the greatest gift we have to offer."

She knew damn well it was a curse.

His lips came closer, and he kissed her on the cheek. The butterflies' flapping dipped between her legs, and a hunger to feel his weight on top of her assaulted her insides.

"Mine isn't as potent as Daggy's since I've already had my child." His fingers caressed the edge of her ear, but she felt them elsewhere. "It will still add to your power."

"Don't touch me, Glaucus." She didn't need his pseudo-affection at the moment. Or his power. And she certainly didn't want his bodily fluids.

Dagmar caught her wrist when she tried to strike him.

"Get away from me, you sick old man." Sarlona screamed as loud as she could—the shrill shriek of a toddler or a dying rabbit. Loud enough that the guards in barracks might hear. She wanted them to hear. Though she doubted a woman's screams would move any of them. "Why don't you just cut off my hands or gouge out my eyes?"

"So dramatic," Dagmar said, using two fingers to pin down Sarlona's opposite shoulder.

"What if he'd made it so you could never lift an axe again?" She yanked her trapped wrist so hard something gave. Pain shot up her arm, and she growled through her teeth.

"Then I'd use my carpal blades to hack apart my enemies. Don't be a child."

Glaucus waved Dagmar back. "She is a child, Daggy."

The Northlander withdrew with a snort.

"You're right, Sarlona." He took her hands. The pain left her wrist instantly but intensified in her heart when he poached her stare. "Our talents were amplified when we became lorkai, and you will lose the greatest of yours." He softened her muscles, and she sank into the bed while her insides railed in protest. "Still, we understand your suffering."

Sarlona huffed.

"My mother and sister killed two of Daggy's brothers when we first met," Glaucus told her. "She heard one die, and the other was drained to death in front of her."

Sarlona broke his gaze to find Dagmar's face.

It was a rock—hard, jagged, expressionless.

"I tormented her for days before releasing her, only to follow her home and terrorize her through the long Northland nights."

"Thank you, sincerely, for not murdering my little brother," Sarlona said. "I still don't want your secretions." He'd made her insides too squishy to summon any edge in her voice. "I can't lose everything I am."

"You're far more than your magic, little one."

She saw no lie in his slight smile. How glowing demon eyes could bathe one in adoration, she didn't know.

"Aunt Dally had Father tortured in front of his men," Dagmar said. "Then Laelia killed them, one by one."

A pang of sympathy punched Sarlona in the gut—a deep, sickening ache.

The thing hovering over her was no victim. Neither monster had shared the full story of how they'd become lorkai with her, but both had spoken of their mortal lives.

She couldn't picture them as anything but aggressors. "What were you doing in the Weald, Glaucus? Trying to conquer and enslave the Gray? And Dagmar. How many villages did you raid before you chopped down the door to a house full of spell-drinkers?"

Dagmar grinned. "A lot."

Glaucus cracked a fresh smile.

"You were both probably violent, predatory assholes long before someone vomited down your throats." Sarlona's voice cracked while she thrashed against iron.

"That's true." As his hand slipped under her shirt, she didn't quite believe it. His fingers massaged her abdomen, and there was nothing violent about it. "Dally was like you. A druidess in training, for the Plains wildmen. Not as powerful."

Warm water spilled from his fingertips and trickled into Sarlona's core. An unnatural calm leaked into her. She couldn't put the urgency into her words that they demanded. "I am my magic, Glaucus. I am. I can't take the Marrow from people. I can't look them in the eye. Talk to them half the time. How am I going to go around touching them and taking from them?"

"Sarlona, you won't need your magic," Dagmar said. "You won't miss it. Your magical power will translate to your power as a lorkai. Once you get used to your body and abilities, you'll be stronger than either of us."

Sarlona didn't lust for any power that came with a hunger to prey on others. "My magic is about more than power. I was supposed to serve…my land and my people."

"Losing your magic will not break your connection with the earth," he said. "And think of the ability you'll have to heal as a lorkai. You'll be able to cure disease and heal injuries with far greater skill than you can now."

Sarlona did think of that. The notion had been keeping her afloat in a sea of despair. "How many will I kill? In my hunger?"

"Hopefully, none. We'll do our best to prevent it." He slid his hand out from her shirt and climbed onto the bed. "My quick won't make you a lorkai." Taking her head in his hands, he stroked her ears with his thumbs. A pleasant shiver crept down her neck. "It's a gift to help make you strong."

He bent, laying most of his warm weight on her. She flushed as he made her drive against him.

"Please, no." Without willing it, she hugged him, clutching his shirt.

"Kiss me, Sarlona," he whispered an inch from her face. His breath caressed her lips.

Her body obeyed despite all her inner protest. With parted lips, she rose to meet his. A pleasant tremor passed through her the instant they touched. Sweetness, like manna, laced his mouth. A taste of what was to come.

His beard tickled her chin as fire raced from the kiss throughout her body. It burned her face and tightened her abdominal and thigh muscles. She throbbed, wrapping a leg around his, desperate to alleviate it. Some buried, primitive voice begged him to fill her.

He kissed her more passionately and spilled his syrup into her mouth. A nudge of his thumb coaxed her jaw farther open.

She swallowed the sweet, bracing elixir, her body ignoring her commands.

It raged through her like electricity, tightening every muscle and stimulating each nerve. At the same time, his warm butterflies spread to all her recesses, their wings beating furiously. He crushed her as if to trap them inside and muffled the cries that threatened to burst from her with a still deeper kiss. Hot, roiling waves crashed against her insides until she shook, and her fingers dug into his flesh.

She whined in agony.

He withdrew his kiss to a touch on the lips and let her explode. She screamed, eyes rolling when all those butterflies flew out of her at once and vanished into ecstasy.

When she reappeared, she lay in bed under a monster with her chest heaving and a thumping spasm deep between her legs.

"Good girl." He kissed her forehead and got to his feet.

Shaking, she sat up. She needed to get out of the bed, out of that room, and she didn't want to look at him on the way out.

"Can I go see Gorgil?" she asked the floorboards.

The lorkai wouldn't let her wander alone, and she couldn't think of anyone else's company she could tolerate. She would've liked to confide in Amenduil. Not after tentacles had burst from her. She planned to stay as far from him and his Abyssal Lord as she could.

"Not yet." Dagmar ripped her from the bed by the upper arm. Gripping Sarlona behind the head, she forced a kiss.

Sarlona tried to lock her jaw and turn her head. But Dagmar's fingers had driven deep into Sarlona's brain. It started all over. She opened her mouth and drank the lorkai concentrate. It scorched through her body, more violently than Glaucus's. She screamed again, mostly in pain this time. Her back arched while her muscles seized and her arms bruised in Dagmar's iron bear hug.

Dagmar released her from the crushing embrace, and Sarlona slid to the floor. The second she could rise, she followed a floorboard by the glow of the lorkai eyes to the chamber door. She slipped out and fell against the door. As if a slab of wood could keep the lorkai inside.

Glancing to the left, she hoped for any guard than the one who stared at her. At least Benton wasn't wearing his stupid grin. "That time, he did get me off," she said.

"Darlin', I—"

She snarled. "Happy?"

He shrugged. "I'm happy *for* you, I guess…"

She shoved him with all her might. He didn't go anywhere. A sliver of that grin slipped free. "I'd be happier if I'd gotten to help."

Her bones sizzled with the heavy, poisoned Marrow of her captors. Jaw and temples aching from how hard she ground her teeth, she snatched for the slippery energy. It was like trying to snag eels from a pail, strands squirming through her grasp, but she held on to some. She shoved him again, this time with her magic.

He flew into the wall with a thump and a grunt but landed on his feet, sword drawn.

She raised her hand, but rather than unleash her rage on him, she pushed her palm at the nearest window. It shattered into a thousand glittering shards. Their tinkling provided a shred of satisfaction. Not enough.

She spun to Dagmar's chamber door and grabbed the air, the top of an imaginary edge. Wood cracked and splintered as she yanked down, and the slab crashed onto the floor.

She marched further down the hall, searching for something to burn.

Chapter Fourteen

Benton stared after her, fingers twitching on his grip, with a bit of dread and desire and a whole lot of the feeling that he should stay the cock out of it. His shoulder blades throbbed from hitting the wall, and his stomach knotted from hearing Sarlona's screams. He and his sword both ached for a drink.

Fortunately, the door beside him opened, before he could decide what to do.

Glaucus stood in the threshold as she set some dusty, faded curtains ablaze.

"You know, if they're gettin' outta bed that pissed off, you ain't doin' it right."

"And if they channel the Abyssal Lord himself?" Glaucus asked in his ever-patient tone.

Benton ached a lot deeper. One of the tentacles that had nearly squeezed the life out of him sprouted in his gut. Sarlona had literally scared the piss out of him, and Dagmar had done nothing short of torture him when she'd returned home. He didn't need to feel bad about that.

Dagmar filled the rest of the doorway behind her father. "There's a lot of...*me* in her now."

Benton glanced at her. "Gods, there ain't gonna be two of you, is there?"

"It's temporary," Glaucus said as Sarlona clutched the air and tore her arms outward. The stairway's inner banister collapsed, and its pieces went crashing down the stairs.

"You gonna do anything about that?"

"No. You take care of her." Glaucus moved into the hall. "Get her outside and help her burn herself out. She'll feel better."

Benton groaned. "Why didn't you drain her?"

"We did," Glaucus answered, patting his shoulder. "It's the

quick."

Benton groaned again, and Dagmar shoved him forward. "Go...
Die."

He growled and jogged after Sarlona, who had disappeared
down the stairs. After sidestepping through a smoldering trail of broken
glass and flame-eaten drapes and carpets, he caught up to her at the main
door.

Cyr half-blocked the exit, which by the doors' yellow glow, he'd
sealed with a spell. She glanced from the doors to him, and Benton was
pretty sure the mage was about to soil his robes.

"Just make sure the fires are out," Benton said as she shattered
the yellow glow with a wave of her hand.

A great crack rang out when the crossbar snapped in half, and
the doors burst outward, showering splinters from around the locking
mechanism. She strode out between them.

Benton followed. "There ain't anywhere to go, Sar."

"Sylvanus will know what to do," she said without whirling
around.

"No one knows what to do with a lorkai's hand around their
throat." He caught up to her and hesitated before seizing her by the
forearm. "Least of all, a robe."

She spun with both fire and tears in her eyes.

Ready for whatever spell she might chuck at him, he let go and
hopped aside. "They'll never let you make it that far anyway."

"At least, I'll get a reprieve." She headed for the gate.

Against his better judgment, he grabbed her again. "You'll just
be torturin' yourself, sweetheart, draggin' it out."

She pivoted, and his heart lurched. Her nose and mouth had
elongated, her eyes had darkened and sunken, and her brow had receded.
Long canines and razor-sharp carnassials gleamed in her open maw. She
roared at him with a hairless bear's face.

"Cockin' robes." He jumped back, expecting her to sextuple in
size and take a swipe at him with a gigantic paw, but her features melted
back into a young woman's. "I'll be glad when you can't do that shit."

She balled her fists, and he braced himself for her to turn on him.

"Will you be glad when I can break your neck with one hand?"
she asked, storming ahead.

He tried not to think about how much power she'd soon have
over him. But if he could coexist with Dagmar, he could coexist with any
version of her no matter how much he pissed her off. "You ain't gonna
do that, darlin'. You're gonna want me more once you're a lorkai."

"Well, you can only go up from where you are now." She eyed

Sal, who stood with his arms crossed in front of the gate.

Benton waved for him to get the hells out of the way.

The bald man stepped aside but loosened his sword from its scabbard.

When she lifted the heavy iron bar that locked the gates, Benton slammed it back in place. "The lorkai told me to burn you out," he admitted as she glared at him. "They said you'd feel better afterward."

"I'm happy to burn out." She curled her fingers toward the sky and the bar flew up, then crashed off to the side. "If I do it escaping Ashmore or razing it. Not lighting up a subjugated alcoholic."

He stuck his boot in front of one of the doors when she tried to pull it open and leaned into it. "Things ain't been goin' your way lately, kid," he said. "And I sure as hells don't need your mercy."

She stared into his eyes, and he tightened his fingers around his grip. The last time she'd looked there, she'd almost squeezed the life out of him.

"It's *pity*, Benton."

His face twitched when he tried to smile. "Whatever it is, don't waste it on me, darlin'. Put me outta my misery if you feel that bad for me."

He imagined she contemplated just that while she stared at the problem boot.

"Except I'm bettin' you scared yourself worse than you scared me when you thought about it the other day."

She glanced at him. "I don't want to kill anyone."

"Great. So go ahead and break shit and have your tantrum until you tire yourself out." He used the same tone he'd take with a child had anyone been irresponsible enough to allow one near him. "Dagmar might be puttin' some vinegar in you, but I know you ain't up to strength. Trust me, darlin', I can take what you've got for me."

"I don't want to…" She yanked on the door again, with more than her body. It smashed into him, and his boots skidded across the gravel. "But if anyone is killed trying to keep me here, I'll find a way to live with myself."

He dashed after her as she slipped through the gate, barely squeezing by before it crashed shut.

"Anchor," she said the instant he grabbed her.

He tried to pull her back toward the gate. She didn't budge.

"Carapace."

His sword wouldn't penetrate, but he drove it down on her foot anyway. The blade slipped off her and stuck into the hard snow, leaking strength from her shielding. He whipped the weapon up and slashed it across her face just to make her flinch.

When he rotated his wrist to do it again, he sensed motion behind him and spun.

A faceless crystalline figure lunged at him with a frozen blade or a razor-sharp arm. It had ice swords for arms. Not for long. Benton severed each weapon as they came at him, then ran the ice creature through the chest. It shattered into a thousand glassy shards, and he swiveled at her.

Snowy feathers barred with chestnut brown covered her skin. She glared with eyes that had grown larger, rounder, and striking yellow. Still lovely if not for the contorting of flesh, mandible, and nasal bone into a beak. He sliced at her right arm-wing, hoping she'd screen herself before he amputated it.

She dropped the transformation and shielded her arm, parrying with the protected appendage.

"That turnin' into an animal shit ain't real attractive, you know that?"

"Good." Her face had returned to normal, yet she appeared like she might retch up an owl pellet. "I'm not obligated to present myself as something desirable to cock, for you or anyone else. Ever. Never mind amid this nightmare."

"It's nice, though."

"Maybe if I turn myself into a giant maggot, I'll be left alone."

He shrugged. "Ain't gonna stop the lorkai any." Then he grinned. "Might not stop me."

She spun, face crinkled, then headed for the distant forest. He had to stop her before she reached it.

"What does stop them? Can they be killed?" she asked as he fell into step.

"You ain't gonna kill 'em, darlin'. Even if you could."

"No harm in telling me, then."

"Fire," he answered. "It's gotta incinerate everything. Right through the bone, like a cremation."

She paused, frowning. "It's hard to get a fire that hot... To sustain it."

"Yeah, so don't bother. You'll just piss 'em off."

With a new franticness in her steps, she marched ahead. He shoved his sword into its scabbard and jogged to catch up. Hopping in front of her, he walked backward with his hands out to get her to slow down.

"Come on, darlin'," he said. "There ain't nowhere to hide. There ain't no help to be had." That did nothing but make her eyes water. He didn't like it when they did that. "Hey, hey," he said, snatching her hands when she tried to sidestep him. "Just come with me, and we'll have a normal day. We'll play darts, dice, or somethin'. I swear, I'll be on my best behavior. I won't have nothin' to drink."

She ripped her hands free, and he let her shoulder by rather than make her skip him across the snow with a telekinetic blast. "I don't want to spend time with you, Benton. I don't want to see your face."

He followed her, so she didn't have to, with a lead ball in his gut.

"Or hear your voice. Or smell you." She glared at him. "I don't want to feel your hands. Ever."

He shrank.

"Or Glaucus's. Or Dagmar's. Or anyone's."

He hoped that wasn't true.

She looked at the snow while the water trickled from her eyes, then traipsed on. "I only want to rest in Tydras's arms. But now, I never will. Unless I can cremate myself alive."

"Don't worry, darlin', there'll be plenty of monster hunters, paladins, and defensive robes happy to help you out if you let 'em know you suck the magic outta folks."

Glaucus had made it crystal clear whose job it was to kill any who got close.

"If my Gods would have me after I've been corrupted. How can I be connected to the web of life if I can't die? I'm supposed to come and go. I won't be part of it. I won't be part of Them."

He shook his head. She was concerned about all the wrong things. "There ain't no 'web,' sweetheart. There ain't no gods."

All the casters he'd known had been eccentric, but none had sounded quite as unhinged as she did now. Amen made more sense.

She stared at the stars. Her eyes were still human, but she saw more than he did up there. "How can you mean that after staring down the Abyss?"

"I didn't say there weren't *hells*."

She glanced at the estate, then at him. "It must be hard being that alone. Is that why you're the way you are? Because you're godless?"

"I'm the way I am because I'm the way I am." It wasn't any of her business. She couldn't truly want to know, anyway. "And, nope, it's real easy. Means everything is what it is, and survival is all that counts." He skipped in front of her, making her look at the face she didn't want to see. "You oughtta get that. After you gave me all that brutality of nature shit."

"Benton…"

Her hands lit up green, and he grabbed his hilt.

"No, it's all right," she said, raising those glowing hands to his head. "Let me help you."

He wasn't sure why he didn't pull his blade. Why he didn't, at least, block her hands when that green light entered through the sides of his skull like warm static. He held his breath, heart pounding as her cold fingertips alighted on his temples. Something fuzzy floated through his brain and enveloped his eyes.

For a second, the night sky brightened. The stars multiplied and rained in a diamond shower, sticking to the trees ahead. They sank through the snow and glowed beneath it, illuminating the ground. Shining extra brightly, they filled her until she resembled a woman-shaped sun behind a thin cloud. And, to his horror, they clung to him. At least, he couldn't feel them.

More terrifying were the billion translucent strands, which the stars coated like dewdrops on spider webbing. Unlike a web, the filaments stretched in all directions connecting everything, including him. They tethered him to the ground, the trees, and the real stars, and most of all, Sarlona. There must have been a million glassy fibers between them alone. She'd trapped him. He breathed again, too hard and fast.

Bringing his arms up between them, he threw them outward and knocked her hands from his head. The night darkened when the sparkling dust blew off, and the filaments were swept away like cobwebs.

"Puttin' pretty sparkles in my head don't prove nothin', darlin'," he said, recoiling. "The gods ain't helpin' either of us. They ain't there."

She frowned and tried to shove past him.

This time, he didn't let her.

"Tydras is real," she said. "He's with me."

"You're just as alone as I am, sweetheart." She stepped to his left, but he mirrored her too fast for her to get by. "Tell yourself what you gotta to get through this. But no one's reachin' across the veil to save you. No one's lookin' out for us. No one's waitin' with open arms when we get done."

He slid right at the same time she did, blocking her path. "You ever watch a man go? They don't see anything, darlin'. They just got terror in their eyes and then…nothin'."

She looked into his eyes. What she saw, he couldn't imagine. "You truly don't believe there's anywhere I can hide? You don't think there's any hope of escape?"

He sighed. "They already beat you at your best, darlin'. Glaucus set you up to prove that they could." That should have been obvious to her. "You get by me and make it to the woods… The lorkai will sniff you out in minutes," he said. "You fly off, they'll run you down. If you disappear somehow, Amen will scry you out. They'll come for you, and you'll be puttin' in harm's way anyone you get to help you."

Fresh, glistening trails trickled down her cheeks. She nodded, head half hanging. For a second, he thought she'd turn around and go with him.

Instead, she opened her arms. The ground parted with them. Heralded by a great crack that echoed through the cold air and a rumble beneath their feet, the earth split.

He drew his sword, ready for what might come at him, ready to leap clear if the ground opened wider to swallow him.

The pit swallowed no more than some snow and the frozen earth that crumbled from its sides and partly caved in. It wasn't much bigger than a grave.

She dropped into the hole, not merely leaking now but crying. He groaned and slumped his shoulders. "What are you doin', Sar?"

"I'm going to rejoin the sands. While I still can," she said, laying down.

"No, you ain't." He knelt and extended his free arm to pull her up. "Come on now, sweetheart. Let's go in and sit by a fire and have some hot food. It'll be all right."

Gazing at the sky, she took a deep breath. A second later, roots burst from the frozen earth around her like snakes seeking prey. She wasn't just pouting and putting on a show.

"Shit."

He jumped into the hole and slashed at the first roots to ensnare her. Catching her under the arm, he tried to haul her up on his left shoulder. She went limp, making herself harder to lift, and the roots wound around her legs anew and his.

Forced to cut the roots off them, he let her go, then shoved his blade into the scabbard. The woody bindings reformed just as soon as he hooked her under both arms again. "Gods dammit, get up."

"Get out, Benton," she said, closing her eyes. "Or die with me."

Holding on tighter, he tried to tear her free from his knees. She wasn't going anywhere. So, when a root slithered over his back, he gave up and let it pull him down on top of her. He didn't think she'd kill him. She'd have done it before if she had it in her. Probably. He was pretty sure she didn't want him on her either.

"I'm sorry," she said, stroking his side while the dirt and snow started to fill in around them. "I hope you can come with me."

He started to think maybe she would kill them both but tried to quash his rising panic. "That's all right, darlin'. I pictured it happenin' a lot worse." Like at the end of Dagmar's claw or alone in a puddle of his vomit. Well before now. "Can't think of a better way than on top of a pretty girl. In one, maybe."

But as chunks of cold earth rained on him, he dreaded dying atop her or anywhere else. Even if the lorkai pulled them out and revived them, he had no urge to experience a live burial.

If he didn't get them up in the next minute though, he wouldn't have a choice…

He smashed his forehead into hers.

The roots retreated like worms sucking back into their holes. He wriggled and fought to get up under the weight of the dirt and the snow while the stars, snow, and dark spun together. Only the shock of the snow that went down his shirt kept them from swallowing him. He grasped her arms and tore her out of the dirt. She groaned when he got his shoulder under her and hauled her out of the hole.

As soon as he dumped her into the snow, she raised her hands and started to pull her arms outward again.

He stuffed them down against her body. "Gods dammit. Ain't you done yet?"

She blinked a few times, then stared at the stars. "I'm done."

He got the impression she meant with everything, not just her latest revolt. Collapsing beside her, for a moment, he could relate. "Come on. I know you druids like to lay around in the snow, but I like all my fingers where they are," he said, squeezing her hand.

She yanked weakly on her arm. "I hope you lose them all." Her voice lacked a trace of conviction.

He climbed to his feet with a groan and tried to hoist her up with him, but she stayed limp. "Get up, darlin'."

She didn't.

"Come on, quit sulkin'." He tapped her with the side of his boot. "It'll be fun bein' a lorkai, once it's all over with."

That seemed to take the fog out of her eyes. She scowled at him.

"You'll be able to kick my ass. That's gotta be worth it."

She cracked the slightest smile, and he offered her a hand.

"You won't have to worry about gettin' sick, or old, or hurt… You'll be Glaucus's granddaughter, nobility."

None of that got a smile. When he grabbed her arm, she let him pull her up.

"You'll be able to heal pretty much anything, anytime."

She nodded and didn't resist when he dragged her toward the house.

"Hey, you'll be able to swim under the ocean all day, without drownin'..."

He tried to think of something else she'd like to do that she couldn't do now, but nothing came to him. Instead, he gave her a few perks he'd be glad of, if he were her. "You can cock all you want without gettin' pregnant... You won't bleed every month..."

She stopped and leered at him. It was the same expression Dagmar got when she thought up a new way to make him miserable. "You know they expect me to make a lot of children?" Sarlona said. "Lorkai children."

"Yeah." A cold pit opened in Benton's stomach. It felt as big as the one she'd created. His numbed skin and shivering bones finally registered.

"With all that Marrow... I'm sure you'd make a fine son."

He let go of her arm. "Heh. That ain't funny, Sar," he said, forcing a smile.

She laughed. Appearing elated, she seized his arm.

When he tried to backpedal, she gripped his shoulder too. He couldn't bear to stare into those big sparkling eyes, but there they were.

She gave him the same grin he liked to give her.

He fought to hold onto his quivering smile and leaned closer, feeling like someone a lot bigger than her had punched him in the gut. "Aww, you're just lookin' for a reason to gimme a kiss."

She patted his shoulders and turned away. "Thanks, Benton. I feel a lot better." Her steps didn't drag, despite taking her in the direction she least wanted to go.

Two strides caught him up to her. "Sweetheart, I know you ain't gonna do that."

"You don't."

"Well, good," he said, wishing he sounded less agitated. "I hope you do it. Then I can go where I want, do what I want, and not worry about bein' sent to the rope afterward. And who the hells don't wanna be immortal, other than you?"

That was a bluff and a half.

He laughed. "Heh, yeah, imagine me controllin' folks' bodies. Controllin' their thoughts. That'll be fun."

His heart skipped a beat when he imagined it himself. A blade gave him all the power he needed. He couldn't be trusted with that.

She gave an almost cheerful sigh. "I'm not in a place where I can care about other people."

He almost believed her. Even if true, it wouldn't last. She'd be devastated if she killed people. Or if he killed people because of her. "That's the best place to be... You'll care about me though." He put on his widest grin and spun her to see it. "We'll be bound for eternity."

She hit him with her sweetest smile and spoke in a sugary tone. "You're going to help me, Benton."

Chapter Fifteen

Benton's steps dragged over the worn oak stairs to Sarlona's room. Constantly depressed, she wasn't fun anymore, and her threat haunted his every sober thought.

He was *pretty sure* she wouldn't follow through on it. Glaucus had promised him it was empty. But he didn't know lorkai Sarlona at all. She might think differently once Dagmar's quick took over.

Helping Sarlona wasn't an option, anyway. If Benton had been willing to betray Glaucus and give up the closest thing he'd ever had to a home, Benton would never pull off their escape. It had taken the lorkai all of five minutes to rip her threat out of his head and make their own.

So, he just lived with nagging anxiety that clawed around in his chest whenever she gifted him one of her rare and now menacing smiles.

He rounded the charred corner and found an empty hall. No Amenduil. The dark mage should've been standing guard outside her room. Instead, his voice droned from inside.

When Benton pressed his ear to the wood, a soft, pained sound mingled with it—crying, or maybe pleading. He barreled into the chamber.

Amenduil sat too close to her on the bed, with one hand stroking her spine. A pool of glassy black water lay in front of them, covering a quarter of the floor like a demonic area rug.

Benton froze, staring into the deepest, darkest, clearest water he'd ever seen. In it, a million black tentacles writhed and twisted and called to him.

The Abyssal Waters. Even a godless heathen like him knew them. Talented as the dark mage was, Benton hadn't believed Amenduil could summon them. Only Vorakor himself was supposed to have that power.

"Go on, my dear, they won't do you any harm," Amenduil said

as he lifted Sarlona's hand from her lap. "They long to meet you."

She glanced at Benton while Amenduil tried to guide her fingertips to the pool. For a second, her eyes looked just like the water. Tears streamed down her face.

Benton drew his sword. "Sar…"

"It's all right, Benton," Amenduil said. "They'd like to greet you as well."

Benton couldn't help peering down. The water's depth and clarity made him feel like he was standing on the edge of a cliff. Falling in would mean a far longer plunge than he could take from any height.

"The Waters are warm… comforting." Amenduil's voice was like silk and honey. "Just what you both need." He stared at Benton. "Step in. Let them take you down for a minute. For Vorakor to cherish. You'll emerge a new man."

He inched closer without willing it. The pool drew him in, called to him, a dozen sweet, sultry voices whispering in his ears. He couldn't make out the words. Just that they were beckoning, inviting.

For a second, he wondered what sliding in would hurt. It wasn't as though dark waters could pull his godless soul away from the light. He had no chance of landing in one of the heavens when he died, if there was such a thing. Marveling at the endless depth, he leaned closer.

The waters swallowed him. Rushed over him, in him. A million tentacles waved in greeting and reached for him.

They were warm, like sinking into a bath or sitting before a tavern fire on a cold night with the right amount of whiskey in his belly. Maybe like a mother's arms. All three at once.

The silky black snakes wrapped around his limbs, cradling him in the perfect embrace. As thinner tendrils began to probe him, trying to find their way inside, he couldn't summon the will to resist.

He blinked, and the waters receded. They lay below him. He hadn't fallen in. It hadn't been real. The warmth hadn't been real. Still, the waters promised him it would be and that he could feel it forever, if he strode into the pool.

He ripped his gaze from the glassy, infinite puddle and jumped back with a shiver. The echo of whatever he'd felt grew icy. The whispers became hisses.

Sarlona's hand hovered just a few inches above the water. A tentacle breached below her fingers as if in anticipation of her touch.

"Don't touch it, Sar."

She strained not to let Amenduil dip her fingers in but didn't seem to be trying to tear her hand away either. Staring at some deep point in the pool, or maybe someplace far beyond it, she appeared mesmerized.

Slowly, a tentacle breached the surface and straightened toward her fingertips.

Benton crow-hopped along the water's edge and jabbed his sword into the thick, ebony tendril. It tore itself off the blade and retracted into the depths, leaving a bone-chilling hiss in his ear.

His hand froze to his hilt. "Knock it off, Amen."

Amenduil shrugged and released her hand. He tapped his foot, and the pool shrunk inward until it disappeared.

She bent over with her arms resting on her knees and her face in her tented hands.

Benton flicked his sword point at the door. "Your shift's up, Amen. Cock off."

He didn't. Instead, he leaned closer to Sarlona. "Let Vorakor help you like your 'gods' refuse to do. Accept his love."

She lifted her head. "Get out."

"As you wish." Amenduil took his sweet time standing and making his way to the door. He opened it but paused before going through. "You're out of time, Sarlona."

Benton shoved his blade in its sheath as soon as Amenduil closed the door. "You all right, sweetheart?"

She dropped her head into her hands again. "No."

Something scooped out Benton's rib cage. He probably should have left or at least sat in the battered chair. Instead, he took Amenduil's spot on the bed and rested his hand where the dark mage's had been. Guilt gnawed at Benton's bowels.

No, *she* wouldn't end up in the Abyss. She'd live forever. And he couldn't have done anything to nudge her toward it anyway. That was all Amen.

"I'm sorry, darlin'." Benton's voice caught in his throat, but he forced it through. "For everything I've said and done that's made this harder for you."

~ * ~

It happened in a blur. Glaucus opened Sarlona's door early in the evening and announced her destruction. Dagmar grabbed Sarlona from behind before his words registered. A ring of candles around a massive granite altar and the lorkai's evil eyes provided the only illumination.

She screamed and thrashed while they stripped her for a few seconds. Then he snatched her hand and made her help undress.

She stepped over the candles then climbed onto the altar with his helping hand. He guided her down until the cold stone kissed her shoulder blades. She lay there, still and naked, the scent of must, tallow, and iron in her nostrils and copper on her tongue where she'd bitten it.

Inside, she screamed, begged, and cursed.

He held her hand and patted her head as Dagmar closed irons, embedded in the stone, around Sarlona's ankles and wrists. Her terror left just enough room for embarrassment to scorch her cheeks as he stared at her.

Putting her back to them, Dagmar disrobed from the waist up. She ejected one carpal blade but kept it bent in on herself at the hinge. Sarlona recoiled as the Northlander drove it through her own chest and ripped it back out.

Adrenaline cut through Sarlona's thighs when Dagmar straightened her bloody claw and turned it on Sarlona.

"Please, Dagmar. No…" She gagged on her tears as she tried to retreat into the stone.

Choked with pain, or perhaps blood, Dagmar's thick voice barely escaped her cavernous thorax. "I'm sorry."

She towered over Sarlona, luminescent eyes glazed over. Blood wept from the deep wound in Dagmar's chest, trickling between breasts that belonged to a softer, more reasonably sized woman, then down her chiseled abdomen.

Sarlona winced as Dagmar inserted the bloody blade into Sarlona's flesh at the clavicle, but it didn't hurt. Glaucus saw to that. Each cut came with a warm rush until she lay decorated with the same blood design Dagmar wore as an ornate scar from collarbone to cleavage.

The carving may not have pained Sarlona, but the sight of so much of her blood did. The knowledge that all her magic was about to be stolen forever did. It trampled her like a feral horse.

Her heart pounded so hard it hurt. "Please… I don't want this. Please don't do it."

She couldn't seem to focus her tear-stained eyes on either lorkai. With candlelight and shadows dancing together across the rock, the underground chamber appeared filled with monsters.

Dagmar trembled, but this time her voice didn't, and she stood as tall as ever. "You'll just be dead a few minutes," she said, bending for a short kiss. "I'll bring you back, I promise." Her muscle-rending quick flowed into Sarlona.

"No." Sarlona's eyes streamed when Dagmar pulled away. "I don't want to come back."

Glaucus took his turn, forcing his quick into Sarlona until, too exhausted to stand, he collapsed beside the altar.

Burning pain exploded into her chest when his hand slipped from her. But ravaged by the lorkai quick and adrenaline, it seemed a distant sensation.

She appealed to the Gods instead of Dagmar. "Please, please help me. Please don't let her do it."

Like the lorkai, they ignored her pleas, allowing Dagmar to take a dagger from the altar instead of fixing it to the stone beside Sarlona's tangled hair. The baleful blade gleamed with a thousand angry threats as Dagmar poised to steal everything Sarlona had and had been promised.

Sarlona told herself she'd be with Tydras, in the Shimmering Sands, after just a few moments of agony. When she tried to picture white sand and sparkling waters, she saw only her mother's face, round and warm, the opposite of the one hovering over her.

The dagger plummeted, its polished steel flashing a vision of hellfire in the orange glow of candlelight and lorkai's demonic eyes.

Sarlona tried to call out for her mother.

The cry died with her.

~ * ~

Sarlona opened her eyes with the pain of her death echoing in her soul. Her body didn't hurt, but *she* did, and for one horrifying moment, she thought she'd been swallowed by the Abyss. Then the grain of pine boards came into focus with eerie detail. Her lightless resting place wasn't eternal damnation.

The scent of soil, rocks, and roots permeated the air. Subterranean insects stirring in their frigid burrows scratched at her ears. How she noticed either over Dagmar's sweet aroma or thunderous heartbeat, Sarlona didn't know.

Frozen, she shut her eyes again and prayed she was in a nightmare. She prayed she'd open them to her chamber's wall. Or better yet, the trunks of trees.

"It's real, Sarlona." Dagmar rapped her fingers along Sarlona's vertebrae. "It's done," she said, sounding relieved.

Sarlona tensed, and her eyes flew open. Raising her head off the monster's chest, she smacked it against the earth-bolstered wood. Her spine hit solid pine when she tried to climb off Dagmar. "Why are we buried?"

"It's a tradition Father insisted upon." Dagmar helped her turn over, then took Sarlona's hands, flipped her palms up, and snapped them back.

With a pleasant release, a single dagger-like claw emerged from the underside of each of Sarlona's forearms, embedding in the wood. The knot in her chest tightened as she gaped at the offenses to nature. She had the lorkai claws.

"Go on," Dagmar said. "Like a turtle hatchling."

What else was there to do?

Shaking, Sarlona smashed both wrists upward, a movement she would've thought weak and awkward, but her claws punched through the coffin lid. She retracted them while the earth filled in around her and crushed the air out of her lungs. The weight of the soil couldn't hold her down, though.

Wriggling through icy roots and abrasive rocks, she rose. The scream she'd trapped to keep dirt from tumbling into her mouth escaped the second her head breached the surface. She crawled a few feet, then collapsed in the snow, bursting into tears.

Glaucus knelt beside her.

She couldn't meet his gaze. Staring at the broken ground hurt. She didn't dare view anything more. The snow showed as countless pieces of crystalline artwork, shimmering in the dark. The dirt had become a stunning field of stones, gems, and fibers instead of brown crumbles.

He took her chin and tilted her face to the stars. They were too bright. She'd go blind or mad. There were too many—the sky swirled with them. She tried to bow her head, but he made her look until the lights stilled, then tipped her face toward his.

Her sight caught every line, every pore, every trim, silver hair. She met his eyes, which flashed a glowing array and held her spellbound. Once they'd cooled and settled on the arresting steel gray he'd been born with, they released her.

He hauled her up and brushed the dirt from the clothes they'd redressed her in. He threw his arms around her and squeezed in a way he hadn't before. "Welcome to the family, Sarlona."

Pure joy laced his tone and his comforting scent begged her to bury her face in his chest.

She wiggled free. Wiping her face on her forearm, she tried to control herself. She had to do what she most dreaded.

After a deep breath, she called the Marrow in the stars, snow, and the distant trees to her hands to come and fill the terrible emptiness that overwhelmed all else.

None answered.

She tried the simplest spell she knew, flicking her fingers to make a few sparks appear.

Nothing.

Shaking, she tried again and added, "flint" for extra oomph. Nothing happened. She fell to her knees. Nothing. There was nothing.

"It will be all right." Glaucus extended his hand.

She batted it away like she would an oversized horse fly. "Undo it."

The smile that skittered into his eyes curled her hands into fists. He was glowing.

As she rose, the carpal blades popped out from a nearly imperceptible seam that ran up the middle of each arm. Narrowing her eyes, she had an idea what to do with them.

He hopped clear, when she struck at him, but her errant swipe wouldn't have hit him anyway. Halfway through its arc, her claw pulled her to the ground, dropping her to her knees. She thrust her claws through the snow and into the earth with no reason but the undeniable urge. Muscles tightening and wrists tingling, some instinct bade her draw in.

Euphoria came with the faint aqua glow that traveled up her arms. For a minute, she forgot everything and savored the perfect connection with the earth, even as the snow around her melted and the ground faded to ash gray.

Only once that blue-green incandescence had spread through her, and was about to overflow, did she withdraw her blades.

"There are few sources of Marrow available to use," he said when she rose, praying for an explanation. "One is the earth itself, taken using our carpal blades."

Ice spread through her veins while she stared at the patch of death. She'd sucked all the life out of it. Sylvanus would be furious. The defilement beneath her feet was nothing short of sacrilege.

"The earth will heal," Glaucus assured her. "But any mortals in contact with the earth you're feeding on will not. You'll drain the Marrow from them as well. So, take care." He pointed to the black circle. "The dead zone is precisely the diameter of your arms and carpal blades outstretched. Understand?"

She peered at the blades, those double-edged alien protuberances that had taken over her arms. Delicately notched on the undersides and shining like ivory in the moonlight, they'd be pretty sticking out of someone else.

She wondered if she could rip them out.

"You'll get used to them," Dagmar said, shaking the dirt from her brassy-blonde hair as she approached.

Sarlona's eyes watered again when a slight flex of her wrists made the blades disappear. Dagmar's unforgiving hand snatched hers.

They started toward the distant manor house, leaving an empty, unmarked grave and four ancient stones behind.

Sarlona surveyed the endless, snow-covered fields. The night couldn't hope to hide the scenery from her reconstructed vision. In fact, she got the best view of it she had yet.

Behind them, the dirt road led from the woods. Fields lay ahead, bordered by more woods with a few cottages dotting its edge. The village, a cluster of homes nestled in the valley with a mill, some larger buildings, and the telltale steeple of a Silsorian temple, looked like it made a tiny dot on a map.

"You can feed from trees and animals as well," he told her. "No source of Marrow is so rich or satisfying as a humanoid with a high capacity for it, however. We can't get all that we need without them."

Dagmar clapped her free hand on Sarlona's shoulder. "Don't worry," she said with a sinister smile. "This next part will be fun."

Chapter Sixteen

Benton's scarred hand hovered over the wrought-iron handle to Glaucus's study. He'd been called there plenty over the last few months but never summoned from sleep.

Come in, Benton, Glaucus whispered into his mind, sending his heart into a sprint.

Benton slowed it too late. The old lorkai would've heard it pound. Heard his sharp breath and his nervous thoughts. Smelled the spike of adrenaline through the door. Just the type of reaction that got Marrow-suckers excited. The way a three-legged squirrel perked up an old dog.

With a sigh, he straightened his ale-stained tunic, tightened his grip on his sword-belt, then pushed through one wide hickory door.

He glanced up to find Dagmar smiling at him.

Throwing his gaze lower, he spotted something he liked even less.

He shook his head, spinning to go right back out the study door.

Glaucus blocked his exit and pinned him in place with a stormy stare. "Sorry to disturb you at such a late hour, Benton. But she wanted you."

"Heh. Well, I knew that."

Sarlona's big, round eyes, with lashes like a horse's, beamed and glowed like a firefly's hind end.

Benton swiped greasy strands out of his face and tried to make those eyes disappear by rubbing his own. It didn't work. "Sorry, darlin'."

Dagmar wrenched his sword-belt from his grasp and tossed his weapon to the plank floor. Almost seven feet of iron woman shoved him into the chair set in the center of the dim room.

He cringed at the sound of the door locking behind him. "If she's gonna be suckin' stuff outta me, it better be thr—"

Dagmar's backhand knocked his mind blank.

Sarlona rubbed the sides of her head. "I don't want to do it. I don't want to hurt anyone."

"Yes, you do." Dagmar grinned at Benton. "But you won't hurt him at all if you do it right."

Hopefully, she'd do it right.

Glaucus took Sarlona's hands and pulled them from her head. "Listen now, little one. You're on the path to making a fatal mistake." He spun her to meet his gaze. "You will do more harm if you deny yourself. You need not kill, but a starved lorkai is a dangerous one. If you go too long without a good meal, you'll lose your mind, lose control, and then, you *will* kill."

Benton wouldn't have thought they could, but Sarlona's eyes grew wider and welled up.

"Shut your eyes, Sarlona. Focus on your other senses for a moment," Glaucus said.

She obeyed, and a tear trickled down each cheek.

They threatened to drown him. "Gods, kid, them tears better not be for me." Benton's glance skipped around the room before his aching stare landed on her again. "I'm the last one who cockin' needs 'em."

She wiped her cheeks and took a slow breath through her nose. Some of the pain slipped off her face. Eyes closed, hiding the lorkai irises, she could have just floated down from the heavens. Dagmar had picked a hells of a disguise to hide a monster in.

The illusion of youthful innocence disintegrated when Sarlona opened her eyes. Benton recognized the expression on her face. He'd worn it plenty himself.

It belonged to a predator. And this time, he was the prey.

"You've some familiarity with the process, albeit from a different perspective," Glaucus said. "Never forget that perspective."

If Sarlona was listening, her countenance gave no indication. She stared at Benton the way he had ogled her.

Cursing under his breath, he turned away. He ran his gaze over leather spines and the golden words emblazoned on them—words meaningless to him. His attention lingered on a dusty bottle of whiskey and two dingy glasses tucked between books on one shelf. A drink would've helped.

"We'll guide you through this first feeding." Glaucus nudged Sarlona forward. "Be gentle now. You're much stronger than you realize."

"Great." Benton sighed. Having known that he'd become a lesser thing to Sarlona—food—hadn't made it any easier. He hadn't pictured it being such a spectacle, figuring she'd just pounce on him in the hall a few times. Then they'd mostly ignore each other. It never occurred to him that he'd be her first meal.

"All right, well, don't be shy, darlin'," he said, patting his lap as if she'd straddle him while ripping his Marrow out. A man could be optimistic.

"Go on." Glaucus prodded her. "Touch his bare skin, wherever you're most comfortable, but don't drink yet."

Sarlona shifted her weight and wrung her hands.

"It's all right, sweetheart, I know I'm hard to resist," Benton said with a shaky voice and the closest thing to a smile he could manage.

Approaching him with hands raised like she intended to grab him, she gazed into his eyes. For too long. He couldn't look away. Her irises flashed from yellow to red to violet through the rainbow.

He missed the ocean blue. "Just...do it, Sar. I don't need a lotta foreplay."

"Okay," she said, probably to herself. She took a deep breath, despite no longer needing air. "Okay."

To his relief, she circled behind him, displacing Dagmar. Maybe he wouldn't have to watch as Sarlona took from him. That would be better. She laid her hands, warm and with no more force than a woman's hands ought to possess, on his shoulders. He imagined them sweeping his hair aside, working their way under his shirt, then coming to a rest just where they were. That might be okay. Not too vulnerable. But after a few seconds, she slid her hands down his arms, leaning over him from behind. Her soft waves brushed against his jaw. They smelled of fresh soil.

She caressed the backs of his hands, and he dug his nails into the wooden armrests.

Her fingertips brushed his skin like warm silk. "Give me your hands."

He pried them open like rusted traps and fought not to squirm when she wrapped her fingers around his and pulled his arms up behind him so his elbows pointed at the ceiling, trapping him.

The hand holding was too intimate. And with his arms in that position, his front and sides were exposed, making him exquisitely helpless.

"You can feel his Marrow," said Glaucus.

"Yes." Her voice sounded strained. "I know what to do."

Benton couldn't tell whether the tremble in his hands was his or hers.

Glaucus nodded. "Go ahead. Tap into it. As carefully as you can.

Try not to drink yet."

They cried out at the same time. Something grasped Benton deep inside, and a sense of impending doom fell over him—a black shadow. He felt like he'd been run through with a cold blade the instant before the pain registered.

Sarlona's cry sounded like one of relief.

"Now, little one, see if you can invade his body," Glaucus said. "Then ease his discomfort."

Benton's chest heaved while he waited to feel his body taken from him. He shook like a young boy and hated himself for being so afraid of what a teenage girl was about to do to him.

She must've figured it out because he jolted, and that cold, painless blade melted into something silky and warm. He made another pathetic sound, but this time it came from relief. His core and his thighs, which had burned from driving his heels into the floor, relaxed. He stopped trying to strangle the hands that held them. His eyelids grew heavy.

Glaucus smiled. "Good."

Despite the fuzziness Sarlona inflicted on him, that smile made Benton ache. Glaucus might have been the one person he'd ever learned to trust, and there the old lorkai stood, beaming as he was about to feed Benton to another monster.

"Now, drink."

When his eyes watered, Benton wished Sarlona would make it hurt. Then he could growl and scream, and his brimming tears would be justified.

She rubbed the center of his palms with her thumbs. "Shhh… It's okay, Benton. I've got you."

Had he been making a sound? Did she think those words would comfort him? He didn't want anyone to have him. Others were dangerous. Especially the three monsters in the room.

She drove a warm, electric spike into his brain. It paralyzed his racing thoughts. The only place they could go was to her.

He lost feeling in his hands or gained feeling in hers. Their hands seemed to melt together until he wasn't sure where he ended and she began. A swell of…something rose out of him, and he had no desire to hold it back. As it passed to her, she rewarded him with a sweet, tender release and made him groan. The transaction didn't stay blissful for long.

He cried out again as Sarlona's consciousness crashed into his. He was laid out, naked, split open, with her fingers probing his guts. *Get out. Please get out. Oh gods, Sar,* don't.

When Glaucus and Dagmar sifted through his being, he hardly

noticed. Sarlona, however, he detected in his mind like a nest of insects sweeping over his brain and palpating it with their antennae. He couldn't have her in there with him. She'd see his crimes. Worse, she'd see his victimization. She'd see the things he ached to do to her.

Please.

She didn't leave. Instead, she embedded herself deeper until she experienced what he felt. She let one hand go, which fell limp at his side. Her fingers crawled up his neck, stroked the stubble on his cheek, and found the tender spot behind his earlobe to caress. He cursed himself for liking it.

Then he slipped, lost in her as she let their minds intertwine. He knew her real mother's embrace and the magic of the sea. Faith in the Gods flooded in, and he sensed the mystery in the stars. Sarlona stole the comfort of a well-balanced blade, the fuzziness of too much ale, and the warmth inside a woman.

Please, Sar.

Her response was to drown him in a serenity so deep he couldn't ask again. She could have whatever she wanted from him. He'd give it to her. His thoughts, Marrow, his life, his soul. He'd offer it all up.

Fortunately, she only took the first two, and after a few more minutes, the rest of him went as limp as his arm. His head lolled to the side, and his eyelids grew too heavy to hold open as his thoughts unraveled.

When they solidified, he lay in his bunk. Groggy and hungover, he half-wondered if it had been a nightmare. If Sarlona was still trapped in the chamber upstairs, a human woman, desperate and afraid.

But his bad dreams and memories were usually one and the same.

~ * ~

Sarlona glanced up from her reading, *An Avenian's Guide to the Flora of Rashiva*. Amenduil stood in the center of her chamber. She would have heard and smelled him coming had he entered any way but magically. "Fortunate I wasn't changing."

"For you, perhaps," Amenduil said, with a devilish twinkle in his eye.

"I don't doubt you scry on me whenever it pleases you," she said as she set the book beside her on the bed.

One of the several downsides to being able to read minds was learning that every guard but Cyr and Lita lusted after her. Being young, at their mercy, and having the parts they enjoyed, she might have guessed.

Some of the animals kept in Ashmore had given it a lot of

thought, however. It made putting her hands on them much more uncomfortable.

"Not for any purpose so raffish as my enjoyment," he said.

"What do you want?"

He stared at the floor. "I just thought I'd see how you're doing. We haven't talked since—"

"What is there to say?"

"Whatever you'd like, my dear."

"I'd like to tell you to go cock yourself," she said. "Then make threats about draining you of every vapor of Marrow and remind you that *I* never made any agreement not to turn you." She grimaced.

Though every fiber of Amenduil's body was pregnant with Marrow, she abhorred the thought of touching him. Despite the sweet, ethereal scent coming off him as if he'd fallen into a vat of cologne, she didn't want to taste him. And much as she would have liked to strip him of some magic, taking it forever seemed too cruel.

"I can't imagine what it's like to lose all that power," he said, unfazed by her half-threats. His face and tone were genuinely sympathetic.

"I'm just as powerful." She thought that was true. "But it's not the same. It's not me. There's nothing Gods-given about this power."

He nodded. "I *am* sorry, Sarlona."

Not sorry enough, but she had no intention of correcting that. She didn't want to make an enemy of him. Avoiding him was the wisest move.

Her unease went beyond healthy respect for the potency of his spells. There was a darkness about him, hidden beneath the contrived gentle aura. A blackness like that which now lurked in the depths of her soul.

His shadows didn't seem buried so deep as her own. They lingered just below the surface, like crocodiles waiting to ambush animals that wandered too close. To crush the weaker creatures in their jaws and drag them down into the abyss. Given his faith and what she had seen him conjure, he surely meant to drag the vulnerable to *the* Abyss.

He crept closer, eying the spot beside her on the bed. "I wouldn't begrudge you the draining if that would help you forgive me."

It wouldn't. She doubted he had any real desire for her forgiveness anyway.

"If that would please you," he said.

Despite what a hearty meal he would make, if she had only killers to feed on and play with, she preferred those who carried their instruments of death at their sides, not in their souls.

And she didn't have to journey to the farthest reaches of his mind—she didn't dare—to know that his was a more sinister evil than Benton and the other guards.

Benton's was a simple sort, born out of misfortune and the world's cruelty. Manifested as the callousness he imagined necessary for survival and the rapaciousness he indulged as a fleeting salve. Compassionless but not malicious. She could understand that. With her new thirst, she even began to relate to it.

Amenduil's darkness seemed a calculating and premeditated sort, and she feared examining it. His immorality was not of chance and need but choice and desire. Benton's blackness commanded him. Amenduil's blackness was commanded *by* him.

The tangible corruption slithering somewhere beneath his disarming exterior made her skin crawl. "I hear you taste terrible."

His brow knitted. "No, no," he said, "Not to you, my dear." His tone turned seductive, sickening. "You would find Vorakor's effluence more agreeable. Perhaps…ambrosial."

Her hunger spiked. Not because she believed him, just because he'd drawn attention to it.

She pinned him with her stare rather than continue floating her gaze about to avoid drawing some aggressive shadow out of him. "Are you implying I'm a darker being than either Glaucus or Dagmar?"

He smiled. "Vorakor has a special love for you, Sarlona."

She locked down a shiver, but she couldn't hold his long-lashed gaze.

His eyes brimmed with conviction. "Unlike the Gods that have abandoned you."

She gritted her teeth, struggling to keep her eyes blue and the blades in her forearms. "My Gods have not abandoned me." That was what she had to tell herself hourly.

"They left all your prayers unanswered. They let this happen to you." He crept closer, like she was a beast that might decide to bite at any moment.

She was.

"They've left you alone, after all your devotion, all your sacrifice." His words were daggers, but his voice was silk drawn across her ears and the back of her neck.

No longer could she use her spells to detect just what he pulsed in her direction. But she sensed the magic on him, active, and she was vulnerable to it. Amenduil masked with spell work the sensation of falling into a dark hole that his aura generated. He projected warmth always. Warmth that allowed him to sit next to her on the bed.

She sighed, exasperated with herself for not running Amenduil through with her claw. And for wanting to.

His seductive shadows caressed her shoulder beneath the hand he set on it. "I think you know whom to turn to if you long to feel loved anew."

Now, she wasn't sure she'd experienced the sensation before.

"I think you know who would never abandon you. Who would hold you in His infinite heart. Who would answer your prayers."

She might have dived right into the Abyssal Waters if he'd summoned a puddle of them then. Just to get away from him, to escape from Ashmore, and to end this stage of her existence.

She stared at the door, knowing her mood would improve if she went through it and found someone to nab. Maybe Benton, again. "I don't hear him."

"You will, my dear."

It was as awful a threat as anyone had ever made against her.

Amenduil leaned close and whispered in her ear, "As you lie alone in this dark chamber... In the dead of the night, ask Him for help."

He punctuated his sentence with a kiss to her ear as soft and gossamer as moth wings. She couldn't help shivering and wiping at the side of her head as though that could undo the kiss and the slither of his words into her ear.

Inching away, she prayed to her Gods that the kiss hadn't been some magical method for making her hear Vorakor's whispers. Fortunately, no evil voices hissed at her from the Abyss.

"And listen," he said with a warm smile when he rose. He went for the door, and Sarlona nearly let him leave.

She should have. "Wait."

He swiveled with eyebrows raised.

She narrowed her eyes. "What are you still doing here?"

Always with a disarming smile. "I'll be leaving for Port Brummit and the Embrace soon."

Good.

"Our Abyssal Lord just asked me to look after you a bit longer."

Look after. She ached to pin him to the door with both carpal blades. On occasion, he had been a mild comfort, a source of information, or someone to commiserate with. Someone to talk to who at least feigned empathy. Yet this wouldn't have happened to her if not for him. The lorkai couldn't have kept her there without him.

He'd kept her there.

Part of her wanted to keep him there. Most of her never wanted to see him again.

"If I asked for help... Would he answer in whispers or actions?" she asked as he opened the door.

He swung around. His eyes always reminded her of a grackle's feathers when they caught the sun just right—bright, dark, and bluish green. Now they just appeared black. His smile should have been fanged.

"Sarlona... Under Port Brummit, in Vorakor's temple, my magic knows no limit."

Chapter Seventeen

Sarlona floated shadow to shadow from the study down to the main doors. She needn't have. With her body as transparent as the clearest glass, Gupson wouldn't spot her. Perhaps if he'd been aware that a lorkai went down the stairs while he came up, he would have spied the crystal woman. His search was for a different lorkai, however. He wasn't expecting her there.

His mind was on his aching left knee and Glaucus. Gupson couldn't finish his ten-hour shift without help. Injuries from his youth complained too loudly on cold nights. He needed Glaucus to ease the pain, let him off duty early, or at least let him sit by the doors.

His mind bled apprehension. What if Glaucus decided Gupson was no longer useful? That if he couldn't perform all his duties, he'd be replaced. What happened to people who knew too much about the Lord of Ashmore when they'd outlived their usefulness?

She lingered, motionless in the dark of the second-floor landing as he limped up the last few stairs to join her. Instead of hugging the wall, she inched back just far enough to let him pass. His scent overwhelmed her when his clothes brushed against her bare skin.

He smelled of everything humanoids secreted—sweat and sweetness. Hundreds of individual chemicals she'd begun to sort out. The collective scent was like bread in the oven.

Beyond that hung the aroma of his individual chemistry, which she recognized from a distance and could've picked out of a large crowd. Over it, the scents of hay and horse manure wafted. They clung to his hair and clothes. He spent more time in the stable than the others.

He couldn't smell her in return. Only lorkai could pick up her scent. And since she hadn't yet learned how to extend her glassiness to her garments, she wasn't wearing any. Her hair, unwashed for a few days, just smelled of Ashmore—must, old burn, and softwood.

Gupson groaned under his breath with his first step up the next flight of stairs, and his bones creaked with the wood as he ascended.

Part of her longed to snatch him. To pin him gently against the wall and tell him he was still valued. To slide her hands under his tunic and tell him his arrows still sought the hearts of his targets, even if some blurred or he couldn't hold his bowstring taut for as long. To promise Glaucus wouldn't discard him as she drew the Marrow from his flesh. She wanted to force Gupson's joints to quiet. Quell their swelling and stifle his pain while she used him.

The remainder won out. She was too shy, self-conscious, and ashamed to do anything but grab a forearm or touch a cheek and say, "I'm sorry."

He had little Marrow to start with anyhow. Without great care, she'd drain all of it, then start sucking out life force. She didn't have much control yet.

Anyway, she yearned for Benton. She loved his Marrow's taste, feeling, whatever it was.

Stronger was her desire for Glaucus's—concentrated and ancient and a hundred times more invigorating than any mortal's. He would give her a taste of himself if she performed her task well. He'd probably fill her with his butterflies too.

She still liked that.

Drifting to the front door, she cursed herself for having become a well-trained beast. But she needed what small pleasures she could take. Those were her incentives to survive. She was worse than an obedient animal—she was Benton.

The crunch of boots on snow along the inner wall of the palisade led her to him. Sneaking up behind him, she followed in the frozen, packed-snow trail as he patrolled.

His divine scent, teeming with Marrow, woke the roiling black creature within. It begged her to devour him. She hovered her hand above his shoulder. Picturing herself ripping him around and rending his shirt to get to the bare skin below, she all but salivated. Her muscles twitched when they came to the section of the wall bathed in the manse's torchlight. An animal ready to pounce, and—she sighed. She couldn't hunt him.

Spinning with impressive speed for a mortal, he drew his sword and jumped. He peered in her direction. "Sar? Is that you?"

The monster inside raged when she stuffed it back into its hole. "Yes."

"For gods' cockin' sakes, Sar. Let me see you."

Why not? What could he do now? It wasn't her body anyway.

Hers was gone. This one was a lorkai's. But her pounding heart prevented her from forcing the pigment back into her skin. "I can't."

His blade flagged, and a grin leaked onto his face. "Can't do the clothes yet, can you?" Squinting harder, he groped for her, but she slipped behind him. His every muscle fiber tightened. Whether they were primed to defend against a hungry monster or attack as one, she couldn't have said. He pivoted, gaze scanning the starry night. "C'mon, Sar, this ain't fair."

The monster thrashed. *Not fair.* She breezed back to where she started. "No. It's not."

Sword tip raised, he swiveled toward her. "Ain't you cold?"

"No." She didn't feel the cold like before. As they spoke, she commanded her blood vessels to stay dilated, shunting her hot blood to meet the winter air. No part of her would freeze, even if she stood there for hours.

"Well, you're makin' me nervous."

Excellent.

Opening the clasp to his cloak, he shrugged himself out of it and handed it to her left.

Surprised by the gesture, it almost hit the snow before she snatched it.

"Thank you." She shrouded herself in black wool, and his scent—stale ale, steel, and leather, perfused with the headiest of Marrow.

His gaze roved over her when she forsook her crystalline disguise. "What're you sneakin' around for anyhow? After a snack?"

"They told me to practice hunting." She'd failed. Glaucus would be disappointed. Gods knew why she cared when she was more determined to hate him than ever. "And I wanted to see you." *Swallow you.*

"I bet you want more than that." He sheathed his blade.

It felt like an invitation. She drifted closer without a thought. He was right. She burned for everything he had.

"Do what you gotta do." His voice thinned. "Just stay outta my head this time."

Guilt and disappointment prodded her heart at once. "It's difficult to keep it from hurting if I can't feel what you're experiencing."

His haunting gaze dropped to the dirt-stained, hard-packed ice on the path. "I'll survive. Assumin' you don't kill me."

Slumping her shoulders, she bit back the urge to remind him who'd helped mold her into humanoid voraciousness. "It would be nice if we could do more than survive this place."

"Well, I'd tell you to take up drinkin', but that won't do you no good now."

She examined the brilliant, multifaceted ice shards that made up the snow. The crystalline graveyard didn't appear as wondrous as it had fresh. The flakes that had retained some shape were but broken survivors among the wreckage of their crushed and melded fellows. "I don't know if I can do this, Benton. Be this way."

Not that the thirst for Marrow gave her any choice. She could either burden it, or the lorkai instincts would obliterate her. "They won't be able to keep me here much longer." But now she had nowhere else to go. How could she return home a monster? "Sometimes, I think it would be easier to go deep into the forest." She peered over the far wall to where fluffy snowcaps resting on pine and spruce crowns peeked above the jagged line, far in the distance. "Let the hunger take me like Glaucus said it would. Just become an animal. Another beast in the wood." Shrugging, she pictured it, the comfort of coniferous shadows. "To survive on the occasional lost hunter. I can't be a druid anymore, but I can be among the forest denizens I safeguarded as one."

The thought had appeal. It might be easier to become an animal in the wood than to walk among her prey, pretending to be one of them.

Benton half-shrugged and cringed, all at once. "You'll be okay, Sar. You're tough." He reached out like he was about to grab a bundle of thorny twigs. "You'll get used to it." Squeezing her shoulder, he did his best to comfort her. "It's only been a couple weeks."

Fire and ash bit her insides. How could she get used to it? Being outside of nature, separate from the cycle of life and death, and removed from humanity? As much time as she'd spent by herself, she'd never been so alone. A hand on her shoulder couldn't begin to erode the emptiness. What could was a mind close to hers. One that glowed for her. Needed her.

She edged nearer. He froze when she laid her head against his shoulder. His scent seemed to flow into her, stirring her as the aroma of freshly tilled soil in the spring once had. "Benton..." He'd snatched her so readily before, eager for every opportunity to trap her in his arms. Now that she didn't fear them around her, his arms wouldn't close. "Please, hold me."

He enveloped her in a frigid, unsteady embrace. His clothes and the skin beneath them had cooled without his cloak. "You know who you're askin'..."

It seemed as much a statement as a question.

"I know who you are," she replied.

A former highwayman who'd earned his spot on the gallows platform well. A boy who'd murdered his family at fifteen. The crimes that had landed him in Ashmore were more terrible than the ones she'd imagined. But having been him, briefly, that first time she'd fed, she couldn't bring herself to hate him as much as she should. Neither could she fear him. Not as a lorkai. He was too fragile an entity.

She lifted her head to admire his face. It glowed violet in the light of her irises.

He rocked back on his heels. "Don't it bother you?"

Of course it did. And it didn't. She wasn't so different now—using those weaker than herself to get by. Besides, he'd been on his best behavior since Glaucus took him in.

That wasn't to say he wasn't the same man. He hadn't changed a lot. Only his circumstances had. Things were good for him. At least as tolerable as they'd ever been.

"I can hardly judge." She lowered her head, speaking into his shirt. As if muffling her words might stop the universe from hearing. "Now that I inflict my needs on the unwilling." Gods, he smelled supernal.

His arms tightened, and he wound his fingers into her hair. Tugging, he tipped her head back so she'd look at him. His gaze delved into hers, maybe searching for sincerity.

She basked in the electric blue of his eyes. "Now that I take whatever I desire." Maybe not *whatever*. There wouldn't be a guard left breathing if she had. But more than she could justify.

A puff of his hot breath hit her face, and he shuddered against her. He stared at her lips. "What do you wanna take from me tonight?" His voice was breathless, and the smell of need permeated the air.

Everything. But maybe she could settle for whatever he offered. She trailed her index finger from his earlobe, across his perpetual stubble, and took his chin between it and her thumb. While coaxing his lips apart, she drove her gaze through his. Its orange glow penetrated far deeper than the matching torchlight reflected in his eyes.

"What would you give me, Benton?" *Nope.* She hadn't meant to ask that.

He grinned and squeezed her, his desire jabbing her between the navel and pubic bone. "Every inch, darlin'. If you think you can handle 'em all."

She buried her burning face in his chest.

He pushed harder against her, then slipped a hand inside the gap in his cloak.

A sweet shiver crawled from his frigid fingers when they alighted on her side. He ran them the length of her waist but stopped at her hip. Evidently, being able to rip hands off may have prevented him from sliding his touch to the front or back.

Her spine fused into an iron rod when he parted the front of the cloak. He stared inside, heart pounding.

Hers thundered when he drifted his quivering fingers to her chest. They landed on the intricate scars Dagmar had left her. Just between her breasts instead of on one.

He traced one delicate curve. "They...cut you...up bad, huh?"

The external scarring was the least of her problems. "You don't like it?"

"No... I... It just seems like it hurt. I like every part of you, Sar," he said. "A lot more than's good for me."

"I know." Maybe that was part of what called her to him like a siren's song. Along with his perfect jawline and the way his battered leather pants hugged his muscular thighs.

Reaching around him, she skimmed one hand low over his backside to get under the hem of his shirt. Her fingers tasted him while she raked them up, and they crossed from leather to hard flesh. It took all she had not to draw in. Not to devour him.

"How can..." His voice was breathy. "You know...*everything* and—" He shook his head, squirming, then met her gaze. "Gods, darlin', don't you hate me?"

Maybe she would have if she'd just been handed an account of all his transgressions. Instead, she'd lived them in his memories. Having witnessed life batter him from his earliest years and sensed the abyss of guilt beneath his feet, she'd leave the hate to others. His victims, lawmen... Dagmar. Why should it be her responsibility, when the hum of his insides narrowed the empty black chasm in her chest?

Sinking into his stare, she caressed the edge of his mind and did her best impression of his grin. "How could I hate you when you taste so damn sweet," she teased.

He smiled. "You don't need another look at all the awful shit I got in here. That ain't gonna make you feel better." He snaked his hands into the cloak again and kneaded her bare hips with calloused fingers. "But I got somethin' that will."

Unable to tune out the delightful ache inside her, she was tempted to let him try. "I'm lonely, Benton. I'm afraid. I just... I need you close." She scraped her fingertips around to his front and traced his granite abdomen. "I won't dredge anything up. Can we just be together for a few minutes?"

He needed it as much as she did. Maybe more so. How his soul had screamed for affection when she'd crashed into him that first feeding.

His shoulders rose and fell as his breaths grew heavier. After his fingers danced on his pommel, he shut his eyes for a second. Opening them, he nodded. "Okay, Sar, but only if you put your eyes to the way they were."

Suppressing her radiant, lorkai irises, she revealed the deep ocean blue she'd been born with.

"That's better," he whispered. "Be gentle, okay?"

"Of course." Slipping her hands around his back, she embraced him. "Always." As she breezed into him, she gave him a big smile. One no one else would be willing to give him. The kind from family waiting upon the shore when they spotted their loved one on the deck of a docking ship.

He put his arm around her, and she rewarded him with tingling heat. Softening, he sank into her.

The nearness dissolved the sensation of falling into never-ending darkness for them both.

But the black, hungry thing that lived deep inside her pined for more. For Marrow.

The thirst tolerated little squeamishness. A yearning that deep demanded satisfaction. While less uncomfortable than mortal thirst or hunger, it was just as urgent and far more pervasive. When the need hit, her body ached for Marrow. Her thoughts were of nothing else, and her heart seemed to burn for it. Its intensity made her take Glaucus's warning seriously—if she fought the hunger for long it would consume her.

She activated whatever strange organ now lived in her fingertips. The light and the extra warmth flooded into them, then into Benton. The energy knitted itself into his, locked into the living net of ethereal nectar that suffused his tissues, and she controlled the flow. Instead of allowing it to float with the rhythms of his body, she drew it to herself, siphoning through her fingers. It spilled into her like heavenly light.

He tensed against the tug, the loss, and the draining of a power he'd never been taught to harness… It wasn't quite painful. Still, she didn't want him to feel it. Or at least notice he was feeling it.

She delved further into him, to a network the other lorkai had been training her to navigate in-depth, mostly on poor Gorgil. Discovering the right strands of webbing, she activated them at her behest, beginning a chemical cascade that flushed the tension from his muscles and made a gentle moan pass his lips. A swell of euphoria wiped his mind blank. When it began to fade, she tickled those strands again.

His legs weakened for a second, and she had to hold him on his feet. "Cock." He moaned louder.

She tugged his strings once more, and he gave himself over. A dam broke, and his Marrow poured into her. He pushed it at her. His blank gaze collapsed into hers, and he squeezed her tighter with a whine.

"Oh, gods, Sar. That's so good." His voice was broken—a small, sweet sound that begged for mercy.

She wouldn't give it to him.

Chapter Eighteen

Benton closed his eyes and took a deep breath in front of Sarlona's chamber door. Four pints had taken the edge off, and the cup in his hand would get him over the threshold, but his fist still shook when he lifted it to knock.

Sarlona's shining eyes would suck him in again.

Then gods knew what would happen to him. Maybe he'd hand over his soul, given how willing he'd been to donate his Marrow and mind. He sighed. Good a place as any for them. Provided he didn't get on her nerves and provoke a Dagmar-like reaction. Assuming she didn't look too hard into his past and decide to create the hell for him that he deserved. He bit his lip. It'd be fine. She wasn't violent like Dagmar. Like him.

There was no avoiding her anyway. Glaucus had ordered Benton to report to her chamber at sunset. So she could 'experiment.'

He took a sip. The pink sky from the hall window laughed at him and his trembling fist. Just as his hand obeyed, the door creaked open. She appeared in the gap, scanning him with eyes that matched the sunset.

"Just couldn't wait to get me alone again...huh, darlin'?"

Same girl. Same heart and soul. Same loneliness. That's what he told himself. He still liked her. It would just take some getting used to—their power reversal.

She nodded, gazing at him with eyes that wouldn't allow him to pretend she was a human woman.

"Thirsty?" He sipped his drink.

"Have a seat." She gestured to the bed and slid around him to shut the door.

"Can't wait to get me in bed either..." He flashed a grin.

"There's no hurry." Her voice was so light, it seemed to fly around the room. "You can finish your drink."

That sounded like a great idea. He took another swallow with one eye fixed on her as she sat to his left.

Her hand floated to him but alighted on his hilt instead of his flesh. She made delicate, sensual circles on the pommel with her fingers. He couldn't help imagining them doing that a few inches to the right.

"Why'd you bring your sword?"

He stared past her—and the way she enwreathed his grip with her fingers—to the window. "Fend you off. Why else?"

A small table had appeared by the sill, draped in a white cloth. A ring of sand kissed its edges. Within stood a fat, white candle, a wide iridescent shell with a splash of water inside, and what appeared to be fish bones. The altar was the first sign he'd seen of her accepting Ashmore as her home.

"Do you still think you could?" Her smile should have been a row of shark teeth.

"No." He might take a few fingers off, but that wouldn't stop her.

"Do you want to?"

On her bed, in her hungry stare, anticipation pricked his skin. "No."

"Remove it then."

He untied his sword belt one-handed and leaned the sheathed blade against the closest bedpost.

"Now, the shirt."

"You first, sweetheart." Grinning, he glanced up to gauge her reaction. That was a mistake.

Her eyes glowed like a blue fire that begged to consume him. Taking another drink, he hid from them.

She leaned nearer and untied the sloppy knot on his jerkin.

He pushed his cup into her hands, then slipped off the worn black leather. "I'll pay my last coin to hear you tell me to take my pants off."

She brought his cup to her face like she might drink. "You can take them off if you'd like."

It wasn't the enthusiastic response he'd hoped for, but he wrenched off his boots. It didn't hurt to be prepared. After yanking the faded black linen over his head, he stood to slide off the dark scratched leather. "Well, it's freezing in here, darlin'. You're at least gonna have to keep me warm."

"Don't I always?"

His gaze hit the floor. She did. Since he first laid eyes on her. That was why she was such a cocking problem.

She set his cup on the nightstand and glided closer, twisting to put her hands on his shoulders. He flinched and braced himself, just in case she drove herself into his mind, temporarily dissolved his rib cage, or made him shit himself. Like Dagmar would do.

All Sar afflicted him with was the warmth of her fingers.

Their heat blossomed and trickled into the rest of his body when she pushed him flat onto the bed. It turned into a hot bolt as she swung one leg over to straddle him. He gawked at this angel-faced, demon-eyed, young woman, whose soft hands roved his naked chest and whose perfect thighs parted over his hips.

"Shit." His cheeks blazed, and the rest of his blood went to his groin. He tried to think of something to stop it. All he could focus on was her.

She could stop it. If she wished to...

Unable to help himself, he snatched her hips. He tried to pull them down on himself, but they wouldn't budge. "Sar..."

She wasn't smiling anymore. But there wasn't anything malicious in her gaze as she stared at him—hunger, maybe, curiosity.

"Gods, I wish all the girls looked at me that way."

"No one can look at you the way I do, Benton."

A pleasant shiver started at his tailbone.

"No one can see you the way I do."

That shiver crawled over him—slow and skin-prickling. He believed her when her consciousness brushed against his. No one else would touch his mind without squealing in horror at what bile came away on their fingertips.

He had no clue how to protect himself. She could have trespassed without him feeling it or barged in, shattering the flimsy locks that nature provided. Instead, she caressed his insides like a warm summer breeze, coaxing him to open the door so he could feel it on his face.

The pressure on his mind grew as she bore down. Like her fingers did into the muscle of his chest, making small circles that promised a tender release.

He closed his eyes, and while he didn't understand how, he opened. She felt too incredible to resist.

Flooding in, she rewarded him with a flush of sweetness that drove out all loneliness. Her smile returned. She had the most wonderful smile.

Her fingertips blazed to life, hot but not burning. She sat up, withdrawing all but one. Her index finger she rested at the base of his throat, in the crook of his sternum. The tugging at his Marrow came a moment later. He didn't fight it. A rivulet of his useless magical reservoir left him, and ecstasy washed in.

Relief spread across her face while she drew her glowing finger down the channel from the top of his sternum to his navel. She looked like she just took that first sip of a hot beverage on a frigid day or the first swig from a pint after a long week.

He made her feel good. For him, that was something. Still, he couldn't help thinking how much better he could make her feel in other ways. "I'm that tasty, huh?"

The fire in her eyes plunged into the depths of the ocean. The light in her fingertips died. Her cool blue eyes did more to relax him than whatever knobs she manipulated on his insides. But he caught a trace of horror in her expression, like she just realized what she was doing. Or remembered she was a monster and hadn't always been one.

"Delicious, Benton." She sat back, careful to rest on his thighs instead of where he wanted her.

Pink fingertips traced his abdominal muscles before retreating. Her pelagic stare roved down his torso, then hopped from the bulging front of his underclothes to his face.

She sighed. "You look pretty delectable too."

He told himself that the beautiful creature straddling him was supposed to be a monster, but he saw only Sarlona.

"Well, tell you what, darlin'… I'll let you see the rest of me if I get to taste a little of you."

Knowing she lingered in his mind, he showed her just where and how he longed to taste her. How much he could make her enjoy it.

She turned as red as he'd ever seen someone without painting them in their blood.

He sat up and slid his hands into her pants, dipping his thumbs from the sides of her hips into her groin. She peered at them as if they were a new life form.

"You can't still be scared of me, Sar." She had reason to be before. Not now.

"No, I can't." She pried his hands from her hips and held his fingers prisoner in her palms.

The sensation of her thumbs caressing his fingertips was too tender. It hurt.

He was afraid. That he'd drown in the depths of her eyes while her presence hung in his mind like a euphoric mist.

He withdrew his hands and wriggled from under her. She didn't budge when he tried to push her over on the bed, half laughing at his efforts.

Her eyes sparkled with light that made him feverish. Straight teeth peeked from what had to be tender lips, standing out against sun-kissed skin. Her beachy glow had faded a little since they'd first met, but the muted hue Dagmar had made permanent was beautiful. It matched that wonderful life-giving smile.

"C'mon, how 'bout we get to some of that experimentin'?" He expected her smile to widen or cheeks to flush again.

Instead, both the light and color left her face. She glanced toward the window. "I don't think so."

He tensed. "What'd Glaucus tell you to do?"

Exhaling like a kettle, she answered, "Possess you, in essence."

He could think of worse things a lorkai could do to him and no one better to be possessed by. Still, he wasn't about to invite it.

"Like I'm a damned demon." Her eyes flashed red, and she looked like one.

"You could never be a demon, Sar." He had no clue if that was true, but it seemed like what she needed to hear.

She snorted. "Your faith in me is overwhelming."

Right, she was still in his head. "I bet you'd make a hells of a succubus," he said, attempting to pull her down onto the bed with him.

To his surprise, she laid beside him and nudged him onto his side. Despite all the unnatural strength coiled in the arm that slithered under his to wrap around him, she didn't crush him. Cautious, flighty, it loosened when he took a deeper breath than the last. He ached for the reverse, to have her in his arms, but in her embrace, every muscle relaxed. Warmth and fuzziness settled in his bones.

Kneading the spot above his stomach where the two sides of his ribcage came together, she filled the emptiness beneath her fingers and sipped at his Marrow. She groaned. "Gods, you taste divine."

The warm rain started again, falling harder and faster and in fatter droplets that burst upon impact.

Being drained shouldn't feel so wonderful. He shouldn't crave her in his head. But the rain built into a storm, and his breaths thinned until he was panting. Her fingertips heated as they ran from his sternum to his navel and returned. She inhaled deeply behind his ear, and he imagined her savoring his scent along with the taste of his Marrow. Her hot breath on the side of his throat when she exhaled quickened his blood.

She whispered in his ear, "I want you, Benton."

That simple admission hardened part of him to diamond and softened the rest. He whined and thrust against her hand, which still tickled him safely around the navel. Fire swept across his skin as he tried to quiet his racing thoughts. His breath caught when her fingers dipped into the waist of his underclothes.

Her palm cradled his hipbone, and his heart raged. He imagined she liked that, the sound of his thrashing heart.

Shutting his eyes tight, he braced for her to wrap her hand around him and make him beg. Instead, she unleashed more of that steady rain. It beat down, drowning him in warmth. Before long, it overtook him.

She should have punished a wicked man with agony as great as she could imagine, not filled him with rapture.

But she was torturing him.

He squirmed. She released his hip and let him flip around to face her.

His attack took her by surprise. Without thinking, he struck like a snake, hitting his mark. At last, he got to taste her. She was just as sweet as he imagined, like the steam that came off a boiling pot of syrup.

Her eyes widened at the kiss, and she stiffened, rock hard but silky smooth, like sanded butternut, when he wrapped his arms around her. He snuck his hands up the back of her shirt and rammed himself against her.

She closed her eyes and drove all ten thirsty fingertips into the tenderest muscles in his back. The warmth threatened to overwhelm him, to melt him into nothing.

Retreating just far enough that he could move his lips, he whispered to her, still bound by the same breath, "I'm yours, Sar."

Returning his kiss, she drew so hard on his Marrow that his bones vibrated, but she smothered the sensation with the perfect embrace and a wave of ecstasy that rolled through him, one end to the other, without dying down.

Trembling and moaning, he pulled himself out of his underclothes and pressed against her as if they might be able to meld together. He grabbed her backside and squeezed like he never intended to let go, driving harder still. Then he slid his shaking hands around to her front and put agonizing inches between them as he fumbled to unlace her pants.

So close to utter relief that when her fingers locked his wrists in iron, tears came to his eyes. "Gods, Sar... I will get on my knees and beg."

After the longest second of his life, she released him to clasp his hips. He tore open her pants, but when he tried to pull them down, his ecstasy swelled, and it took all his being to keep it inside. She fed from the sides of his pelvis as his grip slipped from hers.

"Please, Sar... Don't make me come..." Everything he had fought against it. "Not unless I'm inside you."

The agony subsided, and he caught half a breath. He tore at her pants again, and they came down over those perfect hips. He reached between her legs to where she radiated wet heat.

He wanted her so bad, his head spun, and his insides thinned. And she wanted him too. As he moved to join their bodies in a way he could appreciate, the satin touch on his hip transformed into a rough vise and ripped him backward.

Chapter Nineteen

Sarlona snatched Benton's wrist before Glaucus could tear him away.

"Let him go, Sarlona," Glaucus boomed like Benton had never heard.

Cursing, Benton tried to pull up his underclothes, but they didn't quite make it. He attempted to stand and didn't manage that either. She crushed his wrist as Glaucus struggled to pry her hand free.

"Daggy," Glaucus yelled.

Dagmar appeared within the span of a heartbeat. "Oh, Gods." Grimacing, she twirled from Benton. "Truly, Sarlona?"

"She's killing him, Daggy. Help me."

Dagmar sighed and grabbed Benton's wrist beside Sarlona. "Well, that makes sense."

It didn't make sense to Benton. He groaned. "Get the cock outta here." It came out a whisper. "We don't need you involved."

"Quiet, mutt," she growled as her other hand joined Glaucus's to dislodge Sarlona's.

The grip opened, and Dagmar tore him clear of Sarlona and the bed. Dagmar glanced at him and sneered. Holding him on unsteady feet, she yanked up his underclothes.

He collapsed onto the floor as she let go and pivoted from him without another thought. Exhaustion and confusion stopped him from rising. He couldn't sit up.

When his vision fell into focus, Sarlona had Glaucus by the throat. A maniacal laugh tore out of her chest. Her irises blazed red—twice as bright as the yellow light in Dagmar's or the violet glow from Glaucus.

A chill ran up Benton's spine. He fought to ask what was happening, but the words came out in a rasp into the dusty floorboards.

Glaucus hollered, face twisted in pain as Sarlona's fingers burned his throat and tore blinding blue streaks from his flesh. He strained, red-faced against her, but she was too strong for him. That realization froze Benton's blood. Glaucus, with the slight flick of his wrists, drove her back. She hopped clear of his carpal blades a hair's breadth to spare.

She ejected her ivory swords from her wrists. With an ear-to-ear grin, she stared down Dagmar. "Your turn, Daggy."

Dagmar snorted and flipped out her blades—thick, wide, and long to match the rest of her. "That's 'Mother' to you."

Sarlona snarled. Bleary-eyed, Benton could have sworn she bared fangs. The young lorkai woman lunged, aiming her claws at Dagmar's heart and throat.

Dagmar deflected both blades, barely, above and to the right of Sarlona's head. Benton couldn't follow what happened next.

It ended with Dagmar against the wall, clutching a bloody forearm. Glaucus inched to his daughter.

Sarlona spun on him. "Rethinking your choices yet, milord?"

He skirted the bed with one eye on Sarlona. The other focused on Dagmar. "On the contrary, little one. I've never been more certain in our choice of progeny." He reached for his daughter's arm, from which a sliver of bone gleamed.

Dagmar recoiled. "I'm fine."

Glaucus turned to Sarlona. "You'll be okay, I promise."

Sarlona's eyes flickered and faded to orange. She kept her glare on Dagmar. "You should worry about how you'll be."

"It's normal to lose control when you're so young. We both did." Glaucus drew his blades into his forearms, and they disappeared through a seam too fine for Benton to see.

Dagmar followed her father's example, even as a red puddle formed between her boots. "I left bodies everywhere."

Sarlona eyed them both with a predator's gaze, stock-still as though she was about to strike. Her muscles twitched, taut enough to strain her clothes around the thighs and shoulders.

Benton wished he could get to his sword. Not that he'd be able to do much with it.

Glaucus floated forward, hands open and raised, as if their emptiness made them less of a threat. "You're doing great, little one. Adjusting far better than we thought you would." He flipped his hands over, inviting her to take his. He'd be lucky if she didn't cut them off. "We're very proud of you." She'd at least drain his Marrow reserves. "I'm sorry I interfered with your pet."

Pet? Even the man who had now saved Benton's life twice and been more of a father to him than anyone else thought him an animal.

"But I know you're fond of him and how heavyhearted you'd be if you ended him while in a daze."

Sarlona glanced at Benton, and he wished the Lord of Ashmore had left him out of it. At least she cared about him. That planted a warm seed to sprout amid his misery.

She knocked Glaucus's hands aside and stood on her toes to get in his face. "I've had enough of your placations and wheedling bullshit."

He cracked a smile. *Stupid.*

With a groan, Benton flipped himself over and propped himself on his elbows. "Darlin'…" He couldn't stop himself. "Could you pass me my pants?"

Her eyes dimmed. She dropped to her heels and glanced down. He must have made a sorry sight—weak, pale, eyelids heavy, reclined on the battered floor in nothing but underclothes.

The harsh lines in her face faded. Jaggedness melted to something tender. Fiery eyes changed to lightning bug green.

Sometimes pathetic worked. Especially on women.

Retracting her claws, she withdrew from Glaucus. "I'm sorry, Benton." She glanced at the other lorkai. "I'm sorry."

Benton didn't see why, after all they'd done to her. Maybe that was what was so special about her.

Sarlona scooped up his pants, then him. The room swirled as her chest grazed his, warming his clammy skin. He hadn't meant to end up in her arms again.

She held him on his feet. Her hand burned against his back, tapping into him again. To finish him off. "Here… Have some of Glaucus."

Before Benton could protest, he convulsed like he'd been hit by a bolt of electricity. With a flash of blue, every nerve buzzed. His heart jumped into a thunderous sprint, adrenaline shot through his thighs, and his skin prickled with gooseflesh. The fuzzy lines in his vision condensed into razor-sharp contours. His lungs expanded with cold air.

Then, all at once, he felt incredible, like he'd slept well, without a hangover, and jogged once around the palisade as a warmup. Physically.

Emotionally, his entrails lay on the floor where Dagmar had dumped him.

He swore under his breath and snatched his pants while he slunk away. Sarlona's eyes dulled to ocean blue again. He retreated near the window, putting himself behind her where he couldn't see her eyes. That was safer.

Glaucus proceeded with the wheedling bullshit she claimed to be sick of as Benton pulled on his pants. He tuned the lorkai out while he finished dressing and wondered what the hells he was going to do.

He wouldn't survive Sarlona.

Her growl yanked his attention to the monsters' conversation, and he fumbled to tie his sword belt.

"I can't do it, Glaucus." She didn't sound human. Not even humanoid.

"You've no choice. There's nothing to be done."

"I'm going to *kill* someone like this." Her rumble broke into a girl's squeal. "I—I have to leave. I have to find a way to change back...or get away...from *everyone.*"

Tears streamed down her face. Benton wished he could hide from them or dry them.

"You'll do worse out there." Dagmar jutted her chin at the window. "Where there are innocents."

Glaucus nodded. "It's all right, Sarlona." He inched closer to her, but she crept back. "Benton breathes for *you.* His life is yours."

Benton winced. Breathe for her? He wanted her, that was all. And while he hadn't been naïve enough to believe his life was his own, it felt safer, longer, in Glaucus's hands versus Sarlona's.

Glaucus hazarded a quick step forward and grabbed her arms. "I pulled him off those gallows and commissioned that sword for no other purpose than to keep you safe, Sarlona." Squeezing her shoulders, he gazed into her yellow-glowing eyes. "He's lived an extra seven good years because of you. You can't do any harm."

Sinking, Benton sighed. Maybe his life wouldn't last long with Sarlona, but at least she might value it.

"I'm not built for this," she said, shaking.

Against his better judgment, Benton snaked closer to the lorkai. "Don't you worry about me any, Sar." He'd do that. It was his specialty.

She glanced at him, but her stare drifted over to Dagmar, whose wound had closed, then to Glaucus.

As if to clear it, she shook her head. "You got what you wanted," she said, electric blue eyes beaming brighter. "Now I'm going to get what I want—to leave this place."

Glaucus cupped her cheek. "You need us, little one. You need our guidance and experience." His expression grew soft, sad. "You need a family. A home."

She snarled and shoved him hard. "I had them," she screamed. "You stole them from me."

"Please, Sarlona," Glaucus said, creeping toward her again, "we love you."

"More than anything," Dagmar added.

Sarlona's face twisted, and she flipped her carpal blades out again.

"You belong with us." Pushing his luck, Glaucus pressed on. He walked his cuirass right into the tips of her claws. "You belong as you are now."

"I. Am. Leaving." She tensed her arms, halting Glaucus where he was. "You're both too weak to stop me." Her face hardened to iron.

Dagmar flicked her claws out, with enough force that they clicked when they straightened. The sound made Benton grip his hilt on instinct. "We'll see."

She struck from the side, forcing Sarlona to pivot while Glaucus ejected his blades.

She parried Dagmar and spun in time to lock claws with Glaucus.

Kicking him in the gut, she drove him back. Benton had taught her that. She bound both of Dagmar's claws as they shot for her chest.

Without hesitation, Dagmar smashed her forehead into Sarlona's face.

The girl's nose broke with a pop, and Benton's sword slipped free of its sheath with a metallic scrape. Gods knew what he intended to do with it.

Sarlona retreated, covering her nose. Her eyes burned as red as the blood, her expression more anger than pain.

"You wish to leave so you won't hurt anyone," said Dagmar, tone laced with derision, "but unless you hurt someone, you'll never leave."

Sarlona struck at her, lightning fast. The instant she twitched, Glaucus lunged, forcing her to break off mid-attack and deflect his claws. With her carpal blades raised wide to keep one in front of each older monster, she roared.

"Benton," Glaucus said, his blazing emerald stare locked on Sarlona, claws up and ready. "Fetch the cord on my belt, won't you?"

A coil of iridescent, snot-green string, hung over his left hip. The cord was made of spider-faery silk—a material dragons couldn't break. "You're gonna tie her up?"

Glaucus's attention didn't leave Sarlona. "Just to get her to the cellars." An apologetic note hung in his voice.

There were cells down there, stone and steel cages. Dusty from disuse. One would have to be heavily enchanted to hold a lorkai for long.

"She'll be all right," he said as if he tried to assure them all. "This isn't the first time a young lorkai has become...unruly. We'll all be all right."

Benton couldn't bear to bind Sarlona.

"Benton, I need you now," Glaucus said, prodding him.

I *need you*. Sarlona's voice said in his head.

"Yeah, okay," Benton whispered. In one motion, he raised his blade and drove it through Glaucus's skull.

Glaucus went limp, the tip of Benton's sword protruding from his right eye socket. He collapsed forward, slipping off the blade and onto Sarlona.

Eyes wide and ocean blue again, Sarlona shoved him off her, and the Lord of Ashmore fell like a sack of rocks onto his back.

A crimson pool spread beneath him. The man to whom Benton owed every breath. Blood and vitreous leaked from his punctured eye. The luminescence vanished from the other, and it stared stormily into oblivion.

"Oh, Benton." Dagmar's irises spit fire from her scrunched and reddening face. The veins in her neck and arms bulged. "This time, I *am* going to kill you."

~ * ~

Sarlona leaped between them, twisting to keep one carpal blade in front of Dagmar, and thrust. Before the enraged Northlander could stop, she skewered herself just below the rib cage.

Stunned and bleeding, Dagmar stared at Sarlona.

She gaped, shaking. In a split second, she ripped her claw upward, slicing through ribs and clavicle until the blade emerged beside the left shoulder, just like Dagmar had done to Vosvoshish. The lorkai didn't scream like the merman had. She didn't keel over when the left side of her torso peeled off and flagged, while half her entrails dumped onto the floor with a slurp.

Instead, she grimaced and gurgle-growled with blood seeping from between her teeth and pink fire blazing in her eyes. She grabbed Sarlona by the throat with her fully attached arm and lumbered forward, still advancing at Benton.

Panicking, Sarlona swept her carpal blade up and across, slicing into the Northlander's throat. Dagmar's head rolled down her front, bounced off Sarlona's thigh, and hit the floor with a wet thump. The mass of muscle and blood-soaked hide followed it.

Sarlona backed into Benton, hands clapped over her ears in a futile attempt to shut out the telepathic screams and curses that the severed head spewed. To her horror, Dagmar's face still contorted, her eyes still blazed, her bloody lips still moved.

Then her body lurched, the attached arm stretching across the floor while powerful legs clumsily tried to dig boots into the blood-slick wood. The headless Northlander inched forward, groping, and dragging the peeled-off arm, quarter rib cage, and a hearty portion of guts behind it.

For gods' cocking sakes, one of you put me out.

Spitting profanities, Benton shoved Sarlona aside. He stepped on Dagmar's tangle of bloody hair, pinning her head in place on its side.

"I'm just doin' what you both told me," he said to the head, "lookin' out for her."

He drove his sword point through Dagmar's temple.

Finally, the cursing, growling threats went silent. The light faded from Dagmar's eyes, replaced with boring blue. The lines smoothed out of her face.

The screaming didn't stop, though. This breathy, almost ultrasonic whine hissed in her ears.

He grasped Sarlona's shoulder again. "Darlin'."

It was her. The screams were hers.

"It's all right, Sar. They'll be fine. You'll be fine."

He wouldn't be. Not once Dagmar recovered. His bronze face turned ashen as he stared at Glaucus. "We'd better get goin'."

Sarlona might have protested had she been able to work her voice. Half of what she'd longed to escape was Benton before she killed him. Now, if she didn't do it, Dagmar would. And Dagmar would make it slow and painful.

Chapter Twenty

"How much farther?"

Sarlona glanced over her shoulder as Benton stumbled over a log hidden beneath the snow.

"We've crossed into Treefall." Stopping for him to catch up, she stared high into the canopy.

She was home, but nothing seemed familiar. The stars peeking through the pine glowed like a thousand balls of fire instead of glistening like a hundred magical lights. Each tree was its own alien world instead of a landmark and a friend.

Neither did she recognize the sounds. The snow should have silenced everything but the occasional thunderclap of a frozen tree cracking and the tinkling of the powder itself as their boots plowed it aside. Instead, dozens of hearts beat like drums beneath the snow and in the trees. The caress of owl feathers kissed the snow, and a vole screamed as talons pierced its viscera.

The smells were the least familiar of all. Innumerable plant compounds wafted from every direction. As did the urine and feces of hundreds of animals. Slow decay. Remote smoke. Gratefully, salt still far in the distance. She should have just smelled snow and cold, maybe a hint of pine or spruce.

Overpowering it all, of course, was Benton. His heartbeat, breaths, and chemistry. He beamed like a watch fire, blared like a horn, reeked like essential oil.

Above everything else. "If we walk through the night, we can reach Sylvanus by dawn."

He trudged up beside her. "I ain't makin' it through the night again."

"All right." She zeroed in on a huge hemlock with weeping branches grazing the snow.

It took her about three minutes to dig the snow out from underneath it, build frozen walls to join the low-hanging branches, and construct a nest of pine branchlets.

He crawled into their den after her. "Are you going to be okay without a fire?"

Surely, the lorkai hadn't recovered so soon, especially Dagmar. But Sarlona wouldn't risk drawing attention to themselves just in case.

He grinned. "I will if you keep me warm."

She flashed a smile, but she dreaded touching him. To put her hands on him without draining him seemed impossible. She didn't know if she could draw from him without taking *everything*. "Okay... I'd better feed first."

He snatched her cloak to throw over his legs the second she removed it. After she extricated herself from the shelter and wandered a safe distance, she ejected her carpal blades and found a space with as few trees as possible. Her insides wriggled while pre-guilt wrestled with her need. Feeding from the earth would deaden it. And kill the trees.

Overindulging in the earth, drinking all the Marrow from the forest she could take, staved off some of the hunger for a humanoid meal. If she brimmed with Marrow, there was only so much of Benton she could steal. However much she revered the trees, however just his death sentence had been, his life took precedence over any plant or critter.

She knelt, driving her carpal blades through the snow and into the frozen soil. They sliced through the net of roots and embedded in the ground. With her palms against the needle thatch and the snow up to her elbows, she drew in.

The snow went first, evaporating. Then the shrubs and saplings withered to dust. The tall spruce and spindly maple above her crumbled to ash as she stole their energies with physical euphoria. Their pale particles floated off to join the snow. Another maple then a stately pine farther away soon followed. She must have hit their roots.

By the time she finished, the forest appeared as though a fireball had hit it. She tried not to think about the devastation as she folded her claws in and returned to Benton.

He was shivering. In constant motion for hours, he hadn't been cold before. Now, still and moist with sweat beneath his clothes, he suffered.

His discomfort permeated the frigid air. "Why couldn't we stay at an inn again?"

They'd been over it—so the lorkai couldn't track them by ripping observations from people's minds.

He pulled off his glove and held out his hand. "Get rid of my headache while you're at it."

Almost three days without a drink had taken as much a toll as the endless hike, lack of sleep, and winter cold. At least, that was what his complaining would lead one to believe.

She took his hand and a sip, slaking the craving for him before it hit. Then she sent her tendrils into him.

Tentatively, she heated his skin and extremities. She didn't dare raise his core temperature. The one time she'd tried that, she immediately sensed things...degrading.

Maybe she did need Glaucus and his experience. There was no going back now.

"Thanks, darlin'." Relief flooded Benton's face.

She fashioned an analgesic for his head, and he sighed.

Without releasing her fingers, he lay beside her.

How he could tolerate her touch after what she'd done to him, she didn't understand.

"You think that druid can turn you human?" He squinted at her, eyes dull and hazy, his face drawn.

She didn't have to seep into his mind to know he was exhausted and worried. And doing so was how she'd lost herself.

By conflating their hunger.

"There's no greater healer than Sylvanus," she replied, staring through Benton. "If he can't… I'll go to the Council, but…I'm putting you on a boat to Rashiva alone."

He snorted. "The hells you are."

"They'll be coming for me, Benton, not you."

"For now." He held her hand above his face inspecting her fingers like a toddler, like they were still something new and interesting. "They ain't gonna let me disappear, darlin'. I know too much about 'em." He interlaced their hands and held hers against his heart.

Warmth bloomed in her chest and spread to her cheeks. The delightful pulse against the back of her hand brought a steadiness. It told her the drowning thump in her ears was real and not growing madness. But what did he think she was to him? What did he think they were? She hadn't trod into his thoughts since they'd left.

He tightened his grip. "Anyway, I ain't gettin' on a boat. I can't swim."

"You can't swim?" She scrunched up her face. "You're a grown man."

"I can't read either."

She knew that and didn't find that amusing, just sad. "How could you never learn how to swim?"

"How could I?" he retorted. "We didn't all grow up on the seaside with a tutor."

"How'd you learn how to use a sword?" she shot back but regretted teasing him. "Did you take lessons for that?"

He snorted again. "In a way…" When he looked up at the canopy or some sliver of starlight, he stiffened. "I ain't goin' to Rashiva alone. I'll just fall into the same shit as before." His eyes widened as if the notion frightened him. "You'll just wander into the wilds and become an animal some lord will pay a helluva bounty to have put down."

He'd grown to know her better than she cared to admit.

"All right." She shook her head. "You need to sleep so we can get moving again."

"First…" He glanced at her, then up past her. "Would you…?"

For a second, she thought he wanted something sexual and couldn't help cringing. He would have put his grin on for that. And he wouldn't have had trouble finding the words.

"Before…when you…"

It hit her then, and she didn't make him finish asking. She wound herself deeper into his body and flooded his nerves with the devilish cocktail she'd given him half a dozen times now.

His eyes rolled, and his lips parted. Squeezing her hand, he twisted the moan that started in his chest into a sigh as it came out of him.

Guilt and concern held half her smile down. She liked that she could make someone feel that good. Doing so brought her some joy. Now, when she wasn't drunk on his Marrow and embedded in his mind—experiencing it with him—what she did felt perverse. Never mind awkward.

He mouthed, *thank you, Sar*, with a small sound.

She forced the other side of her mouth into a smile, then dropped it. Patting his arm, she tugged the strings that robbed him of consciousness. His thick lashes met in a kiss. Every hard line melted in his face.

He appeared peaceful, harmless, and beautiful. Two of the three were an illusion, and he'd look that way just so long as she kept the smell of smoke and his younger brother's cries out of his dreams.

~ * ~

They would trip Sylvanus's wards. Without Sarlona's magic, there was no way to avoid blundering through them. A vague scent of spell work, like scorched metal, hung in the air, but her senses couldn't pinpoint or categorize it. They couldn't tell her anything useful.

Better not to catch him unaware anyway.

Fortunately, none of the wards were designed to harm or stop trespassers, but to serve as a warning. They'd send a prickling over his wrinkled, ashy skin, then he'd use the forest denizens to peek at who or what was coming.

A raven fluffed its feathers among the highest branches left on a dead pine. He already had.

"It's just over this ridge," she told Benton. "Maybe you should wait here."

"I'm beginnin' to think you don't want me around, darlin'."

"Beginning?"

She could have gotten home in hours had she not been burdened with a mortal—and walking temptation to kill—slogging along at her side.

"Glaucus was right," he whispered. "The only reason I'm breathin' is so I can keep an eye on you." He pulled his cloak tighter around his shoulders. "Doin' my job is the one hope I've got that he'll keep Dagmar from skinnin' me alive."

Did he think he was looking out for her? His only advantage was years and whatever they told him. "I still think this is a bad idea."

She headed up the ridge. The extra company wouldn't please Sylvanus, but she wouldn't stop Benton from following.

The druid's centuries-old abode came into view as they crested the rise. Sometimes, he kept it under a cloak of magic, weaved the forest over it, but not today. Still, unless one wandered close, they would miss it. The only sign of humanoid habitation was the door built into the hillside and the narrow stone chimney that puffed tendrils of white smoke atop it.

In her fantasies, Sylvanus rushed out to meet her with a smile breaking through his stern features. She knew he wouldn't. He'd never pretended she wasn't a burden. When they approached the entrance, Benton gripped his hilt, and he eyed the worn skulls that framed the door embedded in the earth. Enemies of old, their spirits were now forced to protect that place. They made no move as she opened the door hewn from fallen hardwoods.

She led the way through the short and narrow earthen antechamber that bent ninety degrees to break the draft from the less-than-tight door. It expanded into the first chamber of Sylvanus's two-room home: the kitchen and dining area. The place reeked of drying herbs and spilled potions, but with the walls consisting of earth and roots, neither covered the smell of forest soil.

Or the two humans.

The old druid stood at a small, gray-wood table with his back to them.

"You've returned," he said without turning, his voice hovering between monotone and gruff. As usual. He took a few pinches from his tea chest and stuffed it into a strainer. "And you've brought a guest." For that, he threw a one-eyed glare over his shoulder.

"Sylvanus, I... I— I've— I'm—"

How could she say it? How could she explain what happened to her? That the years of training, all their time and effort, had been washed away in a few minutes. That now, he was prey.

"I know what you are." He glanced at her as he faced the fire glowing in the stone hearth.

Her insides hollowed out. "How?"

"I foresaw it," he said, taking the kettle off the spit.

Benton clutched her shoulder. "He ain't gonna help," he whispered in her ear. "Let's just go."

Her voice shook. "You had a vision? Why didn't you warn me?"

"Knowing what was coming wouldn't have helped you." Firelight casting dark shadows across half his aged face, his words felt particularly ominous. He poured the steaming water into two clay cups and dropped the tea strainers inside. "I had hoped you'd be strong enough to protect yourself when the time came. You weren't."

She couldn't find words or the next question.

He passed a steaming cup to Benton, who didn't take his hand from his hilt or his gaze off Sylvanus's hands. "That's quite the weapon."

Benton accepted the cup with his free hand. "Yup." When Sylvanus pivoted to pick up the other, Benton glanced at her.

She nodded, and he took a sip. The tea was just breeze wort and spirium. But she was surprised he intended to drink it. She'd never seen him drink tea. Somehow it seemed absurd. Maybe he'd grown colder than she'd realized.

"There must be a way to undo it..." she finally said.

Sylvanus sipped his tea, his eyes, a rich brown flecked with green, cutting into her in a way only her father could rival. "There is no undoing what's been done to you."

The pine needle floor fell out from under her. Sylvanus must have seen it in her face.

Sylvanus squared his shoulders. "The corrupted lorkai Marrow resists all natural magic."

"Sylvanus, surely...somewhere, at some point, you've—"

"You shouldn't have returned, Sarlona..."

Her eyes began to flood. Sylvanus hated that. "*Please*... I need your h—"

"You know I don't tolerate dark creatures in these lands." Sylvanus set down his cup.

"Please..."

He raised his left hand, and the fire leaped into it, making a roaring bridge from the hearth to his fingers. When he pulled back his left arm, the flames grew into an inferno behind it.

Her legs turned leaden as she stared into his expressionless face.

He threw the conflagration at her.

Chapter Twenty-One

Benton flashed his sword from its sheath to Sarlona's front before his cup hit the floor. It sucked up the explosion of flames like it hungered for them, but the heat still forced his eyes closed, and his hilt grew so hot it seared his fingers. The spell was too big for the sword to swallow.

He grabbed her shoulder and yanked her around as he flicked the glowing red blade at the old man. Fire ballooned from the sword as Benton pivoted to run, breaking his grip on her. Flames licked at his heels. He rounded the corner out of the room, and the fire streamed into the wall behind him.

Terror bore down on him with the heat. He'd left Sarlona there. Left her in the massive fireball Benton had spit at the old druid. As he braced to shoulder through the cabin's door, it splintered in front of him, and something ripped him through the gap.

He landed face first in the snow with her on top of him, holding him down while wayward flames puffed over them. As soon as the fire died, she rolled off him and stared at the carnage.

The cottage's door had become cinders, and the dead, lower branches of the closest trees dripped flames. Black smoke billowed from the chimney.

The ancient asshole was fine, of course. He strode out of his hovel without a charcoal smudge on his faded green robes.

Benton jumped to his feet. "Let's go." He would have been out of there if he had Sarlona's speed.

At least she snatched his arm again, dragging him east.

Halfway up the ridge, the forest came alive. Ahead of them, the trees hinged sideways, and their roots burst from the frozen ground. The underbrush shook off its snowy branchlets and stretched itself tall, as though it'd always aspired to be trees.

It all wove itself into a great, bottomless basket, fifty feet high, like a messy, towering, sidelong palisade.

She pushed Benton ahead of her, up the first few feet of the living wall, but no sooner had he touched it then the roots and branches were snagging for his ankles.

He threw himself off, hacking at the squirming wood and cutting through a hemlock branch as it snatched his other wrist, then he scrambled away from the wall.

There was nowhere to go. The woods were alive.

She ejected her carpal blades and sliced at the roots and branches as fast as they shot at her.

He worked his sword as fast as he could, but he wouldn't be able to hack that hard and fast for long, especially not when he tripped over the severed plant parts falling around his feet.

"Just let us go," he screamed at Sylvanus. "We'll go south to Rashiva."

Sylvanus kept his icy stare on her. "She's bound to these lands. She could never stay away." A fat root wrapped around her thigh while he wound up with another fireball. "And I could never curse another land with such a blight."

The fireball tore through the grove, leaving a stream of flame behind it. It reduced the base of a maple tree to charcoal and exploded into the snow where she slashed at the crazed flora.

Benton's breath caught. Pine bark popped, and spruce needles glowed and sizzled around the soggy crater where she'd just been.

She couldn't be dead. Reduced to blackened bones maybe, but not *gone*. Even the world's most powerful druid couldn't turn a lorkai to ash with one brief spell.

An inhuman growl from the other direction proved him correct. She chopped at Sylvanus's protective barrier with blood-red glowing eyes as he tried to force her retreat with fiery birds.

She'd gotten out of the way.

Benton hadn't. When he'd thought the fireball had hit her, he'd flinched, hesitated. The roots had coiled around his legs and over his shoulder. They had him locked in place. A birch sapling squeezed his wrist until his sword slipped into the snow.

The woods didn't rip him limb from limb but held him captive. The druid must not want Benton dead. If he had to watch as she burned, though...

And she was on the defensive, backpedaling while slicing through roots as thick as her thighs bearing puffballs that burst with flames instead of spores.

"Cockin' *kill* him, Sar," Benton growled. "Put him down."

Easier said than done, but she wasn't trying. She didn't have it in her despite almost killing Benton twice. When it came down to it, when it truly counted, she couldn't bring down the blade.

Where was her mindless hunger now? Where were her black pit and inky tentacles?

No sooner had the question formed in his head then an ebony tendril slid by Benton's foot, winding through the snow like a snake through the grass. Another slithered past him on the left.

The woods grew darker, shrouded in fog and shadow until she and the old druid became silhouettes. Smooth, black tentacles rose out of the snow like cobras ready to strike. Hundreds of them.

The ball of dread in Benton's gut expanded to fill his whole being. He would have sunk into the snow had his woody bindings allowed it. She wasn't supposed to be able to use magic anymore...

As the ebony snakes struck, twisting over the wooden ones like constrictors around prey, a flock of grackles, which should have flown south weeks ago, descended from the gray sky. They came to a synchronous landing in the shape of a humanoid. Even under a druid's control, real birds don't do that.

In a flash of black-green iridescence, Amenduil appeared. "I should have known she couldn't count on you," he sneered.

The roots and branches ensnaring Benton gave way, rotting and falling to the snow as black decay. He scooped up his sword without a word or glance at the dark mage and ran to Sarlona. Around him, every root and branch entangled with a black tendril crumbled into detritus.

Sylvanus raised a splayed hand at the sky and glowered at her. "Is this the kind of company you keep now?"

The clouds parted above him, making way for bright beams of sunshine. The tentacles in their path withered and disintegrated to black dust. A flick of his fingers sent the rays at her face. She buried her eyes in her elbow with a hiss, and smoke came off her forearm.

Benton circled behind the druid, struck his carapace and managed a few hits before birds of prey dove for Benton's head—a barred owl, a falcon, a red-tailed hawk, then a huge, black-hooded eagle. He dodged the first and struck Sylvanus once more. The second bird tore open Benton's shoulder. The third he drove off with his blade, and the fourth he ran through as it swooped in, razor-sharp, two-inch talons aimed at his eyes.

At last, she charged hard at her former mentor, slashing at his shield with both claws.

He swept her back with a fiery wall. That left his flank open, and

Benton struck again, letting his blade glut on the magical barrier.

Sylvanus called in the real reinforcements.

The woven wall parted sporadically to let them in. First, a bear the size of a shed, then a pack of dire wolves, then a cat that blended in with the snow so well Benton didn't see it until it leaped.

He dove aside, leaving a bright red line along its underbelly but nothing more.

Amenduil spun from the decaying bear carcass. He hit the cat with a shadow, and its hide rotted on impact. Its muscles withered, and its organs fell out of its belly with a sickening thump. It turned on Benton again with an eyeless face and lips drawn into a petrified snarl, then dropped to the snow.

"Don't kill them," she snarled when Sylvanus opened the ground below her and filled the pit with fire. A black tentacle snatched her wrist before she plummeted and whipped her nearer to Benton and Amenduil.

Amenduil grimaced, but as the dire wolves circled, Vorakor's tendrils ensnared rather than strangled them. "Get to the wall, Sarlona."

In a flash, she had Benton by the arm. He shrugged her off. "He ain't after me. Amen and I will hold him."

Her glowing green eyes widened, but she disappeared, leaving a fresh trail of boot prints in her wake. Amenduil spun after her, putting a shimmering black curtain behind him and his dark decay to work on the wall.

Benton wheeled on the druid, catching the next blast of fire on his blade. Charging, he whipped it back, but the flames rolled over Sylvanus's shell, sputtering out as it wrapped around him and kissed the snow. While Benton struck at the shield, he dodged icicles, which sprouted from Sylvanus almost as fast as the lorkai ejected their claws.

The druid looked at Benton impassively, fearlessly, but glanced sidelong at the encroaching shadows with concern in his otherwise stony eyes.

They closed in with a fog of doom and dread. Benton would have to trust Amenduil not to let them swallow him.

His sword absorbed the druid's telekinetic blast, and Benton returned the spell with his lunge, rocking the protective barrier upon the blade's impact.

As the shadows grew thicker, darker, taller, the ebony tendrils reared higher until they seemed to join the forest trees. Sylvanus ignored the assault on his barrier. He spread his hands, and once again, sunlight cut through the thick clouds above. It swathed him in a yellow glow and sent the nearest shadows shrinking with ethereal hisses.

"Benton." Sarlona crouched by a hole in the wall that pulsed as it shrunk and grew, rot battling new growth.

He shoved his sword into its scabbard and ran, hoping Sylvanus was too busy with the wall and the shadows to put anything in his back.

"Hurry," Amenduil growled, his voice strained and arms shaking.

As Benton's legs burned to lift his knees high enough to get his boots through the snow, the forest changed. It died. Instantly. Not with Amenduil's shadowy decay. Only the needles and bark and ends of branches crumbled. The rest was left dry, hard, and sharp. If trees had bones, that was what remained—tangles of staves and spears.

They fell. All of them. Benton swerved toward Amenduil, hoping the dark mage would expand his shield to include him. But Amenduil disintegrated into a cloud of black flies as the forest collapsed.

Benton's shoulder popped when something grabbed his arm. It hit him from behind, slamming him to the ground. Then just sharp, crushing, agony remained.

Sarlona's blood-choked scream rang in his ear. His lungs refused to draw enough air to make his own.

She lifted off him for a second as Amenduil solidified before them, but none of the pain eased, none of the terrible pressure let up. Then she slid down the spears and settled on top of Benton again. A fresh influx of her blood flowed over him to mingle with his.

Amenduil cursed and snatched a vial of glowing blue liquid from his robes—manna. No hope bloomed in Benton's chest as the mage downed it. There wasn't room in there with all the wood. Benton would die in the snow with her on top of him.

At least he wasn't alone.

He just hoped she wouldn't die as well. That they wouldn't burn together.

That seemed unlikely as the world took on an orange glow. Amenduil's eyes darkened to obsidian with the flames reflecting in them. He snarled, and his hands bellowed shadow. That didn't dim the light.

Benton's calves seared as her hands closed around his. The heat crawled up his thighs.

She writhed, and Amenduil winced, twisting his face to the side as he seized her wrists. He growled, shaking, sweating, jaw locked as flames washed over them.

Chapter Twenty-Two

Benton's cheek ground against snow-dusted cobblestone. Amenduil collapsed beside him, pale faced and breathless, and Sarlona rolled off Benton with a groan. She was alive. Safe. Amenduil had done what Glaucus had always claimed was impossible: teleported with a lorkai.

Benton would have laughed if he hadn't been so sure he'd never wake once the pain knocked him out.

He passed out anyway when she grabbed his shoulders, and a wave of anguish smashed through him. But he did wake to a pink sky that churned like a whirlpool and Sarlona's face.

Tears trickled to join the blood dripping from her mouth. She cradled Benton's cheeks in her warm palms, and the stabbing pain of his wounds drained with his fluids. Each unsatisfying breath remained a torment. Much as he ached to gaze at her face for as long as possible before he died, he could barely keep his eyes open.

"I—I can't do it." She glanced at Amenduil, eyes wild. "There's too much…It's too complex… I don't know how."

The mage stared at him. "I have nothing left, Sarlona. Nothing."

She shook. "He's turning blue."

"Just close the flesh." Amenduil cleared his throat. "Keep the heart beating, keep the lungs moving. I'll find a healer. Or a potion."

"He's not going to last that long."

She fixed her beautiful blue gaze on Benton again. She squeezed his face. "Benton… I'm…I'm going to kiss you."

About time. That's what he'd have said if he could. And if he hadn't known what kind of kiss she meant. He wouldn't have believed he could grow any colder with so much of his blood forming intricate streams between the cobblestones. He tried to shake his head. His eyes opened wide to tell her *no*.

"Leave him be, Sarlona…"

She wiped blood from his lower lip with her thumb and coaxed his jaw open. "It's all right, Benton," she whispered. "It won't turn you. Just a swallow."

He wasn't sure why he didn't believe her.

As she leaned closer with parted lips, he couldn't summon any resistance. Even dying, he longed to taste her, even when she was threatening him with her greatest weapon.

He closed his eyes as she pressed her soft mouth onto his and prayed that when he opened them, his irises wouldn't glow. She stiffened, and something like warm, syrupy gin spilled into his mouth.

She covered his nose and mouth when he gagged. "Swallow."

He obeyed with the same dread he'd possessed the day he had stood with the bag over his head and the rope around his neck. It flew off once the tingly quick hit his throat.

A warm and pleasant tremor wound through him. The exhaustion fled, and his vision cleared as he opened his eyes.

The sensation gripped the pit of his stomach and intensified. It dug into his thighs, then everywhere. He screamed into her hand. His tightened muscles lifted him onto his elbows, and his eyes rolled back.

She just smiled sweetly while her quick tore through him. Like what she did to him was innocent. Once he crumpled against the cold stone, she removed her hand.

He sat up, shaking, breathless but not from an inability to breathe.

Thanking her didn't seem appropriate while one last shiver overtook him. He gazed at her perfect face and took a deep breath.

Something was wrong. "You sure that…didn't turn me into a magic sucker?"

She nodded and wiped a tear from her cheek. "I'm sure." Rising gracefully without touching a hand to the ground, she pulled him up with her.

Benton took another long, steadying breath. "Worried 'bout me, huh?" It felt wonderous to have someone worry over him.

She hugged him. That was great too.

"You shouldn't have done that," Amenduil said.

Benton sighed. Right, Amenduil. Benton turned to the dark mage as her embrace unraveled.

More shadow than usual darkened Amenduil's countenance. "Lorkai use their quick for two purposes: to make children and to enslave."

A twinge hit Benton's spine, but he told himself he didn't believe she would do either to him. "Why didn't you stop her then?"

"It spared me the gold for a priest."

Sarlona squeezed Benton's arm. "I just healed you, that's all."

Her lie squirmed in his gut. She'd done something. He felt it...felt *her*.

Benton passed the untruth on to Amenduil. "I feel fine." Strong and clear and...whole. Maybe that should have troubled him more. "You're fulla shit."

His surroundings concerned him.

They loitered on the aft patio of Balis's temple. He recognized the stone and iron railing surrounding the old chapel's cracked cobblestone and the small fountain where rich folk tossed coppers in exchange for a favor from the gods.

As a child, he'd climbed over that railing in the dark, careful to avoid any priests who sometimes prayed outside on a peaceful night. He remembered dipping his hands into the water, no matter how icy, to fish out every copper so that he and Bailey could have something to eat.

Benton didn't like to remember. He did everything he could to forget. As the sun set and left the city's familiar rooftops silhouetted in the sky, he had no choice.

In his second-most desperate moment, he'd been whisked into his childhood despair.

He sighed. "Why in the twenty-eight hells did you drop us in West Ironhill?"

"Because I couldn't carry your dead weight all the way to Port Brummit," Amenduil said, glancing about. He unclasped his cloak and shrugged it off. "Here. Let's strive to be less conspicuous, shall we?"

Benton took the cloak reluctantly. Amenduil was not the kind of man he wanted to be indebted to. He already owed the man his life. Amen would probably expect him to pay with his soul.

As Benton threw the cloak over his shoulders to conceal his soiled clothes, the mage wheeled on her.

She shrank. "Thank you, Amen, truly."

Amenduil scanned her up and down. "You can both thank me by taking the Oath."

Just about bloodless, she shouldn't have been able to blanche. She managed.

Benton wasn't about to pale or thank Amenduil.

Amenduil smoothed out his robes. "I'll save the lecture on just how profoundly foolish you were to go to Sylvanus for once we have the privacy of a room."

She stared at the blood-smeared stones. Where droplets saturated tiny mounds of snow, it resembled gore, like someone had been eviscerated at her feet.

Benton should be dead. Again.

"Take off your clothes," Amenduil said.

Her eyes widened for a second, then she tore off what was left of her cloak and transformed to glass before stripping.

He used her tattered cloak and punctured clothes to wipe up what crimson he could then stuffed the rags into the snowbank at the far side of the patio.

Fortunately, no one seemed to be around for any of it. But Benton wouldn't have noticed if one of Balis's priests peeked out from between the temple curtains.

Amenduil seemed to know where he was going, so Benton followed, keeping his gaze on the man's heels as they shot slate slush over gray stone. He couldn't bear to absorb a familiar failing shop, weathered corner, or, gods forbid, life-battered face.

She kept to the shadows. He couldn't see her, but sensed her close by.

Amenduil led them to the nearest inn and paid for a room. The Jameson Inn and Tavern was the least vermin infested of West Ironhill's accommodations.

Benton shrugged off Amenduil's oversized cloak the second they passed into the room. He started stripping, tossing his blood and slush-soaked clothes on the floor. Invisible, Sarlona floated to the hearth, stirring the ashes for an ember to light the kindling. Amenduil plodded to the farthest bed from the door, one of two, and collapsed onto the straw-stuffed mattress.

Benton stopped short of peeling free his soiled underclothes. He pulled the blanket from the other bed and wrapped it around himself. *Then* he removed his underclothes.

When the fire sprang to life on a bundle of dried grass, the light danced across her translucent skin instead of through her. He couldn't help holding in his mind the image of her naked, glass sculpture crouching in front of the hearth.

"Here," Amenduil said, holding out his cloak while she piled some tinder on the burning grass.

She added a few thin strips of wood atop before the cloak seemed to levitate out of his hand and take a feminine shape. Then she appeared, wrapped in comically overlarge black wool with little more than her bare feet and face peeking out.

Even half-hidden by the cloak's hood, her blue eyes shone red. Her glistening gaze avoided both men, settling on Benton's pile of clothes. She shook out his shirt, but there was no point.

"Don't bother, darlin'." Only his boots and stockings were salvageable.

She nodded at the fire then added a small log to it. The cloak parted enough for him to glimpse a long, muscular leg. Scooping up his belt, she pulled his sword. He wouldn't have trusted it in anyone else's hands. She used his sock to dry the blade as best she could.

"Come here," Benton said from the bed, opening a bare arm.

She laid the blade in front of the fire and stared at the worn-smooth floor when she approached the bed. He wrapped his arm around her the second she plopped beside him.

Benton wished they were alone so he could snake his arm under the cloak. "It's gonna be all right."

She shuddered, and he hoped his arm's warmth offered the same comfort her body provided him.

"He tried to kill me," she said, her voice thick and clouded. Wracked by a sob, she hitched again. "I've known him my whole life… He raised me…as much as my parents."

Benton crushed her. *What the hells do you say to that?*

Amenduil had some ideas. "You should have known better, Sarlona. Sylvanus has always driven the dark creatures from his lands. You've helped him do it."

Her answer was small and broken. "I hoped he'd see I was still me."

"Are you?"

She stiffened, transforming to cold rock under Benton's arm. "Yes."

Amenduil stared at her, calm and silent. "If you wish your magic restored, your humanity, you must come with me to Port Brummit. I'm the only one who can help you. Who will."

Benton's spine froze. "Sar…"

"If you're content as you are," the dark mage continued, "then return to Ashmore and beg for your nursemaid's life."

Benton glowered at him.

"Whatever you decide, it's clear you need adult supervision."

She choked back her tears. "How long before you can get us to Port Brummit?"

Amenduil smiled, but there was no optimism in his voice. "Lorkai resist all forms of magic. You're like an anchor," he explained. "I've no confidence I can teleport with you twice. Especially with Benton in tow."

She ran her hands through her hair. "How far are we?"

"It's a three-day walk," Amenduil answered.

Benton grew cold, like his blood was still seeping into the snow and cobblestone. "Darlin'... No."

She couldn't go to them. Not the Embrace.

"What's your price?" she asked.

Benton tried to turn her shoulders to face him, but she wouldn't budge. "You can't go to a cult of shadow-worshippers for help. They ain't gonna fix anything."

"Take the Oath, and I'll cure you," Amenduil said. "But I implore you to stay with us afterward. The lorkai may seek to turn you again if Dagmar recovers enough of her strength in your lifetime. You may need the Embrace's protection."

Quiet, she stared at the floor.

Whatever gnawed at Benton's gut had icy teeth. "Sweetheart... I know this ain—"

Spinning on him with fiery eyes, an inhuman growl rolled out of her. "I *can't* stay like this, Benton."

"Do you not recall how lovely our dear girl was before?" Amenduil asked.

She was lovely *now*.

"Would you not enjoy each other more as equals?"

When Sarlona went rigid under his arm, Benton did his best not to tremble.

He would enjoy her more if she were human again. If she wasn't a monster, he wouldn't be afraid to... He'd show her everything he felt. And she'd be able to enjoy him. Now, he was a lesser, weaker thing to her. If she were a girl, he'd be a man—strong and able to protect her.

She might marry him someday. They could have children.

With the ice inside him thickening, he retracted his arm. He didn't dare slide over, though. "What...Sar, what *are* you doin' to me?"

She wouldn't meet his eyes. "I just..."

"Don't lie to me. I can feel it." He hated that his voice shook. "Am I turnin' into a spell-sucker too?"

"No. It doesn't work like that." She sighed and put her head in one hand, careful not to lose her grip on Amenduil's robe with the other. "I bound you."

"What the cock does that mean?"

"I'm not sure," she said into her palm.

Amenduil sat back on the bed and crossed his arms. "Slave," he said with the faintest smile on his lips.

"No." She told the floor. "I don't know... It joins us. It aligns your will with mine."

Benton's heart pounded too hard and too slow. In time with the quiver of Amenduil's cloak over her chest.

"What did you do to me, Sar?" Benton demanded.

Her head shot out of her hands, and her eyes burned yellow. "I gave of myself to repair your broken body." The voice wasn't hers. It was darker. "So you might survive. So you might survive *me*."

He wouldn't survive her. He'd known that since he'd first gazed in her oceanic eyes.

The yellow receded, and the sea washed in as he wrapped the blanket tighter around himself.

"My quick is part of you now," she said gently. "It's making you a bit stronger." Her attention sank back to the floor, and she hugged her elbows under the robe. "I can break the bond... If that's what you want."

Benton stared at the side of her face, at the contours of her pronounced cheekbones and her straight nose. At the long lashes that seemed to bat at him in profile. She was beautiful. And she'd shed tears for him. Him. Why would he want to sever his one connection with another living soul borne of affection? Anyway, he could look after her better if he could feel her. Besides, if they were...connected maybe that would stay Dagmar's hand.

"I don't want that," he whispered, hopefully only loud enough for her to hear.

"Or does Sarlona not want that?" Amenduil asked, standing. "Perhaps you can no longer distinguish between your desires and hers?"

"Whose desire is it to shove my boot up your ass?" Picking a fight with Amenduil wasn't the smartest thing, but what else was Benton supposed to say?

Fortunately, the dark mage wasn't riled. "That must be yours, because I know our dear girl isn't so crass," he said, crossing the room. "I'll leave you two to sort this out while I see what I can find to clothe you." The door caught on the floor on his way out and didn't quite shut. He peeked through at her. "Don't feed until I return."

Chapter Twenty-Three

When Sarlona trailed her fingers along Benton's naked shoulder, he shivered. She needed a few minutes to think, to grieve for her old life. To contemplate exactly what she'd created in him. She couldn't do that with questions sitting on the tip of his tongue, his anxiety leaking from his pores, and his desires working through his veins.

A swell of exhaustion rose at her call, and he fell unconscious. She caught him, preventing him from toppling forward onto his face, and laid him out on the bed.

The chamber's flimsy door and loose hardware wouldn't slow the lorkai or Sylvanus for an instant. She forced it closed and bolted it anyway.

To cry.

Sylvanus had never cared about her. Fine. He wouldn't help her. Okay. He wouldn't tolerate her.

She'd longed to check on her family while in Mast Landing. Her mother, at least, had cared about her. She had to have. Now Sarlona would never get near the farm. If the lorkai weren't watching, Sylvanus would be. She'd never see her mother again. Not if she stayed a lorkai.

She had to choose—Amenduil's offer or herself as a monster. What was worse? Connecting with a creature of darkness or being one? What would she have to do if she took the Black Oath? Why hadn't *her* Gods helped her? How could Vorakor be the only God willing to touch her life?

Her thoughts swirled like His tentacles in those dark waters—endlessly writhing and turning over on themselves, ad infinitum. Her Gods had rejected her. So had her teacher.

Humanity.

She was a lorkai, but not like Glaucus or Dagmar.

Alone.

"Sar…"

Before acknowledging Benton, she put another log on the fire.

No sleep remained in his eyes. They were wide and bright and probably boring into her more deeply than she cared to admit.

She matched the color of her own to the flames to hide the tears. "Are we goin' to Port Brummit with him?"

"Yes." She decided in that instant. "I am. I won't ask you to follow me anywhere you don't want to go."

He sucked a breath through his teeth and tipped his head back, then spoke at the thick crop of cobwebs in the corner. "You're all I have, sweetheart." His gaze darted to hers, snatched it and ripped out its fire. "I'll follow you anywhere."

Raising her eyebrows, she smiled. "You have me, do you?"

"I'm gonna have you, Sar." He rose, letting the coarse wool blanket fall half on the bed and half on the floor. "Finally. Tonight. Now."

She kept her gaze on his face, but she could see everything. The blood shot to her cheeks. She'd never seen him. Even with Vosvoshish… she hadn't *seen* anything.

"Benton…" Her protests dissolved on her tongue.

Her old fear of him seemed irrational. Now, she wished she'd let him take her to bed when she was still human. She might have felt all the strength in his narrow, muscular hips. He could have promised that whatever the lorkai did to her, he'd be there for her afterward while he held her in his sinewy arms with her head resting on one of his broad shoulders. Despite it all, she might have felt safe and warm.

As a lorkai, she wondered if she could feel anything but his sweet, pulsing Marrow and the rapid, panicked, weak twinges of a prey animal.

But she could make *him* feel safe and warm. No one else had ever done that for him.

She left the fire and wandered within his reach, still clinging to Amenduil's cloak.

Benton slipped fingers into it, onto her shoulder. "Sar, I need you to know… Before Amen guts me on Vorakor's altar or Dagmar rips out my spine…"

"Benton…"

He swept the cloak off her left shoulder and squeezed the bare skin. His stare hopped from her flesh to her eyes.

"I love you," he breathed out as though the words had been eating at his insides for weeks.

Pretty sure they'd been tormenting him less than an hour, she glanced away. "Benton, that's my quick. That's because you're bound."

She sighed. "It isn't real."

"Nothin' else is real."

Rather than risk viewing conviction in his eyes, she stared at a patch of brown speckles staining the grayed wood above the bed. Blood. Her old eyes never would've picked them out. And her old nose never would have told her they belonged to an adolescent, human male.

The monster had gotten its wish: Benton's devotion. His *love*. She didn't know what the hells to do with them.

"I should break the bond..." She should, but the thought left her empty.

He grabbed her chin, pulling her gaze. "Don't you cockin' dare do that to me."

She didn't fight it when he leaned in and coaxed her lips apart. Heat flashed over her when their lips touched. A jagged bolt of it shook her when he snaked one arm around her waist and cradled her head. The kiss deepened, and the warm butterflies she'd thought only Glaucus could summon took flight.

Benton's lips left her mouth for her throat. "You don't have to say it back," he said between kisses. "I know you care about me." Another kiss landed below her jaw, and sandpaper scratched her throat. "I don't know why the shit you do, but you do."

"Of course, I do." She had no breath.

He seized her by the hips and pulled her tight against him. "I loved you before the quick."

"You loved the chemicals I poured into your blood."

She sat when he guided her back against the bed and sank to his knees at her feet.

"Benton, this isn't r—" She gasped when he ripped the cloak open. "I've manipulated you..." The fire returned to her eyes, coloring Benton's red with their reflection, and a dark cloud sank over them. The blackness rose to stiffen her spine and pull her voice from deep in her chest. "I broke you like a wild horse."

If she'd been hungry, she wouldn't have cared what she'd done to him. She would have torn him apart and made him love it, while she took every vapor of Marrow.

Staring at her chest, he slid his rough hands over her thighs with a growl. "Come in my head, Sar."

He'd never invited her in.

"I want you in me while I'm in you," he said. "I want us to be all tangled up like that first time."

As quickly as the darkness breezed in, it flew out of her. He wrenched her knees apart and stared between them. She lost the shake of her head in a whole-body tremble. There was no way in hells she was going into his mind.

He snatched her behind the knees and hauled her to put himself between them and sit her at the bed's edge.

"Benton, I don't need you to do that." The thought of it turned her stomach.

But prying his hands off her thighs and knocking him over backward so she could slam her knees together seemed overdramatic. She tugged some of the midnight cloak, which had all but fallen off, to cover herself instead.

He threw it aside. "Darlin', you've stared into the darkest corners of my soul. You can let me see your pussy."

There had to be a better word.

"Anyhow, you feed on me damn near every cockin' day. I get to taste you."

Surely blood leaked from her pores. He must have felt her shiver.

As his lips touched her thigh and his warm exhale caressed her most sensitive flesh, her insides became a ball of snakes. Some slithered in excitement, but others... They struck with guilt-laced fangs. He'd lusted after human Sarlona. She wasn't sure that their new bond and addiction didn't play a role in how he needed her now.

His tongue hit its mark, and she forgot her inner turmoil. "Oh, Gods." She glanced at his electric gaze reaching up for her. "Benton."

Sharp pangs of ecstasy bit her between the legs. His stubble scraped her thighs, and his growls seemed to echo through her. She clawed the mattress as he dug into her hips. Her muscles tightened into hot stone.

She leaned on her elbows. "Okay... Okay, Benton." She struggled for breath. "Cock me already."

He didn't stop. She'd explode. His tongue tickled her perfectly, but she ached for lack of him. She couldn't stand the emptiness when he could be filling her. His warm weight could be on top of her.

She could have him groaning in her ear. "Gods, Benton, I need you."

He pulled back and roved his hands up her sides. "I know you do, darlin'," he said, rising and pouncing.

He lifted her, pushed her, and fell atop her all at once. Peppering her throat with ravenous kisses, he squeezed her breast with a small pinch to her nipple.

"Please." Thrusting against him, she arched and lifted him clear off the bed with a moan.

"I don't know, sweetheart." That stupid grin appeared when she lowered her hips. "Maybe I oughtta let you cool off some. So you don't hurt me."

She caught him by the jaw. Or maybe the monster did. Both. "You're going to hurt, Benton. You're going to cry."

She kissed his mouth and swept her tongue over his lips, wrapping a hand around his back to bite him carefully with her nails. Parting her thighs farther for him, she withdrew her kiss. She wanted his gaze.

His grin had gone. He was shaking and breathing hard.

Not quite daring to seize him and sheathe herself, she grabbed his hip instead and shoved him against her. She caught herself before commandeering his body and making his hips do everything she desired.

He kissed her throat again, then her breasts, flicking one nipple with his tongue.

Taking his chin, she urged his lips to hers.

"I want you in my head," he said.

She stared into his eyes, into those living snow pools. "Okay."

Easing into him just deep enough for him to feel her, she ventured into his mind. Just in his conscious present. There was nothing there but his rabid affection for her and the relief, the warmth of feeling her within him.

Then she opened herself and drew him in, so he could hear her active thoughts and feel what she felt. He moaned, reveling in her fondness for him.

Neither of them was alone anymore. In that moment, they were whole.

The intensity with which she wanted him was almost too much for him. His heart swelled, and he groaned, finally putting the end of himself against her. She was more than ready for him.

He buried himself in one slow, powerful thrust, and she cried out. Relieved. Filled.

Watery gaze locked with hers, he drove into her, deliberate but forceful. With each tender stroke, she almost swooned.

"Gods, Sar…" he whispered between feathery kisses along her jaw. "You're heaven." His voice seemed to echo from a realm in which he'd never known the horrors of this one.

He broke when she cradled his face in her hands. Tears rushed to meet her thumbs as she stroked his cheeks.

Not because she made them fall. Everything was too much—the weeks of building desire, the new bond, intermingled consciousness, the sacrifice of his home for her. And he'd never been with anyone he cared about. He hadn't loved at all in almost two decades. It overwhelmed him.

She didn't mind the tears. His vulnerability was his sweetest part, and release extracted them, not sorrow or pain.

They didn't slow his kisses or temper his thrusts anyhow. Those became more unbridled.

It took all her resolve not to grow wild too. Not to forget her strength and crack bones with her embrace.

Or tap into his Marrow.

She couldn't bear the thought of that dark appetite joining them. Not with their minds intertwined like their bodies and their hearts brimming. Even if she'd believed she could control herself this time. So, she tasted him with her kisses alone, savoring his salty skin with tip of her tongue each time she pressed her lips against his throat.

"Darlin'…" He groaned, swallowed by a swell of euphoria. "Gods, I… Sar…" Slowing, he forged as deep as he could, then rocked his hips as he captured her gaze in his electrifying blue. "I love you."

She lost everything but him in a hot red wave that wracked her body and sent an inhuman scream into her throat.

He clapped his hand over her mouth to stifle its escape and grimaced when her muscles seized. His face relaxed with her body, and after a few more achingly delicate thrusts, a claw of ecstasy grabbed his insides. It shook him, rolling his eyes and parting his lips in a protracted groan.

He collapsed on her, then kissed her cheek before resting his scratchy one beside her head. With his eyes glazed and muscles slack, his often-aggravating grin was pure joy.

She grinned, caressing the edge of his ear. Then, kissing his throat, she withdrew from his mind and extricated him from hers.

When he scooped her into his arms, she made fists to keep her fingertips from seeking more of his flesh.

~ * ~

They were still in bed when Amenduil came in. He didn't knock or try the handle. He just unbolted the door telekinetically and strode through. Sarlona doubted he was surprised to see them under the blanket together, though he studied them with raised eyebrows.

"Have you drained your wet nurse to death, or is he just sleeping?" he asked, setting a small crate of supplies on the other bed.

"Neither," Benton answered, opening his eyes.

Amenduil sighed, seeing his cloak tangled up with them in the bed. He called it to him with his hand. A wave cleaned off Benton's blood and everything else.

Amenduil glanced at her. "I hope young men's clothes will do."

Turning herself crystalline, she sat up. "Thank you."

"What'd you get me?" Benton asked.

"A shirt and underclothes." Amenduil threw a ball of bright white linen at him. "And an old jacket. I should be able to repair the rest."

The mage went about just that while Benton pulled on the underwear and shirt, wiping the blood, grime, and dampness from the balled-up leather on the floor. Amenduil knitted his fingers together, and the holes in Benton's pants, jerkin, and gloves closed.

"There," Amenduil said.

Benton scooped up his things. "Thanks."

He dressed while she inspected the clothes and boots at the top of the crate. Nothing more than a corded, cream-colored sweater, hide pants, and well-worn boots. That would be enough.

"Did you steal these?" she asked, shimmying into the pants.

"Just the boots." Amenduil unpacked the rest of the crate— bread, dried meat, and two bottles of mead. "Well, persuaded a troublesome young man to donate them."

She tried not to think about how badly that young man might need them as she shoved her bare feet into the crusty soles.

But among the hundred scents absorbed by the stained leather was an abundance of blood, little of it from their former owner. "We'll pay you back. I promise."

In the firelight, the mage's eyes shone black again. His smile appeared warm and handsome as ever, however. Full lips showed a sliver of bright teeth from within his well-kept beard. "All I'll accept from you, Sarlona, is to see you wrapped contentedly in Vorakor's Embrace."

Transparency hiding her features, she didn't have to suppress her scowl. She dove into the sweater and let the pigments in her flesh spring into existence. "Will I have to kill anyone?" She searched for truth in his twinkling eyes without daring to peer behind them.

"You mean, will you be required to torture a Silsorian virgin atop an obsidian altar before casting her innocent soul into the Abyss?" he asked, tone light with a smile playing at the corner of his mouth. "No, my dear. You may find, however, once you know our Abyssal Lord, that helping others into His warm Waters brings you great joy."

She locked down a shiver and made her face stone.

Benton, meanwhile, exaggerated his and swore as he tied his sword belt.

"Oh, relax, Benton," Amenduil said with a sneer. "You'll fit right in."

Benton just snatched one of the bottles of mead. "Oh, thank the glowin' gods," he said, wrenching the cork out. He drank a quarter of the bottle in one swig.

Amenduil took the loaf of bread and broke it in half. "You *are* returning with me to Port Brummit then?"

She nodded. "If you can truly make me human again." Shoving the half-loaf that Amenduil had set aside at Benton, she met Amenduil's stare. "If Benton and I will be safe there."

"I can," the mage answered, glowing. "And you will be."

Chapter Twenty-Four

They left first thing in the morning despite the big, fluffy flakes floating from the gray sky…and Benton's protests.

Anxious as he was to get where the lorkai wouldn't go and see Sarlona's humanity returned, he wasn't itching to reach their destination.

The Nocturnal Embrace was too quick with its blades. As violent as he'd sometimes been, the thought of hurting or maybe torturing someone for their faith upset his stomach. He couldn't do that. Just watching it would be intolerable. He didn't know if he could listen to it echoing out of some unholy dungeon.

Assuming all the rumors about the evil cult were true.

The thought of praying to Vorakor was almost as abhorrent. Or praying to anything. At best, Benton would be wasting his breath. At worst…What would it mean if there were gods, and they'd all ignored him when he'd most needed help? That his soul was so worthless, they'd deliberately thrown it to the wolves? What if the only god to ever accept his prayers was the god of death and darkness?

Never mind what would happen to Sarlona. Blackness had flooded into her so readily. He'd never forget the black tentacle around his throat and oblivion beneath his feet.

Mostly, as he trudged through the snow and pushed heavy-hanging branches aside, he thought of *her*. Felt her cradling his being.

Cocking Sarlona hadn't cracked the spell she'd thrown over him. If anything, it had strengthened it. They were closer now. That had never happened before—cocking and closeness. There had never been intimacy. Not for him as a grown man.

He'd find a way to cock it up.

"Are you all right?" She grasped his elbow. Her gaze swallowed him whole, and everything swelled at her touch. Even in the storm-muted afternoon light, she glowed.

He'd never been more all right.

But he'd fallen behind again. Keeping up with her was impossible, of course.

Amenduil used some spell to stop from sinking into the snow beyond his boots. To prevent the cold from freezing his cheeks and numbing his fingers. The mage watched them, leaning with one arm against a tree, impatience etched across his face.

Benton offered a real smile and not his grin. "I'm fine."

The breeze shifted. She stiffened like someone had run her through.

"Not for long." A deep, gruff voice was off to his right...with a Northland accent.

Benton spun, and there she was. There they both were. Their eyes were whole and heads attached, if a bit pale. Both lorkai's irises blazed as red as any demon's.

"Benton will *remain* fine," Glaucus countered. "I promise."

The old lorkai stared into his eyes. His hellish gaze tugged at Benton, beckoned him.

A weight lifted from his shoulders. Glaucus forgave him.

The old lorkai couldn't keep an eye on Dagmar all the time, though. Benton wasn't sure the older lorkai could stop the Northlander if she put her mind to ending him.

"You make too many promises." Dagmar's snarl mirrored a great, white bear's more than usual.

"It's time to come home, you two." The trace of the smile on Glaucus's face looked warm, but his voice was stern—the Lord of Ashmore's.

With the building snow steadily accumulating atop their heads and shoulders and their eyes of hellfire, the older lorkai resembled arctic beasts. Dagmar, especially.

"Ashmore is not my home." Sarlona's eyes flared to life with the same bloody glow as her forced family. "I won't go back."

"Where else is there to go now that your mentor has betrayed you, little one?"

"To Port Brummit. Amen says he can make me human again."

A black mist rose around Amenduil and hardened as the lorkai glanced past Sarlona to the dark mage. The shielding made him difficult to see. Benton guessed it made Amen impossible to touch.

Glaucus's stare returned to his granddaughter. "Which is more important, Sarlona, being human or your humanity?" He drifted forward, only sinking a few inches into the snow. "Do not doubt that the cost of one will be the other in Vorakor's temple."

"I've already lost both," Sarlona spat. "Had both stolen."

The ancient lorkai eyed each other, then took their gloves off.

Benton drew his sword before their carpal blades came out.

Sarlona ejected hers too, shredding the sleeves of her sweater. "Leave. Me. Alone."

He expected the lorkai to go for Sarlona. Or maybe for Dagmar to leap at him. Not Glaucus.

With pure instinct and speed he didn't know he had, he whipped his blade out in front of him to deflect *Glaucus's* incoming claw.

Maybe Benton wasn't forgiven.

At least, the lorkai had struck at his thigh instead of his throat.

Glaucus attacked from the left. Benton pivoted with his swipe, too slowly this time. He wasn't strong enough to deflect the carpal blade anyway, not when the lorkai put some muscle into it.

Benton's blade slipped along the claw, and all he could think to do was turn the tip into Glaucus's chest.

Glaucus could have easily skewered his heart. Instead, pain exploded in Benton's left shoulder.

The lorkai wanted him alive. At least for now.

Benton hadn't returned the favor, driving his sword right through Glaucus's chest.

Stupid. He should have tried for the head. Put it in Glaucus's brain again. Spiny insects crawled through his veins as that brutal appendage ripped out his Marrow.

Howling, Benton tried to tear himself off the claw. In another few seconds, Glaucus would start on Benton's life force. He'd fall unconscious, if not dead, into the snow.

Three seconds.

That was how long it'd taken him to fail Sarlona.

But while Glaucus and he snarled into each other's faces, a pulse from his sword reminded Benton he still held it.

The sword was taking *Glaucus's* Marrow. It worked on a lorkai like anyone else, sluggish, but draining. He could use the Marrow to fire off another charge of the last spell the sword had absorbed—a telekinetic blast from Sylvanus.

With a thought, Benton commanded his blade to loose the spell and screamed again as Glaucus's claw tore free, and the lorkai sailed into a tree.

Benton collapsed onto his knees but staggered to his feet. Staining the snow red, left arm useless or not, he had to keep fighting for Sarlona.

Dagmar was on her, or she was on Dagmar. The women were a

flurry of claws and blonde and glowing eyes, like two dogs vying for dominance times a thousand. Benton didn't know how he'd get in there without a stray carpal blade lopping off his head. And in the span of a few heartbeats, Glaucus had picked himself up and joined in.

Where the hells was Amenduil? Why wasn't he doing anything?

As if in answer, a black bolt, like shadowy lightning, exploded into all three lorkai. As one, they crumpled into the snow.

Sarlona was the first to her feet. Just like the last time Amenduil had hit her with a spell, she doubled over and retched tar. Glaucus and Dagmar followed suit.

Benton charged Dagmar, hoping to take advantage of her incapacitation. Even wracked by her heaving stomach, or whatever was in there, the Northlander lorkai got a claw around to her flank and blocked his incoming blade. She spun on him, towering, her face drawn with dimmed eyes and a string of black ooze dribbling from her chin.

He hopped clear of the sluggish claw, slowed as though coated in as much black sludge as her lips but still faster than any steel Benton had parried. Backpedaling, he expected his limbs to drop into the snow in seconds.

Dagmar's boot caught in the otherworldly tar, keeping him out of reach. It trapped all the lorkai's boots, then spread not just out from their vomit. The snow melted into black ooze around them.

Around him. Benton sank halfway to his knees in it.

Amenduil hovered over it.

The mage didn't look human anymore. The whites of his eyes had gone black, and he hung in an aura of shadowy static. A dozen black tentacles sprouted from his back, just like they had from Sarlona that day. Except Amenduil coated his in flame, like he'd dipped them in oil and set them alight. He whipped them at the elder lorkai's throats, narrowly missing Sarlona.

Glaucus and Dagmar sliced through the tentacles with time to spare. While made ponderous by the black goop to a mortal speed, they could still move their feet.

Benton, on the other hand...kept his blade up and ready, but he wouldn't be much help from where he stood submerged.

Glaucus and Dagmar had turned their attention to Amenduil anyway. They advanced on him together, circling in opposite directions, slicing off the ends of any flaming whips that came at them.

The dark mage grew them just as fast.

And Sarlona had his back. She nettled Dagmar with her claws, unable or unwilling to get in a solid strike, but keeping half the Northlander's attention.

Until Glaucus had had enough. One of Amenduil's fiery tendrils came at him, and he just took it around the forearm. With a monstrous growl, he yanked, whipping Amenduil around and smashing him sidelong into a massive pine. The dark mage's shielding held, but the jolt broke his concentration enough that the tar changed fluffy and white.

The lorkai were on Amenduil instantly, hacking at his shielding with speed that made their arms blur.

Sarlona followed them in and grabbed Dagmar by her fur vest and shoulder, ripping her backward.

Like an idiot, Benton charged at Glaucus.

The old lorkai twisted to meet his blade, deflecting it wide at the last instant. Benton's left leg went out from under him, swept away by Glaucus's boot before he could register the kick. He went down hard on his side.

Again, Glaucus could have skewered Benton, could have pinned him dead center like a moth in a shadowbox.

The Lord of Ashmore spun to Amenduil without a second glance.

The dark mage had returned to his feet. He was already casting.

The afternoon sky deepened to twilight, and the forest darkened into a tangle of shadow. An ash tree beside them exploded. Not into splinters of wood but obsidian shards. Jagged black stone flew at the lorkai like spears. Benton threw himself into the snow as a second tree blew up.

A shard pierced Dagmar's hand when she dodged a larger spike that nearly ran her through. One grazed Glaucus's thigh. Sarlona flattened herself in the snow, avoiding them all, and sliced at Dagmar's boot.

The Northlander hopped clear, eluding her daughter's claw, and took cover when a third tree burst.

It splintered other trees and shredded Glaucus's cloak but nothing else.

Twilight withered into night, darker than night, black. The sky, the snow, the trees…even Benton's breath came out as sooty smoke. A loud low sound, more felt in his chest than heard by his ears, made him want to curl into a ball. A sense of impending doom deepened with the dark.

Yet he could vaguely see. Some invisible light source gave every surface a ghostly sheen, including the creatures that poured from the forest.

Some of the monsters made horrifying rattles, shrieks, or dragon-like roars from the blackness. Others slinked in silently, slipping

176

through the dark with feline grace.

No two were alike but for their shadowy skin and wide jaws full of needles.

The one that came for Benton resembled an inky, armor-clad man in a backbend, with its head on wrong, facing front. Its mouth peeled up over its head, revealing a maw of three-inch fangs. Solid black eyes, set off to the sides, locked on him.

It leaped, leading with too-long arms, each bearing claws, some extending a foot.

He threw his shoulders back and hit its claws to the left, severing its first two gnarled fingers. Its mouth kept coming. Twisting right as lower fangs took a slice of flesh from his useless left shoulder, he ripped his blade the way it'd come, lightning-quick, through the terror's neck. Its body slid through the black snow, and its head kept rolling.

As he climbed to his feet, he didn't see the tree-like tribute to thorns. Not until it put three blackened spines through his thigh, and its trunk split down the middle to envelop him in a vertical maw of shadowy spikes.

He thanked gods he didn't believe in when he fell into the snow, and the spiny nightmare bit down on Sarlona's claws and hands rather than his entire body. In seconds, she'd chopped it into hawthorn kindling.

She hauled him to his feet with mangled hands.

But before she could attempt to heal his wounds, three eel-like fish with bear-trap heads shot through the air at her.

"Amen," Benton screamed. "You're gonna rip us *all* apart."

Maybe the dark mage intended just that. Then Amenduil could bring the pieces he desired with him to Port Brummit.

If Amenduil heard him, the mage gave no indication. The flying viperfish circled Sarlona, striking one after another for her glowing eyes. Meanwhile, Glaucus parried the black blades of a tar-coated, three-mouthed mantid.

Only Dagmar seemed to have everything under control, a whirl of blades and muscle, cutting sharp inky pieces off anything that neared. The Northlander hunted deadly monsters for fun.

The one she set her sights on next wore robes.

After bisecting what looked like an upside-down jellyfish with an eye and fangs on each tendril, she rammed both claws into Amenduil's carapace. His spell held, but the force of the blow rocked him against his protection like a sledge to a steel helm. The black flickered. With Dagmar's next explosive strike, the ink bled away.

The nightmare creatures went with it.

Dagmar struck again. Amenduil reeled. A stream of fire burst from his hand, driving her off.

The instant it sputtered, she lunged.

Sarlona leaped at Dagmar from behind, but Glaucus tackled her. His greater weight slammed her atop the trampled snow. And his hands sought her bare wrists and face. If he got them... If he drained her...

Benton stumbled toward them and collapsed. Too much muscle had been severed in his leg. Too much of his blood stained the snow.

Amenduil gazed at him while forcing Dagmar back with another blast of flame. He raised his free hand, and a cloud of shadow spilled out.

It gushed at Benton. He didn't know what the hells it was but tried to scramble clear. "No. Gods dammit, Amen. No."

The shadows grabbed his feet, his legs. Then wrapped around the rest of him, coating him in black electricity. He tried to scream, but his mouth wouldn't move. The fuzzy, crackling force lifted him to his feet and set him charging for Glaucus.

Benton's arm shot out at the old lorkai without consulting Benton.

Glaucus flipped over, pulled Sarlona onto him, and used her as a shield. Benton stopped mid-thrust. The shadows did. He had become a puppet, with Amen's shadowy hand up his backside.

Sarlona ripped herself off Glaucus and sprinted at Dagmar, who'd hit Amenduil's carapace another half-dozen times.

Instead of following her, the shadows went for Glaucus again. The lorkai parried his every strike, claws faster than blades, and Benton found himself spinning like a top to keep Glaucus's carpal blades at bay.

What were probably seconds felt like hours as the shadows used Benton's muscles and their memory. They used his instincts but not his commands, ignoring the searing pain in his thigh and shoulder.

Then Dagmar roared. Fire had blackened her left side, her outer arm charred and bubbling, furs singed, and half her hair a reeking, grayed tangle. Her eyes burned redder than Benton had ever seen them. She leaped at Amenduil.

Sarlona sprang after her, but blood sprayed from half a dozen puncture wounds as she did. Her wrecked hands only grasped the Northlander's vest. The back panel ripped off.

The crack of Amenduil's barrier breaking hit Benton like a hammer. The shadows sucked out of him. Both human men collapsed.

Sarlona caught Dagmar's arm as she wound up to ram her carpal blade through the supine mage's heart. The lorkai women screamed, muscles shaking, and eyes smoldering.

Glaucus slipped behind Benton and set a claw against his throat. "Sarlona." He hauled Benton up onto his knees. "Come now, little one.

Or it is Benton who will suffer."

Sarlona snarled, summoning the strength to throw Dagmar aside. Jaw clenched and chest heaving, she stared at Glaucus, fiery-eyed. She didn't twitch.

Benton didn't want her to.

As much as he didn't wish to suffer or die, he didn't know if he'd survive becoming the reason Sarlona's misery would never end.

"You won't kill him," Sarlona said after a few of the longest seconds of Benton's life. She crept forward.

"I will." Dagmar appeared over Benton's left shoulder. Fortunately, she didn't strike.

Glaucus retracted his free claw and slipped his hand into Benton's collar. Fingertips settled gently across his collarbone. He lurched when the lorkai took control. To Benton's surprise, his pain faded.

Then Glaucus made him scream like a hot iron had been shoved into his gut and contorted his face as though he'd never felt such agony. Nothing hurt.

Eyes wide, Sarlona stiffened.

"No, I won't kill him," the Lord of Ashmore agreed. "I'll do worse things."

Baring her teeth, Sarlona strode forward.

"Sarlona." Amenduil stood not far behind her with an empty vial in his fingers. "Don't be foolish. Now may be your one chance."

She froze but didn't look at him.

Go, Benton pleaded in his mind. He had no idea if she could hear him.

Glaucus made him scream again.

"Okay. Stop. Please..." Her ruined hands shaking, boots silent on the snow, Sarlona inched toward them.

Go.

But maybe everything would be okay. Maybe Sarlona could get used to being a lorkai. Dagmar might not kill Benton. Maybe they could just go home.

Maybe not.

Black tentacles shot out of Amenduil and coiled around Sarlona. They yanked her into the dark mage's arms.

Her wide eyes went blue as they disappeared.

Benton's heart fell out of his chest and into the snow. As good a place for it as any. It broke with the distance between them—hundreds of miles.

Dagmar didn't open her clenched jaw, but a low, terrifying growl rumbled out of her.

Glaucus sighed, pulling the claw from Benton's throat, then retracted it but kept his warm fingers on Benton's collarbone.

"We'll get her back." Glaucus opened Benton's white-knuckled grip and took his sword that he'd made just for Benton.

Heat replaced numbed as Glaucus repaired the damage he'd done to Benton's shoulder. The wounds in his thigh closed next.

Benton wanted to say thank you, to smooth things over, but Glaucus wouldn't let him speak.

The old lorkai patted his shoulder. "It's all right." He said it like he'd say it to a child.

That was what Benton was to them. No, a pet. Without his sword, a toothless dog.

Glaucus squeezed. "We'll get Sarlona back."

Benton didn't want that for her. Much as he desired her. Neither could he bear the thought of her in the dark beneath Port Brummit with Amenduil and the rest of the evil cult.

"What if she's human again by the time we do?" Dagmar asked. "What if I'm not strong enough to turn her back?"

An overwhelming weariness washed over Benton. His eyelids drooped, and his head lolled.

"Everything will be all right," the Lord of Ashmore said.

Benton didn't believe him. His eyes closed.

Chapter Twenty-Five

"Benton."

The high sandstone ceiling echoed his roared name as Sarlona materialized in an unlit chamber with Amenduil's arms around her.

They'd left him. Amenduil had left him.

She spun on the dark mage, but most of her rage evaporated when his hands slipped down her torso and collapsed to the floor. Unconscious. Transporting her that far had drained him as much as if she'd ripped out all his Marrow.

So, she faced Vorakor alone.

Sharp as her lorkai senses were, it took her a moment to conclude that the beast towering over her was a statue. It had no scent but mineral and the mortal reek that clung to it. No heart pounded in its chest. Air didn't whoosh in and out of its lungs.

Yet it seemed alive. The dark shifted around the obsidian effigy that towered atop a marble dais taller than Dagmar.

Loud as some unnamed sense screamed that she should avert her gaze and retreat from the chamber, she couldn't help staring at it.

It was hideous.

And a beautiful work of art. Unrivaled in its detail.

Faint veins showed in its bulging muscles. The clawed hand that gripped a human skull, a real one, bit into the bone. The other hand extended to the front of the chamber; its curled fingers so lifelike it seemed to beckon her.

Striated horns protruded from its temples, curling against shoulder-length hair one could imagine shifting with a breeze. The slender fangs peeking from between its lips could have pierced flesh. Its two great wings swept around it and filled much of the chamber, their rougher texture giving them a more leather-than-stone appearance.

The obsidian monster even had genitals, including an erect

phallus, as if it wouldn't have been repulsive enough without one.

Its eyes, carved of blacker stone than the rest, followed her as she stooped to shake Amenduil.

He didn't wake.

She touched her bloody fingers to his cheek and poked at his brain, trying to heal him to consciousness. With barely the power left to breathe, he was too empty to wake. She sighed, digging deep into herself, and poured the tiniest drop of Marrow from her body into his, secreting it through one fingertip.

His long lashes fluttered, and he sat up with a groan. Despite the strain etched into his face, his labored breathing, and the sweat on his brow, he seemed relieved. "I didn't think I could do it again. So soon..."

"I wish you hadn't." Her voice reflected the icy dark of the chamber.

Black candles flared to life atop a large altar also polished obsidian as he stared past her. Their flickering light reflected in the stone eyes behind it, further bringing Vorakor's tribute to life.

Amenduil staggered to his feet. "I doubt they'll kill him."

His doubt couldn't begin to ease her pounding heart. "Are there other casters here?"

Brushing himself off, he nodded.

She crossed her arms. "Get one of them to take me back."

"None of them could ever transport a lorkai that far," he said with a chuckle.

"Then find some manna and take me back."

Amusement fled his expression. "I've transported you twice in as many days. It will be half a week more before I can do it again. Manna or not."

She put her face within inches of his. "What if I dump Marrow into you?"

"I'm not going to risk it, Sarlona," he said as calmly as one could with a monster's face so near one's own. "You might be willing to die for a stray dog if you could, but I'm not."

"I *must* go back." She snarled, baring her teeth, but water played at the edges of her eyes. Benton wasn't dead, yet. His presence was faint. But for the third time, she feared she'd killed him.

Amenduil frowned and laid his hands on her shoulders. "Then we'll go, my dear... After I've restored your humanity." He squeezed, thumbs kneading knotted muscle. "We'll go together at the height of our power and retrieve him. With Vorakor's blessing."

He urged her shoulders into a half turn, coaxing her gaze to the statue.

She may have imagined it, but the stone monster seemed to shift its weight. The dark magic that thrummed inside the rock she didn't conjure. Even if she couldn't feel it how she used to.

He guided her nearer the altar with gentle hands. She floated to it, gaze locked on the statue's as she tried to decide if it saw her. "How long?"

"It will take me three days to prepare the ritual." Soft and apologetic, his voice nestled in her ears. "Another two to recover from it."

So great was the weight on her chest that she thought the statue had fallen atop her.

Five days.

"I can't wait that long." If she ran, she'd arrive in Ashmore in less than one.

"My dear, if you return to Ashmore alone, you may never leave." He sidestepped her, trailing his hand along her shoulder. "The longer you remain a lorkai, the more difficult it will be to make you human again."

He took one thick black candle, the only one that had failed to light, from the edge of the altar and set it in the center of the blood-red silk that dressed the obsidian. "If they trap you there for too long... I may not be able to change you back at all."

She didn't think that warded chamber would hold her as she was now. But the lorkai might have other ways to imprison her. What if they kept her in Ashmore for years...decades?

"You may never have another chance to restore your magic." He slid out from in front of the altar and moved a smaller, flickering candle to sit beside the large unlit one. "Your humanity."

She stared at the pair of candles.

"Benton, too, was your captor, your tormentor, until a few weeks ago."

Amenduil had also been her captor.

Now she was the tormentor.

"You don't owe him anything." Amenduil couldn't have sounded more certain.

She inched closer to the altar and touched the warm stone. It should have been cold.

Maybe she didn't owe Benton. Nevertheless, she was responsible for him now. She felt that somewhere in her soul.

"Remember your magic, my dear." Amenduil edged his hands to hers.

To her nine mangled fingers, half gore and half shining bone. The pain just started to register.

"Remember what it felt like. How extraordinary it was." His fingers alighted on her less-damaged wrists. "Think of the good you'll be able to do with it, with a few more years under your belt. The power you'll wield."

He didn't care about doing good. Most likely, he'd try to put her power to wicked uses. She did remember, of course, all she was supposed to be. All that'd been stolen from her. Some of it, she could get back.

He came dangerously closer, with warmth emanating from beneath the robes that brushed against her. His breath caressed her ear. "What do you wish to do to me?" he whispered.

Twisting, she peered into the face beside hers. She wanted to tear open his robes and grope him. Despite knowing he had none to spare, she ached to rip out his Marrow, his life force. To leave him as a meat husk on the floor to satisfy her hunger for a few hours. Though he'd saved her life and Benton's only yesterday.

Her hands shook as tears escaped. She hadn't killed anyone yet. But she would.

"You don't owe him anything," he repeated. "However..." He guided her hands forward until her fingertips grazed the candles. "Tomorrow night...take the Black Oath. On the new moon, I'll restore your humanity. And, if you desire it, as soon as we're both at full strength, we'll teleport into Ashmore and retrieve Benton." He released her wrists. "Even if we have to destroy the lorkai to do it."

She took a slow, useless breath then lifted the smaller candle. Its flame swelled as she tipped it sideways. The two wicks kissed, and the dead one flared to life. Instead of brightening by one tiny flame, Vorakor's temple dimmed. Everything but those obsidian eyes. Those flickered along with the last candle.

Or glistened in triumph.

~ * ~

Benton woke to Dagmar pulling him to his feet. He didn't know where he was at first or how long he had slept, but they were indoors in an expansive, rectangular chamber, built floor to ceiling from joined stone, like those that made up Ashmore's cellars. They leached the same oily must, the same old burn. With iron bars at the front of three stalls, chains dangling from the walls and ceiling, and a table outfitted with restraints, this windowless room wasn't a cellar.

It was the underutilized dungeon.

With one arm, she hauled him inside a man-sized cage, a length of chain jangling in her other hand. The silvery bars glowed faintly blue—heavily enchanted. And made of something less brittle than iron.

Her calloused hands crushed his wrist as she slammed it into the first manacle. She pinched his skin when she snapped it shut and, with her fingers rather than a hammer, popped in the iron pin that secured it. Grabbing his other arm, she repeated the process.

He didn't know why she had to be so rough. Or why he had to be chained in the first place. What was he going to do? Break out of an enchanted adamant cage and fight his way past two lorkai and all the guards? Unarmed?

She hung his bound hands from a hook at the top of the cage, then snatched his chin. The blue of her eyes would have bored him if he didn't think he could see all the world's feminine rage roiling in them.

"We can't have you too comfortable. Sarlona needs to feel you suffering." She smiled with genuine delight.

Could Sarlona sense his torment? Did her quick allow that?

"Don't she suffer enough on her own?" He tried to rip his head away. "What the cock's wrong with you?"

Dagmar let go and stepped back. Her smile faded into granite. "The last thing I want to do is hurt her. But if it brings her here, where she's safest, I will." The smile bled through her rock-like features. "If I get to make you scream, that's a bonus."

He stared through her, wishing he could hold in his sweat while Glaucus descended the worn staircase. "Look, I'm *sorry*," he said to the Lord of Ashmore. "I don't know what happened. I just couldn't watch her be tied up."

One corner of Glaucus's mouth lifted, and his storm-cloud eyes twinkled. "I know, Benton. That's all right."

Benton's hilt still peeked over Glaucus's shoulder where the longsword usually protruded.

The sight made Benton feel as if Dagmar had stripped him bare. "That's not why you're down here."

She exited the cage, leaving it open. "You're bait."

His heart raged. They couldn't lock Sarlona up in a smaller, more unyielding prison than before. "We got...close," he said, half-surprised Dagmar hadn't castrated him already. "She ain't comin' for me. She ain't that stupid."

The idea that Sarlona might risk all her hope and freedom for him made him warm and sick at the same time. She wouldn't, though. He hoped she wouldn't.

"Benton. We can smell her quick in you and her intention behind it. You're her Bound," Glaucus said, drawing near the cage. He leaned on the corner of it, opposite the open door. "There's no stronger connection between a lorkai and another soul than the one she shares with a mortal she's bound."

It came to the forefront then, this smoldering tether buried in his gut that brought him agony and ecstasy. Agony because she was so distant. Ecstasy in its assurance that he was hers.

Loneliness was impossible now.

The old lorkai put on a sad smile. "Sarlona feels you now as a beloved part of herself. She will know when you're in distress."

Benton didn't want to know what an immortal's idea of distress was.

Dagmar glowed. "She'll feel you dying."

"She'll either break your bond or come for you," Glaucus said.

The prospect of either made a cold fist close in Benton's chest. Vomit rose in his throat.

Dagmar ducked inside the cage, slowly unfolding a carpal blade from one forearm. His heart strained to pump molasses through his veins.

She slipped her claw under his shirt, the razor-sharp back edge scraping along his abdomen as he tried to suck his stomach into his rib cage. A flick of her wrist cleaved his shirt and jerkin. His relief at her claw disappearing into her arm evaporated when her sprawling hands landed on his bare chest.

She ran her fingers up to his shoulders, then down to the waist of his pants to scare him or tease him. Perhaps both?

"Scream loud," she told him, dipping her thumbs into the hollows beside his hipbones. "In your mind." Her thumbs sank lower, lightly rubbing his skin, and he twitched between them despite himself. "You won't be able to scream aloud for this part."

Certain she was about to rip his cock off, he shut his eyes, shaking and panting. Until he couldn't draw the air to do the latter.

His lungs burned, then screamed, then thrashed.

After three minutes, his whole body tried to breathe, chest fighting to heave but only spasming, blood pounding in his face. But he couldn't open his mouth, couldn't suck air in through his nose. He wanted to kick, fight, do something to get her hands off him, but she allowed no more than his muscles to tighten.

They got what they wished. He screamed and begged inside. Pleaded. Not to Sarlona. Just Dagmar and the universe. Whoever would listen. Finally, he passed out.

A minute later, he took a huge breath, opening his eyes to find Dagmar still standing in front of him. She caressed his heaving torso. His lungs seethed, and his head swam. Just when he'd caught his breath, he couldn't draw another.

Then there was fire in his veins. Acid in his eyes. Glass in his stomach. Cracks in his bones.

He screamed and screamed.

And this time, he was forced to stay conscious. Even as his heartbeat flagged and his body wilted against the pain, his muscles too starved to contract. She only let him take a breath once his thoughts had unraveled too far for him to beg.

Then she started again.

Chapter Twenty-Six

Amenduil had tried to convince Sarlona not to leave the Nocturnal Embrace's sanctuary, rightly fearing that the salt on the breeze and the sharp line on an all-blue horizon might persuade her not to take the Oath. He was clear he wouldn't help her if she didn't.

But she hadn't dipped her toes in the sea in months, hadn't seen the blinding sunlight sparkle off its surface.

Besides, she'd needed to hunt and preferred to steal from a soul she'd never see again than from one of her soon-to-be "brothers" or "sisters." So, she'd left and snatched a young woman who was just opening the alchemist's shop for the morning. She never saw Sarlona, never knew what was happening. Sarlona left the young shopkeeper in the back room, sleepy but unharmed, with no memory of how she'd gotten there.

In no hurry to return to the underground lair filled with friendly killers, Sarlona loitered with her feet in the icy waters of the Avenian sea, the remnants of waves lapping at her ankles.

She prayed, staring out over Tydras's realm. Ritualistic prayers spoken for hundreds of years at least. Prayers she'd memorized at five years old.

No one noticed her on the small, rocky beach north of the docks. Few people went near the water and its whipping winds in the wintertime, and those who did had left at sunrise to work on it. It made for little distraction as she transitioned from recitation to communion.

The sea still held magic, but it wasn't the same. Her vision cut past the glittering surface and into the dark below. The cold didn't hurt. And the briny odor contained dozens of distinct scents packaged together when they were once one.

It didn't feel the same.

Despite her clearer senses, there was a fog between them, her, and the sea. Maybe that had nothing to do with her lorkai mind and body. Maybe that originated from her actions on another beach when those monsters first came for her. Or perhaps her considering Amenduil's offer, which would have her bump Tydras aside for Vorakor, even if only in outward appearance, separated them. Maybe she'd constructed the fog herself, bitter that Tydras hadn't come to her aid in any perceivable way.

She still prayed for the God of the Sea to help and guide her to the right path.

Eventually, her stare went soft and blinded by the glittering sunlight, taken from Balis and converted to Tydras's own.

She was supposed to be one of those sparkles. A glimmer on the waves like all the others that shined so brightly then ended.

Perhaps to gleam anew someday on a different wave.

She wasn't supposed to be part of the unending darkness or live forever.

That was what Tydras told her. What she'd imagined He'd said, anyway.

She and her magic were meant to burn brilliantly for a few years, then go out.

So, when the Serpent or the tendril reached its apex in the sky that night, she'd take the Black Oath. She'd become mortal again, human. Even if it meant marinating in a different type of darkness.

Assuming Amenduil was true to his word.

Then she'd rescue Benton.

Somewhere, he screamed, or writhed in pain.

It broke her heart.

Ironically, it was the lorkai inside her that stopped her from sprinting off to Ashmore as much as Tydras. *He has crimes yet unpaid for,* the monster within her rationalized.

Ironic, too, that the only reason she listened to it was so she could destroy it.

When she turned from the ocean, Benton's agony swelled so high it made her ears whine.

The lorkai wouldn't kill him.

Glaucus wouldn't, anyway. Dagmar wouldn't so long as he was useful.

They had to know how fast she could reach Ashmore. By five days... They might assume she wasn't coming, that he wasn't juicy enough bait after all, and then...

They'd feel it when she became human. Her blood bond with them would break.

As would her bond with Benton.

The thought hollowed her out as she shoved her feet into her boots.

What if the broken bond convinced the lorkai that she didn't care enough for Benton to come for him?

She scooped up a mussel shell encrusted with ice from beside her boot. The brilliant blue, silver, opalescent white, and black made distant memories swirl. She rubbed the ice off between her fingers and cradled the essence of the sea in her hand. The Gods' will. Natural Law. Those trumped all else. As she slipped the shell into her pocket, she glanced once more at Tydras's realm, the perfect blend of dancing light and still depth.

Only shadows danced where she was going next. And its depths weren't still.

~ * ~

The man in ratty wool pretending to be a drunken vagrant didn't so much as raise an eyelid as Sarlona drifted by. His scent shifted, and his pulse quickened, though.

How he knew she was there and who she was without peeking would remain a mystery. If she spun to ask, she might not go inside.

She approached the broken hearth of the rundown house, the dust she disturbed with her boots settling where it'd started with every step. Except for some broken bottles and initials carved into decaying walls, there was no sign anyone had entered that house for years.

Even the heavy must whispered abandoned. Less protected minds might have heard the word as their own.

She pulled the knife Amenduil had given her and stuck it into a crack at the back of the fireplace. As she whispered prayers she didn't mean, the stone below faded until a dim light leaked through it, and she could make out more stone seven feet down.

She slid into the hole and dropped, the rock above hardening the instant she passed through.

A tall, sallow-skinned man with bright green eyes and an aquiline nose lowered the bow he'd trained on her. He offered a half-smile and leaned against the wall.

She couldn't summon a smile in return. Not as Benton twisted in agony.

Her guts squirmed with him while she stalked across the large antechamber/training area and into a dark, narrow corridor. It wound down, then split three ways. Her new room was to the left at the unlit end of the hall.

There were no windows beneath Port Brummit. No light greeted her when she opened the door.

Another scream from Benton stiffened her spine. It mingled with another. This one was fainter and in her ears.

A man was somewhere below.

The Embrace had a dungeon, of course, that held a few Silsorian prisoners.

She slipped her hand into a pocket and rubbed her thumb against the inside of the mussel shell to combat the muffled but terrible sound below. It offered comfort—smooth and soothing but for the few rough grains of sand, like she should be.

They screamed again, Benton and the man. The sound sent her teetering on the edge of the Abyss. Unending dark stretched out ahead and below her, empty but for Vorakor's writhing tendrils and the cries of lost souls.

She closed her eyes and let her forehead rest upon the open door. Grooves in the grain whittled by age dug into her skin, then gouged deeper. The door was made of old wood from ancient trees.

It was all wrong.

She'd have to find another way to get her magic back or endure without it.

Whatever power she was meant to wield, it had to be balanced, light and dark, life and death. She couldn't take the Oath. No matter what Benton had been prior to Ashmore, she sure as hells couldn't wait four more days while the person she cared most for suffered.

Before she went to him, though, she had to visit the dungeon and stop that man from screaming.

She hadn't gone down into that space yet; not wanting anything to do with it. The scents, the drafts, the sounds told her its location. After turning herself into glass, clothes and all this time, she flitted through the abundant shadows, down to an old iron door. It creaked when she opened it, but otherwise, she didn't make a sound.

Chains hung from every surface in the cavernous, utterly black chamber. On its far side lay a still pool. She sensed the life in it, smelled the fish. One finned over as if to greet her. It would have been a gentle sound had she not been sure they were the parasitic species the Embrace held sacred as one of Vorakor's totem animals.

Across from the pool sat a utility table which bore an open logbook, unlit lantern, and an array of sharp tools. Near the center of the room stood another table, nicked, stained, and fit with iron cuffs.

That was where the screaming man lay. Where two shades loomed over him.

The shadows sensed her, tracking her with their eyeless faces as she drew closer. If she'd had her magic, it would've been a simple trick to get rid of them, to destroy them. She could have called Balis's scorching beams into the chamber and immolated them from existence.

She didn't know what she could do to them as a lorkai. At least they couldn't hurt her either.

"Go away," she growled.

To her surprise, one wispy shadow banked to the left, floating over the pool, then fading into the wall. The other simply sank into the floor.

She wrapped her fingers around the man's too pale ones and her consciousness around his battered psyche. He went rigid, expecting greater pain. She numbed his naked, muscled body from head to toe.

Then he thought he was dead, left to drift alone in the Abyss for eternity.

She made him sleep before repairing his body.

That was easy enough. The Embrace hadn't damaged any of the young paladin's organs. All the cuts, the burns, had been made only to hurt and stain him red. To dye his shaggy blond hair auburn. Once his body was whole, she drove out the nightmares that the shades had been drilling into his mind.

Then she sliced through his bonds and left him while she went to tend to Vorakor's other two prisoners.

She approached the older woman first, who teetered in her seat in the corner, ready to fall over flat. Lightly, terrified of what she'd see and feel once Sarlona snuck inside, she touched the woman's bare, yellowed shoulder.

She was one of Silsor's priestesses. Ruthless and righteous, she would have been a templar or paladin had women been allowed. Despite all her light magic, which Amenduil had silenced with his blacker brand, she was full of darkness. Not just that black ooze that had been poured into her. Her own.

She'd done terrible things in the name of Silsor, to Vorakor's servants, and children. Pagans too.

Sarlona retracted her fingers. Leaving the woman there would make her sick.

Setting her loose on the world would make her sicker.

So she went to the man about her age, without cutting the woman's bonds. Unlike the others, he was clothed, and his hands were free, pulling a blanket tight around his shoulders. He was bound at the ankle, tethered to the wall.

He didn't appear sick or injured.

She braced herself as she alighted her fingertips on the light brown skin of his throat.

He was a Silsorian preacher's eldest son—a kind young man. And she was too late to help him. They'd broken him.

His torture hadn't been painful. It had been gentle, sensuous. A torture with feathers, candle wax, and a handsome tormentor's strong hands and soft lips. Each applied to the young man's body amid tender words and sweet promises.

He'd decided that morning to take the Oath. No understanding or acceptance waited for him at home with Silsor if he ever escaped. He'd tell his captor that night after the beautiful man was through with him.

Sarlona withdrew, back to the prisoner who hadn't deserved his punishment, and drank deeply from him. Then she swathed the unconscious man as well as she could in the cloak Amenduil had given her and threw the unwieldy bundle over her shoulder.

The Embrace's sanctum was like a rodent burrow—it had half a dozen cryptic escape holes in case a holy predator came through the main entrance. One lay almost right outside the dungeon, hidden from sight by magic but not from her sense of smell.

After sneaking her rescued paladin through the back alleys of Port Brummit to the nearest Silsorian temple, she left for Ashmore.

Chapter Twenty-Seven

Glaucus brought the cup of water to Benton's lips and let him take as many deep swallows as he wished. "Perhaps she's unable to come," he said to comfort the mortal while he lowered the empty vessel. More than Benton's body hurt. "Perhaps Amenduil has waylaid her in some way."

Of course, the thought of her held or trapped by the Nocturnal Embrace and Amenduil comforted no one. Still, Benton needed to know his pain would end and that Sarlona hadn't abandoned him. Otherwise, he wouldn't last.

Glaucus had expected her to come immediately. Even before Dagmar made her, Sarlona had cared for Benton. However little they both wanted to acknowledge it, they'd felt a deep connection—a bond the Gods sometimes wove between two souls that would draw them together until death.

Glaucus had recognized it. He'd felt it once, almost two millennia ago.

That was why he'd told Sarlona how to bind a mortal. Why he was sure she would come for her Bound, sure she'd walk right into the enchanted, lorkai-proof cage that Glaucus had commissioned for Dagmar centuries ago in her young, unruly years.

"I can't believe you'd lock her up," Benton said, his voice weak from exhaustion and raspy from screaming.

"We locked her up for months," Glaucus reminded him and set the cup on the floor.

"She's one of you now." Benton stood on his toes, unsteady as his legs were, trying to relieve his aching shoulders. "And this is a *cage*."

"I'm sure we won't need to hold her long." Glaucus rested his fingers on Benton's chest, and the mortal tensed in anticipation of pure agony. "She just needs some time to adjust." Instead of pain, he granted

Benton relief—a respite from his aching joints and muscles, his raw throat and wrists.

Benton tried to shrink away.

"I don't know why you're doing that." Dagmar glared, arms folded, from outside the cage.

"Because it's kind, Daggy," Glaucus said without taking his gaze from Benton.

She shrugged. "I'm just going to hurt him again."

"I'll do it this time," Glaucus told her. Benton stiffened beneath his fingers.

She snorted. "You'd deny me the joy?"

"You should be nicer to him." He smiled at Benton. "Benton will likely be family someday. He'll likely be your grandson."

She bristled, and Benton blanched. His heart leaped into a sprint. Swallowing hard, he whispered, "You said Sar wouldn't turn me..."

Glaucus had promised Benton that Sarlona's threat to make him her son was empty. Nothing more than a desperate attempt to convince him to help her.

"I lied, Benton." He let the human's fear rage. Perhaps that would get Sarlona's attention. "Now that she's bound you, it's all but assured."

Benton shuddered. "You can't let her do that. I can't—" He struggled to take a breath and forced his wild gaze to meet Glaucus's. "You know what I'm like..."

He did. Temperance wasn't in Benton's vocabulary.

"Don't worry, Sarlona's a newborn." Dagmar's hand engulfed one of the cage's bars, and she leaned closer. "If she tries it before you're an old man, she'll probably kill you."

One of the coils in Benton's chest loosened. Glaucus couldn't have that. "No. That's why we chose Sarlona. With her power, she can have strong children young."

Benton's heart thrashed in his chest. Pure panic leaked from his pores.

Glaucus squeezed Benton's shoulder. "There's no...need quite like the thirst for Marrow. But... You'll master it, Benton, eventually."

The mortal trembled as images of it flashed in his head—people struggling, then going still as he drained them to death, unable to stop himself. All kinds of people like the innocent and young. Breaking their bodies in his excitement and punching holes in their minds when trying to silence their cries, leaving husks behind.

While Benton's heart fluttered in the grip of terror, Glaucus punched invisible needles into him. One at a time, in his stomach and intestines.

The human's face twisted, and a thin, hoarse scream burst out of him.

"I am sorry, Benton. I don't enjoy bringing you pain." The back of his knuckles dragging against Benton's cheek didn't help. It made the man's eyes widen.

Glaucus stared into them and slid a needle into each kidney.

Dagmar had done worse to him. But to Benton, it hurt more coming from the Lord of Ashmore.

~ * ~

Benton finally shrieked her name. He hadn't meant to. It'd just slipped out, this terrible betrayal. Glaucus's uncompromising gaze and sad smile had twisted it out of him. Along with the worst physical pain of his life.

Benton cried afterward. The pain the lorkai had caused him over the last day had brought plenty of tears. Now though, he cried.

They tore him in half, his desire for Sarlona to descend the creaky stairs into the dungeon and his fear that she would. Her arrival would stop the agony caused by the one man he'd ever trusted.

And there was the anguish of distance.

But how would he live with himself knowing the only person he loved sacrificed everything for him? What if she resented him for it for cocking eternity? If she stayed a monster, they'd never get to have the life together he desired. The life where he got to be the man and…and they had a real family. If she… If she turned him… If she took what little humanity this realm had left in him.

He would become something else. Not like the other lorkai. They had traits that could cut through their monstrousness. Glaucus had all the patience and wisdom of an aged commander. Dagmar had her sheer, stubborn will. Sarlona had her brutal discipline.

Benton, however…was already mostly hunger and guilt. If turned, he'd become that thing Glaucus had warned Sarlona of—that beast lurking in the wilds or beneath the city streets who devoured anything that wandered into his territory.

So when Benton sensed her close, when her nearness sliced through the pain, it kept going and split him down the middle. It made him twitch like an axe had embedded in his brain.

Glaucus saw it in him.

Another betrayal.

Benton slumped, his weight tearing at his wrists as Glaucus retreated from the cage. "She's near."

Dagmar nodded. The shrill, metallic grind of a whetstone on

steel sounded once more before she rose from her seat and sheathed her axe down her back. "I feel her now."

The lorkai took up positions on opposites sides of the cage door and waited.

Maybe Sarlona could overpower them both this time. Maybe.

Despite all his dark thoughts, Benton's heart soared when she appeared halfway down the stairs. The remaining steps didn't make a sound as she floated over them. Her gaze skipped over the other lorkai and fixed on him. She held them blue for *him*.

He shook his head when she strode forward, her face the picture of calm, her movements the image of grace, and a stare the depiction of determination. Without so much as ejecting a blade or pulling a knife, she marched into the cage. She didn't twitch when Dagmar closed the metal bars behind her.

He groaned as Sarlona's arms wrapped around him. Fresh air filled his lungs, and warm water washed over his skin. Just from her embrace. She flipped out a claw and cut carefully through his bindings.

He fell completely into her arms.

"I'm sorry, Benton," she said into his ear. "I'm so sorry. I should have come right away."

He shook his head again when she lowered them to the floor. "You shouldn't've come at all."

She laid his head in her lap and melted his aches with velvety fingers on his cheek.

"Get him some water," she snarled at Glaucus, her eyes burning red. "Some food and a blanket."

Glaucus nodded. "Gorgil is fetching them." He took a breath and let his shoulders slump as it left him. "I'm sorry, Sarlona."

She scowled. "Apologize to Benton."

"I have."

She shot an angrier glare at Dagmar.

The Northlander folded her arms and laughed.

"Sar…" Benton whispered.

Sarlona focused on him, and her eyes plunged into the sea. He just wanted to stare into them awhile. She indulged him, gazing at his face as she ran fingers from the notch in his throat to his pants and back.

Her touch made everything tingle.

"You're beautiful," she told him as she enveloped his mind in a warm fog.

He sank deeper into her and grinned. "No shit."

Smiling, she covered his mouth.

Her smile couldn't last, though. She couldn't ignore the lorkai forever.

"How long can I expect to remain captive in the Lord of Ashmore's dungeon?" She stuck out one claw and sliced at the cage, testing it.

The carpal blade didn't so much as leave a scratch.

Glaucus's eyes looked more dreary than stormy as he answered, "Until you've made peace with your destiny."

The brine in her eyes skimmed over with ice. "For at least the time I've thrown spells then…"

Fourteen years? Fifteen?

Benton wouldn't last years. Even if she didn't inadvertently drain him to death in there or they let him out. He wouldn't survive seeing her imprisoned through the melting snow.

"Will you let Benton out?"

"As soon as he'd like," Glaucus answered.

He must have known Benton had no desire to leave Sarlona's lap now…or to stand.

Dagmar raised her eyebrows. "Do you think he'll be safer out here?" It almost sounded like a question rather than a threat.

"He's suffered enough, Dagmar." Sarlona spat. "For doing the right thing."

Was that what he'd done, the right thing? Too late to matter.

Gorgil appeared then, the heavy thud of his boots heralding his arrival. He carried a green blanket with food bundled in a napkin on top and a small jug hanging from two fingers of the other hand.

"I'm glad you've come back," he told Sarlona and crouched to finagle the items between the bars.

With his brow furrowed and lips pressed so tight they hid his tusks, he appeared anything but glad.

She could have grabbed him. A yank on his arm would have pinned him against the bars. She could have put a carpal blade to his throat and demanded Glaucus let her out. Glaucus might have done it rather than risk the man he'd raised almost like a son.

She didn't think that way. The lorkai knew her too well to believe she'd hurt Gorgil anyhow. So, a perfect opportunity slipped by, leaving bread and moose jerky behind.

Dagmar sighed, shrinking. A crack of softness split her hard features. "Oh, I'm just teasing. I won't hurt your *pet*. Father insists he's part of the family for as long as you keep him bound."

The tension left Sarlona's thighs while Benton's warbled. As much as he desired for family again, joining Dagmar's was an utter nightmare. Despite being at Sarlona's side.

He still didn't understand what it meant to be "bound" either. But it had to be better for Dagmar to think of him as her daughter's pet than the shit on her boot.

Sarlona tucked her fingers under his head, and he groaned when she lifted him into a sit. Scratchy wool hugged his clammy shoulders a moment later. She pushed the small jug into his hands, and he chugged the water.

It was what he needed, not what he desired. He longed for the heat of liquor in his gut and the warmth of her body against his. And he only nibbled at the piece of bread she handed him. Despite his sorry shape, it wasn't what he ached to devour.

"I'd like some cushions," she said to Glaucus while running her fingers up and down the blanket over Benton's spine.

The Lord of Ashmore nodded.

"Some books," she said. "I'm going to need many books."

"Of course, little one."

Benton set down his hunk of bread, his meager appetite already fading.

She was trapped because of him. This beautiful, shining spirit that should be glowing in the woods or waves sat in a cage in a windowless prison.

Because of him.

~ * ~

Sarlona sent Benton from the cage that morning. He'd spent enough time in there. It wasn't safe for him locked up with a newborn lorkai. She didn't have the option of slaking some of her thirst with Marrow from the earth itself.

Never mind the less-than-charming propositions, which were jokes only as long as her eyes flared red in response.

No, if he insisted on keeping her company, he'd have to do it from the other side of the bars.

He did, after a walk around the grounds and a bath, for a few hours.

Glaucus sent him on an errand to the village around midday. By nightfall, the Lord of Ashmore had returned Benton's sword and patrol duties.

For that, she was grateful. He had his life back, with the addition of the leash she'd slung around his neck, which now hung like a lead weight around hers.

The break from him gave her a reprieve from her guilt over binding him, the fear she'd hurt him, her hunger for his Marrow, and the scent of his craving for her. She needed him close but not too close. Not all the time.

She wouldn't grow lonely in the dungeon anyway. Not after she'd spent countless hours alone on the waves or in the woods.

Not when one of the lorkai visited with her every few hours.

Or when she just had to shout into the mind of any guard to make them appear.

Not when she sensed Benton near, felt him with her even when he wasn't standing in the room.

She wouldn't grow bored anytime soon either. True to his word, Glaucus provided her with an abundance of books.

The confinement was what wore on her.

The absence of sunlight, fresh air, trees, and sky. The lack of space to walk and run.

That wasn't to say she didn't get any exercise.

The lorkai's visits weren't just to keep her company. They came to train her. Testing her mental defenses which, with their quick inside her, would never hold against them, and showing her how to assault theirs most effectively.

Sometimes, they brought one of the guards with them and demanded that she practice sifting through his thoughts and finding his secrets. She supposed she was a monster for obliging them. But so were the guards, and each had such interesting stories to uncover, motivations to understand, love, rage, tragedy, and hope to pull apart and study.

That wasn't all she did to Glaucus's men through the bars. She fed, of course, and manipulated their bodies and minds. Practicing, she healed their scrapes and bumps, minor illnesses, and sometimes more serious injuries if they'd done something to irritate Dagmar.

She rehearsed planting ideas in their heads and making them forget, changing them in trivial ways, temporarily. Making them like a food they'd hated before, overcome a small fear, or break a habit.

After Russ had said some especially nasty things to her, she'd made him long for Dagmar for a few days.

And Sarlona practiced causing pleasure…and pain.

She told herself she didn't know why she did it. Glaucus and Dagmar couldn't truly make her. Just threaten her. Down in her dark recesses though, she knew.

The monster enjoyed it. She found it deeply satisfying to make small sounds come out of large men.

Only once they left her hands and retreated without a word or a glance… Once they ascended from the dungeon with a tremor in their steps, did the guilt and shame descend.

Neither ached enough to stop her from doing it again.

The lorkai had stories from their ancient lives for her when they visited. Some from when they were mortals and around the time when they were turned. Often, they didn't just tell their stories. They drew her into their minds and showed her, had her *live* them.

That's how they'd break her.

They'd make her an old friend. Show her how they moved past their transformations to embrace their new lives. They'd get her used to being a lorkai, through their bodies and experiences.

Gods, did that make it hard to hate them. Even when she watched them do things so much more horrible than anything they'd done to her. Doing it with them, with their thoughts, histories, and cultures as the backdrop...made them difficult to condemn.

Like Benton.

Feeling their pains, loss, and trauma along with them convinced her they'd already paid for all of it in full.

Like Benton.

Whom she loved.

She'd at last admitted that to herself. Telling him that seemed difficult, though. Despite the hours he sat beside her cage, nursing a drink with plenty of silence to fill between them, she'd yet to say it.

Why it was harder for her than for him when she'd loved so much before and so recently, she didn't know. She'd loved her parents, brother, Gods...Sylvanus.

There was plenty of time to think about it.

Maybe because it was romantic love. That was new. She hadn't felt anything like that with Vosvoshish. Not when she'd agreed to marry him at Sylvanus's and King Zoshinzin's urging. Not when she had agreed to try to form a living bond between Aven's coastal baronies and the merpeople. And certainly not when Vosvoshish had all but drowned her attempting it.

Maybe that was why. The feeling of cold scales...clawed, webbed fingers...and not enough air that sometimes wafted to the forefront. Or the image of him rent almost in two that floated with his corpse into her nightmares.

Maybe because she didn't believe Benton's love was his own. The infatuation might be. The lust? For sure. But love? She could have planted that there. In her more monstrous moments, she'd wanted to and had thought about doing it. Maybe she had without realizing it.

The bond confused their relationship more. It was difficult to pinpoint where their feelings ended and the other's began. Some things were woven too tightly into that tether.

If she said it, he wouldn't just believe he loved her, but that they were *in* love. That was too cruel a thing to do to him, even for the monster. If it wasn't real.

Or maybe she feared saying it because, if they were in love, then her sitting in that cage, an immortal, seemed asinine while he rotted on the other side of the bars.

What would it mean if she discarded true love in favor of vain determination to return to who she used to be?

Wouldn't her resolve to deny the monster within make her one, if she let a lifetime of love slip away?

That was what she wondered when the air in the room shifted.

Chapter Twenty-Eight

Icy bolts stabbed Sarlona's insides, hellfire scalded her skin, and heavy, wet air filled her lungs. An ear-splitting crack ripped through the dungeon with an explosion of shadow from the middle of the room.

She saw nothing but black for a second.

When it receded, Amenduil stood before her.

The beautiful blue-green had fled his eyes. Shadows raged in its place, and the fiery blue of too much manna burned around them.

"Sarlona..." His gaze locked on her like she was a frail, caged bird.

And he was a cat.

"You broke a promise to me." His voice echoed clear and haunting as if it came from across a lake at night. "You took something of mine."

His feet weren't quite touching the ground, cushioned by roiling shadow. Black tendrils curled up from behind him, around him, then crackled into black smoke, popping in and out of existence.

Her heart crawled into her throat. It never occurred to her that her disappearing act with his prisoner would cause him more than annoyance. She'd never imagined he'd come after her. Couldn't conceive that he'd descend on Ashmore.

But there he was, with death dancing between his fingers.

She had nowhere to go. No chance of dodging his spells in that cage, and no way to get her hands or claws on him.

He pointed two fingers at her. If anyone could conjure flame hot enough to incinerate a lorkai in a few seconds, it was Amenduil.

"Dagmar." She didn't know why she shrieked for the Northlander instead of Glaucus, but the woman burst through the door and skipped the stairs entirely, leaping down from the threshold, axe in hand.

To Sarlona's surprise, no fire erupted from Amenduil's fingertips as she threw her forearms in front of her face. The cage buckled. It crumpled like a tin cup in the grasp of an angry ogre. The top slammed down hard on her right shoulder, and the door's bars nearly smashed into her face, but the whole thing came apart. She slipped through the broken door. He'd freed her, not immolated her.

"Leave," Dagmar growled at him.

"You owe me a soul, my dear." Amenduil stared at Sarlona, features etched in malice. "You owe Vorakor a servant."

What did one say to that?

"You've had too much manna...," she all but whispered.

He overflowed with Marrow. It spilled out of him along with the shadows from around his eyes and fingers, all signs of an overdose. Even the tips of those writhing tentacles dripped blue flame.

He might be spell drunk, not hellbent on revenge.

Glaucus's silhouette appeared in the dungeon threshold. Opposite to Dagmar, he took a step at a time, weapon holstered. "Why don't you let Sarlona siphon off a bit of that extra energy?" His voice was as soft as Sarlona's but didn't quaver.

The last thing she wished to do was drink Amenduil's corrupted Marrow, but the dark mage knew better than to let the other lorkai touch him. Despite what she'd done, he likely trusted her the most.

Glaucus opened his hands, inviting. "Then we can discuss reasonable ways she might make amends."

Amenduil kept his gaze on Sarlona when he replied, "She will make amends in the ways our Abyssal Lord demands." He raised his hand at her again. "First, you must come to Him, my dear. It's clear to me now that your path to Him must be through pain..."

Her blood froze, but she didn't. She was free. "I don't want a fight, Amen. Please."

His fingers and lips were moving. She was ready to bolt as soon as he fired the spell.

Dagmar charged before he got it off, teeth bared and eyes red, muscles tight and ready to hit his shields like a rockslide. He crossed his free arm over his body, beneath his outstretched one, at the Northlander. A telekinetic blast threw her like a ragdoll against the wall.

"This was meant for *you*." Amenduil flicked his wrist, and Sarlona sprinted for the door. He'd anticipated it, spinning as soon as she told her legs to move.

While quick as lightning, she wasn't fast enough. The spell roiled at her back when her fingers grazed the door handle but couldn't grab it. She braced for whatever agony or destruction he'd sent for her.

Instead, Dagmar screamed, going limp just a stride behind Sarlona, then falling from the stairs. She'd thrown herself in front of Sarlona and blocked the spell.

Glaucus screamed his daughter's name, clutching his chest.

Sarlona fell to her knees and nearly off the stairs. A shooting pain tore through her like an arrow had pierced her heart, leaving a hole.

Whatever blood bond she'd shared with Dagmar had been shredded.

Sarlona whirled in horror, sliding off the side of the stairs and scrambling to Glaucus's side.

"Clearly you don't want it," Amenduil finished.

Certain the Northlander was dead, Sarlona gaped when Dagmar's chest rose. A heart beat from inside that cavernous ribcage. She wasn't dead, just different.

Human.

Sarlona shot to her feet. "Gods damn you, Amenduil."

He could have restored her humanity there in Ashmore. Anywhere. And without complex ritual and a five-day delay. Maybe he'd have needed a dangerous dose of manna, but he could have done it.

Her rage froze almost as fast as it had blazed to life. The rim of blue fire had gone from around his eyes, but they were just as black.

He didn't have to say it. The Gods already had…damned him.

Amenduil spread his hands out to his sides while Benton and Grub rushed down the stairs, each with weapons drawn.

"Get out," Sarlona bellowed, adrenaline sizzling through her veins. Much as Benton's blade might come in handy, the battle about to erupt in that chamber was beyond any mortal swordsman.

Benton flinched but hopped down the remaining stairs. Grub didn't so much as acknowledge her.

Sarlona knew the spell. She'd watched Amenduil cast it in her warded chamber. Black water bubbled up from the floor in two puddles, forming pools of endless depth and swirling tentacles—the Abyssal Waters. The way they were eating the stone at their edges, she assumed they'd coalesce to swallow the room.

Led by Gorgil, the other guards streamed in from a hidden passage in the eastern wall.

Glaucus must have summoned them. Lifting Dagmar's huge, unconscious body, he laid her upon two crates against the wall, clear for now of any tentacles slithering from the expanding pools.

Then he turned on Amenduil. "You will leave Ashmore," he said coolly. His eyes burned with demonic rage. "And never return." He strode forward. "Or once we bring you down, Sarlona will turn you."

That was the only thing Amenduil feared, losing his magic.

"I will," she agreed. At first she meant it as an empty threat, but if he hurt anyone, she'd follow through. He'd be far less dangerous as a lorkai. She didn't trust someone like Amenduil to stay dead.

He smiled at her. "I'll leave once Vorakor has your allegiance, my dear…and His fill of souls. To sate His longing for the one you saved."

Amenduil flicked his finger at one of the guards beginning to circle behind him. The bald man collapsed, choking, black ooze leaking from his nose and mouth.

Sarlona leaped for the suffocating man, intending to heal against whatever Amenduil had done.

Sal's face exploded before she touched him. It popped like a bubble full of tar, splattering across the floor and up her boots.

His body went still, and the crater where his face had been oozed like a broken egg filled with shadowy goo. The pool that formed beneath him thinned out, cleared, and deepened.

More Abyssal Waters.

His body floated for a second. Then an ebony tendril wrapped around it and pulled it down.

Her lungs and blood stayed frozen, but she crept toward Amenduil. She and Glaucus had to stop him, or he'd send them *all* to Vorakor's realm.

The dark mage pointed at Benton next. He may as well have plunged a claw into her chest.

Benton's blade flashed in front of him, catching whatever evil thing Amenduil had set upon him before it could do its work.

She and Glaucus charged at once, Sarlona skirting one of the black pools. Amenduil blasted them back, Glaucus into the stairs, which splintered at the impact, and Sarlona between two wicked puddles, her left boot close to landing in one.

Running might be the smartest option. At least getting to open ground. Somewhere where speed was more of an advantage.

As if Amenduil read her mind, the staircase's remnants burned to ashes. One of the cage panels shot to the passage in the wall and plastered itself there, sealing off the other exit.

She and Glaucus could jump high enough to reach the threshold. Getting out anyone else ahead of a spell wouldn't happen.

Now. Glaucus's command cut through her frantic thoughts.

Everyone attacked at once. Cyr hurled some spell that was bound to be useless. Lita threw knives that bounced off the shield in front of Amenduil's throat. Russ fired an arrow at an eye full of night it would never meet. Gupson did the same. The rest of them charged at the dark mage with blades of carpal and steel. Only Glaucus and Sarlona hit shielding before a burst of cold shadow flung everyone backward.

Grub landed with one elbow in a pool.

His eyes went wide with panic as he scrambled to get clear, but black tentacles shot out from the still water. One wrapped about his ankle and another his opposite thigh. He dug his fingers into the grimy stone and strained with all his considerable muscle. The tentacles drew him into the water anyway.

Sarlona might have cut him free if Amenduil's tendrils hadn't shot at Benton.

Benton severed the first, split the second down the middle as it flew for his face, and amputated the third when it caught his ankle. But hinged to free his foot, his blade just nicked the fourth tentacle that went for his throat. It tightened until his eyes bulged, and his face shifted color like a cuttlefish.

Amenduil would have broken his neck had Sarlona not sliced through that tendril. And more zipped at her, exploded at Benton, regrowing as fast as they could cut them back.

So she no more than glanced in Grub's direction as another dark tendril wound its way around his shoulder and yet another coiled about his waist.

Gorgil dropped his sword and dove for Grub, snatching him by the forearm when he was yanked waist-deep into the pool. Despite Gorgil's strength, Grub's descent into the black waters didn't slow. A tentacle soon blasted out and snagged Gorgil's wrist too.

Glaucus darted for them, ripping Gorgil out of Vorakor's hold. As he lunged for Grub, the pool nearest Dagmar lapped at the crates she lay upon. Abyssal tendrils wound up the wood.

When his yank to Grub's arm dislocated the sinking man's shoulder with a sickening pop rather than free him, Glaucus abandoned him to save his daughter.

The black tentacles drew Grub deeper, leaving his strained face hovering above the water, while Glaucus hauled Dagmar from the crates and tried to rouse her.

Grub's garbled scream when one of the tentacles looped over his forehead and pulled his head into the darkness would echo through Sarlona's nightmares for the rest of her life.

However long that was.

With a scream of his own and his dark eyes narrowed, Gorgil rushed Amenduil again. Two arrows, a knife, and a spell followed him in.

The assault drove Amenduil off enough that Sarlona could breathe and Benton could retreat, farther from Amenduil and the pools.

Glaucus got Dagmar on her feet. She shook, paler and more disheveled than usual. After lumbering to the wreckage of the stairs, she snatched her axe out of the ashes.

As Amenduil's tendrils shot for Gorgil instead of Benton, Sarlona barreled at the dark mage, leading with both claws. She hit his shielding like a volley of cannon fire and bounced off like a pebble from a slingshot. But Glaucus, Dagmar, and Benton, with his spell-eating blade, were on him too.

Amenduil blasted them back again and again, charring Glaucus's cloak and searing Gorgil's left side with streams of black flame. He broke both of Gupson's legs with a hand of crooked fingers.

Lita dragged the screaming, fallen man farther from the black pools, and Cyr extinguished his light show to work on healing the injured men.

The onslaught had worn on the dark mage's shielding. At last depleted, Amenduil dropped what remained of it and swept them back a final time.

Then he reached for the crumpled cage as if he were about to palm a melon and shoved his spread-fingered hand at Glaucus. A cage panel flew up and pinned the Lord of Ashmore to the wall.

Glaucus strained and roared, eyes flaring violent red, but the enchanted metal wouldn't give.

Sarlona and Dagmar cursed at the same time.

The whipping tentacles forced Sarlona to sever them each time they snagged Benton or Dagmar instead of charging. Her flurry of claws, Benton's dancing blade, and Dagmar's still-devastating axe were gaining ground, though. Sarlona might be able to dart in fast enough to put a claw through the dark mage's head before he could break the mortals' necks.

He must have seen the thought in her blazing eyes. Pulling a ceremonial knife from his boot, he hollered what sounded less like a spell than an appeal.

Hands coated in black goo burst from the Abyssal Waters. Arms, heads, and shoulders followed. Until five men, two women, and who Sarlona hoped were a pair of brownies rather than children emerged from the waters, covered head to toe in ebony ooze.

She'd seen casters raise skeletons, shades, the decaying dead, and a few ghosts, but she'd never seen souls summoned from the Abyss. They seemed whole. As if they could've been living folk who'd just crawled from a tar pit. The only parts of them not painted sable were their eyes. Those shone as brightly and with as much life as the mortals' eyes around her. One pair sparkled yellow above a squared jaw, borne on a blocky frame like Grub's.

That soul seemed half in a daze.

The rest couldn't keep the black grins from their faces as they lunged, downright ecstatic to sink their obsidian blades into living flesh.

The two smallest tarred wretches succeeded, driving their jagged knives into Russ's stomach and kidney before he could drop his bow and pull his blade. He screamed as he fell, and the miniature villains wasted no time dragging him into the Abyss.

Dagmar took the head off the first abyssal inhabitant to come near her. The pieces dissolved into viscous shadow, plastering the floor. Benton pierced one's heart and the eye of another in a flash. Both melted into black blood at his feet.

Wincing, Sarlona rammed a claw into the chest of the tarred soul resembling Grub. Lita, and Gorgil who was on his feet, put down the two summoned women.

The remaining abyssal servant struck at Benton while Amenduil whipped him with black snakes; one of them wrapped around the hilt of the black knife.

Dagmar hacked at the tentacles, trying to inch forward, sparing a glare for Sarlona.

"Sarlona. Put him down." While deep, loud, and commanding, her growl didn't have the preternatural reverb that it'd once possessed.

Sarlona severed a tendril that came for Benton from behind. It had tried to sneak up from the Abyssal Waters, which now covered much of the floor. This was as he parried that black dagger. A dagger born on a whip, traveling in arcs and changing directions in ways Benton couldn't have faced before.

Glaucus added to Dagmar's shouts. "Sarlona. Or we'll *all* be floating in eternal darkness."

They were running out of floor, and Amenduil didn't appear to be running out of tentacles.

Sarlona set her jaw and took a deep breath, nostrils flaring. Slicing through one last tendril as it wrapped Benton's arm, she charged. She skipped over one tentacle, amputated another, and ducked under the last before plunging her claw through Amenduil's black eye.

Chapter Twenty-Nine

At least, Sarlona thought she had. Amenduil's face evaporated into wisps of shadow.

He'd teleported.

Believing he'd fled, she let her shoulders sag with relief.

Benton's cry obliterated that hope. Ignoring the gash in his face, he sliced at the tendril that had wound around his offhand forearm. The wound ran from his eyebrow to the corner of his mouth, crossing his beautiful right eye.

He grimaced, that side of his face scrunched tight and weeping crimson, but he fought on.

Amenduil's black dagger gleamed with blood. He stood on the surface of the Abyssal pool, the puddles of which had coalesced, as though the clearest glass lay over a black lake. Tendrils swam around his feet, rubbing against them, not grasping but fawning over him.

A tentacle slipped by Dagmar's axe and caught her throat. Sarlona amputated it in a blink.

But the floor of the dungeon had become a pond.

The waters trapped Gorgil against the wall. Lita crouched atop the table with Gup, whom she'd rescued, with the water lapping at its legs, tentacles circling like sharks. Cyr used everything he had left to float above the waters against the far wall.

"Please, Amenduil...," Sarlona said as she retreated from the creeping water. He'd taken three of Glaucus's men. That must have made up for the man she'd stolen.

"Go, Sarlona." Glaucus shifted his gaze, the last part of him left unpinned, to the door above only she could reach.

"Go on, darlin'," Benton hollered.

She wasn't about to leave him, or Dagmar, now that she was mortal, *or* Glaucus, trapped by those bars. Not with the black water creeping toward them all.

"Please."

Amenduil tilted his head to the side, smiling. "One more soul should do." His tone sounded no less warm, no more hateful than he had in the weeks previous.

"All right." Sarlona retracted her blades, eyes wide, heart pounding.

The Abyss had called to her before. Came to her. Maybe that had been her fate all along. It might not be so bad. That black sand Amenduil had sunk her in had been warm. The shadows that had exploded out of her that day in her chamber had felt wonderful.

Maybe she belonged down there. If it could spare Benton, spare more lives... Three men were dead because of her. Damned because of her. Two were awful men, but... It was the right thing to do...

Amenduil's smile widened.

She expected him to cast on her or tell her to wade into the waters.

Instead, the water beneath him exploded with those black tentacles, towering above her head, filling the room...

Not one touched her.

They snatched Benton.

And recoiled into the pool like snakes from a strike.

She dove, grabbing his left hand just before the tendrils could pull his head under. Using every muscle fiber, every vapor of Marrow, every scrap of slumbering lorkai power, she held on.

He growled when his shoulder popped apart, arm torn from its socket. "Cock." His mutilated face twisted in agony. "Gods cockin' dammit."

She twisted into a sitting position, digging in her heels at the edge of the pool to try to keep his face above water.

"You gotta let me go, darlin'," he rasped as the water lapped at his chin. "It's all right. It's where I oughtta be."

She shook her head, tears streaming. "No... No, it's my fault."

"I sent myself down there a long time ago, sweetheart," he said, blanching. His breath came fast and shallow. The eye that still functioned, met hers. "You're—you're the only good thing I ever had, Sar. I'm gonna... I wish—"

"I *do* love you, Benton." Sarlona choked on a sob. "I *love* you. Don't let go."

He smiled. Then let go.

She wouldn't. Couldn't. She'd hold on until her muscles gave out or the tendrils tore him apart. Until they dragged her in too.

A quick yank from the depths pulled him under. It slammed her into the adamantine-glass surface of the pool, ripping him from her grasp.

She shrieked, punching at the invisible barrier. At the pool that wouldn't have her while it took away the man she loved...forever.

The tendrils didn't pull him any deeper. They held him just under the water. Slid over him. Tried to coax his mouth open, urged him to take a breath, as she hacked at the mysterious barrier with her claws, not making a scratch, bawling.

His face was right there. Not an inch below the surface. The hand she hadn't crushed pushed against that heinous glass from the other side, begging for one more touch from her. Pressing against it, she tried to will her palm through the paper-thin forcefield that all her lorkai strength couldn't penetrate. She stared into his perfect electric-blue eye.

He took a breath, and his beautiful eye went wild. His body convulsed.

The tendrils slid off him, retreating into the depths while he thrashed.

Then after a final tremor, his eye rolled back, and he went still.

He looked peaceful as he floated away, then sank.

I love you. She said it into his mind, what was left of it, as their bond dissolved.

Then it was gone. He was no more, and cold emptiness remained, only void and rage.

She screamed and punched the glass, splattering her blood across its surface. Fresh tendrils rose to lap it up, somehow passing through the barrier she couldn't break and dabbing their tips at the droplets. When she lost sight of him, when the speck of him blended into infinite darkness miles below, she shot to her feet, shaking. And locked her stare on Amenduil.

She was on him in three steps. The nest of tentacles he threw at her withered as she grabbed them and sucked the vile magic out. Thick, sweet, and bitter, like molasses, there was so much of it.

She hadn't thought to do that before. The monster came up with it. She was all monster now.

He backed into the wall, getting off one stream of fire.

She sidestepped it, caught him around the throat and slammed him against the stone. The tendrils and pool vanished as his skull cracked against the wall. His eyes turned pretty blue-green.

"Bring. Him. Back."

She had no voice. Something huge, wild, and full of fangs and hunger spoke—a beast. She drank deeply. Too deep. She had to; he had too much. It tasted awful and wonderful, like the strongest whiskey. Burning and singing, it made her drunk. Tears streamed from her face to join whatever black fluid leaked from her nose and splattered like ink on the stone. She speared his gaze with hers, smashing into his mental barrier.

And met…blackness. Nothing more than a swirl of shadow and tentacles in a lake of devotion.

She couldn't make sense of it. Retreating mentally, she squeezed harder and drank deeper.

"Bring him back," she whispered.

Her insides thrummed with dark power. Those black tentacles writhed beneath her skin. Roiling, they begged to burst from her again. All that blackness, it yearned to be free, to explode out of her in a wave of bliss and open a new pit. Maybe if he didn't return Benton, she'd let it. But not until after she'd devoured Amenduil. Not just drained him to death but destroyed him. Coated herself in his blood, tasted it. Saw how finely those carpal blades could slice human flesh.

"I'd need all my power," he rasped.

She ripped more out of him, and he flinched, gritting his teeth.

"You'll have to restore my Marrow." His eyes weren't wide enough. He didn't shake hard enough. "You'll have to give me everything you have."

"Don't," Dagmar shouted.

At the same time, Glaucus bellowed, "No, Sarlona,"

She stopped feeding and loosened her grip on Amenduil's throat, ignoring them. "Let the mortals go."

The cage panel sealing off the room's hidden entrance clanged to the floor. Lita, Cyr, and Gorgil, carrying Gup, slipped through it. "Release Glaucus."

"Not yet," Amenduil replied. "He'll kill me."

He was probably right about that. She should kill him. Now. That was the smart thing to do.

Instead, she brought her face so close that his breath kissed her eyelashes. "If I give you my Marrow and you don't bring him back…"

"I'll retrieve Benton. You have my word." A bead of sweat dripped from his temple into his goatee. "However…you must pray to Him." His voice was steady, careful.

She squeezed his throat. Too tight for him to push words through when he tried to speak.

She loosened her grip.

"It's what our Abyssal Lord desires from you."

"Fine." He was part of her pantheon anyway. She couldn't think of the consequences now. What it might mean, what it might do to her.

Amenduil tried to urge her hand open with his fingers. "It must be now."

She squeezed tighter, reddening his face, and leaned in close to his ear. "If I pray to him... If I give you my Marrow... and you don't return Benton to me..."

He mouthed, "I will," but no voice escaped.

"And you fail to kill me..."

Amenduil tried to shake his head, but he couldn't do that either. His eyes were still calm, like polished, uncut aquamarine—beautiful, shiny, but hard, dead rock. She wished she knew how to fill them with terror.

"If you don't save him but let me live, I will take your magic," she whispered. "I will give you my quick, then I will hunt down *every* one of your brethren." While her lips brushed his ear, she spoke into his mind. "I will execute all Vorakor's children, starting with the nest in Port Brummit. Then crumble his statue and cleanse the pieces in Silsorian holy water myself."

He closed his eyes for a moment, the closest thing to a nod she'd allow. She opened her hand but kept him pinned to the wall with her stare.

"Don't you give him anything," Dagmar growled.

"Ask Him." Throat red and vocal cords bruised, Amenduil's voice lacked its deep melody.

Sarlona didn't close her eyes, but she did reach out...*down*. As earnestly and as far into depth and darkness as she could tolerate. "Vorakor..." Her voice was clear and loud as though she addressed the waves. "My Abyssal Lord, return Benton to me, please."

Black eyes shifted beneath shadow to lock onto her. Tendrils perked, straightened, swelled and stiffened like... A cold claw closed in her chest, and warm water ran over her. The tingling itch beneath her skin intensified. Her muscles shivered, and her breath caught. A hot tongue licked between her legs.

No. That was all her imagination. From the intoxicating thrum of too much Marrow shaking her body and thoughts. She held her plea out there in the universe, kept trying to will the depths to hear it.

Amenduil nodded and *smiled*, damn him. "He's pleased." The dark mage peeled himself off the wall and inched toward her. "I just need the energy to pull Benton out."

"He'll betray you, Sarlona," Glaucus said from behind the crushing bars.

Probably. She didn't see any other way. "Return him then leave.

I never want to see you again."

"I'll leave," he promised, and she took his hands.

Her body raged against it, but she knew what to do. Tapping into his Marrow anew, or where it should have run had she not drained the river, she reversed the flow.

It resisted. Her body, her being, gripped tight to the Marrow. A little at a time, she forced it out, squeezed it from her core and into her fingertips. She jammed it through her finger pads and into Amenduil's riverbed.

It hurt, leaving her insides feeling raw like she was mortal again, and Dagmar and Glaucus fed on her at once.

And made her feel as thin and frail as old bones. She'd endure the sensation forever if it could help rescue the person she loved most.

Once Amenduil's eyes glowed, once blue flame burned in the sockets afresh, no more would go into him. Anything she pushed just sloshed back into her.

She released his hands and stepped clear. Bracing for a devastating spell, she half-hoped she had the strength left to endure or dodge it and half-wished it destroyed her.

Amenduil raised his hands, then paused, the blue flame in his eyes dying down for a second. "I could use this power to restore your humanity if you'd rather."

Sarlona's heart stopped. Glaucus and Dagmar roared in protest as all the darkness of the Abyss closed in on Sarlona. The stone melted beneath her feet. She could escape this nightmare, have what she'd lost. Dagmar was human, and Glaucus couldn't have another child. Sarlona could be free of them forever. She could have her life back.

Not without losing something more valuable.

"Save him," she whispered.

Amenduil's eyes flared before he closed them. Then he held his hands out, palms up. They filled with black smoke while he spoke words she'd never heard in a language that hurt her ears and vestigial bowels. It nauseated her and shook her bones.

Dagmar hitched over, and her black vomit splattered across the stones.

Pure blackness passed through the room, blinding even Sarlona. A cold fog clung to her skin until she let loose a shiver.

The cage panel holding Glaucus crashed to the floor. Amenduil's eyes returned to the color of the southern seas.

But Sarlona saw…*felt* no sign of Benton.

"Where is he, Amen?" she roared, ready to kill him. If she could now.

"Sar?"

She turned to Glaucus. He shook, eyes wide and jaw slack, gawking at his trembling hands.

"Sar..." Glaucus's voice, but weaker, rawer, half a drawl. And he had never shortened her name. Only Benton did that.

With her jaw tightened and nostrils flaring, Dagmar swung her axe in an arc that would have cut Amenduil in half if she hadn't been too slow.

He dissolved into a swarm of black flies before impact. They droned past Sarlona's ears, and he reformed behind her.

"I want Benton's body as well," Sarlona bellowed.

Amenduil snickered. "Well, my dear, you should have specified that."

Glaucus, now Benton, was still staring at his—the Lord of Ashmore's—rich brown and weathered hands.

"Where is it?" Sarlona demanded.

"In solution, Sarlona." Amenduil's tone was confident and patronizing as he retreated. "Be glad his soul was spared. For now."

Glaucus's eyes lit up Marrow blue, and one of his claws flipped out, grazing his chin, leaving a thin red line. "God's cockin' dammit," Benton growled as Glaucus's body dopped to its knees. He tried three times to drive the carpal blade into the stone floor, then split the rock and embedded it in the ground below. "Cock," Benton groaned as a trickle of Marrow wound up the claw and flowed into his arm.

"Where is my father?" The hateful fire in Dagmar's mortal eyes could have melted ice.

Amenduil barely glanced at her. "Gone."

Sarlona bared her teeth. "Bring him back. *And* Benton's body."

"I can't, he's gone. Destroyed." He spoke matter of fact, like he'd incinerated an old, wobbly chair. The words didn't quite land.

"Destroyed..." She couldn't hold onto the thought. "You destroyed his...soul?"

Amenduil sneered as her vision reddened. "Did you think there would be no consequences, my dear?" Creeping backward, he went on, "Did you think you could take a soul from Vorakor, and it would cost you nothing?"

It had cost her a lot before she'd known she'd sacrificed Glaucus. The price may have been her soul after praying to Vorakor.

She lunged at Amenduil with both claws, but he was gone. A swarm of black flies dispersed in every direction as she swatted at them, fleeing through every gap and crack.

The axe slid from Dagmar's pale hands, sickly pale, and clanged to the floor. Her mortal eyes stared into space as tears trickled down her cheeks.

Sarlona stared at Benton, kneeling on another man's—a monster's—knees. He gasped as he ripped out the last vapors of Marrow the dirt below him had to offer.

"Sar." He still shook.

She went to his side and grasped his shoulder. He grabbed her wrist and yanked on her Marrow. Gritting her teeth, she let him take what vapors she had left to spare.

His eyes cooled as he looked at her, with storm clouds instead of lightning. "It hurts."

She patted the aged hand that gripped her arm. "I know."

Chapter Thirty

It had been four days since Benton slept, four days since he'd been human, and he still awakened just after midnight, barely sleeping two hours.

He sat bolt upright in bed the second he woke, heart thundering. His gaze darted around the chamber—Glaucus's—searching for black tentacles slithering across the floor, for black water spilling in through the windows. He found only moonlight—clean, white-blue rays flowing through the window and coating the floorboards, blanketing the bed and illuminating Sarlona. She slept soundly beside him.

Maybe not soundly. One hand had balled a bit of the sheet, and her jaw clenched like an iron trap. She didn't thrash or groan, though. Her long lashes were still. She appeared peaceful overall. Different since he'd last watched her sleep. At least, his eyes saw in new ways. Glaucus's eyes.

Every pore, hair, fine line…speck of dirt…every flush revealed themselves. He saw her heat and electricity. And he smelled her again. He hadn't been able to smell her since Dagmar had stolen that hint of sun, soil, and salt from Sarlona.

But now that he could detect it, her scent was sweeter than it'd ever been. Indescribable, yet familiar. *Familial.* Its nuances painted her moods. As did the pace and thunder of her heart and the rate and depth of her breaths.

The new profoundness with which Glaucus's senses allowed Benton to know her didn't begin to make up for the bond that had dissolved between them, however. That connection…was truer than anything he'd ever known. Perfect. He missed it desperately. With his body gone, he was no longer "bound."

They did share a bond, one of grandfather and granddaughter. So, he felt her distantly. Nothing like he had in his old body after she'd shared her quick.

At least, they were together.

Maybe it would be easier once his human scent faded from Ashmore. Once he couldn't smell himself on her. Those traces his male human body had left before he'd lost it to the Abyss.

The Abyssal Waters he'd been sucked into.

There'd been nothing down there but the black tendrils that had ends but no beginnings. Billions of them going on forever in a dark that he could somehow see miles into in all directions. He'd discovered no forsaken souls, ooze-coated warriors, or demons. No one. The expanse was utter loneliness.

Yet he hadn't been alone. Because those tendrils weren't roots or machines. They were sentient, speaking to him, touching him with intent, belonging to a part of some greater thing. Whether that was the Abyss itself, Vorakor, or something altogether unknown...

Every time the panic rose, each time Benton had taken a breath of the strange substance he floated in to scream, they entangled his limbs. The warm, silky tendrils had worked their way under his clothes and driven the chill out of his core.

Sometimes, they hadn't been satisfied squeezing him. They'd gone inside. They'd split into thinner strands and slipped down his throat, up his nose, into his ears, or... Sometimes they'd buried into his skin. Then they'd wound throughout him, paralyzing his thoughts and body.

Mere minutes had passed in this realm, but they'd felt like weeks in the Abyss. Fortnights with black tendrils that hadn't wanted to give him up when something had drawn him upward. As soon as he'd floated near the surface with bright light blinding him from above, they'd tried to crush him.

He dragged his thoughts out of the black waters, back into the room, where he shared a bed with the woman he loved. She lay on her side in her underclothes, only half-draped in sheets.

He took a few deep breaths, watching her eyelids twitch, her eyes darting beneath them. Damn near all the ribs showed below her tanned skin as her chest expanded and collapsed. While lean when he'd first met her, parts of her had grown gaunt in her last weeks as a human woman. It had taken threats to get her to eat.

She'd slept plenty, though. Mostly when the lorkai had knocked her out. He had loved to watch her sleep. During his shift, he'd sneak in and sit beside her bed in that old chair. Just to watch...well, to sometimes fantasize too that she'd wake and invite him under the covers. That he'd crawl in with her, and her slip would be hiked up, and she'd part her knees... He fantasized about it now.

But he hadn't so much as made a lewd comment to her since he'd been stuffed into Glaucus. They'd held each other. That was it. Benton didn't know if she'd want him in an old man's body. The idea of cocking her with another man's equipment made his insides squirm.

Glaucus's body didn't scream for the warmth between her legs like his had. It was more background noise. Her Marrow, on the other hand, *that* it screamed for. Ceaselessly.

That was why Benton had to get up rather than admire her as he used to. Leering at her made him hungry in ways it hadn't before. Besides, Dagmar kept bitching that he was the ancient one. That he didn't need to feed more than weekly. He had no business stealing the sustenance of a newborn.

Dagmar, however, didn't need Marrow for anything. And she'd probably regenerated by now.

~ * ~

It took Dagmar a second to remember that the face hovering over hers no longer belonged to her father. The face that had until recently brought her more comfort than any other.

Her mind was slower now. Foggy.

She stilled her heart. Fear was pointless. Benton had her arms pinned. His weight crushed her into the mattress. He was going to do what he intended.

Sorrow was harder to quiet. Heartache, knowing that while her father's eyes peered into hers…he wasn't there.

It made her impotent physical form weaker still.

"If you think that body has never been forced on me, you're wrong." Granted, it had been well over six-hundred years since Dagmar woke that night, still a human woman, to the monster who'd been tormenting her for weeks, violating her. He'd given her the first dose of his quick that night. In the way only male lorkai could. "You're not going to break me, Benton." Even if he made her stare in her father's eyes while he tried.

If Glaucus's death hadn't shattered her spirit, only losing Sarlona too could. Not anything Benton could do to her. The creativity eluded him. He was just a cocking animal doing what animals do.

Benton's—Glaucus's—face twitched. "I—*that* ain't what I'm after."

That stupid drawl and terrible grammar in her father's dignified voice made her stomach turn as much as anything else. "Then get your erection off me."

Her height had him pressed against her navel instead of between her legs, and they still had his pants and her underclothes between them.

He shoved his hand down his pants and adjusted himself. For all the good it did. Then grabbed her wrist anew. "I oughtta…"

That was why she despised him.

Whatever he was going to do, she thanked the Gods he hadn't figured out how to truly control a mortal's body so far, their minds, or their feelings. Benton wasn't all that dangerous *yet*. Just a ravenous man with inhuman strength and the ability to suck the life out of people. If Sarlona taught him, though, or if he sunk deep enough into Glaucus's body, the muscle memory would do half the work, and he'd become the stuff of nightmares.

"Well, however much she hates me, Sarlona won't tolerate it," she warned. "So maybe you *oughtn't*."

His face twitched again, and he poked at Dagmar's mind. Even without magical or lorkai abilities, she held a steel wall. She'd had centuries of practice.

That was one silver lining of being mortal. If her body had still been made by the one he was wearing, she wouldn't have been able to keep him out for long. Lorkai children were vulnerable to their parents, bound, by flesh and blood.

Blood that was gone, mercifully.

Or painfully, when she thought of her lost bond with Sarlona.

A newborn…all but alone.

Dagmar growled and struggled, not against Benton, but against fate, the will of the Gods, whatever.

His arms were as immovable as the universe. She thrashed harder, face hot and thick from straining. As a female, she'd been stronger than Glaucus before pouring everything into Sarlona. She would have been stronger again. Against Benton… It had been a struggle not to toss him across the room accidentally.

Now, he snickered at her feebleness.

She snarled. "Will you get on with it?"

He gave her that shit-eating grin using her father's face. "I don't know… This is kinda fun."

She snorted. "Do it before you lose *all* control and drain me to death," she said, much as she didn't wish to feel him delve into her and rip things out that didn't want to go.

"Well, what in the hells do I want you alive for?" The storm flared in his eyes.

She sneered. After nine human lifetimes and accomplishing what she'd put in the world to do, she didn't care if he killed her. Except…

"Sarlona still needs me. You need me."

He clamped her wrists so hard, her bones groaned. "What in the cock for?"

"You're children." He knew. She told him anyway. "You need supervision. You need help. There's a lot Sarlona doesn't yet know about being a lorkai."

"Like what?"

Dagmar gave him the prettiest smile and sweetest voice she'd ever learned. "Keep me alive to find out."

He grimaced but loosened his grip. Sitting up on her, he pulled her hands down in front of them. "Why do I think you'll be a shit teacher?"

"I wish it were Glaucus, believe me." He was the teacher, the mentor, the parent.

The Lord of Ashmore.

Right now, Cyr was doing all the work. Benton stayed inside, and they all pretended the Lord of Ashmore was away.

Jangling her hands with his sigh, he sat up farther. "I… I keep—" He studied the wall in front of him. "Since I came back… I keep seein' a man in my head. I dreamed about him."

She wouldn't have guessed there was room in his dreams for anything but black tendrils. "What man?"

He shrugged. "He's maybe thirty-five or forty. Brown hair, big brown eyes. A little darker skinned than me, than I *was*." Twisting to stare out the window, he ground her knuckles together. "Good lookin'," he admitted, then shook his head. "Great smile."

"A warrior?"

He shrugged. "Built like one. Short sword. Skirt."

"Sounds like Flavius." Her blood ran cold.

Glaucus's brain was still in the skull Benton inhabited. How much of that organ *was* Glaucus? What amount of a person was gray matter, and what was the soul? In the four miserable days that dog with a sword had been wearing her father's skin, he hadn't shown any signs of Glaucus's personality or of the knowledge or memories the Lord of Ashmore had possessed.

Nothing until this.

What if he started acting like Glaucus? What if he saw everything one day? Remembered everything? Including *her*. Everything they'd been through together. "He was Glaucus's First—"

His gray eyes—her father's eyes—widened.

"First Centurion. When Glaucus commanded a century, when he was mortal." Almost eighteen hundred years had passed and Glaucus still thought of him often. Had thought of him. Spoken of him more than his wife or sons or grandchildren. "They loved each other. So much Glaucus would have turned him if he'd been old and strong enough. Idalia tried to do it for him, but Flavius didn't survive the process."

Benton was quiet, staring into space for a damn minute while he sat on her thighs, crushing her hands. "I have his...memories?"

"It would seem so."

He shuddered and stared at her as if he were searching for something beneath the skin. Maybe for whatever Glaucus had seen to make him keep her forever.

Benton probably realized he'd find it...someday.

She shook with him, thinking again that he'd see it all. He'd see her and Glaucus together. Her blood, tears, fear, all of it. He'd see her weaknesses. If not from Glaucus's mind, then from hers once he learned how to use his abilities.

Benton gave a long sigh and loosened his grip, holding her hands just tight enough that she didn't think she could rip them free. She was sinking—that sense of impending doom and that cold claw grasping her chest as he tapped into her Marrow. He drew so hard, she couldn't take a breath. It was like choking and having rough sex and being dragged over gravel at once.

He groaned with relief.

How he could need to feed again after he'd drained Cyr to unconsciousness the previous night and almost killed Lita by stripping her of Marrow that morning, Dagmar didn't understand.

But he'd seen it coming.

He was as he feared he'd be when he'd fretted about Sarlona turning him. Barely able to keep himself from groping every mortal who came within reach. He wasn't just dangerous, but a liability. At this rate, it would take years for him to tune out the urges enough to go into the world. Sarlona would have to start collecting condemned mages for him to deplete—before he drained Dagmar and Ashmore's guards into the ground.

"That's enough, Benton." The room spun. Soon Dagmar wouldn't be conscious to remind him not to kill her.

Half to her surprise, he stopped. Climbing off her, he squeezed her breast, his shitty smile in full force. "Thanks, darlin'."

She would have broken his hands, nose, and balls for that a few months ago. They would have stayed broken until Glaucus or Cyr found him.

Now, raw and faint, she couldn't flip onto her side. "You'd better find a way to master yourself before the SPS finds out what you are."

He froze at the chamber door and pivoted.

"The first of its members who you drain will get you put down like a mad dog."

All trace of his grin fled. "Might be that's for the best."

She sighed, unable to tolerate him feeling sorry for himself. That was all she could do about it. As much as she wanted to kill him, she didn't wish him dead. He had Glaucus's body. Her daughter loved him. And, with his sword and talent, combined with Glaucus's strength and speed, Benton could do a lot to protect Sarlona. If he could pull himself together.

He leaned on the doorframe. "Are you gonna ask Sar to make you a lorkai again?"

She stared at the knots in the ceiling. "Do you think she'd agree to it?"

"I don't know."

Dagmar didn't either. She'd forced Sarlona to be a monster against her will. Surely withholding the power to do the same to Dagmar was the sweetest sort of irony...and vengeance. Besides, Sarlona had to know that if she tried to find another way to become human again, Dagmar would try to stop her. As a lorkai, she had a much higher chance of succeeding.

"If something happened to me...," he said, staring at the scuffed floor. "I wouldn't want her to be alone."

"I don't want her to be alone either." Dagmar made the monumental effort of rolling to face his moonlit silhouette in the threshold... Glaucus's shadow. "Since she squandered her quick on you and dumped her Marrow reserves into Amenduil, I can't have her waste her strength on me right now."

No, Sarlona needed to regain her strength, grow her power. Then, maybe in a few years, Dagmar would ask.

He ran his fingers up the doorframe, staring at it as if he'd never seen one. His gaze flickered green, then jumped to her. "Well, you might be an asshole, Daggy..."

She nearly summoned the strength to leap from the bed and throttle him.

"But I'm beginnin' to think you might be an okay mother too." He shrugged. "Better than mine, anyway."

Those words hit her like a punch to the gut...or the womb. If he didn't idiot his way atop a pyre first, Glaucus's brain might tell him why someday.

"I'll keep trying to be," she said. "Until my dying breath."

He started to turn again but paused and settled back into the threshold. "I truly do love her," he said. "It weren't just the quick like she said...like you said. That bond's gone, and I still love her."

Her sigh was the sound of her tearing in half. Just thinking about what she was about to say twisted her face. "When you do...love her...enter her mind and feed from her while she does the same." Her stomach churned, but a part of her nagged that it would be good for them. That they needed it. "That's how lorkai do it."

He chuckled, but his hands went into his pockets, and he looked at the floor. "Sar ain't gonna... I mean, now... I'm not..."

"She was attracted to Glaucus." Dagmar tried not to think about the conversations she had with her father about how to encourage that. How to use it to manipulate the young woman. "And she loves you."

Chapter Thirty-One

Benton left Dagmar's chamber, for once physically feeling better than when he'd entered. Feeding had taken the edge off the incessant hunger. He hadn't lost control. But the confirmation that he had traces of Glaucus's memories in *his* head had him shaking. Being in someone else's body was bad enough. Being a lorkai...

He wasn't coping well with that either. The thought that a ghost of Glaucus might be inside him, ready to break through at any moment, horrified Benton. He couldn't wrap his head around it.

Where did the brain stop and the soul begin? What if he became two people? Or if Glaucus's old memories, characteristics, and knowledge just swallowed him? Why shouldn't an ancient brain in its own body dominate? What made him who he was and Glaucus who he had been?

What if Benton started feeling things that Glaucus had felt? Started loving Dagmar and that man in his dreams? He could hardly bear his own trauma, what if he had to endure Glaucus's too? All eighteen hundred years' worth... What if Glaucus had done things *worse* than Benton, and Benton had to look at those?

None of it mattered when he reentered Sarlona's/his/Glaucus's bedchamber and gazed at her. If she was with him and okay, it didn't matter. She seemed okay. Maybe that was just an act for him and Dagmar.

Moonlight clothed her like silk, hugging muscular shoulders and hips, draped over a thin waist, and kissing a young, angelic face.

Watching her, he hardened again. It felt...*different* than his old body, but the urge to bury himself somewhere warm was the same. He had a favorite place. Even if he'd only been there once.

They hadn't talked about that. As he removed his pants, he wondered if she'd thought about it since he'd been put in Glaucus's body.

He'd tried not to.

But now… Now he thought of her tightening around whatever cock he was using. And about how much stronger, faster, and more agile he was. About what Dagmar had suggested.

If anything, Sarlona would enjoy it more now. It might be better for him too.

He lowered himself into bed beside her.

Her eyes cracked open. "Do I need to heal anyone?"

"No, I was good," he said, grinning.

She gave him a suspicious glance before her eyelids fluttered closed.

He whispered in her ear, "I need your help with somethin', though."

She reopened her eyes, brows raised.

Taking her hand gently, he guided it to where he strained against his underclothes. The warm pressure tightened his muscles.

Her eyes went wide, and her heart jumped into a gallop. Her peaceful face crinkled.

Maybe not his best come-on.

She didn't retract her soft fingers, however, and a mischievousness crept into her face. "You do, do you?"

"I need you, Sar…"

"Mmm, I know you do."

She cupped her palm, squeezing, and he groaned. It was like she held him tight all over. "Please?"

Her smile glowed as bright as the snow in the moonlight. "Okay."

He pounced, crushing her into the mattress. Catching the sides of her head with dark hands, he kissed her as deeply as he knew how. Heat bloomed in his face when she returned the kiss and drove her hips into him, lifting them off the sheets.

Grinning, he leaned back. "I knew you wanted him to cock you."

She bit her lip, and her eyes sparkled, an expression that made him try to run her through despite the underclothes between them. Looping her arms around his neck, she pulled his face within inches of hers. "I wanted you both to cock me." Her face split into a smile. "At once."

He tried to pull away, unable to decide if he was mildly horrified or more aroused, but she tugged him into another kiss. She was about to get her way, sort of. He slipped his head from her arms and dragged kisses down her throat and chest, then to her breasts. They had to be her softest part, and he'd hardly touched them.

Determined to make up for that, he tugged down the binding she wore to expose them and ran his hands over her, like handfuls of firm silk. His kiss hovered over a nipple as his fingertips played with the other. He slid the other hand into her underclothes, then tapped, pinched, and flicked his tongue at the same time. She moaned, arching.

That sound. He'd heard it before, but now he sensed the depth of its origins. And the scent of her... The pounding of her heart... Her body told him she lusted for him.

He groaned in return, sucked on her, groped her, and rubbed his fingers against her until they came off wet.

Then he ripped off her underclothes—tore right through them—and yanked down his own. He returned his kisses to her lips. She parted her thighs, and he thought he'd shake to pieces. He drove himself into her as accurately and swiftly as he sheathed a blade.

She cried out, the headboard clapped against the wall, and one corner of the bed collapsed.

He froze, afraid he'd hurt her. The lorkai strength had gotten away from him. But when he relented with his kiss, she was trying to hold in a giggle, her eyes filled with laughter.

She held his hips still and squeezed around him, torturing him. "Let's not wake the house..."

He wrested her hands from his hips and slammed them over her head. "Cock 'em."

Thrusting into her again, he shook the room and made her cry out a second time. That sound, and the feeling of her body tightening every time she made it, breathed life into him. The sensation and scent of the tension growing in her had his insides buzzing. Unable to bear it, he broke another bed leg. It still banged against the wall when she cried out once more, longer, harder, insides squeezing him to the point of pain, muscles turning to granite, and eyes rolling.

He paused until the grip on him loosened. Then he rocked his hips, gently this time, his chest fluttering in response to the little thumping throb inside her. She gaped at the ceiling while she caught her breath, then wrapped her legs around him, locking her ankles.

Flames rolled through him as he scooped her up and, from his knees, pinned her against the crooked headboard. Knowing only one would be effective, he lunged with his mind and hips at once.

His psyche collided with her protections and bounced off. Being aching as hard as his body, he groaned. "Let me in..."

Her lips were parted and her eyes gentle, but her mind was steel. "I wanna try somethin'."

Maybe his kiss convinced her—drawn out and tender. She opened, and he eased his way in.

Gods, she felt like going home. Or what going home *should* feel like.

She was full of warmth. All for him. She had the discipline and the practice to shut out or display the thoughts she desired. There was only him. Only that moment. When he withdrew his kiss, his face stared back at him through her eyes. *His* face. A mortal man's.

Caught off guard, he froze.

Part of him liked that she pictured him how he had been as he cocked her. Part of him was relieved by it. The other part worried she hadn't truly wanted...this.

She rested her palms against his cheeks—downy with neat silver hair rather than scratchy with stubble.

He unfroze. When the image in her mind wavered, his face flickering into an old, dark one, he didn't like that much either. He didn't like watching Glaucus cock the woman he loved.

He sighed.

She started to nudge him out of her mind.

"No, wait." He lowered his flimsy barrier. "Come in my head."

She breezed in, bringing a sense of fullness with her, driving out some of the loneliness. He did his best to keep everything but her at bay. To keep the dark water and silky tendrils at a distance.

He tried to repel his longing for his body, thirst, and fear. He attempted to quash the terror that his hunger would kill innocent young girls and helpless little boys. Slay their mothers and fathers. Dread that he'd forget who he was and get swallowed by an ancient Avenian Imperial Commander and Lord of Aven.

He couldn't stifle any of it, not truly.

When he shoved one awful thing away, another popped in. It was like trying to stuff too much into a sack.

She came to his rescue, throwing a foggy curtain around it all. So, instead of him hiding the dark things from her, she helped him conceal them from himself. She was sweet like that. Giving.

After a few minutes, with some effort, only the two of them remained. Them—without all the wicked things that clung to them. They were so close. As near as two people could be. So intimate, he forgot the loss of the bond that had broken between them. All his worry disintegrated.

It didn't matter what he became if he could be with her.

She braced against his shoulders as he went at her harder. He pulled her onto him up to the hilt, then drove her against the wall and headboard.

"Take my Marrow." He didn't know why the hells he should

listen to Dagmar, but if it might bring him closer to Sarlona still, he'd try it.

"You can't aff—"

Her breath caught when he tapped into her power. He groaned as it flowed into him, thrumming every fiber in his body. "Oh, *gods*, Sar, you taste good." Nothing was so sweet or so strong. So perfect.

She pressed her fingertips into his shoulder muscles, and he groaned again when she siphoned his Marrow into her. After a few seconds of tumult, the flow of their Marrow formed a circuit. It spilled from her into him, then from him into her, continuously. All their power threaded together.

He lost himself. Not in the way he feared. In her. In bliss, savoring their perfect connection. She shook, eyes glowing manna-blue and staring into his face, the picture of ecstasy. The softest moans escaped her in time with his hips. Each one made him melt...until there was nothing left of him.

He fell backward onto the bed, overwhelmed, and whined as she toppled onto him, entranced. She stroked his chest, still feeding, while he clutched her thighs and did the same. Her hips did circles, pausing every time the moonlight was about to shatter. Until she had him begging. At last, when his vision narrowed and his grip on her Marrow started to slip, she drove herself down, crushing him to the mattress. He broke into a thousand shards of starlight, shooting up into the sky with the other beautiful things, a million miles from black water and tentacles.

Somewhere, she screamed and convulsed. Her moan echoed in his ear, and the pulse between her legs squeezed him again. Her beautiful face flashed through his tears.

Then he was gone.

Chapter Thirty-Two

By the front cover, Sarlona caught the book Benton threw at her from across the study. The leather ripped off under the pages' weight, and the book hit the floor with a thunk. She glanced from the book-less cover in her hand, to the naked tome at her feet and sighed.

"I don't give a cock about the orcs, Sar." He shoved his chair out from Glaucus's desk and folded his arms in front of him.

She glared at him and stooped to pick up the huge book, filled with decades of Glaucus's notes and maps he'd drawn himself. All about the orcs of Ashmore and neighboring lands. She'd been quizzing Benton over it.

He hadn't done well.

"Well, you have to," she said, tucking the book into its cover.

With Ashmore encompassing land used by two orc clans in wintertime, the Lord of Ashmore had to understand them: their precise territories, migrations, politics, and culture to avoid and resolve conflicts. Never mind that the leaders of both groups demanded an audience with Glaucus. Tomorrow.

"I can't do this shit."

Dagmar, who lounged in her chair by the fire, leaned forward to peek around it. "It's not forever, Glaucus," she said. "Only for a year or so."

His chair crashed to the floor behind him as he spun on her. "Don't you cockin' call me that."

The inhuman bellow shook the diamond windowpanes and made Sarlona cringe. Glaucus had never yelled like that while she'd known him. Benton hadn't either. Not before Amenduil had bottled him in a monster's body.

Dagmar didn't flinch. "You're going to have to get used to it." She shrugged. "The villagers will call you Lord Glaucus. Merchants.

Other lords. The SPS Council…"

Shaking, breathing hard, he strode at her.

Catching him by the shoulder, Sarlona stopped him fast. She tossed the book on the desk and sank her thumbs into the muscle between his shoulder blades. His shake dulled to a tremble while she glared at Dagmar.

He had been prone to solving problems with his blade, but she wouldn't have called him hot-tempered. Now…

Sarlona didn't blame him, of course. He was a wreck. As was she. But she had more time to adjust to her new body, and hers at least looked familiar. No one else's memories intruded on her dreams. If she hadn't joined with his mind, she wouldn't have been able to imagine what he was going through. He couldn't rely on his go-to coping mechanism. Alcohol no longer had any effect on him, other than to make him nauseated.

"I can't hardly read," he said to the floor, shoulders slumping.

She patted them and squeezed. "You're doing great, Benton."

He'd made vast improvements in the last week. Signing his name had once been a struggle. Now he just needed help with a couple words per page. Sarlona didn't know if the lorkai brain or Glaucus's centuries of mastery made learning it easier, but neither helped him focus. Neither helped him give a shit.

"Glaucus was fluent in seventeen living languages," Dagmar said, rising to put another log on the fire. "We're asking you to master the one you've been speaking for your pathetic life."

"Why the cock don't *you* just take over," he said, attempting to stalk toward her.

Again, Sarlona stopped him, snatching his wrist. It seemed like she spent half her time keeping him from Dagmar's throat these days.

She wondered anew if she should try turning Dagmar into a lorkai just so she wouldn't have to defend the Northlander. Spite kept Sarlona from it. And she feared if Dagmar had her old strength, she and Benton would destroy the place with constant brawling.

The Northlander crossed her arms. Weak and breakable as she might be now, she didn't seem it. She looked down her nose at Benton, and her muscles were as big. Mortal or not, she wasn't about to be cowed by him or anyone else. "We've been over this a half dozen times, *milord*."

They had.

The villagers had never accepted Dagmar. It was that simple.

It didn't matter that Ashmore had been her home long before their great-great-grandparents were born. Thanks to the lorkai mind tricks, they didn't seem to notice that their lord and his daughter didn't age, and they couldn't quite remember who had ruled when they were small.

But they couldn't get past that she was a Northlander and not the Lord of Ashmore's blood descendent. Dagmar had never cared enough to go into the heads of all the villagers she had contact with and make it make sense to them.

"He left everything to Sarlona, anyway," Dagmar reminded him with a small smile in her direction. "I have no claim to it."

Sarlona had been shocked when Dagmar had first informed her of that. That Ashmore was hers. So shocked, Sarlona hadn't believed it until she'd read the papers with Ashmore's seal. It made some sense. Glaucus probably hadn't expected to die anytime soon. Though he'd certainly wasted no time taking precautions.

Dagmar was ill-suited to become the Lady of Ashmore anyway. Sarlona didn't doubt the Northlander made a fine leader in battle, but she wasn't a governor, and she sure as hells wasn't a diplomat. Sarlona, at least, had some training in that regard. And she appeared Avenian enough, despite her blondish hair.

"Why don't she just take over then?" Benton stared into the fire.

Sarlona prayed he wasn't thinking about what sometimes drifted into her head when she watched fire now. How it might solve all her problems.

She wrapped her arms around his waist from behind and squeezed him close, taking in his scent with her face against his spine. Her grandfather's scent was comforting. But she missed Benton's.

"I will." She'd do so gladly.

Not that she wished to rule anything. Not even that small fief, but it would give her a sense of duty. It would put some of the years of education and training to use. It would distract her from her hunger and from missing her magic and home.

"There just needs to be a transition period first," she reminded him. "You need to tell the people you're stepping down. They need to see me a little first. Know that I exist."

They could just leave, of course. Abandon Ashmore. Neither of them had suggested it. Ashmore was Benton's home, and they were lost enough without wandering. Dagmar had been the one to bring it up. She'd asked them not to leave. Reminded them of the guards, the villagers, and Glaucus's legacy.

So, they'd stay. Sarlona would rule. Once all the dust had settled.

"At least, it w—" She froze. An unfamiliar, forceful voice, sounded down at the gate with Gorgil.

Benton stiffened too.

"Someone's here," she said, starting for the windows.

He turned to Dagmar. "It's Silas."

Dagmar tensed. "Everything is as it was," she warned.

Just in time. The stranger appeared a second later, inside the large study doors, having teleported in. Not all casters could do that. It took a powerful one.

Stand up straight, Dagmar projected from her mind. *Act* lordly. The command was directed at Benton. Sarlona hoped he was listening.

Be annoyed, Sarlona added. For the moment, she'd trust Dagmar. She had no idea who Silas was, but right now, no one outside of the Lord of Ashmore's estate needed to know whose soul resided in Glaucus's body. *Silas*, she instructed.

"*Silas*," Benton greeted him with Glaucus's commanding tone.

"Sorry to just drop in," the man said.

Sarlona doubted it. Everything about him screamed intentional and dripped confidence—his posture, fine clothes, the arrogant expression on his light brown features.

He slid his doeskin swathed hand into his long brown jacket and produced a scroll. As he passed it to Benton, his deep chestnut eyes settled on Sarlona.

Dagmar dragged them away. "You can't just *pop* in here," she said with a snarl.

"Apologies." Silas plucked a half pine needle from the embroidered gold leaves on his lapel. "Your gatekeeper was being difficult."

As if on cue, Gorgil burst into the room. "Sorry, milord," the guard captain said, out of breath, regarding Benton.

Good man.

"He just," Gorgil waved, "by me."

That's all right.

"That's all right," Benton repeated the words aloud, with Glaucus's more grandfatherly tone. He nodded a dismissal at Gorgil, and the guard captain slipped out.

Benton's predatory gaze fixed on Silas. *Great.* But if the caster roused his hunger anything like Sarlona's, it would take all of Benton's control to keep from pouncing. The handsome mage smelled—*felt*—ten times more potent than Cyr and *far* more appetizing than Amenduil.

Touch him, and we'll all burn, Dagmar roared without sound as she stared Silas down and took the scroll.

With a small, polite smile, Sarlona made sure to keep her gaze on the floor, hands clasped in front of her. The veil of innocence didn't hide her.

"I see now why he was being cagey." Silas edged nearer with eyes narrowed and head cocked. "Aren't you that missing druid? Sarlona Dairnon, isn't it?"

Sarlona's surname struck her like a closed fist. Who was this man to know her? Her face wanted to redden, but she stopped the blood vessels there from dilating. She put on her sweetest smile. "That's right, milord."

The stranger reached out. "Just Silas. I'm an SPS Council emissary."

The Council. Of course. She gave him her hand, and supple leather brought her fingers to full lips. She let herself blush like she always had when someone kissed her hand.

"I heard Sylvanus has been looking everywhere for you."

She frowned as she retracted her fingers. Her insides twisted. She prayed Sylvanus wasn't *still* searching for her, hunting her down. Hopefully, he'd limited his search to the days prior to confirming what had happened. Much as it made his betrayal sting worse, he might have cared before.

"We had a falling out, I'm afraid. Please don't tell him where I've gone."

"I won't, but the Council will w—"

"The *Council* has lost their minds," Dagmar said, drawing his attention. She shook the scroll at him. "There are twelve names on this list."

Silas shrugged. "Who better to rid Aven of dangerous rogue mages—" Cutting himself off, he glanced at Sarlona. "I assume she knows what you are?" he asked, and Dagmar nodded. "Than the lorkai?"

The Northlander rolled up the scroll. "Putting twelve jobs on one piece of parchment doesn't make them one job."

"Well, perhaps that will be it for the new year," Silas said.

Dagmar crossed her arms. "When's it due?"

"There's no rush," he replied. "The equinox."

She snorted.

Sarlona nudged Benton with her mind and gave him something to say. Glaucus wouldn't have stayed out of the conversation.

"Thank you, Silas," he said, taking the scroll from Dagmar. "We'll do as the Council requests, of course."

A dismissal, but Silas didn't leave. He spun to Sarlona. "Sarlona, how did you find yourself in Ashmore?"

Her heart thrust blood at her face, but she kept it out. "Glaucus came to me when Sylvanus was away." Not a blatant lie. "He offered me a position here."

"And *you* decided to end your apprenticeship early to take up a role in the 'court' of a minor lord of a backwater fief, did you?" He glanced at Glaucus in accusation. "You, one of the most promising young casters in Aven, *chose* a Marrow-drinker as your employer."

It hit Sarlona anew while Silas came closer. Everything she'd lost. Her future...blank and never-ending. This wasn't how things were supposed to go. It wasn't the life she was meant to live. "I was tired," she answered, voice thin. "Lord Glaucus is very kind, and I like the quiet."

A sharp pang of missing him hit her—his reassuring words, promises, praise, and his gentle hands. She longed for the warmth he conjured in her chest the most.

"Splendid." Silas glanced at Glaucus again, then Dagmar. "Because if the lorkai brought you here against your will..." His jaw tightened, and his lips formed a thin line. "If they imprisoned you here to feed upon..." He shook his head. "That would be a *grave* crime for them to commit."

Sarlona struggled not to sink into the floorboards.

"I can assure you, Silas," Benton said as instructed by Dagmar. "Sarlona is here by choice."

True. Now.

Silas came nearer and leaned close.

Gods, he smelled good. She bet he tasted better.

"If you need help, Sarlona," he said, looking into her eyes, "just send word." He swiveled to Benton, *Glaucus*, with a cold stare. "The Council would *never* allow the lorkai to keep a caster against her will. Whether she's a member or not."

That would have given her so much hope not long ago. Now...cold and emptiness leaked in.

Hunger flooded in after them.

But she forced a small smile. "Thank you. I'm okay."

Silas smiled back, then turned to Benton. "Until next time, then."

Benton nodded.

With a wave, Silas vanished.

Benton nearly collapsed, hitching over with hands on his knees. "Gods dammit." He tossed the now-crinkled scroll at Dagmar's feet, then rose. Shaking, he stormed to Glaucus's desk and ripped out the bottom drawer. Vials tinkled as he sifted through it and pulled out a little blue one—manna.

He popped off the cork and shot back the potion. The tension in his face and shoulders evaporated.

It would return soon. Manna took the edge off, that's all. Dagmar had warned them they couldn't last on it.

An expensive balm and a waste of a potion.

He inhaled and let the drawer of vials and papers crash to the floor. He put his hands on his knees again. "Cock."

Dagmar picked up the scroll and sighed. "We have many dangerous people to kill in the next couple of months."

Sarlona half heard her. Brushing her mind against Benton's, she touched anguish. Unable to burden his pain on top of her own, she slid away.

He wasn't going to make it. If he didn't surrender to the monster, he'd find a way to end it.

She glared at Dagmar. "If Amenduil could turn *you* human…" Pivoting, she continued, "The Council could help us, Benton."

Adrenaline spiked in Dagmar's scent. "They can't turn you back." Her heart thundered. "Not even the Councilors cast like Amenduil. Vorakor *himself* works through that shadowy piece of shit."

She was half right. "Together, they could do it."

Dagmar scowled. "They *won't* help you, then."

"Silas wanted to help me. He said the Council wou—" She paused, trying to remember a conversation with Glaucus. "Turning me was illegal. A crime committed by their members. They'll wish to set it right."

Dagmar stomped over to the window, shaking her head. "They'll wish to execute me," she said to the snow.

Benton straightened and ran his hands through his hair. "Good."

"Him too," she jerked her head at him. "If they don't believe your whole story."

They'd believe Sarlona. It wouldn't take much to convince anyone who'd known Glaucus that he didn't lurk behind those stormy eyes anymore.

"They won't execute you once they realize you're human," Sarlona said. "They've no jurisdiction over you now." She couldn't know that for sure, of course. Dagmar had no magical ability, though. The Council couldn't just kill or imprison whichever Avenian citizens they wished.

Dagmar paced in front of the windows. "They won't help you. The Council Leader, Kyran, he's been trying to get us killed for twenty years. He hates the lorkai. They're *all* afraid of us."

"Then they'll jump at the chance to be rid of the lorkai forever." A growl slipped out of Sarlona—a bit of that monster. She saw through a pink lens as her eyes flared.

Dagmar snarled in return. "I imagine an inferno would be a simpler spell to cast for that."

All the growl of a Northland bear, and to Sarlona, she sounded small. "You're cynical."

"You're naïve," Dagmar said, facing her. "Either way…that's what you desire? The extinction of a species? Some *druid*."

Sarlona's eye twitched, but she held her tongue. Dagmar suffered too.

"Cock off, you overgrown bitch," Benton said for her.

Sarlona wished he hadn't.

Dagmar stalked to the fire, trembling. A human wouldn't have been able to detect her quiver.

"Ever since his mother and sister fell…all Glaucus wanted was to see the lorkai restored." Dagmar said to the flames. "To ensure we didn't go extinct."

Maybe ending her curse would be spitting on Glaucus's legacy, but Sarlona had never asked to be part of it. She'd been dragged into it, kicking and screaming. It wasn't her responsibility. His spirit couldn't live on through her, not when his spirit didn't exist. He couldn't peek in on her from across the veil, and she couldn't break his heart or shatter his dreams across realms.

Dagmar whirled with tears hanging in her eyes. "We… I…waited almost seven hundred years for the right person." She'd kept her distance since she'd become human, but now she took Sarlona by the shoulders and looked into her eyes. "I waited for *you*," she whispered, squeezing. "The young woman who was supposed to save us." Then, harsher, "Instead, you'll doom us."

"Cock off," Benton said again, ripping Dagmar away.

"And what about *him*?" Dagmar said, shrugging him off before he found skin. "You want to make *that* human?" Face in a sneer, her stare roved over him. "He'll be an old man. With twenty years left if he's *lucky*. While you're *in* your twenties."

"I'm going to retrieve his body," Sarlona said coolly. As if doing so couldn't involve crawling into the hells.

Dagmar snorted. "What will be left of it, Sarlona?" She shook her head. "It's impossible."

"What would you know about it?" The Northlander didn't have a magical bone in her body.

"I know mortals have been trying to bring back the dead since they cast their first spell," Dagmar spat. "I know they raise decaying, corrupted, or mindless monsters *every* time."

"He didn't die," Sarlona argued. If he had, she would have

agreed. Raising the dead and having them be as they'd been... She'd never heard of it. This was different. "He just...went in."

He shook his head. "Don't..." He sighed. "Don't get my hopes up, Sar."

She grabbed his hands and rubbed the backs of his trembling fingers with her thumbs. "You need hope. I'm going to fix this. I'm going to fix everything." Except for bringing Glaucus back. That... She wondered if the Gods themselves could reform an obliterated soul. "I'm going to go to the Council. They're going to help."

Dagmar chuckled as she swung to the fire. It was a mirthless sound, desolate, if not hateful.

Sarlona hugged him around Glaucus's waist. His long black coat instead of Benton's jerkin, and his scent filled her nostrils when she laid her head against the wrong chest. "Everything will be all right."

He closed his arms around her, squeezing. "It'll be all right if I get to be with you."

Liar. His insides squirmed with hunger. He shook harder.

"Go ahead," she whispered into his chest.

He wormed one hand under her shirt to rest at the base of her spine. The other slid down the back of her pants.

Her breath caught as Benton drew in, as that ghostly claw tore a little of her strength away while warm fingers caressed her skin.

"Cocking parasite," Dagmar grumbled over her shoulder.

They all were, in body or heart.

But not for much longer. Sarlona was about to end the species.

Epilogue

Amenduil spun the glass orb on the nicked and stained desk as he finished writing tomorrow's sermon for the uninspiring, short-sighted, pseudo-spiritual Deathmaster. The end of his reign was fast approaching. But Amenduil wouldn't be the one to end it. He'd just be the one to fill the void once Vorakor called the inadequate figurehead home.

Amenduil set down his quill and stopped the whirling orb with one finger. The smoke inside kept turning, a pretty swirl of gray tinged with purple.

It stormed like Glaucus's eyes had but carried lavender petals on the wind. "Now, what in the Abyss am I to do with *you*?"

A lorkai soul had to be useful for something.

Most likely controlling Sarlona. If necessary.

He might not have to do anything more to drive her into Vorakor's loving tendrils. He'd set her down the right path—a dark one.

Glaucus didn't answer, of course. He couldn't speak, hear, or see.

He was nothing now but discordant thoughts and remembrances in a bottle.

One solid spell had rendered the ancient being harmless and out of the way.

Like Dagmar. And Benton was as good as Vorakor's. He always had been. Amenduil would use him again if he had to. As many times as it took.

Later. Now he would wait to see how things played out. *Now* he had to focus on protecting the Abyssal Lord's other children, those far less capable of defending themselves.

Vorakor had shown him another lost woman, one who thought she was Silsorian. The poor, lonely soul.

It wasn't so clear why this one was critical, but Vorakor wouldn't have shown her to him if she wasn't. So Amenduil would work on her next. After he brought the woman home, he'd check in on dear Sarlona.

He dimmed the cool blue light hanging in his lantern shade and scooped up the orb to tuck into the bottom drawer of his desk with the others.

Acknowledgements

Thank you to my wonderful editor, Sevannah Storm, Champagne Book Group for taking a chance on me, and the writing community for all their amazing positivity and support.

About the Author

Kerry loves nothing more than writing secondary-world fantasies with messy romances. Her stories run dark and violent, featuring timeworn estates, leather, and armed scoundrels in place of pretty palaces, fancy dresses, and princes. Glowing-eyed monsters inevitably appear in most of her writing, resulting from a visit by one at eight years old (okay, *maybe* it was a vivid nightmare).

As a lifelong Mainer with a background in ecology, Kerry shares the same reverence for the woods and sea as her heroine. And while she prefers to take down her enemies on roller skates, like her male lead, she loves the feeling of a sword in her hand. When she's not writing, Kerry also enjoys skimboarding, fishing, and spending time with her wonderful husband and daughter.

Kerry loves to hear from her readers. You can find and connect with her at the links below.

Website/Blog: https://kwbernard.com/
Facebook: https://www.facebook.com/kerry.bernard.7
Instagram: https://www.instagram.com/k.w.bernard/
Twitter: https://twitter.com/KerryWBernard

Thank you for taking the time to read *Drained*. If you enjoyed the story, please tell your friends and leave a review. Reviews support authors and ensure they continue to bring readers books to love and enjoy.

~~~

Want more fantasy mixed with romance? And dragons? Turn the page for a peek inside *Sacrifice* by Vicky Walklate.

One dragon god. One human sacrifice. One ironclad rule: they must not fall in love.

Dragon gods rule the realm, demons lurk in the shadows, and a sorcerer hides a dangerous secret. A war is brewing in Jothesia, and the gods have no idea.

Being selected as human sacrifice to the immortal dragon shifters is supposedly an honor, but rebellious Libby doesn't see it that way. When the sacrificial ritual goes badly wrong, she finds herself in a reluctant alliance with eldest god Rhetahn. He's grumpy, cynical, and utterly exasperating …and she can't get him out of her head.

Rhetahn knows there's something wrong with this sacrifice, and it's not just her infuriating stubbornness or the way she makes his jaded heart skip a beat. When terrible misfortune befalls his brothers and renders him powerless, his only choice is to unite with Libby to seek answers.

As they set out on a dangerous quest across the realm, the compelling attraction between them is undeniable, yet doomed. To recover his magic, regain his strength, and prevent the demons from seizing power, Rhetahn needs her blood. He must kill her at the end of their journey, even if it breaks his heart to do so.

But a terrible power lies hidden in Jothesia, one that could destroy everything the gods have built. Libby and Rhetahn's forbidden relationship may be the realm's only hope against utter ruin.

Chapter One

So those were the Shifterlands.

Libby crouched on the summit's edge, the wind tugging her clothes as if coaxing her away. A white-frothed river smashed against a narrow gorge, fed by other rapids roaring in the distance. Shadows twisted amongst ravines and forests, with mountains looming on every side. Some peaks rose so high they vanished into the clouds. Others gloried in revealing every ridge and bluff. Danger branded the shadows, the crests, the sprawling canyons, and mysterious woodlands.

She bowed her head. Beyond the horizon were the exalted dragon gods who ruled the realm from Trivium, their castle stronghold.

"What are you doing here, Lissabet?"

She spun to find Thassa hovering behind her, his black robes flapping and his stare narrow.

Conjuring a meek expression, she sidestepped from the edge. "Forgive me, High Sorcerer. I merely wished to observe the homeland of our divine lords."

"Flat Peak is off limits to all but sorcerers."

"Plus the sacrifice," she pointed out, unable to resist correcting him.

"Indeed. Accompanied by sorcerers."

"And The Three can come whenever they wish."

He crossed his arms. "They send emissaries to collect the sacrifice and that's it. Now come, unless you wish me to inform your parents of your waywardness."

Sighing, Libby obeyed him, skittering over the ridge with the squalls driving her onward. She slowed her pace when they reached the other side, hoping for a final peek at the Shifterlands. He stayed beside her and gestured at the trail, making it impossible to linger without disobeying him. Despite saying nothing as they descended, his disapproval hung in the air like dampening fog.

The campsite at the mountain base teemed with life. Fabric tents dotted the stony ground, each with a fire burning outside. Some occupants rotated spits above the flames, others strolled back with pails of water from a stream, where cobbled horses cropped at the grassy bank. Several people packed luggage on carts in readiness for departure in the morning. Everyone acknowledged the high sorcerer with deferential nods as he ushered her through the encampment.

The Sanctellium sat in the camp's center. The huge ornamental tent, trimmed with bronze cord, housed the council for the gathering's duration. Each sorcerer resided in one of the eight modest compartments surrounding an enormous central chamber. A rectangular spire rose from the roof, supported by wooden pillars dug into the ground. Swathes of material enveloped its sides to create a chimney, allowing smoke to escape from the exposed top. Upon her arrival two days ago, Libby had wondered what prevented the chimney catching fire. The answer was obvious: magic. The Sanctellium was so covered in spells and enchantments, it pulsated with power.

The smell of roasted meat and wood smoke increased, along with the comforting sound of chattering laughter, although four tents remained silent. They housed the aspirants, the twenty prospective sacrifices. One was Karlo, her childhood friend and the aspirant representing her province. Libby drew to a halt, straining to peer inside his tent.

Thassa followed her gaze. "The blessed aspirants are close to learning their fate."

She bit her lip. Being chosen was a tremendous honor, so much that some, like Karlo, volunteered for it. However, it meant death was certain for one. And death, even at the hands of their revered gods, wasn't something sane humans longed for.

"Do you think they're afraid?" Libby ventured.

"Of course," he snapped. "Wouldn't you be?"

She raised her brows at his bitter tone. She knew Thassa better than most. He had lived in her village, Firstocket, before his ascent to high sorcerer last summer. As a human sorcerer, blessed with a long life and the power to command the magic simmering in the realm, he devoted his extended lifespan to The Three. To hear him utter anything other than piousness was rare. Her adopted father, leader of the South Brecks province, held him in high esteem. Libby herself wasn't keen, finding him too intense, too watchful.

"There is no greater honor than to die at the hands of The Three," she recited, half-wondering if he was testing her with his inflammatory tone.

His expression blanked. "Praise The Three."

"Praise The Three," she repeated.

He jerked his head toward her parents' tent. "Return to your father. Ensure you are present in the Sanctellium tonight for the ceremony."

She swung around in surprise. "I wasn't aware I needed to be there. Isn't it only the council, the principals, and their aspirants?"

"Are you not training to be your province's principal?" He strode away, tossing his final words over his shoulder. "You will ensure your attendance."

She ground her teeth. Although some autocracy was expected from him as high sorcerer, his decrees were extra short-tempered when directed at her. She'd given up complaining to her parents. Despite their love for her, Thassa was godlike to them, and his actions were not to be questioned.

Stomping to her tent, her annoyance faded at the sight of two rabbit carcasses roasting on the spit outside. Her stomach rumbled in appreciation. Her father sat by the fire, rotating the handle with steady precision. Some principals of the bigger settlements had brought servants to cook for them, but Jasco Donaire was a simple man and came with just his wife and adopted daughter. He gave Libby a fond smile—one she returned.

Her mother, Alasia, ducked out of the tent and put her hands on her hips. "Where have you been, Lissabet?"

Libby hesitated. "Helping the high sorcerer prepare for the ceremony."

Her father's smile widened. "Excellent. A principal should always stand ready to aid the council."

Settling on the stool beside him, she warmed her hands near the flames and inhaled the tangy aroma of rabbit meat. "He wants me to attend the ceremony. Is that normal?"

Alasia frowned. "To my knowledge, just the principals attend with their aspirants. Are you sure you didn't misunderstand him?"

"He was as cranky and concise as ever." Her quip earned her a censorious tut from her mother.

"Very well," Jasco declared, "you'll attend the ceremony with Karlo and I. He'll be pleased to have you there, and you can help me stand up at the end. My old knees aren't what they used to be."

Libby grinned, edging closer to the fire as the night's chill loomed and the shadow of Flat Peak crept farther across the camp.

Chapter Two

"Stand still, Lissabet."

Libby winced as her mother pinned her hair into a bun. Jasco waited outside their candlelit tent, chatting to a fellow principal. Biting her tongue as another pin scraped across her scalp, she folded the cuffs of her maroon gown, borrowed from her mother. She was shorter than Alasia and it was far too long, yet more elegant than anything she owned. At least the pooling skirts hid her worn ankle boots.

Once her mother finished fussing, Libby went to join her father, lifting the skirts to avoid tripping. The aspirants waited in two silent rows outside the Sanctellium, their simple, cream-colored garments easy to spot in the darkness. Karlo was near the front, clasping his hands together and staring at his feet. She uttered a silent entreaty that her friend wouldn't be chosen, then inwardly apologized to The Three for her blasphemous prayer.

The lingering principals increased in number until all twenty presented themselves, murmuring their greetings. Servants and family members retreated to their campfires to observe the proceedings. Mist snaked around the tents, and clouds covered the stars from sight. She shivered, edging closer to her father. She was debating whether to get her cloak when the Sanctellium entrance flaps swung apart, revealing one of the sorcerers. The young man's gold and turquoise ceremonial robes swirled, producing gasps from the onlookers. Libby gawked too, as spellbound as everyone else.

He waited for the awed whispers to fade then spoke in a clear, strong voice. "The time has come when an individual will be chosen to yield their life to The Three. There is no greater honor." He scanned the observers for a moment, as if daring someone to challenge him. "The blessed aspirants may enter the Sanctellium."

The potential sacrifices filed inside one by one. Karlo's broad shoulders were stiff, his movements lacking their usual easy grace. Many other aspirants were shaking. One woman was weeping. Libby glanced at her father, her pang of sympathy reflected in his eyes.

After much rustling from the tent, the young sorcerer re-emerged. "Those who accompany these aspirants, will now enter in humility and worship."

"Praise The Three," echoed the spectators in one voice.

Heart pounding, Libby trailed after her father into the Sanctellium. Gold and silver tapestries adorned the ceiling and encircled the huge chimney rising above the fire in the center. Sparks hissed and fizzed, the scent of wood smoke blending with sweating bodies and cloying incense. The flames were intense enough she was relieved to be cloak-less. Smoke billowed from the spire, enough escaping into the chamber to make her eyes sting. Several people coughed into their hands. The sobbing woman from earlier cowered next to Karlo, clutching his hand.

Around the outside of the massive chamber, eight openings led to the sorcerers' living quarters. A different council member stood in each threshold, holding a flickering candle. The sorcerer who bid them inside took his place with his own flame. Libby blinked. They weren't candles, but pure magic. Orbs of glimmering light, hovering in their cupped hands.

Magic bubbled like invisible lava beneath the realm, waiting to be exploited by the few who could summon it. To her limited knowledge, The Three were the only dragon shifters with magical ability, although the ice dragons, who ruled the frozen North Sleets, were also rumored to possess some power. Human sorcerers held the same ability, as did some of their descendants. Demons could utilize dark magic, a mysterious element that abetted their pursuit of death and destruction.

Sidling to a rug on the right of the fire, Libby compared the older sorcerers' vivid orbs to the one stuttering in the youngest man's hands. He mumbled to it, as if encouraging it to stay alight. Experience and confidence seemed a significant advantage when dealing with magic.

She and her father hunkered in the back row, farthest from the fire. The aspirants faced them on the other side. She caught Karlo's attention for the first time, returning his rueful smile with her own. Did he regret his decision to volunteer for this? Unlikely. Whether he was selected as the sacrifice or not, his aspirant status meant his family would be cared for by their people. And if he was chosen, the blessing of The Three ensured his spirit was protected from the dark magic hungering for human souls to devour.

The tent flaps closed on the cramped chamber. She wrinkled her nose. Based on the gathering's pomp and formality up to this point, even for simple things like erecting the tents, she wasn't holding much hope for a swift finish to this ceremony.

Thassa strode from his ornate chamber opening, an amber sphere oscillating in his hands. His glorious ceremonial robes were different from his usual somber attire, lustrous peacock-blue in color, embellished with tiny jewels. His blond hair hung to his waist, and his hazel-brown eyes appeared black in the flickering light.

"Welcome, friends. On this glorious night, we give praise to our hallowed gods, The Three, who rule Jothesia with wisdom and mercy. To remain in their good favor and maintain peace across the realm, we will select an individual to gift them with death, restoring their power anew and continuing their illustrious reign. First, the prayer of The Three."

Libby bowed her head with everyone else.

"Oh holy Three," they intoned as a group, "your mercy provides bountiful lands to sustain us; your wisdom guides us into lives of truth and humility, rejecting hate and sin; your strength protects our mortal existence and our eternal sleep. Accept our prayer, Lords; sustain, guide, and protect us, and we will serve you with devotion. Praise The Three."

When the prayer ended, the sorcerers processed through the throng, coming to a halt in a circle by the fire. They sank to their knees, clutching their orbs.

"Two thousand one hundred fifty years ago," the high sorcerer intoned, "brothers Rhetahn, Mhaljett, and Storren led their warriors into battle to destroy Jothesia's persecutor, the demon overlord Kalid'har. The Three were armed with magical amulets, created by this council using human blood and the mighty Rondure stone. Since that triumphant day, they have ruled this realm. In place of the Rondure, destroyed during the amulets' creation, we offer them one sacrifice every twenty-five years, to renew their power and maintain peace across Jothesia."

Hmm.

She fidgeted, glancing around the tent. The tales she'd heard since childhood differed from the official chronicle Thassa recounted. According to whispered legend, the original council refused to relinquish the Rondure to The Three after the battle, frightened its power would corrupt the dragon shifters. As punishment, the brothers killed the high sorcerer's daughter and discovered their magic could be renewed using the blood of a dying human, with no need for the Rondure. They allowed the sorcerers to hide the stone away, on the understanding that in return, Paskyll would provide sacrifices when required. If the council refused, the gods would take the Rondure and subjugate the humans, like Kalid'har before them.

Some didn't believe those rumors, for how could their merciful gods be so cruel, so callous? How could they demand their followers die when an alternative was available? The more pragmatic amongst them admitted it *could* be true, for their gods were not gentle deities, they were dragon shifters, not known for their compassion. A few even sought the Rondure, although none found it, and the council never strayed from their official assertion that the stone was destroyed.

Libby focused on her surroundings again. Thassa was still talking, and she hid her yawn with difficulty. As much as she loved her gods, did their veneration have to be this long-winded?

"The blessed aspirants give themselves freely," the high sorcerer continued, "for there is no greater honor than to die at the hands of The Three. And the spell cast by this faithful council shall choose the one most worthy."

At those words, each aspirant prostrated themselves, palms and foreheads touching the woven rugs beneath them. The principals bowed their heads. Libby copied her father, wispy blonde tendrils escaping from her bun and brushing against her cheeks. She flicked her head in annoyance, just as the sorcerers tossed their flickering spheres into the fire. Except Thassa, who was busy mouthing to his orb. Ebony wisps coiled through the golden ball, and it transformed into a sallow russet color as he threw it into the flames.

She rubbed her chin. Why hadn't the other council members whispered incantations to their spheres? Perhaps this part of the rite was meant for the high sorcerer. It wasn't her place to question it. At least, not out loud.

Smoke billowed in a sibilant rush of power, and she jumped, as did several others. Some coughed, jerking back when heat burst across them. Libby flinched. Colored flame crackled and flashed like a lightning storm then receded as if doused with water. The smoke vanished, leaving behind something that made her gawp.

A whirling ball of magic hovered above the charred wood, twice the size of the sorcerers' hand-held orbs. The principals gazed, speechless, at the amber sphere. Even the sorcerers stared, entranced. The aspirants stayed prostrated on the ground as the glowing sphere floated toward them.

It moved of its own accord, carried by an invisible current, weaving like a divining rod over each aspirant, one after another. When it reached Karlo, Libby held her breath. It hovered for a moment, then floated to the woman beside him, who was sobbing again. Libby exhaled, and her father squeezed her hand. He knew her fondness for their province's brave aspirant.

The sphere reached the last of the aspirants without stopping, then ebbed and flowed toward the principals. Her father stiffened beside her. The sorcerers threw questioning glances at the grim-faced Thassa as the orb performed the same search above the principals, one row at a time. Uneasy whispers filled the tent. An old woman muttered this had never happened before. More people turned questioningly toward Thassa, but he remained silent.

"Keep still, Libby," Jasco murmured. "Something's not right here."

She closed her eyes when it drew close. Heat pulsed above her, and a humming sound resonated in her ears. It smelled sickly sweet with a sour undertone. Rubbing her clammy hands on her skirts, she willed the sphere to move on.

The unpleasant aroma didn't lessen. Neither did the heat, even as chills skittered across her shoulders.

She dragged her gaze up. The orb undulated in place above her, amber hues churning as if trying to communicate.

Thassa pointed at her, his words tolling through the tent like funeral bells. "The sacrifice has been chosen."

Chapter Three

Libby focused on the high sorcerer's finger, her heart pounding with such force, it was deafening. Beyond him, several aspirants clutched each other, gawking at the sphere. Stunned whispers abounded. Everyone appeared baffled, including the other sorcerers.

Thassa seemed unaffected as he rose and gestured at the orb. It floated to him with one final hum, shrinking until it fit into his hand. He closed his fist and the thin auburn tendrils swirled away into nothingness.

"Lissabet is not an aspirant." Jasco's voice was shaky.

The high sorcerer shrugged. "It matters not. The spell was cast and has chosen its sacrifice."

"The orb was not supposed to evaluate anyone other than the aspirants."

"I was not aware you possessed such intricate knowledge of magic, Principal Donaire." Thassa crossed his arms. "Perhaps you should sit on the council in my place?"

Jasco flinched. "I meant no offense, but please, High Sorcerer, she is my only child—"

"You assume she is the first sacrifice to be loved? I wish love could prevent this from happening. It is not enough. She has been chosen to die, and we must treat that as an honor."

"Thassa." Her father clambered to his feet. "There must be something we can do. Perhaps the spell meant to choose Karlo? It paused above his head…"

The attention of everyone in the tent swiveled to Karlo, who sat frozen, a stricken expression on his handsome face. Libby gazed imploringly at her friend. Would he offer himself, like when the call came for aspirants?

He looked away and stared at the floor.

The silence never sounded so loud.

Thassa shrugged again, tying his hair into a loose braid. "Karlo was not selected. The spell we cast is incontestable. Lissabet is the chosen sacrifice and will be taken to Flat Peak in due course. Principals and their honored former aspirants may leave the Sanctellium and prepare to depart the camp at dawn. May The Three grant you safe travels back to your homes."

"That's it?" she burst out. "I was chosen, and there you have it? I wasn't even supposed to be in the tent!" She leapt up. "*You* insisted on my presence. And you addressed your sphere when you threw it into the fire. You planned this, you snake. I knew you hated me!"

"Do not speak to our high sorcerer in such a way, Sacrifice," a council member admonished.

"Don't call me that. Don't bloody call me that."

Her father stepped between her and the sorcerers. "Libby, please stay calm—"

"And you!" She rounded on him. "One weak protest, and you roll over? You've nothing else to say?"

His face crumpled.

The elderly sorcerer spoke again. "The spell was cast. The council's word is the will of the gods. Would you have your father defy our hallowed lords, wayward child?"

"But Thassa engineered this! There are no other family members in this tent! *And* he said something to his sphere when no one else did. Why, Thassa?"

"Enough," the high sorcerer thundered. "Your ridiculous accusations undermine the honor bestowed upon you."

"Fuck your honor!"

A firm grip on her shoulders preceded whispers of magic tickling along her spine. Forcing her muscles to work, she turned her head. Colored tendrils drifted from the wrinkled hands of the sorcerer who'd reprimanded her.

He'd put a spell on her, the bastard. Libby's thoughts slowed and dimmed, like she was dreaming. She tried and failed to move. Her body was no longer hers to command.

"Thank you, Falsten." Thassa sighed, then scowled at the crowd. "I said leave."

The principals departed in a hurry, collecting their former aspirants. Her father's friends tugged him away, and she strained to call after him, to no avail.

She caught sight of Karlo, a relieved smile on his face as he walked hand in hand with the weeping girl from earlier. The woman beamed like a bride on her wedding day, cooing her thanks when he escorted her through the exit. He didn't look back.

Libby stayed with the sorcerers, bound by the suppression spell. They bustled around her, readying themselves for the trek to the summit. Their servants hurried to and fro, straightening the rugs on the ground and assisting the sorcerers. Thassa alone remained stationary, gazing at her with an undecipherable expression on his pale face.

He leaned in. "You hate me now, don't you?"

Her pulse roared in her ears. She couldn't respond.

"Use the hate, Lissabet. Consume it. Let it saturate every inch of your blood."

As she considered his strange words, her shocked mother replaced him in her visage. Despite the spell's confines, a sob escaped Libby. She tried to fling herself into Alasia's arms, to no avail.

"This can't be happening." Tears poured down her mother's cheeks. "Thassa, there must be another way—"

"I already told your husband, there is nothing more to be done. Say your goodbyes."

Alasia flinched, choking back her sobs. Terrible finality washed over Libby. Her mother held Thassa on as high a pedestal as anyone in the land. Even more so since his ascent to the high sorcerer position after Breibern's death last year. He was closer to the gods' grace and mercy than anyone else. Her parents would never risk his wrath, and therefore the wrath of The Three, by going against him.

Libby endured their tearful embraces and vows to treasure her memory, her chest tightening with the desperate, futile need to beg for their help.

She wasn't sure how long she remained standing after her sobbing parents departed. The spell's power increased, lethargy dulling her fear. She focused on Thassa's face with difficulty as it swam into view in front of her.

"It is time," he said. "Don't be afraid. It's an honor, remember that. Remember everything I told you."

He touched her shoulder, removing enough of the spell to sharpen her mind and tense her muscles. She opened her mouth, but nothing came out. He hadn't lifted the spell completely. Determined to defy him, she twisted to run.

"Stop," he commanded.

She froze like a statue, a moan escaping her as her body prevented the desperate instinct to flee.

Thassa nodded in satisfaction. "The emissaries of our hallowed lords are due at dawn. You will accompany the council to Flat Peak."

Out Now!

What's next on your reading list?

Champagne Book Group promises to bring to readers fiction at its finest.

Discover your next
fine read!
http://www.champagnebooks.com/

We are delighted to invite you to receive exclusive rewards. Join our Facebook group for VIP savings, bonus content, early access to new ideas we've cooked up, learn about special events for our readers, and sneak peeks at our fabulous titles.

Join now.
https://www.facebook.com/groups/ChampagneBookClub/

Made in the USA
Middletown, DE
27 September 2023

38814330R00154